SHIFT

Chris Dolley

Baen Books by Chris Dolley

Resonance

Shift

SHIFT

Chris Dolley

SHIFT

Copyright © 2007 by Baen Books

A Baen Books Original

Baen Publishing Enterprises
P.O. Box 1403
Riverdale, NY 10471
www.baen.com

ISBN 10: 1-4165-2140-2
ISBN 13: 978-1-4165-2140-2

Cover art by Alan Pollack

First printing, July 2007

Distributed by Simon & Schuster
1230 Avenue of the Americas
New York, NY 10020

Library of Congress Cataloging-in-Publication Data:

Dolley, Chris, 1954-
  Shift / Chris Dolley.
      p. cm.
  "A Baen Books original"—T.p. verso.
  ISBN 1-4165-2140-2 (hc)
1. Multiple personality—Fiction. 2. Time
travel—Fiction. I. Title.

  PS3604.O436S55 2007
  813'.6—dc22
                          2007015779

Printed in the United States of America

10 9 8 7 6 5 4 3 2 1

CHAPTER ONE

He came out of the darkness in a rush; lights appearing—above, below, to the side—sweeping past him in streaky blurs. He was flying—fast—racing across fields and hedgerows a few feet above the grass. No wind in his hair, no sound, no car beneath him, no plane. Nothing between him and the ground except the blur of speed.

What was happening? Where . . .

A building appeared. A white speck ballooning in size. He was flying straight towards it. Turn! Stop! Pull up!

He couldn't! The walls, the concrete, growing and beckoning. Impact imminent. He tried to raise his hands to protect his face. But he had no hands.

Panic. Time-stretching, gut-wrenching terror. A flash of white as he hit the wall then . . .

He passed straight through, into a corridor, a room, another corridor. Still flying, disorientated by the speed, the blurs, the impossibility. He was flying a few inches above the floor tiles, zigzagging along corridors, a tumbling eyeball with no limbs, no body, no . . .

A sound! Far off and muted but the first sound he'd heard since what seemed like forever. A voice, strange and elongated, slowed down and slurred. And light, suddenly all around him, bright and dazzling. He was falling, falling and then . . .

1

"Now, Peter, tell me what you see."

A room crystallized around him, needle sharp in its clarity: stark white walls, concrete floor, no door that he could see. A solitary light shone from a featureless ceiling. A face stared back at him, questioning. A face haloed in light. A man he'd never seen before.

"It's Christmas," said the stranger, his voice soft and emotionless, his accent unexpectedly English. "You're four years old, sitting beneath a Christmas tree, opening presents. What do you see?"

"What do I see?"

Was the man crazy? And who the hell was Peter? He tried to move but felt the immediate tug of restraints. Straps? He was strapped to a chair. His arms and legs bound. His head too. He could hardly move.

"What's the matter, Peter? What can you see?"

He strained at his ties, pulling, arching his body, pushing with his feet against the bare concrete floor.

"What have you done to me? Why am I tied up like this?"

"It's for your own safety, Peter. You know that."

"I am not Peter! What's the matter with you?" He spat the words out. Disbelief and anger. "My name's John, John Bruce. Don't you recognise me?"

His interrogator didn't reply. He just watched—impassive, unconcerned—looking down at a clipboard every few seconds to jot down a note.

"Who's in charge around here? I want to see someone in authority. Now!"

He was shouting, desperation welling up inside. What were they doing to him? He was John Bruce. The astronaut. The first man chosen to fly to the stars. His last real memory, strapped inside the Pegasus, waiting for the countdown to stop, for the dimension shift engine to engage and send him hurtling into the unknown, spiralling into the higher dimensions. And then? What had happened to him after that? Dim recollections of an all-encompassing blackness, timeless drifting, that weird flight along fields and floor tiles and now here; strapped into another chair. But where? He'd never seen this room before in his life.

And who the hell was Peter?

"It's all right, Peter. Calm down."

"I am not Peter! How many times do I have to tell you? I'm John Bruce, the astronaut."

He was very close to losing control; arms, head, and legs straining against the ties. Like a four-year-old denied a treat, caught in the throes of a temper tantrum, he thrashed and screamed.

"It's okay, John. I'll get the nurse to untie you. You can watch HV if you like. Everything's going to be fine. We'll talk again tomorrow."

Doctor Paul Bazley, senior psychologist at the Upper Heywood Secure Psychiatric Unit, was not a happy man. But unlike most unhappy men, Paul Bazley knew both the reason and the remedy for his state of mind: Peter Pendennis and the killing of Peter Pendennis. Unfortunately, the Hippocratic Oath frowned upon murdering one's patients—however justifiable.

He sighed, leaned back in his chair, and tried to relax. His office stared back at him, sparse and impersonal, like everything else at Upper Heywood—institutionally furnished by a distant bureaucrat on a tight budget; white-painted walls, generic prints, cheap furniture.

The door opened and Anders Ziegler, Bazley's young colleague, bounced into the room. "You'll never believe it!" he said. "Peter's found a new personality."

Peter. It was always Peter. You'd think he was the only patient in the unit. Peter this, Peter that. Why didn't Ziegler see he was being used? Anything Pendennis said was suspect from the moment it left his twisted little brain. He was a liar, a manipulator, a fantasist.

And a killer. As sick as they come.

But to Ziegler—young, enthusiastic Ziegler—he was still a challenge. Something new and exciting, an enigma who hid behind madness and layers of multiple personalities, peeling off one after the other but never showing anything but a glimpse of the monster that dwelt inside.

"I said, Peter's found a new personality."

"I heard you the first time," snapped Bazley, watching his colleague walk over to the small table in the far corner and pour himself a coffee. A conversation was imminent. A long conversation if Ziegler had his way.

Bazley felt the tic above his left eye flicker into overdrive.

"Yes," said Ziegler, stirring in the last of the milk substitute. "Personality number thirteen. John Bruce. *The* John Bruce."

"Who's John Bruce?"

"You know. The astronaut running for President." Ziegler pulled up a chair and placed his coffee on the edge of Bazley's desk. "If Peter thinks he's someone else is that a delusion or another personality?"

Ziegler smiled. Bazley did not. Pendennis was not a subject to be joked about.

"I wonder if any of his other personalities are based upon real people? An interesting line of research, don't you think? But why suddenly latch onto Bruce? You'd have thought that if he were going to, he would have done so two years ago when Bruce first hit the headlines. So why now?"

"Probably fed up inventing his own."

Ziegler took a few tentative sips of coffee. "You don't believe a word he says, do you?"

"Not one."

"Even though he passes every test there is? Hypnosis, drugs, every lie detector we can find. His stories always check out and they're always consistent."

"He's clever."

"Clever enough to keep twelve or thirteen personalities on the go? Separate family histories, separate memories, mannerisms, ways of talking. He even sounded like an American this morning."

"I told you, he's clever."

"But he's not! Look at his old school reports, his IQ tests. He's average to below average. He shouldn't know half the things he does. Let alone express himself the way he can at times."

Bazley was ready to explode. Didn't Ziegler ever listen? He'd told him so many times. Pendennis had never been interested in school or tests. And as for lie detection, that assumed you had some concept of truth. Pendennis didn't. He had no heart, no conscience, no concept of right or wrong. Just a hollow core wrapped in layers of sham multiple personalities. An empty box in a shiny package, reflecting whatever it was he wanted you to see.

That was Pendennis. A manipulator who craved to be at the center of every universe, pushing and prodding until he achieved a reaction. Provoking warders—what did he care if he spent a few weeks in hospital recovering from a beating? He'd won, hadn't he? Sent a warder over the edge, a warder who'd have to be disciplined, a warder who'd never forget the man responsible.

And there might be an inquiry—a chance to widen Peter's circle, suck in a few more people into his expanding world. Social workers, liberal lawyers, nurses at the hospital. Sympathetic ears to soak up harrowing stories, he'd feed them whatever they wanted to hear. Beatings, victimization, a hint that he might be innocent.

He'd crawl inside their heads, pushing everything else aside like a cuckoo in a man's soul. He'd be a puzzle, a victim, a friend. A source of stories that insinuated into your dreams. Stories that beguiled, terrified, made you search beneath your bed before you could sleep, made you stare at shadows in the middle of the night.

And if he got bored, he'd attack—without warning, without reason—130 pounds of feral energy, clawing, biting, gouging with whatever came to hand.

And back Peter would go into solitary confinement and a month or two later it would start all over again. Different victim, different story. The man was so plausible, so persistent, he could cry wolf a dozen times and still find a receptive ear. He had a personality for every occasion, one that he could hide behind later and shout—it wasn't me! I don't even know what you're talking about!

"You all right?"

"What?" Bazley looked up to see Ziegler staring at him across the desk, concern in his eyes. "I'm fine," lied Bazley, uncurling whitened fingers from the arms of his chair.

"Anyway," continued Ziegler, "I was regressing him back to that Christmas when he was four years old. To the time before the first manifestation of multiple personalities. You remember the story he told me of how he found the knives—the set of kitchen knives—meant for his mother and thought they were his?"

Bazley bit his lip. He'd told Ziegler . . .

"I thought it would be interesting to pursue that line. A four-year-old associates brightly wrapped packages with presents for himself. He can't discriminate between gifts for himself and gifts for the rest of the family. He finds a pile of presents and begins to open them all. One of the presents contains a set of kitchen knives, all bright and shiny. Later he believes it to be a sign, a message from God instructing him to use the knives."

Unbelievable! "Can't you see he's playing you?"

"He might be. But if he is, isn't it better to draw him out? The more he talks the more likely he is to reveal something that's actually true. It's got to be better than ignoring him."

Bazley shook his head. Ignoring him was the *only* answer. If it wasn't for the EU and prisoner's rights, he'd have had Pendennis locked away in permanent isolation. Bricked up in a wall cavity, if he could have gotten away with it.

A knock on the door interrupted their conversation. A head peered around the door.

"Sorry to disturb you, Doctor Bazley, Doctor Ziegler, but it's Peter. I think you'd better take a look."

"Why, what's happened?"

"He caught sight of himself in the mirror and went berserk. He's shouting and screaming for a whole bunch of people I've never heard of and we don't know what to do with him."

"He went berserk at his mirror?"

"Yeah. He totally lost it."

Bazley couldn't believe it. His mirror? The one calming influence in Peter's life. The only reason they allowed one in his cell. He'd spend hours staring into it, smiling, nodding, carrying on strange one-sided conversations with his reflection.

Why the sudden change?

Bazley could feel the curiosity surge inside him, just like old times, the rush, the desire to know. Was that what Peter had planned? The whole episode designed to lure him back into Peter's world?

"No." He shook his head. Not again. He'd stayed clear of Pendennis for four months. He couldn't get involved again now.

The warder looked confused. "Doc?"

Ziegler stood up. "I'll come immediately," he said.

Bazley didn't move. He looked down at his desk and tightened his grip on the arms of his chair.

Peter stood in front of the cell mirror clutching his face.

"What's happened to me! My face! What have you done to my face?"

"We haven't done anything to you, Peter," said Ziegler, standing in the doorway.

"I told you! My name isn't Peter, it's John Bruce. Get SHIFT control in here. I want to talk to Harrington. I want explanations."

"Okay, John. Calm down. Let's start from the beginning. What's SHIFT control?"

"You know!" His anger burned. Then turned to surprise. "Isn't this SHIFT medical center?"

"No. This is the Upper Heywood Secure Psychiatric Unit."

A long pause in which Peter's—or John's—eyes traced the small, sparsely furnished cell as if seeing it for the first time.

"A prison?"

"We prefer to call it a psychiatric unit."

Peter looked away, opened his mouth as if to speak then shook his head. He took a deep breath. "In England? Upper Heywood's near Oxford, right? Where the old air base was?"

"That's right."

"Then what am I doing here?"

Ziegler paused. What should he say? Confront Peter with the truth and risk a negative reaction or let the scene play out? Both had their dangers.

He tried a middle way. "You were committed eight years ago."

"What!" Peter's mouth opened and closed in confusion. "But . . . What year's this?"

"2056."

"2056! But that's . . ." He shook his head, turned away, the fingers of both hands flexing then balling into fists. "No," he said, swinging back to face Ziegler, spitting out the words as he fought to keep control. "I can remember August '54 like it was yesterday. And I sure as hell wasn't here. What the *hell* is going on?"

Ziegler didn't answer. He didn't want to guide the conversation.

"You must have seen me on HV." Peter waved his arms in exasperation. "Everyone did. The space launch, John Bruce the astronaut, the SHIFT project, you must know who I am!"

There was a pleading look in his eye.

"We've heard of John Bruce," said Ziegler. "And the space launch, but that was eighteen months ago and you've been here eight years. How do you explain that?"

"I . . . I don't know." He looked confused. And increasingly desperate. He looked from Ziegler to the warders and back again.

"But I can prove I'm John Bruce. Ask me a question, any question. I was born on September 28th, 2024, in Denver, Colorado. My father's Daniel John, my mother's Michelle. Bring them here, they'll recognize me!"

The words came out in a rush and then trailed off as he glanced at the face in the mirror. Ziegler could imagine what he saw. John Bruce had the face and physique of a chisel-jawed superhero. Peter Pendennis did not. Even in his mid-twenties, he still looked like a slightly built adolescent. Sallow complexion, large childlike eyes, scrawny limbs.

"What have you done to my face? Plastic surgery? Was there a fire? Is that it? The launch went wrong and I got burned up bad?"

Ziegler was unsure how to proceed. Peter was becoming agitated again. Was this the moment to tell him the truth? That John Bruce was alive and well and running for the Republican nomination? Or could he deflect him with questions about the SHIFT mission? Test Peter's knowledge, maybe find a reason for Peter's sudden interest.

"Well?"

Ziegler still wasn't sure. Peter was unpredictable and capable of extreme violence in all his guises. And at the moment he wasn't restrained.

And Ziegler was between Peter and the warders.

Ziegler shuffled—imperceptibly, he hoped—back towards the cell door.

Peter advanced towards him, his hands rising towards Ziegler's shoulders. A pleading look in his eye. Or was that an act?

"Tell me!" he shouted.

And then froze. His arms locked in space, stretching towards Ziegler's collar. His face rigid. His lower jaw . . . slowly beginning to twitch. Then his head shot back, his back arched, and his chest pitched forward.

Ziegler threw himself back against the door. He'd seen this before. So had the warders. They rushed past him into the room.

Peter staggered in front of them, legs buckling, eyes bulging, a gurgling sound bubbling up from his throat.

Experienced hands grabbed hold of his shoulders, took his weight. After a few seconds the straining body relaxed and Peter smiled.

"You don't wanna believe a word that Yank says. He's madder than I am."

Then came the laugh. A forced laugh that gradually increased in energy, building and surging until it took control of his entire body, shaking it, shaking the arms of the warders who struggled to keep their grip. Jack was back. Jack enjoyed a good laugh. Trouble was he couldn't stop. Laugh himself into a convulsion would our Jack. And then they'd have to tie him down again. Until Peter, or one of his friends, returned and Jack could go home.

Wherever that was.

CHAPTER TWO

The following day, Ziegler strolled into the canteen. The smell of grease hit him the moment he stepped through the door. The joy of working at Upper Heywood—cutbacks, locked windows, no air-conditioning and a cook who believed that all food had to be sterilized in fat.

He smiled. One day it would be different. One day he'd have his own plush private consultancy, complete with rich, confused clients; wealth; and respect.

And if he could write the definitive book on Pendennis, that day might be very close indeed.

He grabbed a tray and dreamed of future celebrity. There was more than a book on Pendennis, there was the talk show circuit, lecture tours, a film maybe. Pendennis was box office. A killer with his own gang of multiple personalities. A killer who dissected the bodies of his victims, searching for some hidden inner voice that only he could hear.

And that was just the start. Underlying everything was a pattern. An explanation, something that Peter would hint at before changing the subject or being pushed aside by another personality.

But it was there—Ziegler was convinced—and this John Bruce delusion might be the key to its unravelling.

He let his hand hover over the Thai salad before weakening—the steak and kidney pie did look especially inviting today, and that smell of chips and vinegar . . .

He paid for his meal and looked for a table. Bazley was sitting in the corner, reading a newspaper.

Ziegler walked over. "John's back," he said.

Bazley grunted and turned a page.

"And guess what. This time he's given me a list of contacts—names, addresses, even phone numbers. What do you think? Should we try them?"

Bazley shrugged. "Nothing to do with me. He's your patient." He didn't even look up. He kept on reading—or pretending to read—eyes down, tight-lipped, determined not to be drawn.

"Come on, Paul! You were as intrigued as I was about this John Bruce delusion. You know Peter better than anyone. What do you think I should do?"

Another shrug. And an outstretched hand. "Do you want all those chips?"

"Help yourself," said Ziegler, pushing his plate towards his colleague. "But I'm going to phone. I've got a feeling about this one."

He waited until late afternoon to make the calls to America. Couldn't get through to all the numbers but after the third one he didn't have to. They were all dead. Killed in a plane crash.

It was to have been a big surprise. A celebration dinner in Washington, everyone was going to be there: the President, senators, foreign dignitaries. A homecoming dinner for the astronaut hero, John Bruce.

A special plane was laid on at the President's request to fly in John's family and close friends. A kind thought. But that plane needed more than kind thoughts to keep it airborne that night. It was a sad day for America. An even sadder day for a hero.

"Do you think he knew they were all dead?"

Bazley hurried across the car park, pursued by Ziegler and a biting northeasterly wind. Neither were welcome. Clouds scudded low and fast overhead, the occasional flurry of light snow whipped up on the raw winter wind, the continual flurry of questions from Ziegler.

All Bazley wanted was to find his car and go home.

"Convenient, isn't it?" continued Ziegler. "For Peter, that is. He can continue to claim he's John Bruce and no one can challenge him. Though where he got hold of their private phone numbers is beyond me. Most weren't even listed."

Peter, Peter, Peter. Doesn't anyone talk about anything else these days?

He pushed on, his breath coming fast as he picked up the pace. Yesterday had been a mistake. He'd weakened for a second and let that monster sneak back inside his head. Like an alcoholic walking into a bar, one sip and down he went. But not again. Not if he could help it.

The younger man matched his stride, effortless, unhurried, his speech uncluttered by pauses for breath.

"And the way he took the news of his parent's death—you would have sworn he was their son. He's totally convinced—I'm sure of it— that he's John Bruce. But what I can't understand is why, after all that careful preparation he gives me another name—and this one's alive."

"How do you know?" Bazley stopped and turned. Once again, Peter had managed to slide a hook inside his brain.

"Because I just spoke to her. She's coming over tomorrow."

Imagine that, John Bruce! How many years had it been? Twelve? Thirteen? Her first love. The boy next door. She remembered feeling so grown-up talking to her friends about her American boyfriend. To be fifteen and in love.

And how strange. Both the phone call and the timing. It was only two nights ago that she'd had that dream.

Had it been a premonition?

And was that why she'd accepted such a strange request?

Louise emptied yet another wheelbarrow on the steaming muck heap. One of her many daily tasks—mucking out, strawing down, watering, feeding, medicating, and checking. Maybe that was another reason she'd accepted—a break from the monotony of a smallholding in winter.

Funny how he'd changed. John Bruce, that is. Her John would never have entered politics. She could see him as an astronaut; he'd always had that mad desire to push himself into strange inhospitable places. And his family were all Air Force, it was obvious he was going to follow his father into the services when they returned to the States. But standing for the Presidency? Not Johnny Bruce. Not the boy she'd known all those years ago.

Nor the boy who'd floated into her dream the other night. And what a strange dream that had been, even for one of hers. He kept floating in and out, as though he wasn't really part of the dream. He'd be there and then he wouldn't. Just as she felt he was going to take the dream soaring in another direction, he'd fade and something else would take over. She'd be over a mountain range or dipping under the ocean and then she'd see him again—floating, calling to her, imploring. But she could never reach him. He'd blur into the background before she could react.

The unattainable? Was that it? One of those psychological dreams to prove how low Louise's social life had sunk? Condemned to dream about old boyfriends she could never have?

Or was it her subconscious, conspiring with the night to find the excitement that it lacked during the day? The daily grind of milking and feeding, struggling through mud and bottomless puddles carrying endless buckets of water to animals that would as soon knock them over as take a drink.

Why did she do it? A question she often asked herself when the days dragged and her muscles ached. And then she'd see the scars and protruding ribs of her latest rescue case and she'd know the answer. Someone had to do it.

Not that she'd meant to set up an animal rescue center—it just sort of happened. First the donkey, then the goats—before she knew it they'd taken over her life. Who could resist those big sorrowful eyes or refuse to take in the battered and starving if they had the room? Louise Callander couldn't.

She had the space—just. Five acres of Oxfordshire scrub. An oasis of self-sufficiency in the midst of affluence. An affluence that couldn't find a home for its animals once they'd outstayed their welcome.

"You see, he thinks he's John Bruce." Ziegler stopped to open a door for Louise. Smiling, beckoning her through, doing his best to make her feel at ease.

"Like some people think they're Napoleon?"

"Similar. But this one's very convincing and, besides, he doesn't wear a funny hat."

They laughed, the ice broken. It wasn't every day that Louise found herself stalking the corridors of the criminally insane.

"I still don't quite understand why you want me here."

"He asked for you. He wants to prove he is who he says he is. He believes he can do that by convincing you. Little things that only the two of you could know—that sort of thing."

"But why are you helping him?"

"It's . . . part of his therapy."

The corridors seemed to stretch out for miles, a windowless warren of blank white walls and forbidding doors, the smell of disinfectant, echoing footsteps, recessed lights that hummed and flickered overhead. And cameras mounted at every intersection, their lenses turning to track Louise and Ziegler's every step.

"John's dad used to work here, you know?" she said, filling in the silence. "When it was an air base. This *was* part of the old air base, wasn't it?"

Ziegler nodded. "The barracks, I think. Did John live on the base?"

"No, his family lived in Wootton." She paused. "How does he explain that the real John Bruce is alive somewhere else?"

"He doesn't. Not yet. I'm waiting for the right moment to ask him."

"It still seems strange, though. To ask for me. How did he even know about me and John?"

"Thats one of the things I hope to find out.. He's a strange man but you do understand he'll be secured throughout the session? There'll be no danger to you whatsoever."

What?

Had she heard that correctly? The man had to be secured?

Doubt, and a rush of second thoughts. What on earth was she doing? The man had to be secured for Christ's sake! No one had mentioned that yesterday!

A request to help a sick patient—that's all she'd been told. A strange request but nothing dangerous.

Or was securing patients standard procedure? Were they being extra cautious because she was a visitor?

"You all right?" asked Ziegler.

"Yes, fine," she lied, feeling trapped. She'd promised. She was here. She couldn't back out now. "Just feeling a bit funny. I've never done anything like this before. I won't get hypnotised myself will I?"

She swallowed hard, fighting the temptation to turn and run back the way they'd come.

"No, don't worry. You can always close your eyes and cover your ears if you think it helps."

The room was stark and cold. The hum of a solitary overhead light, the only sound besides the slow drone of Ziegler's voice. The prisoner—someone called Peter—lay strapped to a reclining chair bolted to the center of the room.

"I'm going to count to three," said Ziegler, "and when I get to three you will awake as John Bruce. One . . . two . . . three."

There was a pause, then the man's eyes snapped open. He turned his head towards Louise and stared straight at her.

"Louise? Is that you? I knew you'd come." His eyes moved up and down her face. "You've changed your hair—it's shorter."

She froze in the shadows behind Ziegler's shoulder. She'd thought herself invisible and apart from the process. He didn't look anything like John; he was smaller—slighter—and facially completely different. And yet that voice . . .

It was John's. Or as close to John's as she could remember. Out came ribbons of memory, tugged by the sound, long walks in the country-side, winter evenings by a log fire, smiles and laughter.

"It's okay, Miss Callander," said Ziegler. "Come closer, he seems to recognize you."

"Hello." She shuffled forward, not knowing what to say or do.

"You've hardly changed," he said. "What is it—twelve, thirteen years?"

"I think so."

"Have they told you what's happened?"

"Not much."

"It's going to be hard to believe. I'm not sure what's happened myself but you're my last hope." He paused, his voice lowering. "You've heard about my parents?"

She nodded.

"I don't know what's going on. It's as though everyone who was ever close to me has been killed. Like someone's trying to erase all memory of me from the human race—as though I never existed. You'd better watch out too."

"I'll be fine."

"I'm serious, Lou. Be careful."

"I will."

He breathed out hard. His face relaxed.

"Do you remember what I gave you for your eighteenth birthday?" he asked.

Louise looked at Ziegler, unsure how she should answer.

"It's okay, Lou," said John. "I'll tell you what the present was. You tell the doc if I'm right. A Saint Christopher on a white gold chain. To keep you safe on your travels. You were about to go to university. To Exeter, to study biology. I never knew how you did. We'd returned to the States by the end of your first year there. And now, here you are. How'd I do?"

The two men looked at Louise, awaiting an answer, but she was too shocked to speak. It couldn't be! He sounded so real, so convincing but it was impossible. She was flustered, struggling to marshal her thoughts. Other people had known of her present, could one of them have told him? What was there that only she and John could know, that neither of them would have told anyone else . . . And that she could talk about in front of Ziegler?

Funny. She was already beginning to think of him as John. It was Ziegler who she considered the stranger, the one she couldn't talk in front of.

"Who was Bunny?" she asked.

"Bunny?"

She could feel the concentration in his face. His eyes twitched, a slight but rapid movement, almost as though they were being bombarded with fast-forwarding images as memories cascaded into and out of view.

"The dog!" He remembered in a flood. "The dog from across the road. That's it, isn't it? You were the only one who called him Bunny. His real name was Jason but he'd tag along with us and you'd tease him, calling him Bunny because he liked to chase rabbits. We'd walk over the fields behind the village and he'd be running around like crazy chasing rabbits that were always too clever for him. That's right, isn't it? Isn't it?"

They returned along the corridors in silence. Ziegler could tell that Louise was shocked and was willing to give her time to come to terms with her feelings. God knows, she needed it. It's not everyday you meet an old boyfriend trapped inside the body of a crazed murderer.

Ziegler needed time to think as well. Things were moving rapidly into areas beyond his understanding. He expected Peter to be plausible, almost convincing at times, but not *that* convincing. Either the two of them were in collusion or . . . or what?

He took another look at Louise. Did she look like a groupie? One of those strange women attracted to notorious prisoners?

He didn't think so. She'd have to be a consummate actress if she were. And Pendennis wasn't allowed private correspondence.

Which meant . . .

His mind began to race. No. It couldn't be! A higher dimensional effect? John Bruce had been the first man to travel through the higher dimensions. Could that have affected his mind? Dimension Theory remained a mystery to Ziegler—he stood firm with the traditional wing that denied its preeminence in the field of psychology. But there were many that expounded it as the key to the understanding of the human brain. He felt out of his depth. He could see his book on Pendennis fade with every new thought.

"What happens now?" asked Louise as they neared the exit. It was the first words she'd spoken since he'd ended the session. She looked lost and subdued.

"Er . . . I don't know," he said. "I'll need to talk to my colleagues about this. Thank you very much for coming." He didn't mean it but the words came out as a dismissal. Perhaps, subconsciously, it was. He needed time alone to think things through.

"Is that it?" snapped Louise. "Thank you and good-bye? *You* brought me here. *You* got me involved. What the hell happened back there?"

She was close to tears and starting to shout. Two guards at the reception desk had stopped talking and were looking their way. Ziegler shifted his weight onto his other foot.

It was then that he made his mistake. He gave her a name. Nick Stubbs, professor of applied astropsychology, one of the gurus of the Higher Dimensional lobby.

"He might be able to help."

As he watched her climb into her battered pickup, he cursed himself for thinking aloud, giving a name to a line of thought that was merely passing through. Bazley would hit the roof. There's nothing so intense as the rivalry between two factions of the same profession. They were incompatible. You could not believe in one without disbelieving totally in everything the other stood for. And he had just given the other side an entrée into the world of Peter Pendennis.

CHAPTER THREE

What did she think she was doing? Driving to Oxford, searching for some obscure professor, all because of what? Some madman and his delusions? And yet it had all seemed so real in the hospital. Outside, she wasn't so sure.

And even less sure after her visit to St. Olaves. She'd found the astropsychology department, but no Professor Stubbs. He was spending the month at Framlingham Hall, out on the Banbury Road.

"You can leave a message if you want but it could be days before he checks his messages. Always out and about, that one," the receptionist had told her.

Was this fate giving Louise another chance to back out? What was it her mother used to say? That fate gave everyone three chances to change their minds. Three chances and then the page turned and the future set.

Was this her third chance?

She could easily back out. She hadn't committed herself to anything. She and John had drifted apart years ago. What help could she be?

Of course their parents had kept in touch, cards at Christmas—that sort of thing. Little notes saying this and that, how they were doing, what was Oxford like these days? With little pieces of news thrown in—how proud John's dad had been when he followed him into the

Air Force, John's transfer to NASA, his selection for the SHIFT mission. After that who needed cards? John was headline news. The first man to travel the new space, the quiet-spoken hero. And then the political John Bruce, the master of the photo opportunity, the born-again darling of right-wing Middle America.

But the hype had never registered with Louise. She'd known the boy, not the man. As far as she was concerned, it could have been a complete stranger on the holovision. But today . . . she'd met the boy again.

It must have been that which drove her down the Banbury Road, that and her love of abandoned animals. For, whoever it was that inhabited the recesses of Peter Pendennis's brain, whether John or not, they'd been abandoned there as much as any neglected dog or goat.

She pulled up outside Framlingham Hall, one of those early Victorian statements of wealth: gothic, grey, and rambling. She climbed down from the pickup and looked up at the crumbling facade: the dirty grey stone, the cracked windows, and paint-peeling woodwork. It couldn't have been lived in for years.

The gardens showed the same level of neglect. Once-formal regularity replaced by haphazard colonization. Lawns grown wild; long grass and nettles folded over by winter snows, yellowed by frost and crisscrossed by nocturnal paths. Leaves and broken branches left where they fell.

She crunched along the gravel drive and stopped by the entrance porch. Her last chance to turn back. An ugly brass knocker stared back at her, daring her to knock. She grasped it with her right hand and rapped twice.

A silence followed. Louise glanced back towards her pickup and wondered how long she could wait before giving up. A few seconds, a minute? Shouldn't she just turn round now and let John become someone else's problem?

The door opened.

"Professor Stubbs?"

"Yes?"

He was younger than Louise expected, and scruffier. He looked like a student straight out of the '40s—tall and lean with long unkempt hair and a straggly beard. And a fashion sense to match.

Not that she could claim to be an expert on fashion. Her wardrobe came straight off the shelves of Two Counties Farmers. Discount clothing for the rural poor, hard-wearing and cheap.

She held out her hand. "My name's Louise Callander, I was referred to you by a Doctor Ziegler—from Upper Heywood?"

His eyes widened. "You've escaped? I always thought Upper Heywood looked after their patients better than that."

"No, it's . . ." She was flustered. "It's not for me. I was only visiting . . ."

"That's what they all say, Ms. Callander. Now tell me, are you very, very violent or just mildly homicidal?"

Nick Stubbs was enjoying himself. An amusing interlude in an otherwise boring day searching for phenomena that steadfastly refused to be found. And it had promised so much—a week ago. Come out and have a look at Framlingham Hall, they'd said. One of the most haunted houses in Britain. Guaranteed apparitions from dusk to dawn. They're knocking it down at the end of the month so it'll be your last chance. Can you afford to pass it up?

Nick Stubbs couldn't.

His was a simple philosophy—never pass up an opportunity for who knows where it may lead. A philosophy that had served him well. He'd had his fair share of falling into life's open sewers but generally came up smelling, if not of roses, then of something only marginally less fragrant.

And now, here he was, standing under a musty, cobwebbed door frame talking to an attractive young woman. The day was looking up.

Louise looked less sure.

"Maybe this wasn't such a good idea. Perhaps I should—"

"Nonsense. Ms. Callander. Please come in. I insist."

He beckoned her inside with a theatrical bow and then wished he hadn't. The poor girl was on the verge of running away as it was. One day he'd learn to rein in his eccentricities.

But not any day soon.

He led her through the dark and musty entrance hall, over the bare, echoing floorboards, past the peeling wallpaper, and into the light of a large front room. Library, morning room, study, billiard room—it could have been anything in a previous incarnation. But today, stripped of its former elegance it was just another empty room: four walls, imposing marble fireplace and a high, moulded ceiling.

And an array of tripods in the far corner. An oasis of modern technology in a desert of emptiness and decay.

"They're mine." He'd noticed her interest. "Higher dimensional imagers. Cameras, if you like." He walked over and patted one of them, feeling like a proud parent amongst strange misshapen children. "Now, how can I help?"

She looked nervously towards the door.

"Please," he said, trying to put her at ease. "If Anders Ziegler referred you to me, it's got to be important." Earth-shatteringly important. The two men barely spoke.

"I'm not sure where to begin," said Louise.

"Then just start talking and we'll work it out from there."

She started slowly, nervously stringing facts together and then becoming more animated. Nick listened, fighting the urge to interject. John Bruce, multiple personalities: he could see so many possibilities, so many unexpected avenues of research.

He waited until she'd finished and then jumped in.

"Interesting. The involvement with John Bruce in particular. Did you know most of my instrumentation came from the SHIFT project or offshoots from linked research? Well, no reason why you should. Higher Dimensional research owes a lot to SHIFT. And if John Bruce was subjected to a bombardment of higher dimensional stress—which is not that implausible, there was supposed to be adequate neural shielding but then again it was early days and more trial and error than proven fact. Given all that, could the extreme stress of the launch have had some adverse effect on the higher dimensional component of his mind?"

Louise raised her hands. "Whoa, you've lost me. That Higher Dimensional stuff passed me by. When I left school, it was still Newton and Einstein."

He was only half listening. Thinking of all the different ways a personality could split and still remain viable. Was it possible? Was any of it possible? All thoughts of the nonexistent Framlingham ghosts had been firmly put aside. This was something new. Something with potential. And it was his for the solving.

He looked at Louise. Suddenly aware of her existence. Wanting to hug her for opening such an unexpected door. Rescuing him from boredom and frustrated inactivity. Feeling like Sherlock Holmes on one of his bad days, with Moriarty dead and not the hint of an interesting crime on any horizon.

But how could he explain it to her? This dark-haired woman waiting nervously for an answer while all he could do was witter and play the fool. And he was getting worse. He knew that. What had started out as playful affectation had all but taken him over. Sometimes he'd find himself saying things that even he couldn't believe, making impossible connections, playing the wayward genius like a ham actor in a bad amateur production.

And that was another thing—tangential leaps in his thinking processes. He'd start thinking about one thing and end up God knows where, with no idea how he got there. A brain stuffed full of butterflies, all of them flapping at once.

And then Louise came back into focus, still looking at him, still waiting for an answer. How could he explain things to her without first taking her through an introduction to Higher Dimensional Theory?

"You see you've got to know the context."

And then he was away. Switching into lecture mode, recalling facts and personalities, reeling off the talk he'd given so many times before.

He told her about the search for a unified theory. How the laws of gravitation, electromagnetism, quantum mechanics, relativity, and possibly a few others besides had all been brought together under the umbrella of Higher Dimensional Theory.

"You see, the universe is not just the three physical dimensions that we see around us but ten—can you believe that—*ten* physical dimensions. Eleven if you count time. Isn't that just amazing? Here we are—barely coping with length, breadth, and depth—and suddenly we've got another seven to worry about.

He was in his element now, pacing and expounding, arms windmilling. Like a child let loose in a toy factory, flitting from one subject to the next. But with a structure this time. A practiced discipline that held the speech together. Taking Louise through the labyrinthine twists and turns of a complex subject. Passing on his excitement as only a true enthusiast can.

He talked of acupuncture, he talked of dowsing. He explained how they accessed the hidden—the higher—dimensional component that all matter was composed of. How so much material was hidden from the five physical senses. How telepathy, near death experiences—maybe even ghosts someday—could be explained by reference to HDT. Senses and skills that exploited the hidden universe.

"And just think of the implications for space travel. How for years we've only considered the three axes of movement—up, down, left, right, forward and back. But in eleven dimensions we've got another seven. Astounding, isn't it. Unfathomable! How can we, trapped inside our three-dimensional thought, conceive of what these other seven axes look like?"

But Nick Stubbs could. Tracing pictures inside Louise's imagination, he drew her deeper and deeper into his strange world.

"Imagine a two-dimensional universe. Like a picture on a piece of paper, it has no depth. Imagine this world as a blank piece of paper inhabited by little stick men—just like a cartoon. The stick men can move left and right and up and down across the page but they can't move forward and back—that's the third dimension that doesn't exist for them. They would have no concept whatsoever of this third dimension, the same as we have no concept of our extra seven."

He hoped she could see it. The imaginary paper world he held fluttering before her. And then, with a flourish, he screwed it up into a tight little ball.

"You see, the universe is no more flat than the Earth."

He stared at his creation, breathing belief into it. A tiny paper ball universe balanced on an outstretched palm of thought.

"We still have our piece of paper and stick men who can travel only on the surface but now we have something else, don't we? With our three-dimensional knowledge we can see that many points on the paper have been moved closer together. Not for the stick men, because they'd still have to walk along the surface of the paper, but if they had a three-dimensional capability they could reduce the distance dramatically and travel directly through the ball. That was the driving force behind SHIFT, to reduce the vast interstellar distances that we've measured in three dimensions by utilizing some or all of the other seven. Forget all that 'no one can travel faster than the speed of light' crap and fly to the stars in a matter of minutes!"

He paused, breathing hard.

"Now, of course, not everyone believed that was possible. For years it was thought these extra dimensions had to be minute—rolled up upon themselves, no bigger than an atom. They had to be or else we'd see them, right?"

He waited for Louise to nod. And then shot her down as he'd done to a thousand other students.

"Like we can see infrared or ultraviolet?" He shook his head. "We're adapted to sense a fraction of what's out there. The fraction we need to get by and that's it. I can't sense a magnetic field but give me the right machine and I can show it to you. Same goes for the higher dimensions. Those cameras over there. They're calibrated to display the higher dimensional energy spectrum.

"And guess what . . . some of those higher dimensions are as infinite as our physical three."

Another pause for effect, another sweep of his arms.

"What followed was one of those golden eras of scientific discovery when the interests of politicians, big business, and science all coincided so that everyone could pull together and make the thing work. You know—national pride, promises of new industries, new markets, undying fame. All other areas of research put on hold.

"Which is why we now know more about travel in the higher dimensions than any other aspect of HDT. Take my research—we know little more about the mind today than we did fifty years ago. There are still eminent doctors who deny the existence of HDT or its relevance to psychology—your Doctor Ziegler, for one. If we'd had the same resources put into our research as SHIFT it might have been different. But I'm not complaining—far from it. As I said, most of my machinery comes from SHIFT or SHIFT-related research. These higher dimensional imagers and translators—all SHIFT-based technology."

He patted one again, noticed a speck of dust and brushed it away. Then he was off again. Talking of the mind and its mysterious higher dimensional component.

"You see, most of the body's higher dimensional matter is located in the area of the brain. What we see—the visible part—is but a small component of the whole. It's like . . ." He searched for a suitable analogy, his eyes flashing and flickering. "A mushroom! Just like a mushroom. You have the fruiting body aboveground—the visible component—and a vast array of tendrils and God knows what else spreading and permeating about underground—the unseen component, so easy to overlook but absolutely essential to the understanding of the organism.

"Which brings us to John Bruce. He was supposed to be fully shielded during his journey. All his bits picked up and brought back. But what if the shielding was flawed and not all of him came back. What then?"

"Wouldn't he die?" asked Louise.

"Depends which bits he lost. My profession used to advocate lobotomies—you know, surgically removing bits of the brain. Many who had lobotomies survived. Who's to say you couldn't lose some higher dimensional matter and survive—quite likely really. The only problem with that theory is that SHIFT were so thorough, I can't believe they wouldn't have picked up an anomaly like that when comparing the before and after scans. Otherwise—nice theory."

"Are you saying that John Bruce might have lost a part of his mind during the voyage and somehow that lost part has surfaced within Peter Pendennis?"

"Was I saying that?" He thought for a while, trying to remember. Sometimes his brain moved so quickly he lost touch with his thoughts once he'd committed them to speech. Or so he liked to think. He always fancied himself as something special, something exceptional. Others were less charitable and said he talked so much drivel it was no wonder his memory was too embarrassed to store it all.

"It's one possibility," he said, regaining his thread. "One of many, I should think. The voyage might have affected John's higher dimensional abilities—accentuated his telepathic skills, for example. Pendennis might be a receptive, a medium, who can pick up telepathic messages. Or the shift through the dimensions might have ripped at John's mental fabric—maybe dislodged a bubble of memory so strong that it could exist independent of its owner. Who knows?"

And what fun it would be to find out. He could see months of research opening out before him, maybe even years, maybe even a new branch of science.

"And if I could get hold of John Bruce's brain scans, there might be something the SHIFT team overlooked."

"I don't remember hearing about any other SHIFT missions after John's. Couldn't that be proof that something went wrong?"

"What?" He was half in the room, half racing into the future. "Oh, that. No, that was down to navigation problems. The craft was supposed to slip into the higher dimensions and then return. A short journey just to prove that flight was possible. Trouble was it came back fifty miles away from where it was supposed to. Spectacular sight, mind you—one second it was there, hanging in space, a couple of thousand miles above the Earth, then . . ." He clicked his fingers. "It winked out of existence and reappeared fifty miles to the left."

"So it did go wrong?"

"After a fashion. They knew about the navigation error long before John got anywhere near the craft. But it wasn't seen as a problem. You see, they experienced the same magnitude of deflection during the unmanned flights. It was predictable. They didn't know where he was going to reappear but they knew it would be about fifty miles from the start point. And it wasn't as though he was going anywhere. Just nipping into the void and back."

"Seems one hell of a risk to me."

"Ah, but you didn't have half of Washington breathing down your neck. SHIFT could have been cancelled if there were any more delays."

"Still seems a crazy way to run a project."

"It's a crazy world. Anyway, SHIFT's on hold now until they sort the navigation problem out. No point venturing to the stars if you can't find your way back, is there?" He paused, thinking. Then smiled. "I don't know though. It does have that certain appeal, doesn't it?"

"So SHIFT was cancelled after all?"

"No, not cancelled—put on hold. The funds are still there. If and when they crack the navigation problem"

"So, what do we do?"

He didn't answer immediately. He stood, staring vacantly out the window, mulling over the possibilities. What was the best plan of action? Rush off to the States and try to persuade John Bruce to submit to a brain scan? What chance was there of that? And what if the whole thing was a fake? An opportunist telepath reading Louise's mind and regurgitating events for . . . for what? Attention? Prestige? Some strange twisted plan that might never be fully understood?

"Tell you what, I'll get in touch with SHIFT and, in the meantime, let's have a look at Mr. Pendennis before Ziegler changes his mind."

"Do I have to be there?"

"Definitely. If there is a telepathic link between the two of you, end of story. I can calibrate the imagers to pick up even the weakest telepathic bond so there'll be no chance of him faking anything."

"And if there is no link?"

"That, Ms. Callander, is when it starts to get interesting."

CHAPTER FOUR

Nick tossed his car key onto the dining room table and switched on the HV. It was all he could think about on the drive over. Go home, call up every John Bruce holocast you can find and see if there's a change.

One that nobody had noticed.

It would have to be something subtle. Maybe a slight loss of motor skills—was that why he'd left NASA? Or gaps in his memory, or . . .

The HV prompt light came on. All he needed now was the remote which, as usual, was hiding—probably buried beneath last night's Indian takeaway. Or was that the night before's?

Someday he really had to find the trigger to his tidy gene.

He found the remote, wiped off the red sauce, and switched to voice input.

"John Bruce," he said and selected "news."

A news anchor materialized in the corner of the room—the image, half life-size and floating two feet off the ground. She smiled at Nick and spoke in a soft Southern drawl.

"John Bruce will be leaving the campaign trail today to attend a SHIFT reunion in Florida. The thirty-one-year-old former spaceman is currently trailing third in the polls in New Hampshire but—"

Nick froze the image and asked for a list of every John Bruce appearance, with titles and dates. The news anchor disappeared to be replaced by columns of text scrolling through the air. Nick selected a handful either side of the launch date and flipped between them. Did Bruce show a discernible change?

He walked around each image, flipping between the slightly nervous but always smiling spaceman and the relieved hero. All the interviews looked staged and undoubtedly were. NASA was fixated on image, paying as much attention to public perception as they did to their programs. John Bruce would have been coached from day one.

Nick extended the search into entertainment, documentaries, and beyond. There had to be some candid shots surely, some unguarded moment away from his NASA minders?

Text scrolled and faded. Images flashed. There were a few extended interviews, some passing appearances on live documentaries. But Bruce always appeared guarded. Impeccably polite, quick to smile, friendly . . . but he never really opened up.

Even when he talked about his religious experience . . .

Nick felt like slapping himself. How could he have forgotten! John Bruce had one of those religious born-again experiences during the SHIFT flight.

He froze the image. "New search. John Bruce. Born-again."

He tapped at the remote, extended the search into the God channels. A new list appeared. Shorter. He selected the first. No good. The second . . . the third.

John Bruce materialized in front of him. He was sitting in a chair, on a stage somewhere, being interviewed. He looked dumbstruck—eyes wide open, mouth slightly parted.

"It was incredible," began Bruce, his voice slow and wavering slightly. "I saw this white light, brighter than anything you can ever imagine."

The holocameras zoomed in on his face, ballooning John Bruce's head to twice normal size. Nick could see the spaceman's eyes tearing up, the slow bemused shake of his giant head, the faraway look.

"And suddenly I felt this rush. So much joy, so much peace. It was like I was bathed in light. All my sins, all my worries being washed away. It was then that I knew I wasn't alone in the *Pegasus*. God was with me."

"Hallelujah," shouted a disembodied voice from the studio audience.

Nick agreed. Hallelujah, indeed, and froze the image. White lights, feelings of euphoria. Everything you'd expect to see if the brain came under stress during the flight. Distortions of the visual cortex, a massive release of endorphins. Was this the proof he'd been looking for?

He bounced to his feet and paced around the frozen image. He so wanted it to be true. Just thinking about the possibility made his brain salivate. There were so many ramifications. Not just for John Bruce, but for science. If a fragment of Bruce's memory could become detached and find its way into another person eighteen months later, then where had it been in the meantime? Had it been preserved in the higher dimensions? Had it drifted on hitherto undreamed-of upper dimensional currents? Had it snapped back to Earth immediately and spent eighteen months trapped inside Pendennis's head?

And was it more than just memory? How much of John Bruce's personality had gone with it? A vestigial remnant? Louise said he talked like John. Could a complete subpersonality have ripped away?

Or was the great Nick Stubbs deluding himself?

Every week thousands of people saw bright white lights. Near-death experience, anaesthetics, drugs. Why should this one be any different? John's brain had come under stress. So what? He was being shot through new space. Everyone expected his brain to come under stress. He saw a white light as he started to pass out then came to. End of story. Pendennis was a con man who'd tapped Louise's mind and John Bruce was as whole as the day he'd joined NASA.

Nick slumped back onto the sofa. Why did rational explanations always have to be so boring? Why couldn't he live in a universe where the simple answer was invariably wrong, a Heath Robinson universe of elegant complication, magic, and imagination?

He grabbed the remote and pressed Play. Maybe the interviewer would ask about Bruce's childhood and the spaceman wouldn't be able to answer.

John Bruce stuttered back to life.

"And when I returned to Earth, I was amazed at how beautiful everything was. It was like I'd been wearing dark glasses all my life. Suddenly everything was brighter, the colors deeper, the sounds sweeter. Life was beautiful. It still is. If only people would take time out and look around."

Nick froze the image and leaned forward. How long had it taken *Pegasus* to return to Earth? Two days? The white light effect doesn't last that long. If Bruce was still experiencing a disturbance in his visual cortex two days later . . .

He jumped to his feet.

Not the primary visual cortex—that was at the back of the brain, too far away. But the temporal cortex. Right place, right function. It handled some of the visual processing and it was close to long-term memory and hearing. A single localized rupture there and . . .

He was off again, spiralling into the wonderful world of conjecture. He could see it all. A section of higher dimensional matter ripped away. Not enough to kill or critically impair, just enough to mildly distort some of Bruce's sensory functions.

He paced as he thought, kindling his brain, greasing his synapses. Think, think, think. If only he had a scan of Bruce's brain, he could prove it. He could generate a map, work out exactly what would have been lost, and . . .

He needed that scan. He grabbed the remote, zapped John Bruce, called up a list of his SHIFT contacts, and then tried to calm down, taking deep breaths. He had to sound relaxed. A casual voice mail inquiry to a fellow scientist across the pond. Do you still have the full spectrum brain scans from before and after John Bruce's flight? Did that sound innocent enough? What if there really had been a cover up? What if they knew he'd been damaged?

He tapped his fingers nervously on the remote. What choice did he have? He needed those scans. If SHIFT knew there were problems with the neural shielding then no concocted cover story would convince them to give up the data.

He voiced in his request and played it back. Then recorded it again, bringing the timbre of his voice down from slightly manic to somewhere around borderline normal. Happy, he appended his contact details and pressed Send.

Then another thought hit him. What if Pendennis didn't need to be telepathic? What if John Bruce had talked about Louise in an interview and everything Pendennis had told Louise was in the public domain?

"New search," he asked. "All areas. John Bruce and Louise Callander."

He waited, feeling stupid. Shouldn't this have been his first search? Had he lost the ability to see the obvious?

The search took in the whole net: the holocasts, the web, the groups, the boards, homespace. Several hundred hits, but nothing linking the astronaut John Bruce to his Oxfordshire sweetheart.

Which was a relief.

He tried Pendennis next. There was something familiar about that name.

"New search. Peter Pendennis. Upper Heywood."

A list of titles filled the viewing area. *Angel-faced killer gets life. The Butcher sent down. Butcher guilty.*

Nick stared at the list. Now he remembered. He'd been out of the country at the time but had caught some of the Spanish-language holocasts. It had been big news worldwide. For a month or two.

He selected the first entry to refresh his memory. Back came the friendly news anchor.

"The angel-faced killer, Peter Pendennis, was sentenced to life imprisonment today for the murder of eleven people."

Eleven people in two months. Nick listened to the litany, watched the images of each victim flash and fade. Wedding pictures, holiday snaps, smiling moments from happier times.

Then the horror. Cold words delivered off camera while pictures of grim-faced policemen stood guard outside people's homes. Five houses around Oxford broken into, the owners drugged, killed, and dissected.

Tearful neighbors came into shot, friends, family members— ashen-faced accounts of how the bodies had been discovered. Not bodies, corrected one of the witnesses, pieces. Then he broke down.

Nick swallowed hard. Pieces. Strewn over carpeted floors. No attempt to hide or conceal, just left where they fell like cuts of meat. Except for their noses, which were always missing—bitten off, presumed eaten.

Nick looked away. *This* was the man he was going to see?

Did Louise know? Should he tell her?

He looked at his phone.

What if she pulled out?

Anders Ziegler was standing by the window staring out at the car park. They'd be arriving soon.

Big mistake.

But what else could he have done?

Twice he'd rung to cancel and twice he'd changed his mind in mid-call. What if there *was* a higher dimensional component to Peter's condition? Could he risk not finding out? Could he risk discovering later—maybe many years later—that he'd had the answer within his grasp but had turned the opportunity down because of theoretical differences?

Straw grabbing. The day was going to be a disaster and everyone knew it. Bazley had washed his hands of the whole affair and Security were obsessed with the equipment Stubbs was bringing with him. Not only had they insisted on a detailed specification of each item coming in but they were going to scan the lot for drugs and explosives.

"Why's he need all those tripods?" the chief warder had asked. "Bet they're hollow. You know how much contraband you can fit in one of those extendable legs?"

He did now.

The day couldn't end soon enough.

Louise watched as Nick set up the last of his equipment, completing the circle of tripods and black boxes. It was the same room she'd been taken to before. A bleak room with what looked like a dentist's chair at its center. Except this chair had straps.

She shivered. Everything about this room was cold. The bare white walls, the concrete floor. It felt like a larder. One of those old farmhouse cold rooms, lined with slate and facing north to keep the food fresh.

And the atmosphere didn't help. The two men weren't speaking. Ziegler kept looking towards the door and checking his watch while Nick stomped around his equipment and glared.

And any second now a lunatic was going to walk into the room.

Could the day get any better?

Louise looked towards the door. Perhaps she should just leave? Reschedule for another day, another year . . .

The door opened.

Pendennis shuffled through. Dressed in a red tracksuit, chained hand and foot, smiling, confident, flanked by two warders, he looked like a boxer on his way to the ring, nodding to invisible supporters, smiling at invisible friends.

Louise stepped back. The room had grown colder.

The warders sat Pendennis in the chair and strapped him in. He looked so small. A tiny red figure, pinned to the center of the room.

The lights dimmed then went out. On came a new light, a pencil-thin beam that played across Pendennis's forehead. A few adjustments, the whirr of a projector motor, and the beam changed shape. It pulsed, slow and rhythmic, sucking the consciousness from Pendennis's brain. Ziegler's voice—monotonous, droning, persuading—worked in harmony with the light. Sight and sound, prising resistance apart; penetrating, probing, smoothing, and calming.

"John? Can you hear me?"

Only the electric motor replied, humming to itself from its housing above the door. Louise could feel her heart thumping in the foreground, waiting . . . waiting for something to happen.

And then John arrived, pushing into the darkness, unsure . . . afraid. The light caught the wildness in his eyes. His red suit wriggled in the chair like a maggot on a palm.

"What's the matter, John?" asked Ziegler.

John struggled to speak. His teeth clenched. "Lou," he grunted. "Where is she?"

"She's here, John," said Ziegler beckoning her forward.

Louise shuffled closer until she was alongside Ziegler. A few feet away, John struggled against his ties, the webbing digging into his forehead, the skin on either side white with the strain.

"What's the matter, John?" Ziegler asked again.

"Got to warn her." The words came out in a rush. He grimaced as if in pain, writhed, threw his head from side to side. "He's coming. He knows we're here."

"Who knows we're here?" asked Ziegler.

John's eyes bulged, his face was blotched. He threw his head far over to one side, as far as the ties would allow, as if trying to bury his face in the back of the chair.

He mumbled something into the fabric.

"I'm sorry, John, I can't hear."

John's head snapped back. Louise jumped. He was staring right at her, eyes imploring, breathing hard, his lips moving silently against clenched teeth.

Ziegler adjusted the light.

"I'm taking you to a safer place, John. Back to your childhood. Do you remember a place where you felt safe?"

John shook his head and shouted. "No! Can't leave. He's everywhere. Don't have much time." His head jerked back to face Louise. "Tell now. Must."

He strained to move closer, his eyes watering, sweat beading his forehead. His teeth clenched in a rictus grin.

"Listen," he said, his voice almost incomprehensible.

Louise edged closer. He looked terrified. She reached out to touch his shoulder. "It's all right, John."

It was the gentlest of touches. She half expected him to flinch, but he didn't. He closed his eyes, stopped straining, and took a deep breath.

"You're real," he said. "I wasn't sure." For the first time he sounded like John.

"What message do you have for Louise, John?" asked Ziegler.

John looked into Louise's eyes and smiled. "It's for her, Doc. Only her. Come closer. He can't hear if I whisper."

"Who can't hear?" asked Ziegler.

John turned to look at the doctor. "You know, Doc. He says you've always known."

"Peter? Have you been talking to Peter?" Ziegler's voice lost its emotionless edge. It quickened and rose a few notes.

John shook his head. "No, the other one."

"Which other one?"

John ignored him and turned back to Louise. "I saw her, you know. On the *Pegasus*. She was waiting for me by the bright white light."

"Who?" Louise and Ziegler spoke at the same time.

"Your mother. She told me to tell you . . ."

Louise felt like she was going to collapse. Her mother had died five years ago. The memory still raw. The chemo, the weight loss, the helplessness.

"What did she say? What . . . "

John's mouth formed as if to speak but nothing came out. He looked drained, his face streaked with sweat. His eyelids began to droop.

"John, what did she tell you?" Louise felt like shaking him. She'd driven through the night to get to her mother's bedside. Ran from the house the moment her father had called from the hospital. Driven through the rain and the tears only to miss her by a few minutes. One lousy red light that should have been green. She'd never been able to say good-bye. Never been . . .

John said something. Barely audible. Louise leaned forward, straining to hear, her ear bathed in a gentle exhalation of his breath.

And then her world shattered.

Teeth clamped around her left ear. The pain excruciating. A wild animal growling beneath her, throwing its head from side to side like a crocodile, trying to rip the ear from her face, tear it to shreds, kill, destroy, maim.

She screamed, grabbed hold of something—the chair, Pendennis, she couldn't tell. Shock. Disorientation. Liquid running down her neck. Blood and saliva coagulating together, piercing pain ripping at her insides. Pain piled upon more pain piled upon panic and fear and hatred and . . . why couldn't she faint? Why couldn't she close her eyes and disappear into some other world where all pain had been abolished and . . .

Time dilated. Reality rolled up inside a long dark tube with Louise at one end and all manner of hells at the other. Guttural sounds, shrieks, and shouts.

And then darkness.

Mick Harris—warder, blue shift—ran into the room. The main lights flashed on. Confusion. A woman was screaming. Doc Ziegler was standing over her, trying to drag her off. There was someone in the chair . . .

Recognition. He saw the red-clad legs. Peter Pendennis! He should have known. It was always Peter Pendennis. If ever someone should have been "lost" out of an upstairs window—it was Peter bloody Pendennis.

He ran over, looked for a glimpse of red torso in a gap between the writhing bodies, and hit it hard. And kept on hitting it. For Sarah and Siobhan, the Jacksons, little Tracey, and all the others. For everyone who'd ever had the misfortune to come into contact with that sick murdering bastard.

More warders, more shouting, running feet amongst the cries. Someone prised Pendennis's jaws apart and pulled the woman off. Blood everywhere. Pendennis laughing, looking right at him, shrieking, the woman's blood running down his cheek.

"Bastard!" The warder swung a crunching left into Pendennis's face. Then another. An arm grabbed his from behind, pulled him back and away. He wrestled free, charged forward again. Pendennis still laughing at him, spitting blood in his direction.

He swung and missed. Knocked off balance from behind, he almost fell on Pendennis. A brief hope surged. If he could crack his forehead against the bridge of Pendennis's nose? He brought his head back ready. But was pulled sideways, rolling across the chair and onto the floor.

Why didn't they let him finish the little bugger off?

He struggled. Two, three men on top of him, arms and legs locked. Everyone breathing hard. And Pendennis shrieking from the chair. Laughing, mocking.

Another lunge, desperate and futile.

"Leave it out, Mick," said someone. "He's not worth it."

Mick was on his feet now, straining against his fellow warders, the group moving crablike towards the door.

He saw the woman, ashen-faced, her hand pressing something white against her ear. She was leaning against the corridor wall, Ziegler supporting her elbow.

Pendennis screamed at her from behind. "So much for your Yank boyfriend, whore! You'll never see him again now, will you? Peter's killed him! Peter's killed him!"

A red mist descended. Like all the previous red mists. Mick struggled to break free. Why didn't someone shut the bastard up! Just one more shot. Just one. Maybe he'd get lucky and break the bugger's jaw.

Force of numbers bundled him into the corridor. Behind him, a door slammed shut.

CHAPTER FIVE

Louise sat in the passenger seat of her pickup and simmered as Nick drove her to hospital. The whole side of her face throbbed. She felt used, violated, and stupid. He'd used her mother to get to her! That hurt more than the ear. Her mother's memory raped by that sick bastard.

She pressed the bandage harder against her face. Why hadn't someone told her!

She darted a glance at Nick. "Did you know?" she snapped.

"Know what?"

He kept his eyes on the road. He'd barely looked at her since the attack.

"You knew, didn't you? About Pendennis being the Butcher."

Nick swallowed. "I only found out yesterday."

"And you didn't tell me!"

"I thought you knew."

"You thought I knew! What kind of idiot do you take me for? I wouldn't have gone within a million miles of him if I'd known."

Silence, broken only by the constant beat of the windscreen wipers as they fought to keep pace with the rain.

"Sorry," said Nick. At least he sounded contrite. "I thought, being local, you'd have known."

"Well this is one local who doesn't watch the news as much as she should, okay!"

She turned away and stared blankly at rows of rain-streaked houses. Was it her fault? Should she have known? Should she have at least checked before agreeing to see a patient at a secure psychiatric unit?

And what was Ziegler doing even entertaining such an idea! Letting that sick bastard loose on the public again. She couldn't believe it when the nurse had told her.

"You know who he is, don't you?" she'd said while bandaging Louise's ear. "The Butcher, that's who. He tried it on me once. Pretending to be all nice and friendly. But I've seen what he does to people. He's worse than sick. He's evil."

The Butcher. She remembered the news reports from eight years back but not his real name. He'd always been referred to as the Butcher, not Peter Pendennis. Not that she watched much news back then—she was always too busy.

Pain shot through her ear again. She'd have to have stitches. Maybe a shot or two . . .

Panic. She swung to face Nick. "He doesn't have PIRS does he?" Or AIDS or CJD or God knows how many other blood-borne killers.

"No . . . "

"How do you know? Don't they gang rape prisoners all the time?" And drugs. Pendennis would have to be a junkie. Shared needles, tainted blood . . .

"I asked," said Nick. "Pendennis is kept away from the other prisoners. . . ."

"But not members of the public," she shouted. "Not me!" She hit the dashboard with the heel of her hand. She wanted to hit out at everyone. Her anger bouncing from target to target. "Not me," she repeated, quieter this time, and slumped back in her seat.

"Pendennis was given a clean bill of health last month," said Nick.

"Lucky him."

Quiet descended. Louise stared straight ahead, unfocussing her eyes and letting the world swish back and forth in time to the wipers.

"And there's something else," said Nick.

"Thrill me."

"It's about the readings I took . . . of Pendennis. I was only monitoring one of the imagers at the time but from what I saw the readings were incredible. Huge spikes right across the spectrum. Far more higher dimensional matter than you'd expect. Pendennis has got one of the most abnormal brains I've ever seen."

Louise turned and glared at him, incredulity turning to sarcasm. "You think?"

Nick waited for Louise while she was being treated. And braced himself for her return. His normal reaction to raw emotion was to walk away as quickly as possible. Not easy in a car.

And the guilt didn't help. He should have told her about Pendennis. He should have watched out for her. But he'd been too busy being mesmerized by the spikes and flares coming from the scan screen to see anything else.

And it had been incredible. No one had thought to give MPD patients a full-spectrum brain scan. At least not that he'd heard. Would they all exhibit such incredible diversity?

He itched to return to Upper Heywood, collect his equipment, and process the data. But duty kept him nailed to the waiting room chair.

Eventually, Louise appeared in the corridor. With the bandage removed and her earlobe sealed and microstitched, no one could have told she'd been injured. Only the garishly bloodstained jumper and slightly matted hair gave her away.

"What were you saying earlier about Pendennis's scan?" she asked as she came nearer. "Tell me the last two days weren't a complete waste of time."

"Time spent in the pursuit of knowledge is never a waste . . . "

She stopped him with a look. "Just tell me."

"I need to process all the data first—the imager I was monitoring only analyzes part of the spectrum—but I can say there was no attempt at telepathic bonding. I had an imager trained on him from the moment he stepped through the door."

"But that doesn't mean that there wasn't the first time."

"No, but why stop? He wouldn't have known what my equipment was there for. And if he was trying to lure you closer to him why didn't he try to read your mind to gauge how he was doing or plant telepathic suggestions? It would have made things easier for him."

Louise shook her head. "So, where was John? Ziegler didn't do anything different today. So, why didn't John appear? How come we got that . . . that thing instead?"

"Hypnosis is not an exact science. He might have had John at the beginning but, if it had been me, I wouldn't have been happy about his level of distress."

"Why?"

"It can interfere with hypnotic control. Ideally you want your subject calm and submissive. Too much emotion and—zap—the subject's flooded with adrenaline and you're liable to lose him. I would have taken John deeper, established a solid baseline, and then begun."

Hindsight. The second greatest power in the universe, after chocolate.

"So, you don't think he was faking it the first time?"

"I like to keep an open mind. But from what I saw today, Pendennis has a far greater agglomeration of higher dimensional matter around his brain than any subject I've ever encountered. And most of it looks distorted, ripped even. Now, is that because his MPD has segmented his mind? Was I looking at the billowing strands of a fractured consciousness? Or is there another cause? I can't wait to analyze the rest of the data to find out."

"How long will that take?"

"About thirty minutes to process the data, an hour or two to map and analyze." Not to mention the drooling and speculating while the numbers crunched. "I'll start as soon as I've dropped you off."

"You'll start sooner if you call a cab now. I'm perfectly capable of driving myself home."

Nick's equipment was waiting for him, packed and roughly stacked in a corner of the Upper Heywood reception area, along with the implicit message "Never darken these doors again" etched in the atmosphere. Two warders glared at him from behind glass screens. The same two warders who'd made him take everything apart earlier so they could scan and tick everything off against their ridiculous register.

"You'll have to sign for it first," said one of the men.

Not before he'd checked the crates, he wouldn't. He squatted next to the stack and began the inventory, making sure that everything was present and that nothing had been broken or reset.

"I'd check the big crate at the bottom," said the other warder. "Peter likes to play hide and seek."

Highly amusing, thought Nick, though somewhat disconcerting for a man whose hand happened to be hovering over the big crate's latch at the time.

He flipped the catch and peered inside, jumping only slightly at the shout of "Boo" from over his shoulder. He shook his head and tuned out the laughter, and sifted through the crate. Everything present, intact, and functioning.

It took several journeys to carry everything over to his van. No offer of assistance was either offered or asked for. Nick staggered while the two men watched. At least they'd stopped cracking jokes.

Once on the road, Nick relaxed and started planning his schedule. He'd use the computer he'd taken to Framlingham Hall. It was faster than his home system and he'd been using it for the past week to process imager data—all the presets were programmed in.

He swung the van into the Hall's gravel drive then backed up to the front door. At least the rain had stopped, he could see the first stars twinkling through gaps in the cloud. He opened up the Hall and switched on the lights then ferried the crates into the large front room that he used as his base. Soon the room was humming to the sound of cooler fans and the electronic whirr and click as each imager disgorged its data into the central processor. Nick checked his watch—6:17PM—another half hour and he'd have the results. He sent his mind skipping into the future, imagining what he'd find: a map of a brain ripped into twelve, or however many personalities Pendennis was supposed to have, pieces? Or twelve separate entities—pieces of psychic flotsam washed up on Peter's wrecking shore? And if the latter, what form and extent would they take? A few cells of memory, an entire subpersonality, a jumble of ideas and thoughts?

The prospect was so vast. And begged so many questions. How did they get there? Why *there* and not somewhere else? Was it a process happening all the time? Was that why memories degrade with age—were we constantly shedding experiences into the higher dimensions? Maybe into a vast collective unconscious, a species memory girdling the planet like a ring, helping shape the development of future generations.

He paced up and down the echoing boards. What a time to be alive. The dawn of a new age of discovery.

That's when he heard the noise. Not the settlement creak of an old house. Or the whirr of a computer. But a distinct thud. And it came from upstairs.

A manifestation? His first thought. A spirit? After all these weeks of inactivity had something decided to materialize? He glanced at the display bank in the corner—no warning lights. All the so-called "hot" rooms were monitored—sudden temperature change, sound, infrared, ultraspectrum, higher dimensional fluctuations.

Had something happened in one of the other rooms?

Another thud. He grabbed one of the wide-spectrum imagers, moved towards the door, then looked back. Should he leave now? Wasn't the Pendennis project more important?

But when you're hot . . . Why not stun the scientific world with two major discoveries in less than an hour?

He moved through into the hallway and listened. Distant traffic noise hummed from outside. Should he switch off the hall light? Use the screen from the imager as a guide?

He looked up the stairs. The wide wooden staircase wound along the outer walls of the hallway—three floors and two half landings. Cobwebs hung from the undersides of the stairs, draping the upper sections of a wallpaper that had long since faded and peeled along every join.

He turned off the lights and let the house sink into darkness. A pale light shone from the imager's display screen, a view of the stairs—like several pictures overlaid—a two-dimensional representation of a ten-dimensional object, using color and luminosity to portray the different planes. To most people it would have looked like a jumbled mess. To Nick Stubbs it was like second sight.

He ascended slowly, keeping to the outer, less creak-prone, edge. He let the imager pan before him, turning slowly at the half landing to take in the next flight. Nothing. The display rippled slightly with the motion of his hands, the extreme sensitivity of the imager warping the picture like a desert heat haze.

He reached the first floor, corridors running to the left and right, a door straight ahead—open. He stopped and listened. Distant traffic, still the only sound. He swept the imager in a slow arc through 360 degrees. Nothing moving, nothing anomalous, only bare walls, floor, and ceiling.

And the cold smell of decay. The house hadn't been heated for years and damp had penetrated deep into the fabric of the building.

A thud from upstairs to his left. He swung round, instinctively pointing the imager at the sound. A ceiling rippled back. An ordinary color-soaked ceiling.

He turned and took the stairs, quicker now, still keeping to the edge but not checking the imager. Not yet. He stopped a few steps from the next floor, reached out and placed the imager on the landing floor, turning it to point down the left-hand corridor, tilting and angling the display screen back towards him. The corridor snapped into focus, psychedelic but sharp.

And empty.

He rotated the imager to point down the right-hand corridor. Also empty.

Another thud. Closer this time. One of the rooms to the left. Maybe front, maybe back—he couldn't tell.

He scooped up the imager, crept along the corridor, hunching down, his eyes glued to the display screen. He paused at the first set of doors. One left, one right, both open. He held out the imager and scanned into both rooms. Nothing. He leaned further in, stretching to scan behind the doors. Still nothing. A light from a passing car tracked across the ceiling then disappeared. Darkness and silence.

Thud. Closer still. It had to be from the next room. The next room at the front.

Back into the corridor, hunching lower still. Wasn't the White Room along this corridor? He'd been told the third door from the stairs. That's where he'd set up his equipment. What if they'd told him wrong? Or included the door at the top of the stairs in their count?

Had he been monitoring the wrong room?

The imager shook in his hands. Nerves, excitement, the sudden appreciation that he was alone in a dark, deserted old house.

With a history of death and hauntings.

Thud. Or was that more of a bang? He fought to place the sound. Wood striking wood? A door banging?

He edged closer, colors dancing in the monitor, a few more yards, feet . . . He froze, then slowly bent his legs, sliding his back down the wall into a squatting position. His hand reached out, placed the imager on the floor to his right as noiselessly as he could, just clear of the doorjamb and pointing into the room.

The display screen filled with color. Something was inside. Something he couldn't quite make out. He narrowed his eyes, peered, leaned as close as he dare. The screen showed a mass of color. Not moving but complex—a large projection into higher dimensional space but too obscured to be recognizable. Was it a ghost?

A rush of cold air came from the room. Nick swallowed, his eyes fixed on the screen. If anything started to move towards the door . . .

Bang. Nick jumped. Definitely a bang this time. From well inside the room. And was that something moving on the screen? Something at the rear by the windows.

He steeled himself, reached out, and grabbed the imager. He needed a shot from another angle. And he wanted to be on his feet—just in case. He pushed himself upright and held the imager out at shoulder height into the doorway. Whatever had been moving had stopped. And the mass of immobile color was now at floor level, low and long, a few feet from the door.

Shit! He couldn't keep his hands still. The image danced and rippled. Did it look human? A second ago he was almost sure but now . . .

It was man-sized but why was it lying on the ground? Weren't apparitions supposed to walk? Or was he totally misreading the image?

He closed his eyes for a long second, took a deep breath, and stepped into the doorway.

His eyes flicked between the screen and the grey murk that filled the doorway. He could see a shadow, a slightly darker grey outline on the floor. And a mass of orange, yellow, and red from the screen.

Something was lying on the floor.

There was a bang and another rush of cold air. Nick jumped, pointing the imager at the sound. A window? An open window banging in the wind?

His hand steadied for a second. Colors stopped dancing. It had to be a window. But they'd all been locked. He'd checked them himself only a few days ago.

His attention switched back to the shape by the door. Was it a person? A tramp or junkie looking for a place to crash for the night? The shape looked right. But shouldn't there be some movement? Breathing, a sound?

He had a bad feeling, a very bad feeling. He felt for the light switch, flicked it on and . . .

Froze. A man's body lay sprawled on the floor, face upwards.

His nose was missing.

CHAPTER SIX

Panic! Pendennis, the bitten-off nose was his trademark. He must have escaped. Was he still here?

Nick threw himself back against the open door, slamming it against the wall, darting glances left and right. What if Peter was still in the building? Hiding. Wasn't it likely? The body was still in one piece. Pendennis always stayed to cut them up.

He forced himself to look at the body. It wasn't just the nose. Both eyes had been gouged out. And—he swallowed hard, forcing himself to continue—both ears were either missing or obscured by blood. Thoughts of Louise percolated to mind – that madman clamped to her ear. It had to be Pendennis. The ears, the nose . . .

And the hands. Both had been severed.

He vomited. Uncontrollably. Then ran, flapping his hands at light switches but not stopping if he missed, ducking at the slightest noise— real or imagined—running for his life, stumbling, tripping, throwing himself down the stairs. He had to get out. He had to get out now!

The front door wouldn't open. He dropped the imager, grabbed the door handle with both hands—turned, pulled, rattled, and wrenched the door open. Running again, the wind cold against his face, gravel crunching beneath his feet. Not safe yet. He needed open spaces, people, streetlights. Pendennis could be anywhere—hiding in the house, the grounds, that shadow by the gate.

He flew across the road, not heeding the traffic, ran to the nearest streetlight ,and turned, breathing hard. No sign of Pendennis. Yet.

He activated his phone, shaking fingers pressing the buttons at his wrist. "Police," he said, his voice ragged. "Now! There's been a murder at Framlingham Hall."

He called Louise next. No answer. Shit! Shit! Shit! Was Pendennis already there? Was that where he'd come from?

A sudden noise made him jump. Something metallic being knocked over. The wind, a cat, Pendennis? He ran to the next streetlight. Keep moving. Keep visible. Maybe flag down a car?

Who'd stop for a wild arm-waving stranger? He wouldn't. Not at night.

On to the next streetlight. Then the next. Another call to Louise. Still no answer but he'd leave a message.

"Call me. Lock all your doors and windows. Don't answer your door to anyone. Pendennis has escaped."

He checked his watch. How long would the police take? Was that a siren?

Five minutes later the police arrived, lights flashing, siren wailing. He tried to flag them down but they drove past, stopping outside the Hall gate. He crossed over and ran towards them, calling. He had to warn them.

They were outside when he caught up to them. Two uniformed officers. Was that enough?

"Stop!" he shouted, slowing to a breathless halt. "He might still be in there."

"Who?" said the older of the two officers, eyeing Nick suspiciously.

"Pendennis," said Nick. "He's escaped."

The two policemen looked at each other. "*Peter* Pendennis?"

"Yes, Peter Pendennis. Look, there's a body in there with its nose ripped off. Who does that remind you of? And he's severed both hands. He must have been cutting the body up when I disturbed him. He might still be in there."

All three men turned to look at the house. It sat grey and silent, set back from the road and bathed in shadow.

The two policemen conferred. One went back to the vehicle. Hopefully to call for backup. The other switched on his lapel recorder.

"Now, sir, for the record, what's your name?"

Nick gave his statement, glancing towards the house whenever he thought he heard a sound or caught a flash of something moving out of the corner of his eye.

The other policemen called over from the car. "Nothing on the system about Pendennis breaking loose."

"Call Upper Heywood," said Nick. "They might not have missed him yet. And get a car over to Lower Hillside Farm, Mickleton. Check that Louise Callander's okay. Pendennis threatened her. He attacked her this afternoon."

Another shared glance between the two officers, followed by a click as the lapel recorder was turned off.

"I think you should show us the body first."

Great, thought Nick. They don't believe me. "Ring Upper Heywood. They'll confirm it. Or the A&E at Oxford General. They treated her."

A hand propelled him from behind. They were going to force him back into the house. Playing into Pendennis's hands, they were going to walk in unprepared.

"At least arm yourselves," he begged. "He could be anywhere."

The older policeman patted the baton strapped to his belt. "Don't worry, sir. Anyone gets out of order . . . we know what to do."

Even better, not only didn't they believe him but they were getting ready to take him round the back and play bad cop-bad cop on his ribs.

"I'm telling the truth!"

"Of course you are, sir."

They walked in silence. Nick pushed from behind into the lead, steering a course along the exact centre of the gravel drive, wary of every shrub and shadow. He skirted past his van, reached the open door and ushered the officers through.

"Second floor, turn left, second door on your right."

"We'll follow you."

Nick closed his eyes. He could be walking to his death. No one would care. The police would blame Pendennis. *Our officers couldn't have foreseen the danger. A tragic turn of events for all concerned.*

Not that it was much safer on the porch. Pendennis could be under the van, waiting for the police to move off.

He took a deep breath and pushed the front door wider. At least the lights were still on. He stepped though, his eyes zigzagging, trying to cover every inch of the hallway. Empty. Except for the imager he'd dropped earlier. He bent down to pick it up.

"Is that a camera?"

"Yes, it's mine. I dropped it earlier." He set it down on a windowsill and looked towards the stairs.

"The police are here," he shouted. "More are on their way."

"Come on," said the younger officer, nudging Nick in the back. "The sooner you show us this body the sooner you can get out of here."

Nick began the climb, trying to think positively. At least with the lights on, anyone hiding would cast a shadow. That thought took him to the first half-landing where another thought was waiting. What if Peter was hiding behind a door or perched on an upstairs banister waiting to jump on him from above.

Nick crouched instinctively, and looked up. Nothing.

"What's the matter?" said a voice from behind.

"Nothing," he lied. What was the point? They wouldn't take him seriously until they saw the body. Or Pendennis jumped them. Scenes from every horror film he'd ever watched fluttered to mind. The hero walking into a trap. Deranged killer lurking in the shadows. Cue suspenseful music, cue unexpected death. What was the betting if he turned around now he'd find only one officer left? The other garrotted and whisked silently away, only to reappear in a future scene, cut up and flayed.

He'd never—*ever*—watch another horror film again.

He listened, straining to hear two footfalls following his.

Or was one Peter's?

He glanced back—he had to. Two policemen were in his wake.

For now.

Calm down. You're nearly there. All the lights are on. Pendennis'll be miles away by now.

Encouraging words. But one floor away was a mutilated body. Dozens of hiding places in between. And a crazed killer who could be hiding behind every door.

"Come on," urged a voice from behind. "We haven't got all night."

Nick ascended, swallowing hard, the first-floor landing approaching, his eyes darted from side to side. Was that a shadow? Was that a footstep?

He hovered on the top stair then took off, grabbing onto the handrail and pulling himself across the landing and up onto the next flight of stairs, away from every door and hiding place, as quick as he could.

Then slowed. Deep breaths. Nearly there. One flight of stairs, one corridor and five doors to go. Another glance back. Still two policemen behind him. No crazed axe-man rushing at them from the shadows.

Yet.

More deep breaths. His mouth was dry and why had that window stopped banging? Had the wind dropped? Or had someone closed it?

A creak made him start. He looked up, trying to judge if it came from the attic or the landing above. Roof timbers settling or a floorboard shifting under a killer's bloodstained foot?

Calm down. One step at a time. Nearly there.

Up he went, hugging the wall, counting down the remaining steps. Nine, eight, seven. The landing looming, a moth fluttering around the bare light bulb at the head of the stairs. Three, two . . .

One.

He stopped. Every sense on alert—the slightest sound, the smallest movement.

The window banged.

He closed his eyes, one last deep breath and . . .

He was moving—swiftly, purposefully—along the corridor, jumping past the open doors, not pausing to think or breathe, just aiming for the other side of *that* doorway, *that* room.

He glanced inside as he leapt by. It was still there, lying on the floor. For one awful moment he'd expected to find it gone. But it wasn't.

"It's in there," he said, pointing into the room. "The vomit's mine."

It was a relief to be believed. Suddenly, action was taken. Backup was requested, CID, forensics. A car was sent to check on Louise. And, hopefully, Upper Heywood too. Within twenty minutes the Hall was alive with people and light and voices and away went the fear. Pendennis would be miles away by now.

Time dragged. Nick was put in the room across the corridor and told to wait, someone would interview him later. All his requests to be allowed to wait downstairs so he could check on his work were denied.

Great. Forty minutes ago he was on the verge of two major discoveries. Now, he was on the verge of none. The house crawling with heavy-handed coppers, poking into everything. What if someone pressed a reset button and cleared all his data?

Or had Pendennis already done that? Was that why he'd left the body? To lure Nick away so he could wipe all the data?

Shit! Shit! Shit!

The door opened. A man—plain clothes, early forties, sharp-featured—stepped inside. He reminded Nick of an old schoolteacher he'd once had. It was the glasses and the way he stared—a long, silent, appraising look as though he was looking deep into your soul and judging it flawed.

"DCI Marsh," said the man. "Are you ready to give a statement?"

Nick was more than ready. He waited for the lapel recorder to flash red then reeled off the events from the moment he entered the Hall that evening.

"Are you the owner of this property?"

"No, I'm from the university. We've been using the Hall."

"What for?"

Ah. This was not going in a good direction. One sniff of the word *paranormal* and he'd be labelled a crackpot. The general public hadn't absorbed the huge advances that had been made in the last two years. Higher Dimensional Theory to them was still SHIFT and space travel. They didn't realize the extent of its application.

"Research," he said, hoping the interview could move elsewhere.

"Into what?"

"Astropsychology."

"Which is what in layman's terms?"

"The study of Higher Dimensional Theory and its application to psychology."

There was a pause. If Marsh asked for an explanation of HDT he'd refer him to a textbook.

"Where does Framlingham Hall fit into that?"

Marsh was definitely like Nick's old teacher. He could never be deflected either.

"Look, I'm doing 'blue sky' research. I take an idea and run with it wherever it leads. This house is supposed to be haunted. I've been monitoring some of the rooms to see if there's a higher dimensional explanation."

He recognized the look. It may have been fleeting, but it was there. Who can trust a witness who sees ghosts for a living?

"And before you ask, I wasn't monitoring that room. You'll find my equipment in the room next door."

"Convenient. Did you recognize the victim?"

"No."

"You've never seen him before?"

"Never. Look, have you seen Louise Callander yet? Is she all right?"

"She is now. After two of my officers spent ten minutes reassuring her that Pendennis was still locked up."

"He is?"

Nick couldn't believe it. How . . .

And then another thought. Would Upper Heywood lie to protect their reputation? Stall the police until they'd got their stories straight? Or had someone sneaked Peter back in?

"Are you sure?" he asked. "Has anyone actually seen him?"

"We don't need to. Peter Pendennis is not part of this investigation."

"But it's his MO. The nose, everything."

Marsh shook his head. "The vic's too clean. Pendennis leaves his saliva over every body part. He licks them. This one's clean."

Nick swallowed. That was information he'd have been happier not knowing.

"And the body's intact," Marsh continued. "Peter likes to cut his up."

"He was interrupted."

The detective shook his head again. "That never bothered him before. That's how we caught him. We found him sitting on a basement floor with a severed head in his hands." He looked into the distance and clenched his fists. "He had its nose in his mouth, can you believe that? And he just looked at us. Didn't try to run or anything. Just looked up as though what was happening was the most normal thing in the world. And all the time his cheeks were going in and out as he sucked on that wretched girl's nose."

"Sucked?"

None of the holocasts had mentioned that. A stray synapse fired somewhere in Nick's brain. A connection. Something he'd read a long time ago. Rituals—Egyptian? Polynesian?—something to do with sucking the spirits of the dead out through their noses.

"And killers don't change their MO," said Marsh.

"Killers with MPD might. He's got twelve personalities so why not have twelve different MOs?"

"You seem to know a lot about Peter Pendennis."

Back came the appraising stare.

"I was at Upper Heywood this afternoon. I saw him."

Marsh narrowed his eyes. "Do you often visit Mr. Pendennis?"

"No." Where was this going?

"My officers said you had a camera with you when you found the body. Were you taking pictures?"

"No! I was using it to see by. It's got night-vision capabilities."

"Why not switch on a light?"

"I didn't want to risk losing the manifestation."

"You didn't want to risk losing the manifestation."

Marsh sounded like a cross-examining barrister echoing Nick's testimony to an incredulous jury. Nick squirmed. Okay, so all the other HDT researchers were out there doing sensible things with their imagers like helping develop stronger, lighter, cheaper alloys. And, yes, he was having fun, pointing his imagers at anything and everything he could think of. But that's what real scientists were supposed to do—to shine light where no one had ever thought to look before, to push, probe, and question.

There was a knock at the door. A young man leaned into the room. "Sorry to disturb you, sir, but we've got an ID on the vic."

"Sergeant Kelly enters the room," said Marsh for the benefit of the recording. "Close the door, Mike. What have you got?"

The sergeant closed the door and read from a note pad. "Name's Vince Culley, twenty-nine, local man with two previous convictions for burglary. Petty, opportunist stuff. Probably after the cameras downstairs. They're easy to spot from outside."

A burglar? Nick hadn't considered his imagers a target. Though, thinking about it, he should have.

"So, if the cameras are downstairs," asked Marsh, "why was his body found up here?"

"The window was open in the room I found him in," said Nick. "It still is."

The sergeant shook his head. "Unlikely point of entry for our Vince. He's strictly a ground-floor, brick-through-the-window type of crim. And we found a broken pane in a door at the back."

"So," said Marsh, eyeing Nick like a predator about to strike. "He breaks in downstairs to steal the cameras. You catch him at it. There's a chase."

Nick started to remonstrate. Marsh ignored him, raising his voice to drown out Nick's objections.

"You trap him in the room opposite. There's a fight. You hit him too hard, panic, then try to make it look like Pendennis. Is that how it happened?"

"Where's the blood?" Nick shouted, holding out his hands, showing his nails, gesturing to his clothes. "Whoever cut off his ears must be covered in the stuff."

"We'll check the bathrooms," said Marsh. "And the bins. If you cleaned yourself up we'll know."

An hour later was Nick was formally arrested and taken to the station at Summertown where he was scanned, DNA-swabbed, and had his fingernails cleaned. Then he was given a virtual lawyer, who explained his rights and talked him through the procedures. Don't say anything, don't sign anything, and don't let them search your property. Probably the wisest words he'd heard all day.

A succession of detectives took it in turns to interview him. Nick sat through it all, biting his tongue. He'd tried the cooperative route and look where that had got him.

He was released at nine AM the next day without charge. No apology, no explanation, just a grudging "You can go'" from the desk sergeant.

Once outside, he called Louise. Had the police really spoken to her yesterday? They'd spun so many stories at him the previous night he didn't know what to believe.

The phone rang endlessly. Where the hell was she? He left another message then called a taxi. He'd pick up his van from the Hall then drive to Louise's.

The cold bit through his clothes. He wasn't dressed for being outside. He folded his arms and tried to squeeze some warmth into his chest. The taxi arrived, he climbed inside.

"Framlingham Hall," he said. "And turn the heater up as far as it'll go."

Streets flashed by. Inside, Nick rubbed his hands and replayed scenarios. What the hell was happening? Was Pendennis on the loose or paying a copycat? Some sick scheme to reopen his case?

And had the police impounded Nick's equipment? Had he lost all the data from the night before?

The taxi slowed as the Hall came into view. There was a police car blocking the entrance, a tape strung across the drive.

"Drive past," said Nick. "I'll get out around the corner."

The taxi dropped Nick off a block away. He cut down a side street and over to an alley that led to the back of Hall. There was a door in the long stone wall that ringed the Hall grounds. Nick slipped inside, out of sight of the police at the main entrance, and ran across the rough grass towards the back of the house.

Great, the grass was wet. He looked down at his trousers—soaked from the knees down. So much for looking inconspicuous. He made his way to the back door by the kitchen. The police had said Culley had broken a pane in the back door. Would anyone have fixed it overnight?

No one had. He stood by the door and listened. It didn't sound like anyone was inside. He slipped a hand through the broken pane, turned the key in the lock, and gently opened the door.

He stepped through, closed the door behind him, and tiptoed to the front of the house. Still no sounds of life within the Hall. He paused at the bottom of the stairs, looking up, senses on high alert. The police must have gone, left a couple of officers to sit outside to keep the onlookers away.

Damn! He noticed the empty windowsill. He'd left one of the imagers there last night.

He ran to the front room. How much had they taken?

An array of imagers, monitors, and processors filled one corner of the room. Were they all there? He counted them, walking around, checking they hadn't been damaged or reset. Only the one imager was missing.

He rummaged through one of the boxes looking for a blank data cube, found one, and quickly inserted it into the main processor. The download began. He glanced to the window. Anyone walking by would see him. Were the two officers supposed to patrol the grounds?

He tapped his fingers on the top of the unit. Come on! A few more seconds . . .

The data cube ejected. He thrust it into a pocket. And stopped.

Curiosity. He was here, the data was here, the monitors were here. Okay, the data hadn't been fully processed yet. But the imager data would have been merged, enough for a composite picture. Could he wait another hour?

He ran to the side of the window, squatted down, peered back towards the gate. The police car was still there, nothing moving.

He checked his watch. Five minutes. That's all he'd risk.

He called up the files, sifted through the ones he could use, and ran the programs. A composite scan of Pendennis's brain appeared on the screen. It was staggering. He viewed it from every plane, zooming in and out, flipping and rotating. Colors flared and sparked. He'd need more time to calibrate the results and run comparisons but the initial results . . .

So much mass. What was it—three, four times the amount of higher dimensional matter you'd expect? Though what *was* normal? They'd sampled such an infinitesimal section of the human population, who could say what the normal ranges were?

But what a sight! It looked like the brain had been ripped in several places and then expanded. Was that evidence of additional matter— an outside source for the extra material—or was it part of the brain's natural healing process? An accretion of new matter like new bone being created at a fracture site?

He definitely needed John Bruce's brain scans. Had they arrived yet?

He rang the university computer, dialled into his office, and checked his mail. Nothing from SHIFT. Maybe his usual contact was on holiday? He rang off and called up his home computer. He'd resend the request and tag on a couple of extra addresses. One of his contacts at SHIFT had to be at work.

There was a sound in the distance. Outside. Nick ducked down, tapped in the confirmation, and sent the request to SHIFT. Time to leave. He could finish processing the data at home. He grabbed an imager—one of the full spectrum models—and stuffed it in his pocket. Who could tell when the police would release the rest?

He retraced his steps back to the Banbury Road, wet-legged, a considerable bulge in one of his pockets, but exuding a practiced and smiling innocence.

"Hi," he told the first policeman. "I've come to collect my van."

He showed his ID, waited to be photographed, finger-scanned and cleared with HQ.

And then collected his van. He could feel the impatient stare of the two policemen burning into the back of his neck as he took his time, walking around the van, looking inside, underneath and checking the back. Images of the previous night were still fresh. If Pendennis had escaped yesterday and made his way to the Hall, what better mode of transport than hiding in Nick's van?

A car horn sounded from the gate. "Come on, we haven't got all day!"

Nick opened the driver side door and climbed inside. One more check of the backseats and he was away, waving good-bye to the police and Framlingham Hall. He tried Louise's number again. Still no answer. Was she avoiding him? Or worse?

He didn't want to think about worse. He'd go home, load the data, fire off the analysis programs, and leave them running while he drove over to see her.

And maybe drive to Upper Heywood afterwards. Demand to see Pendennis and see how Ziegler reacted.

He parked outside his two-bedroomed terrace, slammed the car door shut ,and jogged the few yards through his almost nonexistent front garden.

And stopped.

His front door was ajar. Had the police searched his house after all? He reached out a hand and pushed the door wider. He expected to see his belongings strewn all over the floor but the carpet was clear. He could see up the stairs to the landing and the hallway through to the kitchen at the back. Nothing looked out of place. No damage, no muddy boot prints from overzealous officers.

A more worrying thought. If not the police . . .

He crept inside. At least it was daylight. And there were people nearby. Houses on both sides, a street only yards away.

But would Pendennis care about that?

He glanced into the lounge, the same mess he'd left it in. But at least it was *his* mess. He turned back. The kitchen light was on. *That* was wrong. It had been daylight when he'd left yesterday. No reason for the light to be on at all.

He stepped back and grabbed an umbrella from the hall stand. Not exactly a baseball bat but at least it was something.

He edged closer, leaned back, and pushed at the kitchen door with his foot, watched it slowly swing open, holding the umbrella two-handed in front of him like a kendo staff.

He braced himself.

There was large saucepan on the kitchen table. It drew his eyes. He hadn't left it there. A burglar wouldn't have left it there. . . .

It had to be a message. Someone playing a game with him. Take off the lid and look inside. Except the moment he did, he knew it wasn't going to be good. He didn't have any pets, but the children next door did. A little voice cried out for uncertainty. Let whatever it was inside that pan stay in whatever state it wanted to be. Alive, dead, undetermined.

He edged closer. Sniffed the air. No smell of freshly cooked meat, thank God. He reached out. Let his fingers hover a few millimeters above the lid. No heat.

He drew back. He'd call the police. Let them open it. Or was that what they wanted? They couldn't get a search warrant so they broke into his home and left this knowing that he'd be so freaked after last night that he'd have to call them. Then they'd have access. No need for a warrant as they'd been invited onto the property.

Was that how they worked?

Or was he being stupid, irrational? It was only a saucepan for Christ's sake! He couldn't leave it there forever.

He rose on the balls of his feet, reached out, ready to spring back in an instant.

He closed his fingers around the wooden button at the center of the lid, took a deep breath and started to lift . . .

Inside, two hands were cupped in prayer. An eyeball nestled at their base. Maybe two. He'd dropped the lid and looked away by then. He turned, threw up what little he had left in his stomach, and fled.

CHAPTER SEVEN

Nick struggled with the van door, yanked it open, and threw himself inside. One thought. Drive. He had to get away. Fast.

The engine responded, the back end of the van sluing from side to side as Nick floored the pedal, accelerating between the lines of parked cars.

He braked hard at the end of the street, turned a corner, then another, navigating as fast as he could along the myriad narrow city streets.

Was he being warned, set up, or played with?

He hit the brakes. He shouldn't have left that pan for the police to find. His fingerprints were on the lid, probably all over the pan too. He had to go back, get rid of the evidence. The police could arrive at any time.

Doubt. Wouldn't that be part of Peter's game? He'd want Nick to go back, waste time removing evidence, digging himself deeper when all the time there was something else—the ears, the nose, God knows what—hidden in a drawer, the fridge, or under a pillow. Nick running around like a rat in a maze while Pendennis watched and laughed.

No, he couldn't go back. The police would be on their way. A tip-off. All part of the game. One that he was *not* going to play. He gunned the engine. He needed space, time to think. A place Pendennis and the police couldn't find. And he needed to find Louise. She'd be next.

If she was still alive.

He hit redial at the next junction. Why didn't she answer?

Louise started at the noise—a creak from upstairs. Any other day she probably wouldn't have noticed. Old houses were never quiet. But since Nick's message she'd been unable to settle. And being told by the police not to panic hadn't helped—if there was nothing to worry about, why had they driven all the way over to tell her?

Pendennis. She could see him whenever she closed her eyes: his grin smiled in the embers of the fire in the lounge grate: he pursued her into her dreams. He was the cause of every unknown sound and inspiration behind every fear.

She shivered. The room was cold. The heat from last night's fire had all but gone and she couldn't afford to start another one until this evening. Finances, lack of. She grimaced and took another look at the figures on the screen. Surely last month couldn't have been that bad?

But it had. Another month with more going out than coming in, the gap ever widening, her savings diminishing. Just what she needed—doing the monthly accounts was supposed to take her mind off Pendennis, not depress her further.

She stared at the screen wondering where all the money had gone. Well, it was late winter. Her vegetable plot at its bleakest—only the leeks and winter cabbage producing, the early broccoli another five weeks away, her stores of usable potatoes and onions dwindling. Not to mention the extra fuel bills and the feed for the animals.

A sudden noise from outside made her jump. A chain saw starting up. Someone out hedging or cutting up logs for firewood.

Or looking for someone to massacre.

Stop it, Louise, she told herself. You're being ridiculous. But she listened all the same, listening for the whine of the motor to come closer.

It didn't, stopping instead after a fifteen-second burst. Louise kept listening, all other senses on hold, her eyes unfocussed, her body stock-still. A goat bleated from the front field breaking the spell. No doubt Bonnie, the young Anglo-Nubian, complaining that it was too cold, too muddy, not enough food, and she was bored.

Try living my life, thought Louise. And took another look at the figures. Maybe it was time to get a part-time job? Though how she'd fit it in was beyond her. The vegetable garden took up all her spare time from April to September and rescue cases could arrive at any time. If she cut down on the rescues then she'd risk losing donations and charitable status. If she skimped on farm maintenance—the hedges and the buildings—she'd lose her Countryside Stewardship Grant.

She was stuck. With no good way out. All logic said downsize—sell the farm, buy somewhere cheaper, get a proper job. But this was her *life*. And her last link to her father.

She sighed. Anchored to the past, that's what she was. By the farm, the land, and the dream. They'd found the property together—she and her father—both falling in love with the nut-brown thatch, the eyebrow windows, the leaded lights, the massive oak beams, the buttermilk walls that hadn't known a right angle in over four hundred years. They'd made an offer on the spot, and moved in two months later. It was to have been their refuge from a world that had taken away a wife and mother, their hope for a new, simpler, self-sufficient life.

She sniffed away a tear. Her father's ashes were scattered around the base of the old beech tree by the barn. His favorite spot. He'd sit beneath its massive canopy for hours watching the sun slowly set.

Memories like that could not be quantified. Nor outweighed by numbers or logic.

She'd never leave. And that was that.

The chain saw started up again. Or was that a car? She glanced toward the window but couldn't see anything. And whatever it was it had stopped. She rose from the chair and started to walk to the window. Then the hammering started: someone was pounding on her front door.

"Who is it?" she shouted, standing well back from the door, her legs braced to run.

"It's me. Nick. Open up."

She unlocked the door. Nick burst in. He looked shaken, and out of breath.

"Are you okay?" he asked. "Has anything happened?"

"What . . ." She stopped mid-sentence, he'd pushed past her and run into the kitchen. "What are you doing?" she asked, hurrying after him.

"Checking," he said, his eyes darting everywhere. "Has anyone been here? Left anything?"

"Only the police," she said, folding her arms. "What the hell did you think you were playing at last night? You scared the shit out of me."

He didn't seem to be listening. He pushed past her again this time into the hallway. "Have you looked everywhere?" he said over his shoulder. "Would you notice if someone broke in and left something?"

"Like what?" She followed him into the lounge. "Nick, if this is some kind of joke . . ."

He turned. "Do I look like I'm joking?"

He didn't. Louise's day edged another notch downwards. She'd checked the news reports—both last night's and this morning's. All they'd said was that a body had been discovered at Framlingham Hall and the police were treating the death as suspicious. No one had mentioned Pendennis, and last night she'd been assured that he was still locked up.

But Nick's face said different.

"What happened at the Hall?" she asked.

He told her everything. The body, his arrest ,and the remnants on his kitchen table. She listened, her pulse quickening. This could not be happening.

"Now do you see?" said Nick, bouncing forward in his chair. "You're next."

"No." She shook her head. There had to be some mistake.

"Think about it," urged Nick. "He's playing with us. First the dead body, then the scattered body parts. Where do you think he'll hide the ears?"

She found her hand rising to the side of her face, her injured ear tingling.

"But Pendennis is locked up! The police said—

"The police!" The chair could no longer contain him. He was on his feet, arms waving in frustration. "They think *I* did it. Dead body, suspicious character at the scene, why look any further? I doubt anyone's even been to Upper Heywood to check."

"But why would Upper Heywood lie? They couldn't hope to get away with anything as stupid as that."

"Oh, no? They call it news management. You wait and see. In a couple of days someone'll come on air and say that Pendennis has been recaptured and how they couldn't release the news earlier because of the unnecessary panic it would have caused and how the police investigation would have been hampered by thousands of mistaken sightings. It's what government agencies do all the time."

Louise felt besieged. She could see the logic in what Nick was saying but there had to be other possibilities. If only he'd slow down and give her a chance to think.

"Couldn't it have been someone else?" she asked.

"Who? Someone left a mutilated body at a house only I frequent. Then they go to my home and leave body parts on my kitchen table. I'm being targeted. Now, how many Mafia bosses have I pissed off this last week?" He raised a finger to his cheek in mock deliberation. "Hmmm, let's see . . . none. How many serial-killing murdering bastards have I met? Oh, just the one. Do you think it could be him?"

"There's no need to be sarcastic."

"He attacked you, Lou. He tried to rip off your ear. That body last night was missing two ears . . . and a nose—which is Pendennis's trademark. What more do you need?"

"The police said—" she started.

"Sod what the police said. We've got to get out of here." His hands swung towards the front door in an exaggerated shooing motion. "Now, come on. Pack whatever clothes you need. I know a place we can hide . . ."

"No," she said, gripping the arms of her chair. "I can't leave. I won't."

He stared at her, incredulous. "What do you mean you can't leave? Pendennis could be here any second. He might already be here."

She felt like one of those poor families on the HV broadcasts. You saw them all the time. In the midst of floods, lava flows, insurrection, and hurricanes. An interviewer on the doorstep, asking why they refused to leave. All reason weighted against them. But still they clung to the forlorn hope that their home would be spared, their valley saved. Some miracle around the corner. Some miracle that never came.

"No," she said, looking away from him. "I have responsibilities. I have animals to look after."

"Don't you understand? The man is a butchering maniac."

"No, *you* don't understand." She glowered at him, stabbing a finger towards his chest. "I can't just run off. Someone's got to look after them." She pointed at the window, towards her fields and animals. "It's my job. It's my *life*."

She could feel the catch in her throat, her lip trembling. And then Nick replied, his voice for once calm and reasoned.

"And what do you think Pendennis is going to do to them?"

Her hand flew to her mouth. Her animals! She hadn't thought. "I'll call the police. They'll protect us."

She started punching numbers on her wrist. Nothing happened. Her wrist-phone was still switched off from last night. She flicked it back on.

"Louise." Nick's hand closed around her wrist, covering the dial-pad. "They won't listen. And even if they did, they'd only protect you, not your animals."

She struggled to pull her wrist free and then stopped. He was right. To the police, animals were property, not living beings. They'd park a squad car in the yard and watch the house but not the paddocks. There were five acres of fields. Pendennis would use that. He'd get to her through her animals. Make her wake up to find a butchered corpse in the front field.

She shook her head. No, she couldn't let that happen. She'd spent her life protecting animals. She couldn't endanger them.

"We've got to go," she said, pushing him away, rising to her feet, already starting to plan the hand over. "I'll ring Karen, see if she and Jane can take the sheep and goats. There's a girl in the village who might be able to take the donkey."

She hurried towards the bureau by the door. She'd have to draw up a diet sheet. Who liked what, when, and how much.

Minutes passed, maybe tens of minutes. Louise running from room to room, phoning friends and acquaintances—explaining, cajoling, begging, packing—while Nick played with her old HV set in the corner, bringing up images of Pendennis and monitoring the news reports.

"At least no one's found the body parts on my kitchen table yet," he shouted up to her as she clicked her battered suitcase shut. "We should be able to get a clear run out of Oxford."

"Which reminds me," said Louise. "Where exactly are we going?"

He didn't answer. Louise called louder. "Nick?"

Still no answer. Louise froze. She could hear the drone of conversation through the floorboards—the holovision?—but nothing else.

She hurried to the stairs—no point trying to be furtive in a house where every floorboard creaked—and flew down them. She grabbed her father's walking stick by the coat rack and burst into the lounge.

Nick was over by the holovision set. Two of him. One, a grainy head-and-shoulder shot floating two feet off the ground. A woman reporter was talking in the background.

"Police have yet to confirm that this is the same man they held for questioning last night but informed sources . . ."

Nick muted the commentary. He looked dazed. "They've just found a tongue and a pair of ears on my desk at college."

CHAPTER EIGHT

Nick stared at his grainy image. At least one of him was smiling. The unsmiling one held his head in his hands. He'd been stitched up so tight the join was seamless. Body parts at home, body parts at work. Who needed a confession? There was a trail of blood running through every building he frequented.

And they'd be looking for his van. He'd have to keep to the unmonitored roads away from the street cameras. And switch off his phone.

"Come on," said Louise, pulling him to his feet. "Have you disabled your van's GPS transponder?"

"What?" said Nick, confused.

"The security tracking device. If you haven't disabled it, all the police need is the van's code and they'll know exactly where we are. Have you disabled it?"

He shrugged. "How would I do that?"

"Never mind," she said, pushing him towards the door. "We'll take mine. You follow me in the van. I'll find a quiet place away from here where you can dump it. I know where all the local cameras are."

"You do?" He started to feel inordinately dense. He hadn't thought about transponders or how easily he could have been tracked. The police might have started already. His van was outside now, pinging its whereabouts into the ether.

And did he infer correctly that Louise's pickup had had its security transponder disabled?

Louise ran upstairs and returned with a battered suitcase. "Come on," she said. "I thought you were in a hurry."

He followed her out, hanging back while she locked up. "Why would you disable your security transponder?" he asked.

She smiled at him as she walked past. "You're not the only one with secrets."

Nick followed Louise to a lay-by on the outskirts of a large village five miles away. He parked the van, locked up, and ran to the waiting pickup.

"You'll have to tell me where we're going," said Louise.

"Head for Devon. Back roads all the way."

Louise drove, navigating a circuitous route along twisting country lanes, single-track roads, and barely metalled farm tracks. Several times they had to turn back. A major road up ahead or a large village. After half an hour, Louise hit the brakes. Hard. The pickup screeched to a halt.

"What?" shouted Nick.

Louise nodded to a flashing red light on the pickup's dashboard. "Camera up ahead," she said, already throwing the pickup into reverse.

Nick clung to the edges of his seat as the vehicle swung into a quick three-point turn. "You have a camera detector? Aren't they illegal?"

Louise didn't answer. She looked straight ahead. "I think there was a left turn about a half mile back."

"Lou, why do you have a camera detector?"

"You don't want to know."

"Yes, I do."

"No, you don't." She pointed to a junction ahead. "There. That should get us past the village."

On they went, crisscrossing the county out of Oxfordshire, through Berkshire, and into Wiltshire, taking any small road heading south or west. Navigating by the sun, knowing that if they switched on the pickup's computer it would give away their location in an instant. Nick ducked down, obscuring his face as a line of oncoming traffic approached. He pretended to read a book on his lap, covering the side of his face with his left hand.

Time stretched. More traffic, more about turns, more anxious minutes. Anything could be happening back in Oxford. The police could have raided his house, issued an arrest warrant, started a nationwide hunt. If only he could find out.

He tugged at his wrist-phone. If he switched it back on he could call up the news, see if they'd found his car, made the connection to Louise . . .

And give his location away. A simple triangulation of the phone masts. The police would know his position to the nearest centimeter. Enough to set up a perimeter, roadblocks, a search grid for the surveillance drones.

He sank lower in his seat, peered into the sky, listened. Were the drones already airborne? Were the police waiting to see where he went?

Nothing. Nothing that he could see. He opened the window and stuck his head outside, turning in his seat to check behind. Still nothing. The sky was clear except for a handful of ivory-colored cumulus clouds.

"What are you doing?" asked Louise.

"Looking for drones," he said, ducking his head back inside. "Couldn't see any."

An hour later they pulled over by a farm gate to switch seats—Nick's turn to drive. They crossed the county border into Devon soon after. Only an hour or so more to go.

The mood began to lighten. They were almost there. Oxford was miles away, they'd avoided every camera and hadn't seen a single police car. Maybe the murder wasn't such a high-profile case? Maybe Nick had already been cleared of any involvement?

"Is there any food at this place we're going to?" asked Louise.

"Plenty," said Nick. "No need to stop to stock up on anything."

"What kind of place is it?"

"It's a clinic. One of those private homes for the confused children of the very, very rich. You know, the kind of place where you pay someone else to look after your teenage delinquents once they've burnt and bombed their way out of all their other homes."

"And you've got a room there?" She sounded surprised.

"Two actually. The owner's a friend and I rent an apartment—well, a couple of rooms—over the garage."

"Why?"

"Research."

"Into teenage delinquents?"

"No."

"Into what then? Ghosts?"

He turned to look at her. Could he tell her? Or would she be just like the others?

"Let's just call it blue-sky research into an interesting aspect of Higher Dimensional Theory."

"Which you couldn't do in Oxford?"

He searched for the right words. A part of him just wanted to come straight out with it. Another part held back.

"Let's just say I needed somewhere I'd never be interrupted. Which is why we're going there. No one else knows about it."

"What about the clinic staff? If your face is all over the HV. . . ."

"No one'll see us arrive. There's a back way to the garage. And the apartment's set back from the house. We'll have the pickup locked away and be inside before anyone notices."

Nick drove up to the garage annex and jumped out. Louise shuffled across into the driver's seat while Nick unlocked the door to the end garage. She peered over at the main building. A Victorian rectory by the look of it—three floors of solid grey stone—with a two-story annex forming an L at one corner and ending in a garage block. She eased the pickup forward as Nick raised the door then accelerated into the garage.

The door to the apartment was at the end of the block. Nick had it open by the time Louise joined him.

"It used to be the housekeeper's flat," said Nick as he thumped up the stairs. So much for keeping quiet, thought Louise, wondering how far noise would carry in an old place like this. "Then it became a storeroom, then it became my research lab."

Nick turned left at the top of the stairs and started pushing boxes and clutter aside. Louise watched from the hallway. The room was a mess. Cardboard boxes, packaging material, tripods, papers, electrical equipment. Everything scattered over the carpet like a random archipelago of clutter. In the corner was a bed. Unmade. She peeked into the other rooms while Nick cleared a space and set up the HV. More chaos. Another room that looked the twin of the first and a kitchen, with three large boxes of what looked like food. God knows what the sell-by dates would be. It looked like someone had returned from the supermarket, dumped the shopping on the kitchen table, and left.

At least she couldn't smell anything—other than the usual stale mustiness of a room that hadn't known an open window for months. She poked through the first box of shopping. Pasta, tins of tomatoes, vegetables, and soup. And a supermarket till receipt dated five months ago.

Music sounded from the HV in the other room. A short burst she recognized as the introduction to BBC News. Louise checked the second box of groceries—breakfast cereal, tins of ready meals, baked beans—then walked through to join Nick.

"They've found the body parts at my house," he said.

But they hadn't found his van. Or made the connection to Louise.

At least, no one had said so.

"Look at that," said Nick gesticulating at a wild-eyed head shot of himself rotating double life-size above a small island of bare carpet. "I look like Rasputin . . . after he'd been poisoned, shot, beaten, and drowned."

Louise smiled. There was a resemblance. The long straggly hair, the wild look. "They do say the camera never lies."

"Then *they've* never heard of editing. I never looked like that in my life."

But there was one slice of luck. The murder was moving down the news schedules. A celebrity sex scandal and a drugs cheat sports star had knocked it off lead spot. Maybe by tomorrow it would be old news.

"Is there any mention of Pendennis?" asked Louise.

Nick checked. Nothing on the news channels for over a year.

Louise watched as he widened the search, trawling the groups, the forums, the web, looking for anything written in the last two days. "Someone might have heard something and posted to a forum," said Nick. "Maybe one of the warders at Upper Heywood developed a conscience."

Louise didn't say anything. All the doubts she'd held in check during the car journey began to resurface. What if Pendennis hadn't escaped? What if Nick was wrong? She'd abandoned everything—her animals, her home. All for what? Nick's insistence that Peter Pendennis had escaped. The only proof being a gruesome murder that someone was trying to frame Nick for.

Or so Nick said. She watched him as he stabbed a remote at the HV. What did she really know about him? He was a professor who studied ghosts and looked like Rasputin. He seemed harmless enough but . . . who could tell? You heard so many horror stories these days. Killers whose own wives hadn't thought them capable of hurting a fly. How could she—a person who'd only known him a few days—really know what he was capable of?

Guilt. It crept up on her. What was she doing? Doubting a man *she'd* put in danger. Without her, Nick would never have met Pendennis. She'd brought them together. It was her fault. She should never have accepted Ziegler's invitation in the first place.

Rage. At her own stupidity, at Ziegler, at Pendennis, at John Bruce and the world. Why? Why? Why?

Text and images flashed and scrolled before her. The few recent hits Nick found were deadends. Kids listing their top ten favorite serial killers and extracts from weird song lyrics.

"The government might have blocked access to all the relevant files," suggested Nick.

Louise shook her head in disbelief. If she heard one more conspiracy theory . . .

Then she had an idea.

"I'll phone Ziegler," she said. "He owes me." Her hand reached instinctively for her ear. "If I ask him to let me talk to Pendennis he can't refuse."

Nick looked incredulous. "Of course he can. And the moment you phone you give away our location."

"I'll drive somewhere else and make the call."

"It's too risky. You might be seen. The pickup might be seen. And it's not only the police who are looking for us."

"You don't know that!"

He rolled his eyes. "We've been through this . . ."

"*You've* been through this."

Out came the resentment. The feeling that she'd been railroaded into leaving everything she held dear, her voice rising in both volume and pitch.

"You're not listening!" hissed Nick. "Pendennis has escaped—"

"You don't know that!"

"But I can find out."

"How? By searching the net?"

"No, by—"

He stopped mid-sentence and looked away.

"By what?" she pressed.

He looked uncomfortable. He took a deep breath. "Look, there's something I've got to do first. But as soon as I've done it I'll tell you."

Louise shook her head. She was not going to be fobbed off.

Nick held up his hand. "I'm not stalling. I really do know a way. But there's something I've got to show you first."

Nick loaded the data cube of Pendennis he'd brought from Framlingham Hall.

"It'll take about fifteen minutes to finish the processing but . . ." He paused while he tapped in a series of commands into a box attached to the HV system. "In the meantime, take a look at this."

A half-life-size image of Pendennis strapped in a chair flashed into life. Louise jumped. It looked so real, the image so sharp, floating there a few feet distant. She wanted to look away but felt drawn. At least his face was turned away. And the image was frozen. She wasn't sure if she could stomach looking into those eyes again.

"You'll note I've tuned out Ziegler and everyone else in the room," said Nick. "I'll tune out the chair next but I need you to see something first."

He shifted position, kneeling down to tweak at a control box—one of the many sleek black boxes stacked either side of the HV unit.

"What you're seeing now is a three dimensional representation of Pendennis and the chair. The three physical dimensions. Let's call them x, y and z. Now, thanks to the wonders of science—and some pretty amazing programming—how would you like to see the same picture from the higher dimensions?"

He paused, expectant, like a father on a Christmas morning waiting for his son to open his special present—a working model of a spaceport, the one with all the extras and the programmable docking module.

"Go on," said Louise, indulging him.

Pendennis disappeared. As did the chair. Louise stared at the new image. It looked like a chunk of coral, a wild misshapen chunk of coral with tendrils radiating in places half a meter from the center. The whole colored in a wash of light blue.

"Forget about the blue color," said Nick. "That's just there to help visualize the object. We could have chosen any color. The important thing to note is the position of the object. Watch."

He flipped the image back to the original and then back again. "See where the higher dimensional matter is located. It's centered on the brain."

He flipped the images back and forth once more. Pendennis's head morphed into the blue coral and back again.

"Now, what we're seeing here isn't a complete higher dimensional representation. Remember how I told you that there were seven extra dimensions?"

Louise nodded.

"Let's call them a, b, c, d, e, f, and g. Well, what you see here"—he waved a hand at the holodisplay—"is only a, b and c. A three-dimensional subset of the higher dimensions just to give you a flavor."

He checked his watch and then gazed towards the bay he'd loaded the data cube into. "Another ten minutes or so and I'll be able to show you the rest. Swap the axes in and out and show you how amazing the universe is three dimensions at a time."

"How does any of this help determine if Pendennis has escaped or not?"

"I'm coming to that."

He bounced to his feet and fetched a computer screen from the corner of the room.

"Now we're switching to two dimensions," he said, setting up the screen on a box and turning it on. "We're going to use color to portray the higher dimensions. It's a bit confusing at first. But it's the best way we've found so far to visualize the entirety of a ten-dimensional image."

He flicked switches on another control box and voiced in a series of commands. A multicolored image appeared on-screen, the colors so dazzling it looked like a psychedelic cartoon.

"That," said Nick, "is the image of a normal brain." He smiled. "Well, as normal as anything about me could ever be described as normal. Maybe a tad larger than the average man or woman in the street's brain and chock full of—"

"I get the point," said Louise, cutting him off.

"But will you get this point?"

He turned off the screen, flicked a series of switches, and voiced in a new set of commands. A new image appeared on the holodisplay—a life-size human brain slowly rotating through space.

"That's me," he said. "I've transferred the image to the HV display. Now watch as I flip to the abc representation."

Back came the blue coral. But smaller and more regular, the tendrils even and of similar size.

"Pendennis's brain is bigger than yours?" asked Louise.

"Not his physical brain. That's slightly smaller but the rest of it . . ." He billowed his arms. "I've only seen a subset of it so far but it's massive. Like someone's dipped his brain into a blender and then teased it out into all kinds of fantastic shapes."

He checked his watch again. "Another few minutes and we'll be able to see."

"You still haven't—"

"I'm getting to it." he interrupted. "Look."

He pressed a button on the remote and the image changed. A succession of images followed. Strange shapes, like exotic sea creatures. Corals, sponges, jellyfish, shapes she couldn't even describe. Nick flicked through the dimensions three at a time, varying the combinations: c, d, and e; a, b and d; c, e and a. His brain morphing about its axis.

"Now, watch this," he said. The image disappeared. "That's the g axis. For some reason we haven't found anything that protrudes into it. Animate or inanimate. The same for the f."

He pressed the remote again. "Now look at this."

Another exotic shape appeared. Irregular and edged with what looked like fronds. Nick froze the image.

"This is the x, y and b representation." He stretched a finger into the viewing area and pointed to a dark line near the base of the image. "Do you see that?"

He pressed the remote and rotated the image—slowly. "It looks like a crack, doesn't it? And note its extent. It rings the base of the image. Separating the structure into two: the small area at the base and the larger mass at the top."

It did. An irregular black line sliced through the base of the image as though it was a piece of blue ceramic that had broken apart and been badly glued back together.

"Now, here's another. Again I'm mixing two physical dimensions with one higher and . . . same result."

He was definitely in his element. He looked like a stage magician producing rabbits from places no one dreamed a rabbit could ever appear from. His eyes screamed, "isn't this amazing?"

It was, but where was it going?

He flicked through image after image. Each one showed a dark line—or fracture as Nick now insisted on calling it—running through the base of the image.

"Now we flip back to a purely upper dimensional representation to refresh our memories and voila—no fractures anywhere. You only get a fracture when you see the brain straddling the upper and lower dimensions."

He slowed his delivery to emphasize the last sentence. *You only get a fracture when you see the brain straddling the upper and lower dimensions.*

He paused as though expecting a light bulb to ignite over Louise's head.

"So?" she asked.

"So maybe that fracture *is* the boundary between the upper and lower dimensions. A separation point between the physical world and the other—the universe of the higher dimensions."

Louise started to feel inordinately dense. What did any of that mean? There was a boundary and it was marked. Nice. But what bearing did it have on anything happening in the real world?

"Don't you see what that means?" he asked. "The brain is split in two."

She felt like saying "so" again but decided upon another approach.

"Go back to the xyz display," she said.

The familiar shape of the physical human brain returned. "Freeze it there," she said, walking over and pointing to the dark line that separated the right and left hemispheres of the brain. "What's the difference between your 'fractures' and that?"

"There's every difference. They're different kind of lines for a start. One's at a dimensional boundary."

"They look the same to me."

"That's because you're looking at it with your head and not your heart. And, anyway, you haven't seen my other set of pictures."

CHAPTER NINE

He returned with another data cube, one he'd dug out of a box by the door. Louise wondered what kind of filing system he kept.

"Prepare to be amazed," he said, loading the cube.

A half-life-size image of Nick lying on a bed materialized in mid-air.

"That's me," he said. "Five months ago."

She recognized the bed. It was the one pushed up against the far wall.

"Now, watch as I strip away my ruggedly handsome features."

First the bed then Nick's body peeled away—feet first—until all that was left was his brain. It flickered for an instant then jumped to twice life-size.

"Ready?" he asked, once more resembling a stage magician. A stage magician poised to present his showstopper.

"Should I get the popcorn?" she asked.

"Only if you want to miss the most amazing thing you'll ever see."

He pressed the remote and the image vanished to be replaced by nine smaller images in a three-by-three grid.

"Come closer," he said, beckoning her forward. "You can't afford to miss a thing. All these are different views of my brain. The one in the center is the purely physical representation, top right is purely upper dimensional—the abc image—and those others are a mix of higher and physical axes—note the fracture lines."

Louise dutifully did.

"Now, I'm going to fast forward in time—let's not forget the ubiquitous fourth dimension—until . . ." He paused, his eyes riveted to a display panel on one of the control boxes. "Now!"

He pressed the remote and sat back on his heels. "Watch this. You'll be amazed."

Nine stationary objects floated in the ether. Some were the size of a large cauliflower, others smaller; all were bizarre. Even the physical brain—the more she looked at it. What a weird collection of twists and folds.

Louise blinked. Was that movement? The one at the top right, the chunk of blue coral. Did one of its tips move?

It did. And again. The whole structure seemed to shudder. But the physical brain hadn't moved an inch. She looked at Nick. He smiled back.

"Astounding, isn't it?"

"How are you doing that?" she asked. "Are there muscles that cross into the higher dimensions?"

He didn't answer. Only smiled and pointed to the image. There was more to come.

The blue coral appeared to stretch, the appendages elongating. And the other images too. The movement barely perceptible, a shimmer, a slight ripple along the surface. Only the physical brain remained stock-still.

Louise watched, fascinated: what was going to happen next?

There was a sudden shudder—across all the blue images—every surface rippling and then . . . movement. Each image stretching and elongating just as the coral had and . . .

Louise's mouth opened in surprise. The dark fracture lines were widening. The basal areas remained stationary while the rest of the image pulled away, maybe as much as an inch, two inches.

Louise leaned in closer, lowering and tilting her head to peer through the crack of the nearest image. It had almost split in two. The upper portion pulling away but still connected by a thread. The thread distorting under the pressure, looking like a piece of elastic pulled close to its limits. It had to be seven, nearly eight inches long now. The other images showed a similar deflection. Nick's brain was being pulled apart at the higher dimensional level.

She threw a glance in his direction. Had it hurt? Had it . . .

Another shudder. She caught the movement out of the corner of her eye. The blue images were wobbling just like the bubbles of detergent she'd loved blowing as a child. Then they snapped back. Every image restored to how they had first appeared.

"Well?" said Nick, switching the display off. "What do you think of that?"

"What was it?"

"You mean besides history in the making?" He paused. Something that Louise had begun to recognize as his customary pause after a rhetorical question. "That was my attempt to prove a theory," he continued. 'And a good attempt too. Did you see the degree of separation I achieved?"

She had but what did it mean? "Separation?" she asked.

"Of mind and body. Weren't you watching?"

Alarm bells went off in Louise's head. Separation of mind and body? Was Nick about to say he'd just filmed his soul? She started to shake her head. Religion had no place in her life. Religion, God, souls. They were anathema. If there was a God why did He look the other way when her mother got sick? When she was wasting away in front of everyone's eyes? When she died?

And if He hadn't looked the other way—if He'd watched—that was no God she wanted to know.

"That was not a soul," she said, jabbing a finger at the empty space where the image had been.

"A soul is only a name . . ."

"No, it's not. It's a belief. You'll have every zealot using it as an excuse to get creationism back on the curriculum. Don't you remember the chaos that caused?"

"Okay," he said, raising his hands in attempt to calm her down. "Don't worry, I'm the last person who wants to go public with this. Not until I fully understand it. And at the moment I see two possibilities, neither of which involves a deity."

She calmed down. "You do?"

"The way I see it it's one of two things. Something from the past or a glimpse of the future."

She was puzzled. "How do you mean?"

"Well, think back in evolutionary history to the birth of consciousness. Now, could that have come about because of a chance meeting millions of years ago? Two beings—one physical, one higher dimensional—combining together in a symbiotic relationship to produce the hybrid we know today? The higher dimensional component bringing consciousness and an increased potential for learning. The physical being bringing all the wonders of sensation—sight, sound, taste, smell, and touch."

Louise was skeptical. "How would it breed? How could you transfer the higher dimensional component into future generations?"

Nick shrugged. "I haven't worked out the detail yet. But if it happened far enough back in the evolutionary process maybe the higher dimensional component fused with the corporeal being. Maybe *it* was that spark that brought life to our planet all those billions of years ago. Maybe our bodies are more like shells that the higher dimensional component animates and the fracture that I showed you is the vestigial join between two ancient entities."

"What's your second theory?"

"That we're on the verge of an evolutionary quantum shift."

She looked at him. He appeared deadly serious.

"What kind of evolutionary quantum shift?"

"Ascension."

She wasn't sure if she'd heard correctly. "Ascension?"

"Our next evolutionary step. Discarding our corporeal form. Not in this generation, maybe not for several generations. But the mechanics are being put in place."

"Who by? God?"

"No, by random chance. All we need is that evolutionary push. The same motivation that whispered in the amphibian's ear—nice legs, now how about trying them out up there?"

"You think the human race is about to fly off into hyperspace?"

"I think a lot of things. One being that with the right motivation we can do anything. If the planet became uninhabitable—nuclear catastrophe, climatic meltdown, you name it—and I had the option of dying or flying, I know which I'd choose."

She didn't know what to say. It was all so . . . unreal and yet she'd seen the images.

"And it's already happening," continued Nick. "Think of near-death-experiences. What's that but a natural stress reaction? A precursor, if you want, of evolution's tap on the shoulder."

"I thought NDE was brought about by anaesthetics."

"That's the bright white light. Distortion of the visual cortex. What I'm talking about are the cases where a person finds him or herself floating above their body, looking down at the scene. There've been hundreds of accredited cases. Several where a patient was unconscious, their eyes closed, and yet they could recount everything that had happened around them—the conversations, what people were wearing, even the bald patch on a doctor as tall as a basketball player. They were up there," he pointed to the ceiling, "looking down the whole time."

"Is that what you were trying to do? To move your mind to the ceiling?"

He nodded. "And it almost worked didn't it? You saw how much it moved."

"But it didn't separate. You only shifted what . . . eight inches?"

He shrugged. "It was an early attempt. With practice I know I could do it. A little self-hypnosis maybe?"

"Why would you even want . . ."

A lightbulb blazed into life inside Louise's brain. He wasn't? He was. She could see it etched in every contour of his face.

"You're going to fly to Upper Heywood?"

He smiled. "And I won't be knocking on any doors."

She still didn't appear to understand. He'd explained the position he was in. On the run—from the police *and* a crazed serial killer—with only one person believing in him—Louise—and even she was having second thoughts. What else could he do? He had to prove to her that Pendennis had escaped.

Okay, so perhaps there was an element of the untried and the experimental about his suggested approach but didn't she see the elegance, the potential, of what he was proposing? If it worked he'd be able to see and hear everything going on around him, to bypass security, locked doors. He'd be able to search every cell and listen to every conversation. If Pendennis was missing, he'd find out. And then track down whoever was in charge and listen to whatever they had to say. A high-profile prisoner like Pendennis going missing was bound to generate a lot of audio traffic.

That had to make more sense than phoning Ziegler and trying to shame him into telling the truth. The man's job would be on the line. He wouldn't say a word.

"But it's a one hundred and thirty miles to Oxford! You can't even fly eight inches."

"I didn't have the motivation then. I saw the images of my brain stretching on the HV and panicked. Now I'm motivated. Believe me."

Back and forth the argument raged. Yes, there were risks but what choice did he have? Give himself up and put his trust in the justice system? With all that evidence against him and a deranged killer ready to manufacture more?

Or stay in hiding? How long would that last? Two days? Three? Certainly not a week. Louise was on the verge of walking out already. She'd be climbing the walls by next week. And he had a career, a vocation. He couldn't drop out forever and devote his life to something else. He had to clear himself now. Take the initiative and prove Pendennis's guilt.

"But what if it doesn't work? What if that elastic thing snaps and you can't find your way back?"

"Look, Lou, I'm not insane. I'm not intending to fly to Oxford on my first trip. I'll test everything thoroughly first. A trip to the ceiling and back to make sure I can reconnect. And I expect that membrane or whatever it is to snap. There's no way it could reach the ceiling. And when it does break it'll make subsequent separation easier."

"You don't know that!"

"I can infer it! Thousands of people have had near death experiences. And thousands more have experienced out-of-body flight. I'm not inventing anything new. I'm just bringing the light of science into a long neglected corner of our understanding."

And taking a sledgehammer to a centuries-old wall of scientific dogma. *If it doesn't accord with our understanding of the world it cannot be true.*

Well, sometimes it could, even if shifting opinion was like trying to turn an ocean tanker with a rowing boat.

"Look, let's agree to differ for the moment," said Nick. "Don't you want to see Pendennis's scans?"

He retrieved the new Pendennis file and fed it into the simulation matrix.

"Watch this," he said, turning his head to speak to Louise. "Look for fractures."

And count them. He crossed his fingers. Thirteen fractures were what he was looking for. One along the physical boundary and one for every personality. Wouldn't that be amazing? The first ever clinical test for MPD. An incontrovertible proof!

And maybe an explanation for Peter's newfound memories of John Bruce. A chunk of higher dimensional matter adhered unconformably to Pendennis's brain. A chunk that he could map back to a missing portion from John Bruce—if NASA ever forwarded that brain scan he'd requested.

Pendennis appeared—half life-size—recumbent in his chair.

"I'll strip the chair away in a minute but look at this first."

He tapped at the presets, switched out the z axis and brought in the c. A blue image appeared, recognisably Pendennis and the chair but different, looking like a corroded statue after centuries on the seabed, the shape distorted by decay and accretion.

"See how the chair itself—both the metal and the fabric—protrudes into the higher dimensions. Not much, but enough to give it substance and shape. The same for Pendennis's body."

His eyes raced towards the head. He could make out the boundary fracture but was that another? He leaned closer and peered. Difficult to make out at this resolution.

He hurried on to the next preset. Switched out the c axis and replaced it with the e. The chair disappeared. So did the body.

"This is the e axis. See how it's only the brain that exists here. If I wanted to pass through a wall all I'd need do is shift a few centimeters, maybe as little as a few molecules, along the e axis and there wouldn't be a wall to stop me."

Louise didn't answer. Her mouth was set and her eyes told him to get on with it.

He turned back to the image, recentred it on the brain, and ramped it up to twice life-size. There was more than one fracture but . . .

He rotated the image. The fracture wasn't complete. It was about six inches long on one side with nothing corresponding on the other. He flipped between the dimensions, swapping axes in and out. Similar results. Pendennis's brain was crazed with cracks but only one— along the dimension boundary—penetrated all the way through the structure.

Was he viewing the image correctly? Was there something he wasn't seeing?

Images flashed and morphed. Pendennis's brain was incredible. Wild, distorted, ruptured, lacerated. And looking more closely, were some of those cracks almost complete? Not slicing though the structure to the other side but looking like the crack you'd get if you removed a chip from a piece of knapped flint and stuck it back together again.

Or pressed a piece of gum onto the surface of a bowl.

He strained to make sense of the images, increased the magnification. Did it look like Pendennis's brain had grown through accretion or by being teased apart? If only there was a mechanism for weighing higher dimensional matter or probing inside—some kind of higher dimensional ultrasound that he could use to map the fractures and discover their depth and extent.

But there wasn't. This was as far as the technology had developed.

"What does it show?" asked Louise.

God knows, thought Nick. Those cracks could be minor rips or the mouths of large pockets. Large pockets containing chunks of discarded memory or personality that had been sucked inside and absorbed. Or they could be healing fractures, the last outward signs of a personality ripped into thirteen pieces and now slowly growing back together. Who could tell?

Without dissecting Pendennis's brain.

Late afternoon passed into evening. They ate, they talked, they surfed the holovision. And planned. It was dark outside, too dark for a debut out-of-body flight across the countryside but that didn't mean he couldn't practice. He dragged the bed out of the corner and placed imagers on either side. If he fed the imager data direct into the HV he could use biofeedback to help him separate.

"You're mad," said Louise.

"I'm desperate," corrected Nick.

He felt like a boxer who'd walked into two right-hands before he'd even known he was in a fight. Now his head was clearing and he was out to prove to Pendennis and the police that he was both faster and smarter. The higher dimensions would be his edge. And he was going to use every inch.

He lay there, legs out straight, fingers laced across his stomach, eyes staring up at the holoimage he'd beamed above the bed. His brain stared back at him from the ceiling. A profile shot showing the fracture line along the boundary divide. All he had to do was concentrate, imagine the crack widening, and think it into happening.

Minutes passed. He concentrated. He imagined. He tried to suck the ceiling towards him. Nothing. Not even a wobble. He closed his eyes, tried to float, tried to fill his mind with thoughts of weightlessness. He was a feather, a bubble of air, a floating spaceman.

He cracked open an eye. His brain stared back. The crack nothing more than a wafer-thin line.

"It's not working," said Louise.

He ignored her and tried harder. He squeezed his eyes shut, concentrated, pushed with his mind, strained. More minutes passed. Time meaningless in the struggle to break free. Pain. A pain behind his eyes. Was it concentration or something else? The membrane about to snap?

Panic. Suppressed but growing. What if the membrane wasn't meant to be broken? What if all those NDEs came from people who didn't have membranes? People who were genetically disposed to separate? People not like him? People ready to ascend?

More panic. Not only was he in danger but now he was defective. A Neanderthal trying to pass himself off as Homo Superior. Soon to be a comatose Neanderthal with mind and body irreparably cleft in two.

He opened his eyes, sweat beading his forehead. The image of his brain still sitting above him, the crack still wafer-thin.

He turned his head towards Louise. "Well?" he asked. "Did anything happen?"

She shook her head. "Some rapid eye movement but that was all. The image didn't change."

He tried again and again, failing every time. Perhaps the conditions weren't right. Perhaps he was trying too hard. Or it was the presence of Louise and all her negative energy. He could feel her, sitting on the edge of that box, looking as though she was about to pounce on him and drag his mind back to earth the moment it started to break free.

He'd try again tomorrow.

CHAPTER TEN

The first rays of morning sun teased open his eyes. He was half awake, drifting in and out between dreams and thought. He knew he had something important to do, but couldn't put a name to the task.

And where was he? There was an imager by the side of his bed, already mounted on a tripod and pointing directly at his head.

Recollection. He was at the rectory clinic. Louise would be in the room next door.

He stared at the ceiling. Why couldn't he reach up there with his mind? Other people could.

He closed his eyes. Maybe if he relaxed more. Maybe if he bolstered his belief with self-hypnosis. Told a few lies. *Separation was easy. He'd done it many times before. A simple stretch of the mind and he'd be free.*

He drifted back into the twilight realm between sleep and waking, imagined himself floating on an invisible sea, lifted up and down by slow, undulating ocean waves. Up . . . and down, up . . . and down, each wave lifting him higher than the former, his mind feeling as light as a feather, his body sagging, until . . .

Until nothing. He opened his eyes expecting to see his body laid out beneath him but saw the ceiling instead.

Why couldn't he separate? Thousands of people had had near-death experiences? What was different about them?

Easy answer—death—or at least its proximity. The body close to the point of shutting down, the mind reacting to the extreme stress.

Something he could replicate?

Was he that desperate? Could he really put his life in danger? Throw pills down his throat, hold his head under water?

Or was there an easier way?

A surge of excitement. He could simulate an NDE with self-hypnosis! Put his mind into a receptive state then slowly think himself closer and closer to the point of death. It wouldn't have to be dangerous. His mind was incredibly receptive. One of the most susceptible minds to hypnotic suggestion around—everyone said so. And he'd build in safeguards. Okay, he'd never attempted anything as extreme as this but it had to be worth a try, didn't it?

He didn't give himself time for doubt. He closed his eyes and worked out the script. He'd keep it simple—visualize his body on a hospital life support unit. A nurse standing by, watching the entire process, ready to intervene at the slightest danger. And then she'd start turning the dial, reducing life support, taking it down slowly, reading off the numbers from the dial as she did so—ninety-five, ninety-one—all the way down to zero.

And then he'd be clinically dead. But only for a few seconds. Just time for him to separate and fly free. And underlying everything would be the knowledge, the certainty, that the finest medical team in the world were observing close by. One word from them and the dial would be cranked back up to one hundred.

It would work! He knew it would!

He memorized the script, burned it into his subconscious. It wasn't words any more, it was real. He could smell the hospital ward, see the nurse.

Down he went, taking himself deeper, following his prepared script of self-hypnotic induction. The hospital ward sharpened, overhead lights, sounds from the corridors. The nurse smiling as she counted—eighty-three, seventy-five. A feeling of light-headedness. Vision clouding, sounds elongating.

No! This was wrong. His chest was tightening, his breathing labored. Stop! Pull back! Enough!

The nurse smiled through his failing vision, started turning the dial back up, reversing the count.

No! A strengthening resolve. He couldn't back out now. There was no other option. He had to go on!

Doubt and conviction, fighting within his mind—grappling, tumbling, slashing. The count stuck on twenty-seven, the words like a mantra repeated over and over.

Then descending. Twenty-six, twenty-five. It was the only way. He had to succeed!

But at what cost? His life? For a gamble? Something deep inside him rose up, fighting back. Instinct, self-survival. Breathe! God damn you! Breathe!

The count oscillated in the low twenties, the nurse's hand turning the dial back and forth. Live, die, breathe, try.

One last push. His face contorting. He had to go through with it. He had to, he had to!

Twenty-one, twenty . . .

The light-headedness returned, the elongating sounds. Se-ve-n-teeee e e e n . . .

Now! Rise up. There's nothing to hold you down. You feel compelled to rise. Your body expels you.

He was rising, floating free. He opened his eyes and . . .

There was something wrong. He could see too much. He could see the ceiling, four walls, the floor—all without moving his head. And . . . was that his body?

He peered through the twilight gloom. Everything was so dark and hazy. It was definitely his room at the rectory clinic and it had to be his body four, five feet below him but . . . why was it rippling. Why was everything rippling?

And why was he looking in every direction at once?

He tried to reach out with an arm but . . . nothing happened. Not even to the body on the bed. Did he have no form in this existence?

He tried to turn his head and . . . the room shifted. His bed moved towards the wall, the window moved closer—a bright rectangle of light and color.

Was he moving along the ceiling? Was he flying?

He willed himself farther. The room lurched, the window grew. He could see outside now. Trees, lawns, greens, blues and browns. The whole streaked and shimmering as though the window was covered in a wash of pouring rain.

He was free! He'd separated.

And he could move just by looking and thinking himself there.

Excitement—pure and unrestrained. The window beckoning, the sky, the clouds. One thought and he'd be away, flying with the birds . . .

Ow!

Pain hit him the moment he willed himself through the window. One second his world was awash with light, the next he was being dragged back inside the darkened room. He'd never experienced a pain like it—sharp and intense, and coming from what appeared to be every inch of his being.

Was it the membrane? Had he stretched it to its limit and it had pulled him back like a piece of elastic?

He tried the window again, slower this time. Thinking himself closer, willing himself forward . . .

He felt the resistance like a dull ache. An ache that sharpened into pain when he stretched and eased when he retreated.

It had to be the membrane.

Shit! To have come so far . . .

He glanced towards the window. It was out there. The possibility. Flight without limitation. One stretch and he'd be there. All those stories of out-of-body flight couldn't be wrong. Okay, all the volunteers he'd tested had been fakes or honestly deluded, but that didn't mean they all were. The stories had to have originated from somewhere. So many accounts from so many cultures. There had to be some basis in fact. *Someone* must have succeeded.

And it was so close. A stretch away. All he had to do was break the cord. Doctors did it every day. Umbilical cords. That's what it'd be like. A brief moment of pain then freedom.

Or death.

What if he couldn't reconnect to his body? What if the membrane was essential to the process? He'd be cast out, a ghost, sucked up into the first bright white light and scattered to the eleven horizons. He had to stop the experiment, go back, it was too dangerous to continue.

But if he didn't try . . .

This was his last hope, his edge, turn away now and he might never get the chance again. It had taken him months to get to the ceiling, who could tell if he could ever re-create this situation again.

Indecision. He edged back and forth along the ceiling. Where to next? The window or back to his body?

Or prison? Indicted for murder, no chance of parole. Or worse, chopped up and licked by that sick little pervert, Pendennis.

He hovered over the bed, one last glance at his body then . . .

The window. He held the rippling image in his mind, looking through and beyond, looking for a tree, something on the other side that he could focus on, aim for, fix in his mind, and pull towards him as fast as he dare.

He saw a branch, tuned everything else out, concentrated, braced himself. *There! Now!*

Light hit him from every angle. And pain—searing, debilitating, screaming-at-the-top-of-your-lungs pain. He was tumbling, falling, screaming—the sky, lawns, grey stone walls, clouds, and trees blurring all around him.

But he was outside, dozens of yards from the window, and the pain was receding fast.

And he could fly!

It was incredible. He was like a flying singularity—no mass, no shape, just an eyeball in the sky looking everywhere at once.

He circled the clinic grounds, diving, soaring, accelerating. This was true mind over matter. He could turn on a thought and accelerate at will. No need for wings to beat or thermals to soar on. All he needed was to think, *move*, and he moved; think, *fast*, and he accelerated; think, *there*, and he was on his way.

He climbed, he soared, he swooped. He changed direction in an instant; no G-force, no screeching tires, no mechanical roar. Think and turn, think and accelerate, think and stop.

He stopped. Hovering hundreds of feet above a shifting landscape that shimmered and swayed. Was it his eyes? Features were sharp one second and blurred the next. Maybe that's what passed for vision in these higher realms, maybe he needed time to acclimatize? It was like peering out at the world through a rippling veil.

Not that any of that mattered. He could fly!

He focussed his mind on a cloud, pulled it towards him, barrelled through, a sensation of mist and whites and greys and . . . he was out the other side. Into the blue above, a vast blue that stretched from horizon to horizon. Below him, if there was any such direction as below anymore, dabs of white cumulus marched across fields of green and brown. The whole—the sky, the sun, the earth—presented to him as one all-encompassing image. 360-degree, up-down, left-right, back-and-forth vision.

Incredible. Unfathomable. And it was all his. He could fly!

He compressed his mind, imagined himself an arrow, sleek and fast. *Down*, he commanded. *Down fast!*

The world lurched, the blues dissolved into foggy white then streaky green. The ground rising fast. He turned at the last second, the last microsecond, pulling up, cresting a tree, descending again, dipping into fields, pulling up over woods and lines of houses. And then he was rising again, spiralling and blurring into and above the clouds. How fast could he go? How high?

He pushed his newfound ability to the limit, accelerating and accelerating, the world reduced to a stream of color and then . . .

Blackness.

He stopped dead.

Everything had gone—colors, features, everything. Had he flown into space?

But if so where was the sun? He couldn't have flown that far could he? Where were the stars?

Panic. What if he'd travelled along another axis? The f or the g or any of the higher dimensional axes for that matter. What if he'd been gliding along the edge of the dimensional divide—a few centimeters, a few microns within the higher dimensions yet still in contact with the physical world? And then veered off course, pulled away from the boundary into a world where his senses didn't work. He could be surrounded by features he couldn't see or feel.

And which way was back?

He didn't dare move. He had no bearings, no idea which way he was facing or from which direction he'd come. The world he knew could be a few centimeters away or a million miles. With ten axes of movement to choose from, which way was home?

He concentrated harder. There had to be something out there. Maybe if he waited long enough his vision would clear?

He waited. Everything was so black, so silent. No smells, no sounds, nothing.

Or was there? It was more of a feeling than an image but was that something in the distance? A patch of grey amidst the black. Small, barely discernible . . .

He embraced it. Not stopping to think, not wanting to think. Blotting everything out except that tiny patch of grey and wishing it larger and larger, focussing, pulling, sucking it towards him.

It grew. Discernible now. A patch of grey covering a sixth of his vision, with other patches within it. Lighter shades of grey, maybe a hint of blue.

He pulled harder, making it grow and grow until . . .

He tumbled through. Above him was a cloud, below were fields or was that a wood?

He stopped. He was back. Not above the clinic, or anywhere he recognized. But at least it was Earth.

Relief. If he'd had lungs he would have cried out.

He hovered for a while trying to work out his bearings. He was
maybe two hundred feet above the ground. Everything below looked
calm and peaceful. Not a sound . . .

Which was when it struck him. He hadn't heard a sound since he'd
left his body. Not a bird, a car, nothing. And there were no smells. No
feeling of wind as he flew. The only sense that appeared to function
here was sight. Or what passed for sight in these upper realms.

But how was he going to get back? All he could see below were
woods and fields. It could be anywhere in England. Or Northern
Europe for that matter. Should he gain height and look for a town?

And risk flying off into the void again?

Definitely not. He clung to the visible surface of the planet, dropping lower to just above tree height. If he kept going in one
direction—aimed for that clump of trees across the field—he was
bound to find a road eventually and from there a larger road until he
found something he recognized.

He advanced, slowly at first, making sure he didn't lose contact
with the physical world, then accelerating, little by little, as his confidence returned. He became aware of plowed fields, a barn, a house, a
track, a road.

He turned sharply, dropping down between the high grass banks
that bordered the road, a country lane by the look of it. He swept
along it, a few feet above the metalled surface, twisting and turning
between high banks of grass and hedge. His world contracted
between the hedgerows, his all-round vision reigned in by turf and
twig.

And then he saw it. Flashing yellow and orange on the periphery of
his perception, lighting up the leafless gaps in the hedgerow.

He stopped—curious but apprehensive. What the hell was it?

He rose slowly above the line of hedge. A hundred yards away, a
giant snake of pulsing fire cut across the fields from horizon to horizon, its image sharp and clear, its edges distinct. The only shimmer
coming from the pulses of yellows and oranges that shot along its
length.

What the hell was it? Was it alive?

He dropped lower, using the hedge as cover. Fire trickled through
the gaps like a long line of setting suns. Could it be power lines? It was

straight enough. Did electricity seep into the higher dimensions? Did it become visible?

Or was it a ley line? He bobbed above the hedge line for a second before dropping down again. It could be either. It could be a higher dimensional killer worm for all he knew.

But if it was a ley line . . .

He tried to reconcile the fiery line he was seeing now with the segment of blue line he'd captured once with an imager. Of course the blue was irrelevant. But there'd been no indication of a pulse. Or anything like the power that this fiery line appeared to radiate. Leys were seen as weak lines of unknown energy. An energy with a higher dimensional component, something that you could map with an imager or dowse with a rod but . . . nothing on this scale.

He bobbed up for another look. Had the line shifted position at all? Power lines and ley lines wouldn't move. . . .

But neither would a killer worm . . . if it was asleep.

Indecision. Reason versus imagination. An imagination fuelled on every science fiction film he'd ever seen. It would be a snake, a worm, a gigantic tentacle of an even more gigantic planet-sucking beast.

Or something harmless, something natural—a new energy source that could revolutionize science.

He drifted along the road, continuing his journey, keeping down below hedge height, monitoring the flashes of color from his right. The road twisted to the left then swung back to the right. Back towards the line. He could see it now, up ahead, crossing the road at hedge height. He floated towards it. The slightest change in its position and he'd blur himself into the sky.

But it didn't move. It hung there, a glowing pipe of color, a man's height in diameter.

He looked for a pole, a pylon, something to prove it was a power line. Nothing. What proof was there for a ley line? A link to an ancient monument? An old church?

What proof was there for a killer worm? Instant immolation, snapping jaws?

He ascended, using a tree by the side of the road as a guide. The line spread across the road and beyond as far as he could see. And was that another? Over to the left, running almost parallel along the far horizon.

Curiosity. Cat-killer and beguiler of scientific minds. Could he really return home without checking this out?

He drifted away from the road, following the line into the field. It wouldn't take long. A quick trip along the line and back. A minute at the most. He could turn back at any time.

He set off, paralleling the line's course. Accelerating. It was so much easier to follow, so bright, so sharp, its features didn't blur and streak like the rest of the world.

And it was no longer straight. It curved slightly and dipped. And there was its companion. Another pulsing line of fire swinging in from the left. Were they going to join?

He gained height, fixing his sights on two objects—a cloud above and the line below—marvelling at the fact that he could focus on two objects at the same time almost 180 degrees apart. Using the cloud to gain height while keeping the line in sight—his anchor to the physical world, his protection against straying into the void.

Hazy patchwork fields spread out below, their colors drab against the brightness of the two lines that swept together, curled around each other then separated again. Both lines tracing a similar path—sometimes separated by inches, sometimes by hundreds of meters—cutting a broad straight channel from horizon to horizon. That was no power line. But neither was it typical of a ley. Some lines were twinned but most were not.

He was reminded of something. Something he'd read a long time ago. Norse mythology was it? No, druidic. The Nwyrve, that was it. Twelve serpent lines that were said to encircle the Earth. What could look more like a serpent than that?

Curiosity again. He had to follow the lines further. He couldn't leave halfway through a mystery.

He tracked them from above, keeping to the cloud line, shadowing their sinuous progress, the two lines twining and separating, never quite touching and never drifting more than a half mile apart.

He increased his speed, focussing on the point where the lines touched the horizon and sucking it towards him. The ground streaked beneath him. Speed beyond dreams. And then . . .

What was that?

He slowed. The light had intensified. A ball of light on the horizon. Like the first rays of a rising sun. But not *the* sun. That had already risen. And was that another line? Streaking in from the right. And another from the left? Four lines? Did they meet at that crescendo of light?

He accelerated, watching the ball of light grow—it *was* where the lines met, he could see that now. And something else, at the intersection, its features obscured by the brilliant wash of light.

He slowed again, dropping down from cloud height. It looked like a brightly lit roundabout at the intersection of two major roads. A circular rim of pulsing light connected to each of the—he counted—six lines that fed into the intersection. The twin line separating again and continuing its journey on the far side of the junction, the single line crossing it at right angles. It was amazing.

And now he came closer he could see other lights—dots—forming an avenue that flanked the twin line's approach. He dropped lower still, aiming for tree height but unable to make out any trees—the light from the lines was bleaching out every other feature.

He dropped as low as he dared, looking along the lines now, looking at the dots in profile. They weren't dots anymore but rectangles and the intersection, it wasn't a circle but a rim raised off the ground on . . . stilts?

Or were they stones? Large, luminous, irregular . . .

A stone circle!

His eyes took in everything at once. Standing stones, everywhere, glowing, flanking the twin lines approach and holding up the rim of light. Or were they marking its position?

He flew closer. There *was* a gap. The rim of light was hovering above the stones, not touching. And the stones, though luminous were several magnitudes of brightness dimmer than the lines. Not that that diminished their effect. They were magnificent. Fifteen to twenty feet high in the ring and only slightly smaller along the avenue. And these were no hazy images of the physical world, no ghostly specters but sharp and fast like the lines themselves.

The lines had to be leys. With a stone circle at their intersection what more proof did he need?

His mind raced. There were so many ramifications. So many things to comprehend all at once. This had to be proof that ancient man knew how to separate mind from body. The stones were markers. They had to be. Markers that some ancient architect had erected to delineate the site, to glorify, to map, to mirror the way the energy lines circled the intersection.

And which stone circle was this? There were so many.

He started to circle the site, trying to tune out the lines and the stones, peering into the bleached featureless gaps in between. It didn't look like Stonehenge.

But it did look inviting. And the more he looked at that perfect rim of light the less natural it looked. It was too regular. The ley lines swung and bucked their way across the countryside but this . . . this looked machine perfect. And it shone. More white than yellow and pulsing faster.

He climbed and swung over to a position directly above the centre of the circle. A perfect circle, a hundred meters at least in diameter, without a kink or a curve out of true. Could it have been manufactured? *Who* could have manufactured it and why?

He descended into the center of the circle, all around him the light pulsed and . . . was that a sound? Something crackling, something humming, the air suddenly electric, the light hypnotic.

And there was something else in the circle, if he tuned out the glare of the lights, he could make out other shapes. A physical world of grass and roads and . . . was that a car? Something flashed by. Something large and red. And then another. He drifted closer, peering through the glare. It *was* a car. He was standing in the middle of a road. A road passing through a stone circle. How bizarre. Was it real or was he looking through some kind of portal to somewhere else?

And then he remembered. Avebury! The main road ran straight through the stone circle. He knew where he was.

And how to return to the clinic. He'd driven the route many times before, it was practically on the way between Oxford and the clinic.

He paused, one last lingering look around the circle. He'd come back when all this was over. With his imagers, with everything. Conduct a proper investigation.

And then he was flying—ducking under the dazzling rim and following the road south. Accelerating—by car, the journey would have taken him an hour and a half—this time it would take minutes.

He ate the miles, swinging left and right around bends, fixing his mind on the road up ahead or a distant car and pulling it towards him. Only slowing when searching for his next turn, not caring about speed cameras or police cars.

Or gates. He veered off the road the moment he recognized the hazy outline of the rectory against the skyline, swooping low over the neighboring field before hurdling the clinic wall. Almost there. Only the window to negotiate. The one at the end above the garage.

He stopped, hovering for a second above the window ledge before stretching inside. The light level dropped immediately and the world shrank. His infinite up-down, left-right, all-around vision constrained by the room's walls.

He floated towards the bed, wondering what to do next. Would his mind be sucked back inside his body as soon as he moved close enough? Or had that possibility disappeared the moment he snapped the membrane?

He hovered above his chest, waiting. What if he'd been away too long? What if there was a time limit? Reconnect within four minutes or you're brain dead?

Panic. He didn't look dead. But he didn't look alive either. He looked asleep. His eyes were closed . . . but was he breathing? He couldn't tell if it was breath lifting his chest up and down or the heat haze that passed for sight in this realm.

And why hadn't he considered this *before* he separated?

Not the time for recriminations. Concentrate! What did the literature say? All those accounts of out-of-body experiences. Something about the top of the head? A hole in the top of the head that drew you down and sucked you inside?

He moved closer, along his face towards the hairline. Should he feel something now? A tug? Or was that what the membrane was for? His ex-membrane flapping limp in the ether.

Nothing. He was practically touching his scalp. How close did he have to get? Did he have to . . .

The room sharpened into reality. Objects took shape, sound everywhere—birds, a tractor, a barking dog—and feeling, he could feel his clothes, the slight breath of air against his skin as he moved his face, his hands . . .

He had to tell Louise. He threw back the quilt, grabbed his jeans, a T-shirt, and . . . fell over, rolling over onto his back while struggling to push the other leg into his jeans. Why did it always happen when he was in a hurry?

He flew into the hall, his smile so wide it almost wedged in the doorway. He tried the kitchen first then the bathroom. Where was she? He ran down the hallway and banged on her door.

"Lou!"

No answer. He turned the knob, threw open the door. "Lou, you'll never believe . . ."

He stopped. The room was empty. She'd gone.

CHAPTER ELEVEN

Louise checked the mirror. Was she far enough away yet? She'd driven close to thirty miles.

She pulled over onto a grass verge and took a deep breath. Time to phone. She couldn't face another night like last night. Not with those dreams, every one of them filled with slaughtered animals and grinning maniacs. If she didn't phone home in the next hour she'd explode.

She tapped in Karen's number. She should have finished the feeding by now. If anything terrible had happened Karen would have heard.

"Karen!" said Louise, interrupting as soon as she heard her friend's voice. "It's me, Louise. How are the animals?"

"Louise! How are you? Oh, they're fine. We've moved them all now except for Jasper. But how are you? Are you all right? Running off like that!"

"I'm fine. I'll explain later—why couldn't you move Jasper?"

"Need you ask? Jane needs another day to check the fences in that old paddock of hers. You know how she is about animals escaping."

"But Jasper's okay? You've seen him this morning?"

Louise couldn't bear to think of anything happening to Jasper. The donkey had been her first rescue case.

"He's fine." Karen laughed. "I took him some carrots for breakfast. Made his day. Oh, and I almost forgot, I met your brother."

"My brother?"

"Yes. Is it family problems? He looked worried. Really put out to have missed you."

"What did he look like?"

"Your brother?" She hesitated. "Fine, I suppose. Worried but . . . Is there something wrong? Why do you want to know what your brother looked like?"

"Because I don't have a brother, Karen."

Louise split into two people. The one on the phone, calm and asking all the pertinent questions; and the one inside, dissolving.

"Oh! Oh dear!" said Karen, flustered, her voice rising. "What's happening, Lou? Are you in trouble?"

"What did he look like?" Louise repeated. She had to stay calm; she had to keep Karen calm. "Was he short, tall, what?"

"I don't know. I . . . average I suppose."

"What about his age? How old was he?"

Louise held her breath. How old was Pendennis? He looked about nineteen.

"About our age?" said Karen without conviction. "Maybe a bit older. Late thirties maybe?"

Relief. No one could describe Pendennis as late-thirties.

"Who is he, Lou? An old boyfriend?"

"No idea. Did he say what he wanted?"

Karen breathed heavily into the phone. "He . . . he just appeared in your yard. I'd just topped up Jasper's water when . . ."

Karen stopped talking.

"When what, Karen?"

"Oh, I'm so stupid! He called *me* Louise. That's the first thing he said. I should have realized, shouldn't I. Oh, sorry, Lou. I shouldn't have been taken in like that. It's not as though we're alike, is it? Oh God, it's nothing to do with . . . you know, is it?"

"No, it's not," said Louise, quickly burying the subject. They were talking over an open line and she'd already got enough people in trouble without adding to her tally. "What exactly did he say, Karen?"

Louise could hear Karen fighting to compose herself, her voice trembling, her sentences punctuated by large intakes of breath.

"Something about . . . being sorry he missed you. Did I know where you were? When were you coming back? And something about a professor. Chubb, Stubbs, something like that."

"What did you tell him?"

"Nothing. I didn't know anything *to* tell."

"Did he say if he was coming back?"

"No, he just turned and left. Like I said, he looked upset."

Or angry. Insane-copycat-killer angry. Louise fought to hold herself together. Couldn't there be an innocent explanation? A reporter following up on the Framlingham murder?

"Do you want me to call the police, Lou?"

"No!" Louise almost shouted the word into the phone. Not the police. Not yet. "Only if he comes back," she continued. "And tell the others. Don't answer your door to any strangers. Understand?"

"You're frightening me, Lou. What's happening?"

"I wish I knew."

Louise disconnected the phone and slumped back in her seat. She was shaking. What had she gotten herself into? What had she gotten her friends into?

And then she was driving. She had to get away fast. People could be monitoring her phone. And she had things to do. Shopping for one. If she was going to be holed up at that rectory for any length of time she'd need fresh fruit and vegetables and some proper cleaning materials. The kitchen was a mess. The cupboards, the drawers, the fridge. And she'd need to stock up now before her face hit the headlines.

She found a market on the way back, parked outside the monitored zone, tucked her hair inside the hood of her coat and pulled the drawstrings tight. No one would recognize her now. All anyone would see was an ageless woman wrapped up against the cold. She pulled on her gloves. Not even a fingerprint would be left.

Nick started at the noise. Someone was running upstairs. Louise?

They reached the top of the stairs at the same time. "Where have you been?" he asked as she pushed past him into the kitchen. "I've been going crazy . . ." He paused in disbelief. She was weighed down with four heavy shopping bags. "Have you been shopping?"

He couldn't believe it. There was enough tinned food in the kitchen to feed them for weeks.

"We've got a problem," she said hoisting the bags onto the kitchen table.

"Someone saw you?" He was incredulous. Had the woman lost her mind? After all they'd gone through yesterday avoiding cameras. The detours, the about-turns. She'd compromised everything. And for what? French bread and some oranges as far as he could see.

Louise took a deep breath. "No one saw me. It's worse. Someone turned up at the farm this morning pretending to be my brother."

"How . . ." he paused, not believing what he was hearing. "Please tell me you haven't driven home." He glanced towards the stairs, panic building. Had someone followed her back?

"It's all right," she said, starting to unpack. "I phoned. And before you shout at me I drove to the outskirts of Exeter. If anyone monitored the call they'd never trace it back here."

Nick felt like arguing the point but was curious.

"Did you get a description of the man?"

Louise told him what Karen had said. "Don't you see?" she said. "It *wasn't* Pendennis."

"So?" said Nick, failing to see the significance. "It'll be someone from the police."

"No." Louise was adamant. "I've been thinking about this for the last hour. The police would have accessed my ID card picture from their records before coming out. They wouldn't have mistaken Karen for me or pretended to be my brother."

Nick disagreed. "You're assuming a level of competence and forethought way above the average overworked copper. He was probably a junior officer not even working on the case who was rung up by his boss, given sketchy details, and told to drive over and see what he could find out."

"So why did he get upset?"

"Maybe Karen was mistaken . . ."

Louise slammed a tub of margarine down on the table. "No! If the police thought you were hiding at the farm or there was evidence there of your whereabouts they'd have got a search warrant."

She had a point. They'd been quick enough to arrest him. And to give his name to the media.

"Okay, so it was a reporter," he suggested.

"I thought about that too, but how did he find me? The only people who know about you and me are the police, Upper Heywood, and," she stabbed a bunch of bananas in his direction, "the person trying to frame you. He broke into your house, didn't he? Could he have found something there with my name on it?"

"No," he said, shaking his head. "We've been through all this. Pendennis is the person trying to frame me. And he already knows about you."

"He's in prison, Nick!"

"He's not. And I can prove it."

"Oh yeah," she said sarcastically. "When?"

He looked at his watch and smiled. "Oh, I'd say in about an hour."

"You flew to Avebury?"

She still didn't appear to believe him. He'd told her everything, except for the pain and the snapped membrane. But the rest—the flight, the ley lines, the stone circle—out they came as a breathless monologue as every experience of his flight came tumbling out of his memory in whatever order they presented themselves. Who wanted to be lucid? He was the man who could fly!

"Did I say fly? Delete that thought and replace it with . . . soar." He let the word fly too, encouraging it into flight with a sweep of his hand. "Can you believe that? Me? Isn't it incredible? Isn't it just amazing?"

He wanted to hug her, he wanted to hug everybody, he wanted to share his joy and bounce belief into her. She wriggled free of his grip, looking uncomfortable. Probably thought he was drunk. Which he was—drunk on success and the exhilaration of flight.

"Look, I can prove it," he said, taking her hand again and leading her towards the HV. "Watch the images. You'll see the separation. And . . ." Another idea. An even better idea. He let go of her hand and darted across the floor. Where did he keep that box of paper? Ah, there it was. He grabbed a sheet and handed it to Louise.

"Write something on it. Print as large as you can. I can't see too well up there."

Louise took the paper and looked around for a pen.

"Put the paper wherever you want. Somewhere I can't see from the bed but could from the ceiling. And make sure the writing's facing upward. This is mind projection, not magic."

He switched on the imagers, checked the connections, showed Louise how to use the remote. Then jumped on the bed, shuffled into position, took a deep breath, and tried to relax.

Doubt. Would it work? Would he have to think himself into a near-death experience again?

He slowed his breathing, prepared a vent to drain all doubt. Things were different now. He'd snapped the membrane. Separating would be easy. A piece of cake.

He closed his eyes, imagined success, conjured up images of his mind as a separate entity, held that image, strengthened it, imagined it lifting, rising, floating free and . . .

The bed appeared . . . and the ceiling, the boxes, Louise. His 360-degree up-down, all-around vision was back. He'd done it!

Where was the note? He froze in mid-air and tried to stabilize his rippling vision. There was something white on a box in the far corner. He sucked it towards him. The room shifted in an instant. He was hovering over it—words, letters dancing at the edge of his perception. There were five words, one much longer than the others. He tried to blink; he tried focussing his vision to the side of the note. Nothing appeared to work. The words washed up and down, patches clearing—was the first word *Pete*?—then hazing over again. The third word was *is* the second had *dennis* in the middle. Peter Pendennis? More patches cleared, two or three letters at a time. The message unravelling. *Peter Pendennis is in prison.*

He flew back to the bed, lined his mind up with that imaginary hole in the top of his head and let himself be sucked inside.

"Very funny," he said, opening his eyes. "And you misspelt *isn't* because Peter Pendennis very definitely is *not* in prison."

Louise stared at him openmouthed. Which pleased him. A round of applause would have been better but openmouthed astonishment was always appreciated.

"You really did it," she said, glancing back to point at the holo-image of his brain. "You disappeared for about a minute. You just lifted straight out. No stretching membrane. Nothing. Just *whoosh* and you were gone."

Whoosh . . . he liked that. Whoosh and soar. And in a few minutes time he'd be whooshing and soaring again. This time all the way to Upper Heywood.

But first he had to prepare. He'd need to memorize the roads around Upper Heywood. And maybe take a look at that ley line. Didn't someone compile a ley line map of Great Britain a few years back?

He searched the web, skimming through the twilight zone of crank pages that anything to do with the paranormal attracted until he found the site he'd been looking for: *Ley Line Atlas of the United Kingdom.*

"What are ley lines?" asked Louise, leaning over his left shoulder.

"No one knows," said Nick, aligning the map. "At one time they were thought to be old roads—straight tracks linking important prehistoric sites. But they're far more than that. And more widespread. Everywhere you look—Europe, America, Polynesia, China—you'll find references to lines of power and dragons."

"Dragons?"

"Large animal, serpentlike, breathes flame . . ."

She punched him on the shoulder.

"I know what a dragon is!"

"Ah, but this is the old type of dragon, before Renaissance painters and Disney got hold of them. These are the wyrms, far more serpentlike. Imagine you're a prehistoric shaman on an out-of-body flight and you see a ley line for the first time. What's it going to look like to you? A fiery snake stretching from horizon to horizon? Cue dragon legend."

"It really looks like a fiery snake?"

"Depends what you've been smoking. But Norse legend has stories about fiery serpents—wyrms—that encircle the world. The druids called them Nwyvre—serpent lines—and the Chinese called them *lung mei*—dragon lines of Earth energy. And this line—" He paused to magnify a section of the holoimage, "—used to be called the dragon line because it linked so many sites with dragon legends."

He froze the image and stared at it. There it was. The ley line he'd followed to Avebury.

"They call it the Michael and Mary line now—after all the churches called St. Michael along its route. Early church 101—if you have a local dragon legend to contend with, name your church after a dragon-slaying saint."

"And Mary?"

"A later addition when the line was found to be twinned. Two lines coiling around each other—one's got to be male, the other female, right? The classic yin and yang. So along came Mary."

He traced the path of the line. It rose from Land's End in Cornwall and bisected the country until sinking into the sea off Norfolk. If he'd kept going from Avebury the next stop would have been Glastonbury. Would he have seen a spectral Camelot glowing in the higher dimensional haze?

"But what are they?" pressed Louise. "Hasn't anyone analyzed what they're made of?"

"What with? We've only just developed cameras that can *see* the higher dimensions. Analysis is years away. And up until last year no one had even thought to point an imager at a ley line. That is until a certain boy genius stunned the scientific world and proved their existence."

He turned to face her. "I might win an award, you know?"

Louise groaned. "For what? Lying about your age, boy genius? And, anyway, what are you doing looking at ley lines? I thought you were planning your route to Oxford."

"I am. Ley lines are the shining interstates of the higher dimensions. You can see them for miles. All you have to do is focus on the horizon and pull them towards you whereas on the road you're limited by bends and having to slow down to look for turn offs and read road signs."

And they were sexy. Why travel by road when you could fly by ley?

He zoomed in on a section of the line where it transected Devon and superimposed a road map. The apartment was only a few miles north of the line. If he headed southeast from the bedroom window he couldn't miss it. He ran his finger along the line, scrolling the image past Avebury towards Oxford and Upper Heywood. It passed within a dozen or so miles. All he'd have to do was count the number of ley intersections and then slow down until he hit a road.

And hope the map was accurate. But even if it wasn't it couldn't be that far out, could it? He traced the route he'd travelled earlier. The map showed three lines intersecting at Avebury. Accurate so far.

"How are you going to recognize Pendennis if you can't see that well?" asked Louise.

"It's not that bad. You just have to concentrate and be patient. Anyway, Pendennis stands out. He's the only one who looks like an evil twelve-year-old."

"But what if you miss him? You've got to stop off at every room and wait for your vision to clear. What if Pendennis moves from one room you hadn't seen to one you'd already checked? You'd come back here claiming he wasn't there when in fact he was."

"Upper Heywood's not that big. Anyway, I'll be thorough. If . . . *when* I find that Peter's missing, I'll check out Ziegler and the governor. Someone'll be panicking."

But would they be talking? And would he be able to hear them if they were? He wasn't going to say anything to Louise but the lack of sound in the higher dimensions worried him. There was nothing in the NDE reports that suggested hearing was impaired. Maybe he was upper dimensionally deaf? Or maybe sound didn't penetrate that far into the upper dimensions and he had to position himself closer?

He pushed the negative thoughts aside. First he had to find Pendennis's empty cell, the rest he could worry about later.

He flew straight out the window, aiming southeast this time, using a large oak tree by the road as a guide. He accelerated, blurring the ground beneath him as he raced towards the skyline, slowing momentarily as he caught sight of the ley then swinging to the left and aligning his trajectory with the golden line.

Speed. Infinite and exhilarating. The ley line so close he could feel every turn and dip, leaning into bends like a downhill racer, the landscape and the sky a blur. Intersections flashed by. He counted them: two, three, four. Not even slowing for Glastonbury or Avebury, noting their brilliance as passing dots—knots on a golden thread that traversed the country, the entire globe for all he knew.

More intersections, more speed—he could probably circle the world in a matter of minutes if he really cut loose.

Or disappear into a featureless void.

The last intersection flashed by. He slowed. The world slowing with him, streaks becoming blurs, blurs becoming houses. He accelerated again, keeping his speed in line with his ability to see. The map showed three major roads crossing the line somewhere in this vicinity. Any of them would do. All would take him north towards Oxford. He slowed at the first road junction—too small—the second—only a spur road—the third—a dual carriageway.

He took it, rising to above tree height to extend his field of vision, selecting a distant lorry and pulling it towards him, latching onto the next, clawing his way to Oxford and beyond.

Upper Heywood lay beneath him. Low, flat-roofed buildings laid out in bays and blocks. You could still make out the runway and the line of the old perimeter fence from when it had been an air base. He circled the site, spiralling lower, wondering which wall to penetrate first. Should he start at the main entrance and proceed clockwise? Or should he be more selective? Wouldn't there be some sort of security control room—a place where all the feeds from the surveillance cameras were routed to?

He drifted through the glass reception doors, past the guards, through the security doors into a long corridor. Slowly, he stretched to his left, into the fabric of the corridor wall and beyond . . . into a room. He stopped. He was straddling two worlds: the room and the corridor. Looking at both at the same time. The effect was . . . astounding. He drifted further to the left. The corridor disappeared. He drifted back to the right. It returned. How thick was the wall? Nine inches, more? If he could span that then . . . what kind of eye did he have? Not a singularity. And it didn't feel as though he had more than one eye. Could his entire surface be a receptor? One giant imperfect eyeball that could span a wall?

A little voice coughed from somewhere deep within his mind. Research could wait, now there was a job to do.

He quartered the first bay, straddling the walls to cover both corridor and rooms at the same time, stopping whenever he saw someone, taking time to let their faces clear then racing off again. He proceeded bay by bay. Some bays were cell blocks; others were offices, storerooms, wards, canteens, recreational blocks. All joined together by a labyrinth of near-identical white corridors.

He turned into the next bay: a long central corridor with an avenue of paired doors—cells, no doubt. He stretched into the first room and froze. Someone was sitting cross-legged on the floor. Someone in a red tracksuit.

Nick strained to see the man's face. Pendennis had been dressed in red when he'd attacked Louise. It wasn't the normal prison uniform—everyone else he'd seen so far had been in green or orange. Was it peculiar to this bay? Was red reserved for high risk prisoners?

Or just Pendennis?

He stifled the thought. It couldn't be Pendennis. Pendennis had escaped.

Hadn't he?

The figure on the floor didn't move. Nick floated closer, swinging to the left to get a better view of the man's face. Was it Pendennis? He looked the right size. Small, slightly built. But that could apply to any kid, maybe Upper Heywood were taking in juveniles now?

The face rippled before him, the forehead clearing then the chin, a shifting heat haze obscuring then revealing then . . .

. . . shattering every presumption that Nick had constructed over the past twenty-four hours.

Peter Pendennis was sitting cross-legged on the floor. And even worse. He was smiling. His eyes looking straight at Nick.

Nick shot to his left. Only a few feet but he had to make sure. Would Pendennis's eyes follow? Was he really looking at him?

The room flowed and rippled. Teasing glimpses, then slowly Pendennis's face cleared. His eyes hadn't moved. Neither had the smile.

CHAPTER TWELVE

Louise wasn't surprised at Nick's news.

"I've been thinking while you've been away," she said. One of the byproducts of an hour spent cleaning the kitchen. Plenty of time to allow the mind to wander. "Remember you asked me who else could have a motive to frame you?"

Nick grunted a reply which Louise took for a yes. He hadn't moved from his bed since he returned. Now he was sat on its edge, head in hands and looking like a sad bloodhound whose owner had just died.

"You forgot about the Americans," she said, waiting for a reaction.

"What Americans?" said Nick, his face still buried, his voice distracted.

"Think about it. You send a message to SHIFT asking for John Bruce's brain scan and the next day someone frames you for murder."

Nick looked up. "I hardly think NASA—"

"Why not?" Louise jumped in. "If something happened to John Bruce during the SHIFT flight and they covered it up—"

"No." Nick tried to wave Louise's argument away. "NASA may be obsessed with image but they're not going to kill to protect it."

"You don't know what they're capable of."

"But why kill? All they'd need do is doctor the scans and the problem goes away. No need to kill anyone."

He looked tired and frustrated but Louise pressed. She'd been thinking of nothing else for the past hour and knew she was on to something. If only because nothing else made sense.

"Couldn't you tell if the scans had been doctored?"

"I'm an astropsychologist not a computer scientist."

"But they wouldn't know that. You could be talking to anyone. At the college, friends . . ."

He shook his head then reverted to staring at the floor.

"Okay, so what about this." Louise switched the HV back on. "I was checking this when you rematerialized."

A picture of John Bruce arriving outside a restaurant appeared.

"That's from two nights ago. He's attending a SHIFT reunion."

Louise waited for a response. Her turn to play the stage magician.

"So?" said Nick.

"So that was the day you sent the query to SHIFT. What would be more natural than an old colleague passing on a warning?"

Nick looked baffled. "What warning?"

Louise rolled her eyes. Was he being deliberately obtuse?

"Think about it. He's in the middle of an election campaign. How's a request for his old brain scans going to be viewed? Someone's going to think dirty tricks. If not John then one of his handlers or backers. And I've seen some of the organizations that are supposedly backing him. Right-wing extremists."

She had his attention. "John Bruce is linked to right-wing extremists?"

"Some of his supporters are. I'm not saying John's an extremist but he's attracted money from unsavory characters. And that's all it takes. One madman who hears about your inquiry and sees it as an attempt to discredit John Bruce by saying his brain was damaged in the SHIFT flight."

"But why frame me for murder? Why not frighten me off? Two large men on the doorstep would have sufficed. A bribe would have been nice."

"You're assuming these people were thinking straight . . ."

"No." He jumped to his feet. "I don't buy that. If someone wanted me out of the way why not kill me? And why not do it quietly? Scattering body parts all over Oxford is a surefire way of attracting publicity. And If I'm still alive I can shout dirty tricks and point my finger at John Bruce. That would be the last thing they'd want."

She'd thought of that too. "What if the point wasn't to kill you but to warn you off? Think about it. They don't know if you're working on your own or with a group. So they send everyone a message. Back off or it'll get a hell of a lot worse."

He paced between the boxes before swinging round and shaking his head.

"But I didn't get the message, did I? I thought it was Pendennis."

"But they wouldn't have known about Pendennis. You said it yourself, remember? *How many Mafia bosses have I pissed off this week?* Replace Mafia with 'dubious right-wing organizations' and you'd have your answer. And think about the victim's tongue being cut out. An obvious warning for someone to keep quiet."

"And the nose?"

That was a problem . . . but she had an answer.

"Maybe that was a message too. Don't speak, don't look, don't touch, don't listen, and don't poke your nose where it doesn't belong."

Nick shrugged. "What's the point of a message you need a Ph.D. in lateral thinking to understand?"

"But they wouldn't see it like that, Nick. These people are obsessives. They eat, drink, and sleep politics. To them everything would be about the campaign and they'd assume you were the same."

Nick sighed. "Maybe you're right."

He didn't look convinced.

Nick commandeered the HV remote while Louise prepared lunch. Maybe there was a news item on Pendennis's recapture. *Something* to resurrect his failing theory.

He voiced in "Pendennis" and selected "recent news." An apologetic news anchor appeared. "Sorry," she said. "We have nothing on that item."

He slumped forward, feeling the weight of the world once more pressing down upon his shoulders. Had Upper Heywood managed to keep Pendennis's escape and recapture a secret? Or was Louise right—he hadn't escaped in the first place?

Doubt. Despite what Louise said he was reluctant to let go of Pendennis as a suspect. He'd seen Pendennis in action. He'd seen the body. He'd seen the newsreels.

But . . .

He grabbed the remote again. Who were these dubious backers that Louise had talked about? He voiced in "John Bruce" and "organized crime" and selected "news" and "documentaries." Back came the apologetic news anchor.

He expanded the search into the web and beyond. Hundreds of hits. He sifted through them, page after page of junk.

He returned to the news and documentary channels, replaced "organized crime" with "right wing" and added "campaign" and "backers." This time he found several hits, including a documentary from two months ago entitled *John Bruce: Where the Money Really Comes From.* He clicked on it.

An excited reporter spent the next forty minutes trying to tie John Bruce to a right-wing plot to put Christianity at the heart of a future education system, replacing the three Rs with the three Cs: Christianity, creationism, and chastity. It was trial by association. Yes, John Bruce received donations and occasionally shared platforms with members of the evangelical right but there was nothing to show he endorsed their ideals.

Not that facts featured very highly in the documentary's agenda. It was a typical preelection hatchet job. Bruce was a committed Christian and a Republican, so trot out every right-wing scare story and attempt to trace a link to John, however tenuous or fanciful.

If anything John Bruce came across as politically naïve, someone in desperate need of campaign funds who was trying hard to please everyone he met.

Nick voiced in a new search. "Extreme right" and "terror campaigns." Was there a history of framing people for murder?

Back came the matches. Bombings, shootings, stabbings. From the sample he saw, the extreme right favoured the direct approach—denounce, intimidate, beat up, and kill. Surely if he'd been a target they'd have confronted him directly—firebombed his house, lobbied the college for his dismissal, attacked him in the street. Framing someone for murder was not their style.

Not that that ruled out a twisted fellow traveller. The ubiquitous loner with a warped imagination and a desire to see John Bruce as President.

He stabbed a finger at the news button. Time to check the news from Oxford. A series of headlines flashed over the viewing platform. The murder had been relegated to ninth in the list of headline news. But it was something else that caught his eye. The story in second place.

Republican candidate endorses preemptive strike v. China.

He clicked on the story. A picture of John Bruce appeared. It was night. He was getting out of a car, pausing to smile at the cameras and wave to well-wishers.

The voice of a female news anchor spoke over the action. "This was Republican candidate John Bruce last night on his way back to his hotel in Manchester, New Hampshire."

A throng of reporters pushed forward and surrounded Bruce as he tried to walk across the pavement between his car and the hotel steps. They fired questions at him and thrust microphones in his face. *John, are you confident of winning New Hampshire? Will you drop out if you don't come in the first three?* Bruce smiled and kept pushing through the crowd. The questions continued, Bruce answering with a nod or a shake of his head. Then came *the* question. *What's your policy on China? Do you think a preemptive nuclear strike against them would be a good thing?* Bruce paused and the holocamera zoomed in on his face. Nick couldn't believe it. He was actually thinking about the question. More microphones lurched forward, all other questions forgotten. What was the man going to say?

"It's an option," said John Bruce.

The pavement erupted. Every reporter talking at once, shouting questions, asking for clarification, turning wide-eyed to camera and asking their producers, "did you get that?"

And at the back, pushing wildly towards their candidate was an apoplectic campaign staff.

Nick called Louise through. What had Bruce been thinking? Reporters doorstep politicians all the time. It was part of their job. Something that Bruce would have been aware of. He'd been through the NASA publicity machine and, surely, his campaign team would have coached him even harder. All he had to do was smile and wave, and ignore any question he didn't want to answer. Had he misheard the question?

Not according to the media. The Bruce camp had been given several opportunities to clarify their candidate's position on China and although they initially issued a statement saying he'd misheard the question, that was withdrawn an hour later. Then the media feeding frenzy really began as prominent Bruce supporters and campaigners were tracked down and asked for a reaction. Most kept quiet, some expressed surprise, some denied he'd even said it, but a few backed his stance calling it brave and clear-sighted.

Nick flicked through the American news channels. Very little else was being discussed. Condemnation was coming in from all sides of the political spectrum, most pundits agreeing that Bruce's campaign was over.

"He was never a credible candidate," said one. "He's never run for office before and tonight it showed."

A few tried to find excuses for Bruce. He was confused, misheard the question, or was answering an earlier one. Some even blamed the journalists.

"The only purpose of a question like that is to entrap the candidate. We, at home, heard the question because it was spoken into a microphone but would John Bruce? With all those reporters screaming in his ear? The whole thing was staged."

Only one pundit supported Bruce. A gnarled conservative on Fox's late-night election campaign roundup.

"John Bruce only said what millions of Americans have been thinking for years. We've had six decades of being the sole superpower and wasted the last two trying to make the rest of the world like us. Well, wake up, America! It didn't work. Now our forces are underfunded, our weapons research virtually nonexistent, and we're sinking into a new Cold War. Except this time it's not America that has the technological and economic edge. It's the Chinese.

"Our country has never been so vulnerable. Even if we started today, rebuilding our military strength is going to take years and, in the meantime, any candidate who doesn't consider a limited preemptive strike an option isn't fit to run for office."

"That's not John," said Louise, staring at the holographic scene of John Bruce outside the hotel. "He'd never condone a nuclear preemptive strike against anyone."

"People change," said Nick, lying on his bed reading something he'd downloaded into his handheld.

"Not that much," said Louise.

She continued surfing the library of John's post-SHIFT appearances as she'd done for most of the afternoon. Every now and then she froze an image, zoomed in on his face, walked up to it and stared at every detail. He *was* different. There was a zealous naïvete that the old John—her John—had never had. She could see it in his eyes. That childlike look of wonder as though every experience was new. The certainty in his voice whenever he talked about God and his great vision for the future. He just looked . . . wrong.

"He's been born again," explained Nick. "That's what happens."

"It's more than that," insisted Louise, unable to take her eyes off that image hovering before her. "I haven't seen him laugh. Not really laugh. He smiles a lot and grins but . . . doesn't he look vacuous to you?"

She turned to quiz Nick. Surely he had to see it too.

He didn't.

"Maybe that's the persona his image makers told him to project," he said. "Honest country boy with a big smile and a firm handshake."

Louise glared at him. Was he playing devil's advocate or did he really believe what he was saying? And what was he reading? What could be more important than understanding what had happened to John? She turned back to the smiling face of the presidential candidate. That wasn't a persona being projected. That was real. You could see it in his eyes. There was no calculation behind them anymore.

"The John I knew had a quick wit and was always telling jokes. This one just smiles a lot and talks about a better tomorrow."

"You don't get elected playing stand-up."

"But look at his eyes! There's no playfulness there. No mischief. He looks like he's on tranquillizers. He looks . . ."

She stopped and stared at Nick. "You said he might have lost a part of his personality during the SHIFT flight. Could he have lost the part that reasons?"

Nick scratched his chin. "It doesn't quite work like that . . ."

"Isn't there a reasoning part of the brain—some place that filters thoughts and ideas? Like whether to answer yes to a journalist asking about nuking China?"

"Not exactly . . ."

Louise wasn't listening. She could see exactly what had happened to John. He'd lost the reasoning part of his brain during the SHIFT flight, leaving him open to religion and politics and the unscrupulous manipulation of others intent on using his name to forward their own political ambitions. John was nothing but a pawn in their hands.

Nick disagreed. "Look," he said, putting his handheld down. "If he were a pawn, the campaign team would have had him back on those hotel steps within minutes explaining how he misheard the question. The fact they didn't tells me that not only does he believe what he said but his handlers can't persuade him to back down."

"But that's not John!" She felt like she was banging her head against a brick wall. Nick didn't know the real John; the media didn't know the real John. But she did!

"Could he have been split in two?" she asked. "Could the good bit have gone into Pendennis and left the bad bit behind."

"Next you'll be saying that Mr. Hyde is standing for the President of the United States."

"Well, is he?"

Nick sat up. "No. Mr. Hyde is a Victorian concept. We're not composed of two selves—one good, one evil—locked in a fight for dominion over our soul. We're far more complex than that."

"But you said part of his personality could have been ripped from his brain during the SHIFT flight . . ."

"And it could. But it wouldn't be entirely good or entirely evil. It would be part of a subpersonality. Maybe an entire subpersonality."

Louise was confused. Personalities, sub-personalities, personas. Weren't they all describing the same thing?

"So he lost the subpersonality that controls reason?" she asked.

Nick took a deep breath. "I see I'm going to have to explain this." He shuffled closer to the edge of the bed and rested both hands on his knees. "Think back to your childhood. I bet you were a different girl with your friends than you were with your parents."

Louise nodded.

"That's because you, like most children, learned to adopt different personae according to where you were and who you were interacting with. Now, as you get older these subpersonalities change. Some fade away, others appear. You flit between roles: mother, wife, lover, friend, child, colleague, boss, and however many other personae your life-style demands. Now, John spent most of his adult life in the forces. Maybe, and I'm using retrospective psychoanalysis here, maybe that led to him developing a subpersonality to cope with a highly structured, disciplined regime. Moving to NASA and the SHIFT program would have accentuated that. The same discipline but this time extended into his off-duty hours. He'd be a twenty-four-hour ambassador. For NASA, for SHIFT, for his country. The first man chosen to fly to the stars couldn't be seen behaving badly.

"So, over the years John's work persona assumes the dominant role in his life. But what happens if that persona—the highly disciplined, professional John Bruce that made up say seventy-five percent of his life—is suddenly ripped away. He wouldn't turn evil but his other subpersonalities would suddenly be forced to cope with the unexpected exposure. And how would they react? Wouldn't they feel freed? Maybe even reborn. All that rigid discipline and constraint suddenly removed. Which could explain the new John. He's lost the rational straitjacket and become reacquainted with the child, the friend, and all the other subpersonalities that he'd been repressing all these years. Which is why when someone asks if it's a good idea to nuke China he'll answer off the cuff. Well, yeah, it's gotta be an option."

"So I *was* right," said Louise. "He's lost his reasoning sub-personality."

"No, he's still reasoning but employing a different set of priorities. His 'work' personality would place a high priority on behaving well at all times. His 'friend' personality would care more about being popular. They'd both employ reason but with different goals."

"But isn't that dangerous?"

"Only if he gets elected, which he won't. You heard the news. His campaign's finished."

"But what about John? Shouldn't someone tell him he needs therapy or something?"

Nick smiled. "And be accused of orchestrating another dirty tricks campaign? How many more murders do you want me accused of?"

CHAPTER THIRTEEN

Karen clapped her hands together; even with her thick mittens the cold penetrated. There'd be a frost tonight. A heavy one.

She checked the lane again before entering Louise's yard. No parked cars, no strange men lurking. Thank God. She'd had the chain on her door since this morning. What had Louise gotten herself into this time?

The yard crunched under foot. Ice was beginning to form in the ruts. Would Jasper's water be frozen too? She looked over towards the farmhouse. Maybe she should fetch a bucket of warm water? That would at least give Jasper a few hours before his water iced over again. And save her from having to hook out fragments of ice with her bare hands.

She trudged back to the farmhouse, dug Louise's spare key out of a deep coat pocket, and opened the door. The house felt cold—only marginally warmer than outside. Louise on another economy drive, no doubt. Karen wondered if that was why she'd had to leave. Money problems. Maybe even threats from some dubious loan shark.

She stood looking out the kitchen window while the bucket filled. Looking at the field gate and wondering where Jasper was. The donkey knew his meal times off by heart. It was unlike him not to be waiting by the gate.

The bucket filled, she hoisted it out of the sink and carried it carefully through the house and into the yard. Still no sign of Jasper. She peered along the hedge line. It was so unlike him to be away from the gate. Especially in winter. There was no grazing anywhere in the field. Could he be in his shelter?

She called his name. Nothing. Normally he'd bray and come galloping over. Was he asleep?

She unlatched the field gate and poured the warm water into his bucket. And then called again. Still nothing. Nothing moving or making a noise for miles around. It was one of those cold, still winter evenings with patches of mist filling hollows in the landscape—like at the bottom of Jasper's field where the pasture sloped away. Could he be down there?

She checked the shelter first—fresh droppings but no Jasper. She was confused. He couldn't have escaped. The gate was still fastened and the field well-fenced. She stared at the misty hollow at the field bottom. He had to be down there.

Was he hurt?

She started to run, her feet jarring on the uneven frozen ground. Please don't let him be hurt! Not Jasper.

The ground fell away, she descended into the mist, calling, peering through the fog. Was that him over there? That dark shape in the corner?

She veered towards it, stumbling, her arms flailing as she tried to run and keep her balance at the same time.

A shape formed out of the mist. Jasper; backed up against the hedge, hunched down, ears back, shaking. He looked terrified. She slid to a stop.

"Jasper, what's the matter, boy?"

She crept forward, her right hand extended. "It's all right, boy. It's only me. Smell my hand."

Something moved on the periphery of her vision, the mist in motion as the slightest breeze rippled through the hollow. Karen shivered. She felt a sudden icy touch against her skin—on her left side just below her rib cage. One of her many layers of clothing must have untucked itself in her dash across the field. She stopped to rearrange herself.

The icy touch moved, slithering across her back. She flapped at it, bending her arms behind her back, swivelling on the spot. Panic. Had something slipped down her neck? Ice? A snake? And then she was moving—upwards, lifted off her feet by something she couldn't see, rising ten, twelve feet in the air, hovering for an instant and then . . .

. . . slamming hard against an invisible barrier, like a wall of glass in the sky.

Disbelief mingled with pain. She swished through the mist, a dozen feet off the ground, slamming into that invisible wall in the sky. Once, twice . . . too many times.

Far too many times.

A rag doll tugged in a direction it just couldn't go.

Louise stared at the image on the holovision. Her farm, her yard . . .

"It might not be her," said Nick softly.

Louise barely registered his presence. All she could see was her home and boundless despair. What had she done? It had to be Karen. Poor innocent Karen.

The picture changed. An overhead shot from a circling camera drone. The farmhouse at the center, the yard full of emergency vehicles, Jasper watching them from the gate. The camera zoomed in on a stretcher being carried from the field.

"This was taken earlier today," said a somber news anchor.

Louise clutched Nick's arm as she watched the stretcher balloon in size. The person's face was covered but . . . that coat. It was Karen's. She'd seen her wearing it a thousand times.

"Police have named the victim as Louise Callander, a thirty-one-year-old charity worker . . ."

No, no, no, no, no! She felt like screaming. "Why do they keep saying that?" she cried. "Why?"

"Because it's your farm and . . . maybe she didn't have any identification on her."

"But we don't look anything like each other! And the police saw me only two nights ago."

Nick looked away.

"What?" she asked. "Why are you looking like that?"

He took a deep breath, started to say something then changed his mind.

"What? What are you not telling me?" She punched him hard in the arm. "Tell me!"

He took another deep breath and touched her hand.

"Maybe they're having trouble making an identification."

Louise thought she was sinking through the floor. "No!" Not that. Not Karen. Not anyone. She was on her feet, wanting to run but not knowing where to. She stumbled over a box, turned, and kicked it.

And kicked it again. Stupid, stupid boxes all over the floor. Nick grabbed her, she pulled away. This was not happening. This was definitely not happening.

Maybe it hadn't happened? She'd phone and Karen would answer. They'd laugh about it later. A silly mistake. That's all it had been.

Her right hand flew to her wrist-phone.

"What are you doing?" asked Nick.

"Phoning Karen . . ."

He dived towards her, grabbed her wrist. "No! Not here."

She pulled her wrist away. "I've got to phone Karen. It's not her."

She tripped; another stupid cardboard box—why didn't he ever put things away? He grabbed her again, clamped his hand over her wrist, and pushed her towards the door.

"Come on. I'll drive. You can make the phone call but not here."

She tried to pull away. "I've got to phone." Her one thought.

"I know, I'm going to help."

Time progressed in jerky dreamtime. Louise disembodied from herself—maybe this was what it was like to separate?—watching a sad girl helped outside and into a car. The girl cried a lot—she could hear the wailing grief—but no tears fell. Her face wouldn't allow it. Tears were for the weak, she said, and for private moments when the world wasn't looking. The sad girl preferred a mask instead, its features fixed and blank.

Time danced, waltzing into the future quick and slow. Louise followed in its wake, connecting and disconnecting with the sad girl and her mask.

"Are we there yet?" the sad girl asked, her voice sucked dry of emotion.

"Another ten miles," said Nick.

Ten miles. She counted them off in her head: one, two . . .

"Are we there yet?"

Nick glanced over. The sad girl couldn't see the concern on his face—she was staring straight ahead at the wash of countryside—but Louise could. "Another six miles," he said.

"Six," said the sad girl, already starting to count. No, said Louise, ripping the mask away. They'd travelled far enough. She had to phone now!

She tore at her wrist, her fingers all thumbs, hit the wrong button, hit the right button, swore at both . . .

"What are you doing?" asked Nick.

She didn't answer. Wasn't it obvious? He reached across; she pulled her wrist away, turned her body towards the passenger door and pressed herself against it. The number was ringing. She could hear it, the dial tone repetitive, insistent, mocking.

"Come on!" she shouted, willing Karen to be at home, praying for that cheery voice to echo down the line, for death to be cheated—just this once. Was that so much to ask?

The phone rang on.

The car must have stopped. Nick was leaning across her. She shrugged him off.

The phone rang on.

The passenger door opened. Nick was outside, his hand closed around her wrist.

The ringing stopped. Louise buried her face in her hands, drew her knees up, and folded herself away.

Louise disappeared into her room the moment they returned to the apartment. She didn't want anything to drink, she didn't want anything to eat, and she didn't want company.

Nick went to the window in his room and stared outside. Everything was dark grey and black. If only it had been a few hours earlier. He could have flown to Upper Heywood and checked on Pendennis. Maybe discovered he'd escaped.

Or maybe not.

He stayed there motionless for several minutes, wondering if he could navigate at night. The leys would be easy enough. Maybe if he drove to a location where the ley crossed a road?

But could he guarantee the roads at the other end would be lit? Upper Heywood was in a rural location. Most country roads didn't have streetlights. And it was hard enough navigating the higher dimensions by day, one centimeter in the wrong direction and he could slip into the void.

He decided to watch the news instead.

By late evening the police had changed the victim's name to Karen Hawkins. Her picture appeared, closely followed by one of Louise. Police wanted to interview the thirty-one-year-old charity worker.

Nick watched, waiting for his picture to appear. They must have made the connection by now even if they weren't releasing the information to the press.

He flicked through the other news channels, sampling perspectives but finding little extra. No one was sure whether Louise was a suspect or another victim, one whose body had yet to be found.

He switched to the Framlingham murder, expecting the worst but finding the story unchanged. No updates since yesterday. The police were still looking for Nick Stubbs and still showing that ridiculous Rasputin photo.

He blanked the display. And deliberated. It *had* to be Pendennis. Framing Nick for murder, killing Louise's best friend. The killer was playing with them. Forcing them into hiding, robbing them of their homes, their work, their friends. That wasn't a warning, that was torture. Death by a thousand cuts.

He glanced over to the window. If only he could fly to Upper Heywood and find out. Maybe if he took it slow?

Then he had another idea. Bruce might have dropped out of the campaign by now. It was afternoon over there. Plenty of time to make an announcement. And if he had, wouldn't that exonerate anyone on his staff from being involved in Karen's death? No one would worry about a potential smear campaign when the candidate had already quit.

He surfed the American news channels. Nothing in the headlines. He clicked on campaign news, sampling five-second bursts before toggling to the next. There had to be something on John Bruce surely.

There was. The results of a WCN poll conducted since last night's statement had just been announced. John's numbers had dropped but not disastrously.

"It's a sympathy reaction," suggested the station's political correspondent. "I think some people felt that John got a raw deal yesterday. But I can't see him holding onto those numbers come Tuesday. America may love the underdog but they never vote for him."

The anchor repeated the numbers. Bruce's support had dropped from 21 to 13 percent.

"Senator Warren McKinley is still out in front with forty-eight percent, a nine-point gain over the week."

The Manchester Dome wasn't packed but it was lively. Two thousand banner-waving McKinley supporters being exulted to give it up for their man, the Senator from Ohio, the next President of the United States, War-ren Mc-Kin-ley.

Senator McKinley stood in the wings. He didn't have the physical presence or the looks of John Bruce. He was a small, craggy sexagenarian who looked as though he'd been pickled in the smoke and grime of a lifetime in politics—too many late-night committee rooms, snatched meals, and hotel bars.

His stomach rumbled. Not from hunger—hunger was something he'd never suffered from as his ample stomach testified—but from nerves. He'd always had a nervous stomach, even as a boy. His insides bubbling and churning as everyone around him complimented him on how cool he was under stress, how old Warren could handle anything thrown at him. Good old Warren—tough as old boots and a stomach to match.

If only they knew.

He crunched another tablet, cracked his face into a smile, and marched on stage. Music blared, people jumped up and down, and banners pumped. But all Warren could see was the giant face on the screen. His. He looked terrible, he knew the makeup would be a mistake; he looked like a reject from mortician's school. Why couldn't they let him be himself?

He waved to the crowd, plugged his speech into the lectern, and waited for the cheering to abate. A sharp pain stabbed at his abdomen. He gripped the sides of the lectern to dull the pain and tried not to grimace. Maybe he should shorten the speech by a few minutes, cut out some of the larger passages and see how he felt? After all, the hard work had already been done—he'd made the deals, he had the votes— this was just the icing for the holovision networks.

The first few words rattled out much as normal. He had never been a rousing orator, so no one paid attention to the strain in his voice. By the second sentence everyone did.

The last word came out as a cry. Pain. Intense and building. His stomach felt tight to the point of bursting, a bloated feeling spreading to his lower abdomen and chest. He hunched forward, gripping the lectern. It was as though something—something enormous—had crawled inside him and was now trying to stretch its way out.

The pain spread throughout his body. Incredulously, he could feel his calves stretching; he could hear knuckles popping, ribs cracking. A larger man was materializing inside his body. Slowly. Both bodies fighting for the same space, coresident yet separate. A larger man pushing in from another plane of existence, stretching into the physical world, a bit at a time, squeezing into McKinley's space, pushing him out.

Blood seeped from every pore of his body. His clothes moved by themselves, buttons popped, seams split. Dark patches enveloped his suit. His hands awash, his face a parody. He staggered, stumbling towards the front of the stage. An internal pressure building up behind his face, threatening to crack it open from ear to ear.

It was one of those moments that stick in the memory of a nation. Millions of people watching live. Sitting at home, unprepared, nibbling at food, shouting at their kids, waiting to zap to the next channel. And then hologram hell exploded in their living room.

Tiny shards of holobone cascaded over a million carpets, bits that looked familiar, bits of a face that would come back and haunt their dreams for the rest of their lives. If they could ever sleep again.

Some said the senator's skull expanded a full two inches before it finally blew apart; most just wanted to forget.

CHAPTER FOURTEEN

Nick awoke to the news. It was the lead story on all the holovision channels. And a mystery. How could a man be killed like that?

Manchester police didn't appear to know; neither did the FBI or Homeland Security. All took a similar line—the investigation was in an early phase, no stone would be left unturned, the perpetrator would be brought to justice, and speculation about the cause of death at this point in time was inappropriate.

The media disagreed. Speculation was not only appropriate but essential. And they had the experts lined up to prove it. Weapons experts, medical experts, political analysts, research scientists. Everyone dissecting the evening's events and providing their own interpretation. A compressed-gas bullet, nanoexplosives placed inside a dental cavity, a focussed energy wave, a low-frequency sound gun.

Nick flicked between the channels. One even found a link between McKinley and a cosmetics company, Nanotech Industries.

"Is it true," asked an excited reporter, "that Warren McKinley was being administered rejuvenating nanotechnocytes even though NTCs have yet to be cleared by the FDA?"

An equally excited former McKinley aide admitted that it had been discussed.

"Warren was no oil painting and some of the polls showed a marked voter negativity towards Warren's looks, especially in the upper quartile eighteen-to-thirty-four-year-old group. Some people thought that if we could get Warren to undergo some minor cosmetic surgery it would be worth ten points in November."

"Did he undergo cosmetic surgery?"

"No, but he did have talks with Nanotech. I know they were lobbying hard for FDA approval to commence human trials. According to them they were ready and all you'd need was one injection and all those NTCs would start rebuilding your body from the inside out. As soon as I saw the Senator's death on HV, I couldn't get the idea out of my head. Had someone injected him with NTCs? And had it all gone horribly wrong?"

The reporter turned to face the camera. "A question the whole nation is asking. Craig Sorrensen, WCN News, reporting live from Manchester, New Hampshire."

More experts, more channels. It was an accident, it was a contract killing, a political assassination. Everyone had a theory. Even John Bruce.

He stood on the same hotel steps where he'd been besieged the previous evening. He looked somber. It was the first time he'd been coaxed out of his hotel suite all day.

"Senator McKinley's death is a tragic loss to the nation," he said. "But not unexpected."

There was a whole second of dead air as the reporter, caught by surprise, tried to frame the follow-up question whilst several excited voices shouted in her ear from the studio. "How do you mean?" she asked.

"Because the senator was doing so well in the polls and it's in China's interest to see the President reelected. They can't afford a change in American foreign policy."

He turned to face the camera. "McKinley was a threat. He had to be removed."

Nick blurred past Avebury. He had to check on Pendennis despite his growing doubts. Peter had no interest in whether McKinley lived or died. But John Bruce did. Could Louise have been right all along?

He didn't want to believe it. John Bruce was a hero; the first man to pilot a craft into new space.

But if he'd been damaged, if part of his brain had been ripped away . . .

And that comment on China the evening before and the way he blamed China for McKinley's death. *McKinley was a threat. He had to be removed.* A threat to whom? China or John Bruce?

The wheel of doubt turned once again. What if Bruce was right about China? There was tension between the two countries and there were probably factions within China who viewed political assassination as a legitimate tool if the national interest was threatened.

Which begged the question: Was McKinley a threat to China? Nick hadn't heard anything to support that assertion but what did he know about politics? It was something he spent most of his life avoiding.

The last ley junction flashed by, Nick slowed and scanned ahead for the Oxford road. Maybe McKinley's death had nothing to do with John, Pendennis, or the Chinese. Maybe the man really did overdose on rejuvenating NTCs.

Upper Heywood blurred into view. Nick swung around to the main entrance, lined himself up with the doors, and sped through, dropping to floor level as he did so. He blazed along the main corridor, counting the bays—seven, eight—turning at the end into the east wing, more bays, more counting before slowing as Pendennis's cell approached.

He stretched into the wall, drifting slowly from corridor to cell. A red shape was standing by a mirror. Nick slid along the wall to the side. Was it Peter?

The man didn't move. He looked like he was talking to the mirror, standing there chatting to his reflection. And it *was* Pendennis, Nick could see that now. Which meant . . .

Which meant Pendennis had to be innocent.

Unless he had an accomplice.

Or a way of slipping in and out of Upper Heywood at will.

Louise was waiting by his bed. He'd barely had time to blink and focus his eyes before she spoke.

"Have you seen this?" she asked, her voice agitated, her arm pointing to an image of Warren McKinley on the HV. "We've got to do something. Tell the media. Tell someone. We can't sit back and let him slaughter his way to the White House."

She was breathing hard, eyes blazing. A different woman from the zombie he'd helped from the car the previous evening.

"Do you really think John's capable of—"

"*That* is not John." She stabbed a finger at the HV. "Did you hear what he said about McKinley? He's in a dream world. McKinley was no threat to China."

"Wasn't he?"

"Of course he wasn't," she snapped. "All the mainstream candidates preach accommodation with China. No one wants an arms race. Except . . ." She looked like she could barely bring herself to speak his name. "That thing calling itself John Bruce. He'll plunge the world into nuclear war. All it needs is suspicion. And if China thinks he's going to get elected and order a first strike against them what do you think they're going to do? Wait for his inauguration or strike first?"

She was agitated; arm-waving, finger-stabbing, table-banging agitated. Which made Nick nervous, supine as he was. He shuffled up the bed into a sitting position, his back against the headboard. He could see the logic of her argument but doubted the premise upon which it was built. How many Americans would vote for John Bruce?

"Who's going to vote for a candidate advocating nuclear war?" he asked.

"If he's the only candidate left standing—millions."

"But—"

"No buts, Nick. You saw what happened to McKinley. Take out a few more candidates and no one's going to be asking about rejuvenating NTCs, they're going to be screaming for revenge and if the only person giving them answers is John Bruce they're going to listen."

"That's assuming he doesn't make a mistake first and get caught—"

"How many's he killed so far? Three? And who're the police looking for?"

"You don't know he's killed anyone. In fact he couldn't have killed Culley or Karen. He wasn't even in the country."

"He could have ordered it," she screamed between clenched teeth. "He's the only one who benefits from all three deaths."

"How does he benefit from Karen's death?"

"I don't know!" she shouted, kicking the nearest box. "He must have thought she was me. The killer he hired must have thought she was me. *Someone* must have thought she was me!"

She turned away and kicked a path towards the window, scattering Nick's filing system as she went. Nick decided to let her burn her anger off. He still couldn't see how Louise could be viewed as a threat to Bruce—except by association—which assumed the killer had somehow traced her though him. But how? If he'd been followed to

Louise's home they'd have seen Louise too. So no reason to kill Karen by mistake.

Which meant . . . which meant what? That either Karen was another message or they'd traced Louise another way. Phone records, visitor logs at Upper Heywood, or by something he'd left in his house—address logs, notes . . .

Notes. He'd written Louise's name on a Post-it note and stuck it to the fridge door—along with the date and time of their rendezvous with Ziegler, so he wouldn't forget. Whoever left the body parts in the saucepan could have seen it.

But it wasn't the only note on the fridge door, or the only name. There was nothing to make it stand out.

Unless you were an old boyfriend.

Or someone who knew John Bruce's life inside out.

He glanced towards the window. Had she calmed down? He couldn't see her face but she hadn't kicked anything for ten seconds.

"What about members of Bruce's campaign?" he said. "They'd have a motive if they were expecting a top job at the end of it all. Or some fanatic with a John Bruce fixation . . ."

She turned away from the window. "How many of them would know there was a problem with John's brain scan?"

"We're not totally sure that there was—"

She stamped her foot and stabbed a finger once more at the HV. "*That* is not John. *That* is what you're left with after you rip away all the decency and the . . ."

She started to cry. Maybe it was delayed shock over Karen's death, maybe it was an excess of emotion.

Maybe it was just time.

"Do you want anything to eat?" asked Nick an hour later, knocking on her door.

The door opened. "I'll cook," she said, attempting a smile. She felt better, ready to greet the world again. The last hour had been cathartic.

"Are you sure?" asked Nick. "I'm a dab hand in the kitchen."

"No you're not," she said, pushing past. "You warm things up. And don't you get sick of all that processed food?"

"No." He followed her through into the kitchen.

"Well, you should. It's not good for you."

"It's even worse for the vegetables," he joked. "Think of all those carrots happily sunning themselves in the garden, a light breeze playing through their leaves."

She almost laughed. If only she could prolong this moment of normality. Two people engaged in light conversation, no thought about the past or the future or anything that might be happening beyond the walls of the room.

Nick shattered that wish in a second.

"I've been thinking about what you said earlier," he said.

Louise ignored him. She pulled a chopping board down from an overhead cupboard and looked for a sharp knife.

"I think there is something we can do," he continued. "It won't be easy. It might not even be possible but . . ."

She stared at him, barely daring to hope.

"Do you think you might put down that knife?" he asked. "I find it hard to be brilliant in front of an armed audience."

CHAPTER FIFTEEN

He'd been thinking about the possibility for the last day, mulling it over, reading associated literature. In theory it ought to work. But the mechanics of putting that theory into practice . . .

"You see, what we really need to do," he said, "is find a way of reuniting the two parts of John's consciousness."

"You can do that?"

"I don't know but I can't see any reason why it shouldn't be possible. After all, if we're right it's already happened once. All we've got to do is reverse the process. Persuade the part of John inside Pendennis to disconnect and then—somehow—reconnect with the real John."

"Would he be able to reconnect?"

The sixty-four-million-dollar question. In theory yes but no one tell the British Medical Authority.

"I think so. I'm making a guess here but I don't think we need perfect alignment. I don't see this as delicate neurosurgery where you need to reconnect every nerve and blood vessel back to its sister. I see this more like a skin graft or setting a bone. We position John's missing subpersonality as close to the top of his head as possible and let nature do the rest."

"What if it didn't?"

"We'd try again. Look, when I reconnect all I do is position myself over a mythical hole in the top of my head and think myself inside. I don't even know if I'm facing the right way. But it works every time."

"But your head's empty when you do that." She heard what she'd said and rolled her eyes. "Sorry, but you know what I mean."

"Pendennis's wasn't. You've seen the scans. If John can connect with Pendennis, surely he can connect with his old self."

She smiled, a genuine broad smile. The first time he'd seen her do that in ages.

"It could work, couldn't it?" she said, her excitement growing. "And if John's whole again then he'll come to his senses and pull out of the election . . . and retract all those things he's been saying. But how would you get him out of Pendennis? Hypnotism?"

Nick hesitated. Should he tell her? He decided on a compromise. "That's the plan," he said. "Though there are problems. Even if I do manage to persuade him to separate, I don't know if I'll be able to see him. When I try to look at myself in the higher dimensions I see nothing. Now, is that because I'm one giant eyeball or is it because I'm invisible?"

"Couldn't you tell where he was from his voice?"

That was the bigger problem. She was in such a good mood at the moment. Positive and focussed. Exactly how he needed her to be. But if he told her he was deaf in the higher dimensions, that he couldn't hear and probably couldn't speak either . . . how would she react then? How can you hypnotize a subject who can't even hear you?

"I don't know," he said. "But there is a way I could find out. In fact, I think it's essential if we're to have any chance of ferrying John across the Atlantic."

"What?" she asked.

"I need you to separate."

"I'll do it," she said, the words flying out of her mouth. "Whatever it takes." Anything to get this nightmare over with. For Karen, for the John trapped inside Pendennis's head, for the world, for everyone.

Ten minutes later she was having second thoughts. Hypnotism was fine—for other people—but she was too practical, too suspicious. When Nick told her to close her eyes, lie back, and relax she immediately tensed. She couldn't help it. She felt uncomfortable, and vulnerable, her head filling with stories of dubious stage hypnotists and the humiliation they put their subjects through. Not that she thought Nick would, but the idea once implanted wouldn't go away. And the harder she tried to shift it, the tenser she became.

Nick's voice droned on, telling her to relax, to imagine herself somewhere peaceful where she felt safe. A week ago that would have been her yard, sitting under the beech tree watching lambs racing and bouncing across the field consumed by the pure joy of being alive on a warm summer day. Now her yard was a place where emergency vehicles parked, where murderers stalked, and Karen . . .

Poor, dear, sweet Karen. And with that thought came the guilt. Guilt that she was alive and Karen wasn't. Guilt that here she was with a chance to do something about the situation and all she could do was build barriers and wallow in self-pity. Why couldn't she relax? Why couldn't she lie back and allow herself to be hypnotized? Why couldn't she *do* something!

She thrashed and turned. She struggled. She tried to force her mind to blank, shoving and squeezing at thoughts that refused to budge. She . . .

"This is no good," she said, getting up and pushing Nick away. "I want to help. I really do. But not now. I'll try again later."

She tried again later. And again. Perhaps if she got drunk? But there was no alcohol in the fridge, not even a bottle of wine.

"Perhaps if you tried self-hypnosis," suggested Nick. "Maybe you'd find that easier."

He gave her a few exercises to try. Some basic self-hypnosis routines to help her relax.

She tried. She really did. But nothing seemed to work.

"Perhaps it would be better if you were alone," said Nick. He cleared a space on the floor next to the bed and lay down. "I need to see what happens to the ley line when it hits the coast. We may be able to follow it across the Atlantic. You relax. I'll be back in about an hour."

She watched him lay back and stare at the ceiling. And then he was gone. Or so she supposed. His breathing had lowered and he wasn't asleep. Unless he'd learned how to sleep with his eyes open.

She sighed and turned back to her own problems. She had to master this. People's lives depended on it. She rolled her eyes. That's all she needed. Extra pressure. The fate of the entire world depends upon you, Louise Callander. Now relax.

A whirring sound came from the kitchen—the fridge freezer. She hadn't realized before how noisy it was. And was that a tap dripping in the bathroom? She lay there, feeling hypersensitive, sucking in faraway sounds from the apartment and the grounds—a dog barking, a passing lorry, a pigeon in the woods.

Relax.

A voice in her head. Funny, for a moment it sounded like Nick but it couldn't have been. He was still off enjoying himself in the higher dimensions. She glanced over towards his body to make sure. It lay there, silent, his lips not moving.

Relax.

That voice again, lapping over her consciousness; the second syllable elongated, ending like the distant sound of a wave crashing on an empty beach.

A gently shelving beach. The sun shining, the sea lapping, the sand warm beneath your feet, pressing through the gaps between your toes as you walk.

Yes, she could feel it now. Soft, warm, fine-grained sand.

A gentle breeze blowing off the sea, a tang of salt in the air.

She could taste it too. And smell it. Salt, ozone . . .

. . . and a deserted beach. No one else about. Just you, the sand, and the ocean.

The ocean. She could hear the waves crashing far out to sea, the water surging up the gently shelving beach, then receding.

Nibbling at the sand beneath your feet.

Yes, she could feel that too. The tingling, tickling sensation along the soles of her feet. The sand excavated beneath her heels and toes.

The water rippling over the tops of your feet and ankles. The water warm and inviting, the sun hot on the top of your head.

Yes, it was hot. She could feel the slight burning on her scalp and shoulders.

But the water's warm. The perfect temperature. You can feel it rising up your legs as you wade deeper. It's becoming harder to walk, resistance from the water, slowing you down, lifting you up . . .

She rose with the wave, lifting her arms, stretching onto tiptoe.

You lie back in the water; let the sea take your weight, arms outstretched . . .

Floating, the sky as blue and deep as eternity.

Floating, almost motionless, the gentle rise and fall of a summer sea on a windless day . . .

Floating . . .

The sun so bright you have to close your eyes.

Floating . . .

You can feel your mind drifting away into deep, fathomless sleep.

It was working! Nick looked down on Louise's shimmering form on the bed.

"You're feeling relaxed, calm, and confident," he said, forming the words in his mind and willing them into Louise's head.

"Yes," she said sleepily, her voice like a whisper from deep inside his mind. No direction at all, just there—nestling within him. A few minutes ago, when he'd first heard her voice, he'd almost shot out of the window. He'd been hoping she could hear him. It had been his plan all along. Kill two birds with one stone. See if he could hypnotize Louise from the higher dimensions as a dry run for Pendennis. He'd thought *speak* and willed Louise to hear him, hovering as close to her head as he dared. And then he heard her. The sudden sound of her voice breaking the perfect silence of the higher dimensions. And the shock . . . he was so used to sound having direction but this sound appeared to emanate from inside him as though injected straight into his brain.

He knew that telepathic communication was possible, even filmed it, but it was something else to actually participate in the process. It was incredible.

And from then on it had been easy. Far easier than any corporeal session. Louise's defences were nonexistent. She was open, receptive.

But now came the hard part. Could he persuade her to die?

He took her deeper, counting through the levels, bolstering her confidence. And then introduced the hospital ward, the life support unit, the nurse.

"You'll never be in danger," he promised her. "And remember you're doing this for John . . . and Karen. They're both counting on you, willing you to succeed."

All the cards were now in play. Nick moved the nurse's hand towards the dial and began the count.

"Now," Nick urged. "You feel your mind rising. Your body lets go. It expels you, forces you free."

He waited. Scanning her face, the area above the bed. Would there be anything to see? Would there . . .

A shape! He saw it. A vague outline, a pale cloud rising from Louise's head. A pale cloud now composed of myriad tiny specks of light.

Not a shimmering mirage of the physical world but something sharper.

He watched transfixed. It rose, its edges wobbling like a football-sized bubble. A bubble filled with a thousand points of light; some blue, some red, some sparkling white, like miniscule stars trapped inside a shifting membrane. What were they? The imagers had hinted at nothing like this.

He called to her. "You're feeling relaxed, calm, and confident. Nothing can go wrong on a perfect day like this. Now, slowly open your mind to your surroundings. What do you see?"

"It's dark."

"Look closer. Let your vision adjust to the level of light. What do you see?"

"I see . . . me on a bed and . . . Nick. But I can't see too well, there's something in my eye."

"That's because you've separated, Louise. You're looking down on your body from above but there's nothing to worry about. Everything is fine. Can you see me? I'm out-of-body too, floating a few feet in front of you."

"Something hazy? Like a speckled lampshade?"

He rose to the ceiling. "Does it move?"

"Yes, is that . . . is that you?"

"Apparently. Now, when you want to move all you have to do is imagine yourself moving and you will. We'll start slowly. See the window over there? Let's move towards it. Start off slowly and follow the talking lampshade."

He took her to the window. Next came the difficult bit.

"See that tree overhanging the wall by the gate?"

"Yes."

"We're going to go there. Fast. You'll feel a slight pain for about a second as we pass through the window but you mustn't worry. It's something that has to be done. For John and for Karen. They know you'll be brave. I've given you some painkillers and even now you can feel them swimming through your mind, deadening your pain receptors. You'll hardly feel a thing."

It had to work. Hypnotism had been used to deaden pain during major surgery. This was nothing in comparison.

"Are you ready, Louise? Fix that overhanging branch in your mind and imagine yourself flying towards it as fast as a bird. Go!"

She blurred through the window. He followed. Not a scream, not a whimper trailed in her wake.

He caught up with her by the branch. "I'm going to count to four, Louise. As I count your mind is going to clear. You're going to remember everything from the moment you separated. As for the separation itself—that was easy, you didn't even have a membrane to break—and any time you want to separate in the future all you have to do is close your eyes and think your mind free. One, you're beginning to wake up. Two, you're feeling relaxed and confident. Three, you forget what I told you about pain and painkillers. Four."

"I've really separated?" she asked.

"Like you were born to it. Now take in that view and follow the devilishly handsome lampshade."

It was amazing. She was swathed in views. The 360-degree, up-down, all-around vision that Nick had told her so much about. It was almost too much to take in.

"Come on," he said. "We'll practice flying in tandem. Fix your mind on me. Imagine we're joined by a wire. Where I go, you go."

He started slowly at first, flying at walking pace parallel to the ground; then slowly accelerating, adding dives and swoops and sharper turns. Louise followed, fixing her mind on Nick's image and thinking *stick close*. Limpet close. She repeated the words like a mantra.

She passed through clouds, she joined a flying V of geese, she saw ley lines and flaming circles of stone. She flew at speeds she never dreamed she could achieve.

"Exhilarating, isn't it?" said Nick as they blurred along a fiery ley.

Louise didn't reply. There were some things—like giant roller coaster rides and rope bridges thrown across impossibly deep chasms—that were best viewed through the small gaps between one's fingers. This was another. She didn't even have eyelids she could close. It was all right for Nick, he had a bright ley line to fix his mind on, all she had was a fuzzy lampshade. And the knowledge that one centimeter was all that stood between her and the void. One slip and she could be lost forever.

She hung on, persuading him to slow down, persuading him that maybe there were other things they should be doing besides trying to set new speed records.

"Like seeing how far apart we can go and still communicate," she said.

He liked the idea. He slowed and then suddenly veered away from the line. "There's a house over there we can use as a reference."

He positioned himself at the base of the house's front door and told Louise to climb away from him, counting as she went, throwing her words as hard as she could towards him.

She rose up the face of the building, past the top of the door, past the first floor window, the gutters. "Can you still hear me?" she asked.

"Loud and clear," he replied.

She climbed higher, aiming at straight up but finding her course deviating and then, in panic, deciding to follow the roofline instead, hugging the red tiles. She reached the ridge and stopped.

"Can you hear me?"

Silence, then Nick appeared at the base of the roof. "Eight to ten meters, I'd say. We can give it another go back at the rectory. Do you think we've got time to visit Stonehenge?"

"No!"

They spent the rest of the afternoon planning. Nick downloaded a map of America's eastern seaboard and started committing it to memory.

"You can't memorize the entire map," said Louise.

"Don't need to. All I need to know are the rough locations of the major coastal towns. Then as soon as we hit land, I'll follow the coast until I see a city I recognize. The rest is easy. Follow the coast north past Boston then follow the road signs for Manchester. John's itinerary for tomorrow is available on the web so I'll commit that to memory too, along with the relevant portions of the Manchester street map."

It all sounded so easy. Too easy. Hypnotize Peter, free John; use hypnosis to keep John pliant, train him to fly in tandem with Nick; head west, cross the Atlantic, find Manchester, track down the other John; more hypnosis, reunite the two Johns, and then return.

"I'll need to start at first light tomorrow," said Nick. "I'll need as much daylight as I can get."

"What happens if you can't get back in the light?"

"It's always light somewhere. Maybe I'll follow the sun and keep going west."

She envied him his confidence. But it worried her too. Was he taking things too lightly? There were so many things that could go wrong.

"Do you think you should wait another day?" she asked. "Maybe have a dry run across the Atlantic and back?"

He shook his head. "We don't have the time. There might be another death by tomorrow. And the longer we leave it the harder it might be to free John. Who knows what's happening inside Peter's mind? Is it healing over? Is there a time limit beyond which John's subpersonality becomes so well fixed inside Peter that it would take another SHIFT flight to rip it out?"

She hoped not.

The afternoon progressed in growing optimism. John had two engagements the following day; both were in Manchester, both easy to find. And Nick found a room plan of John's hotel. There were only three VIP suites. John Bruce had to be using one of them.

Even Louise found the optimism catching. Nick's plan was no longer fanciful but something that could work. Everything could be over in less than twenty-four hours.

Then the apartment phone rang.

CHAPTER SIXTEEN

They both froze, their eyes fixed on the red flashing light on the HV unit. Who could possibly be calling? Had someone traced them via the HV? The police? John Bruce?

"Don't answer it," snapped Nick. Not that Louise needed telling, she backed away from the unit. "Should we turn everything off?" she asked.

Nick didn't answer; he kept staring at the light.

The ringing stopped after thirty seconds.

Nick turned to Louise. "It could be a wrong number."

And pigs might separate.

Louise knew exactly who it was. Someone looking for Nick. Someone who'd found out about the apartment or traced him via the HV connection. Her hand flew to her mouth. His inquiry about John Bruce's itinerary and hotel floor plan. Could that have tripped some kind of switch? People monitor those sorts of things, don't they?

"Switch it off," she said. "Disconnect everything."

The doorbell rang.

A second of hesitation then Louise was running. There were knives in the kitchen. She grabbed two: one sharp, one large; started to run back to the lounge then stopped. Should she have chosen something longer, heavier? A mop, a broom handle? Something she could wield from a distance?

The doorbell rang again. She was standing at the top of the stairs, two knives in her hands, staring at the door, her hands. Where was Nick?

She ran into the lounge. He was lying on the floor, motionless, his eyes wide and staring. Was he . . .?

She dropped the knives, bent down by his side, felt for a pulse. He was breathing—barely—and his pulse was almost nonexistent.

His eyes fluttered. Then he smiled. "It's okay," he said. "It's Adam. He's a friend."

Louise kept both knives close while Nick went downstairs to answer the door. He may have been confident that he'd recognized the person at the door when he'd separated just now, but Louise was less sure. It was getting dark outside and how well could he see from the higher dimensions?

Voices came from the front door. Louise listened, tightening the grip on the knife in her right hand.

Laughter rippled up the stairs. She relaxed.

Nick introduced her to Adam Llewellyn, the owner of the clinic and an old friend of Nick's from his student days. The two men couldn't have looked more different. Adam was well-groomed and smartly dressed. Nick wasn't.

"Does anyone else know we're here?" Nick asked him.

"You mean like the police?" Adam said, arching his eyebrows then smiling. "Don't worry, I haven't told anyone. The idea of you dismembering anyone is laughable." He turned to wink at Louise. "He can't stand the sight of blood."

"What about your staff?" pressed Nick.

"I expect they know someone's here. You can see the kitchen window from the rear of the clinic. But no one knows who you are. As far as the outside world is concerned you're someone from the city who rents the place for weekends and holidays. Just as we agreed."

Just as we agreed. It seemed so clandestine to Louise. Almost as though Nick knew he'd need somewhere to hide when he'd first taken out the lease.

"Do you want coffee?" asked Louise, remembering her manners.

"No, thank you," said Adam. "I only popped round to make sure the apartment hadn't been invaded by squatters." He adjusted his right cuff and glanced around the room. "Though with Nick's sense of decor it's always difficult to tell."

"Clutter is the hallmark of a creative mind," said Nick.

"Then you must be a genius." He smiled and made his farewells then stopped by the lounge door and turned to face Nick. "Oh, and next time you're on the run you might choose to close the curtains and remember to keep the lights turned off at night. Hardened criminals swear by it."

Nick turned to Louise and rolled his eyes. "I'll see Adam out. There's something I need to arrange with him. Won't be long."

"Arrange what?" she asked, but he was already thundering down the stairs.

She waited, checking her watch every other minute. After ten minutes, the front door latch clicked and Nick came running up the stairs. He was carrying what looked like a large black briefcase. He placed it carefully on top of a box in the lounge then ran back downstairs to fetch another.

"What are they?" asked Louise, bending down to examine the nearest one. There wasn't a label anywhere.

"Portable life support units," he said, beaming. "Aren't they great? These are the new ones that even I can use. You plug in the unit, stick a few patches on your skin, and the LSU does the rest. Monitors your vitals and tops up your fluids."

Louise was confused. "Why on earth would you want something like that?" And then concerned. "You're not ill are you?"

He smiled. "Not me. It's insurance in case it takes longer to get across the Atlantic and back. I want to make sure I've got a fit, healthy, and undeniably alive body to come back to. It's one of the reasons I chose to base my research here. All clinics have to have portable LSUs these days. And maintain them. Handy for when I need to borrow one."

"Why have you borrowed two?"

"Didn't I say?"

She had to admit it made sense. She didn't like it. But it made sense.

"I know I can hypnotize Peter," explained Nick. "And there'll be no membrane of John's to break. The connection to Peter's body will be tenuous at best, but . . . it's persuading him to disconnect and not freak out that worries me. He trusts you. He's more likely to stay calm if you're around and more likely to do what I say if you tell him it's okay."

All true. And as Nick said, it could easily turn into a long trip across the Atlantic. He might have trouble keeping John under for that amount of time.

"But if you're there," he continued, "you can help keep an eye on him. And if we have to stop every few minutes to push him deeper under you'll be able to help with that as well."

"Why didn't you say all this earlier?"

He grimaced. "Mea culpa. I had the impression that you're the type of person who does better when they don't have time to dwell on a problem."

She opened her mouth in surprise. Was she that transparent? Did she have "compulsive worrier" tattooed across her face? Or worse—"Louise Callander, Worrier Princess?"

"When did you plan on telling me then? A minute before we were due to leave?"

He attempted a boyish smile. "Maybe over breakfast. But I was quite prepared to leave without you. I still am. But . . ." He paused, his face turning serious. "It makes sense for you to come along. I need to know that I'm talking to the real John and not some caricature that Peter's hatched up. I need you to quiz him first. Otherwise . . ."

He didn't have to finish the sentence. Mr. Hyde as President was bad enough but Mr. Hyde and Peter Pendennis on a joint ticket . . .

It was time.

Louise stood by the window looking out at a dawn breaking grey and overcast. She'd been awake for hours. Anticipating.

And practising. She'd separated twice before breakfast just to prove she still could.

She stared unfocussed into the distance. This was a day she wanted behind her.

"Ready when you are," said Nick from the other side of the room. He'd been playing with the LSUs for the past half hour: checking instructions, untangling cables, making sure all the drips were full and correctly installed.

Louise turned away from the window and walked like a condemned woman to the bed that was now lying alongside Nick's. He handed her the long-sleeved green vest that came with the LSU. She peeled off her own T-shirt and put it on.

"Lie down and I'll hook you up," said Nick, holding an array of tubes and wires in his hands.

She obeyed without thinking, her mind on autopilot. He knelt by her bed, clipping the various tubes and wires into the connectors on her vest. She stared up at the ceiling.

"One more connector," he said. Click. "Now adjusting the levels." He moved to the head of the bed, bent down, and tapped in a series of commands.

"Okay, switching on. You could be gone for a week and not even feel hungry. All your fluids topped up, nutrient levels balanced—the lot. Though, don't ask me how it finds a vein—Adam told me once and I'd have preferred he hadn't. Suffice to say—it's clever, computerized, and hidden away in that miracle vest. Though, I think they could have come up with a better color than olive green."

He flicked another switch, tweaked a few wires, then stood back. "There, everything's connected and working. You're alive, Miss Frankenstein."

She forced a smile.

"Watch out for the blood pressure monitor," said Nick. "It's activated on a timer. When mine first came on I thought some higher dimensional bogeyman had grabbed my arm."

She tried to maintain her smile but it was morphing into a grimace. She closed her eyes and waited. She heard Nick climbing onto his bed; the *tip-tap* of fingers on a keypad; the click of cables being connected. And then silence.

"Okay. Let's go."

She almost hit the ceiling in the rush to be free. This wasn't a time to be tentative, this was a time to get the job done and over with quick. Like swallowing something unpleasant.

Nick's voice boomed into her head. "Ready?"

"Ready."

They flew out of the window, Nick taking the lead, Louise following. One slow test lap of the rectory and then they were away, two clouds of thought accelerating across the countryside: cresting trees, houses, dipping into fields, flying low and fast then climbing, then banking as the ley line swept in from the horizon. They accelerated again, gliding along golden strands, weaving past forgotten monuments to the dead, ancient hill forts, burial mounds, temples, and churches. Then slowing as Oxford approached, looking for the turnoff, finding it, hitching lift after lift, clawing their way through the traffic until . . .

Upper Heywood: its warren of low flat-roofed buildings sprawled out ahead of them.

"When we get to Pendennis's cell I want you to follow me in," said Nick. "But think *silent*. I don't want Peter to hear anyone's voice but mine."

"Okay," said Louise.

"Then as soon as I contact John step in and help. Think your voice inside his head. Let him know who you are, keep him calm, then ask him a question that only the real John would know. If he passes the test, start persuading like mad. We want him out and away from Pendennis as quick as possible."

"What if he doesn't pass the test?"

"I'll take Peter deeper. Into a coma if necessary."

They drifted through the roof into reception, passing through the concrete and the timber and the ceiling tiles. They found the main corridor. Everything white: the walls, the floor, the ceiling; even the overalls of the cleaner pushing a mop over the floor. Louise followed Nick, the scenery unchanging, every entrance to every bay looking identical. They turned at the far end, passed into another corridor then stopped.

"This is it," said Nick. "Think yourself silent and invisible."

Up went her walls. She imagined herself a soundproof fortress, with twelve-foot-thick walls of padded stone.

Nick floated further down the corridor then slipped though a wall. Louise followed.

Pendennis was inside, a red shape lying on a bed. He looked asleep, his eyes tight-closed.

"So tired," whispered Nick, elongating his voice. "So-o . . . ti-red."

Louise hovered by the side of the bed, trying to keep hold of her thoughts. She could hear Nick. Would she be able to hear Pendennis?

"Sleep," whispered Nick. "You feel so tired you could sleep for a week."

Silence. Was Pendennis already asleep? Could you hypnotize someone who was already asleep?

"Sle-ep," repeated Nick. "Every part of you is asleep except the tiny part of you that can hear me. Can you hear me, Peter?"

Louise waited, the silence excruciating. Her mind alive with concerns that she was terrified to express in case Pendennis overheard them.

"Yes," said a very small voice. "I hear you."

"Good," said Nick. "You're drifting deeper, drifting into a sleep so deep, so warm, so safe that you don't ever want to leave. Can you feel how peaceful it is, Peter?"

"Yes," came the reply, sibilant and sleepy.

"You feel it like a heavy blanket impossible to move."

"Yes."

"Is John there?" Nick asked.

Silence.

He asked again. "John?"

Behind her walls, Louise began to panic. What if John had been absorbed? Or killed? Or was too frightened to answer?

"I need to talk to John Bruce," said Nick.

If anything, the silence deepened. Louise couldn't take it anymore. She opened a window in her walls and sent a name flying through the ether towards the body on the bed.

"John," she whispered, then louder. "John, it's Louise, I've come for you."

No answer. She drifted closer, tore down her walls, imagined her voice inside Peter's head, planted it there, gave it power, life, breath. "John!"

"Louise?"

His voice exploded inside her head. *His* voice. John's. Unmistakable.

"Yes, John," she said. "It's me. I've come to get you out."

"Where are you, Lou? I can't see you." He sounded nervous and worried.

"I'm . . . I'm outside in the corridor," said Louise, thinking quickly. "I have a friend with me. We've come to help you. Do you . . . do you remember the name of my best friend at school?"

Up went her walls. Her best friend's name hidden away, pushed to the deepest dungeon of her memory. Come on, John! Remember. Let it really be you.

"Is she with you?" asked John, confused.

"No, she's, er . . . it's another test, John. I want to make sure your memory hasn't been impaired. We're worried about you."

Louise took a deep virtual breath. Please, John, just answer and get this over with.

"Suzie?" said John. "Suzie Onslow?"

Yes!

"Okay, John," she said. "I want you to close your eyes and relax. My friend's going to talk to you. He knows how to get you out. Do what he says and you'll be free. We'll take you home."

"Can you do that, Lou? Can you really take me home?"

"Yes, John. We can."

"Are your eyes closed yet, John?" asked Nick.

"Who are you?" A hint of panic. "Where's Louise?"

"Calm down, John," said Louise. "He's a friend. Listen to him."

"Okay, Lou, if you say so."

"I'm taking you back to the *Pegasus*," said Nick. "You're weightless again. Do you remember how that feels?"

"Yes."

"You feel totally relaxed. Your body has no weight, no substance. You're floating without a care in the world, drifting, drifting into a deep, deep sleep."

Silence. Was the lack of response good or bad?

Nick continued. "You're floating weightless inside the Pegasus. Your body horizontal, your arms and legs by your side. Now, as I count, I'm going to gradually turn on the artificial gravity. Do you understand?"

"Yes," came the sleepy reply.

"As I do so your body is gradually going to feel heavier. One, your arms and legs start to droop. Two, you feel your body start—ever so slowly—to drift down towards the floor. But not your mind. You feel light-headed. Your body's getting heavier but your mind is still weightless. You like the feeling. You want to let go and let your mind fly free. Three, you feel a breath of wind between your mind and your body. You feel your mind start to lift as your body sags. Slowly at first. Rising gently on that breath of wind. Can you feel it?"

"Yes."

"Feel your mind lift higher, John. Feel your body sink away."

"Something's wrong," said John, his voice sounding frightened. "Turbulence. There's something wrong with the *Pegasus*. Lou!"

"Calm . . ."

"Lou, help me! I'm being ripped apart. Louise!"

Shit! Had Nick tapped into a memory? They both spoke at once—Nick and Louise—both trying to calm John down, both failing.

John screamed. The sound reverberating inside Louise. So loud, so painful.

"John, listen to my voice," Nick urged over the screams. "You are not in the *Pegasus*. I'm taking you back to a time before the launch."

"There's no time. The ship's breaking up! Everything's blurred. Louise, help me!"

"I'm here, John. How can I help?"

"I need to get to the escape hatch. But something's pinned me against the far wall. If you can help get it off me, I know I can get out."

"I help you, John. I'm pulling you clear."

"You're not! I can't see you! Why don't you come to me?"

"I am with you, John. You can hear me."

"But you're too far away. I need your strength for one last push and I'll be free!"

"You don't need it, John. A surge of energy runs through you. You have the strength. Can you feel it?"

"Yes, I'm . . . I'm free of the back wall. I've reached the escape hatch. It's opening. My hands are pushing through. I'm reaching out to you, Louise. Take my hands—your friend too—if you pull me through I'll be free."

Louise concentrated hard; thinking, hoping, praying that this would be it. One more encouragement and John would be free. A new lampshade-sized cloud of thought hovering above Pendennis's bed.

But something else happened instead.

Someone started to laugh and everything went black.

CHAPTER SEVENTEEN

Nick awoke. Someone was shining a light in his eyes. He blinked and turned his head away. Then saw Louise. She was lying in the next bed, a drip attached to her arm. But not the one he'd attached. This one was hanging from a stand high above the bed. And the room was different. It wasn't his apartment. It looked . . . it looked like a hospital? White walls, white ceiling.

"Do you know where you are?" asked a male voice.

Nick swung his head around. A doctor stood over him—a man, mid-thirties, no one he recognized—he was holding a pencil light in his hand.

"Where is this?" asked Nick, trying to sit up. The doctor pushed him back down on the bed. Nick lacked the strength to resist.

"It's best you take it easy for a while," said the doctor. "You've been out for some time."

"Where is this?" Nick repeated, his eyes darting around the room. It looked like a hospital room—two beds but . . . where were the windows?

"You're in hospital," said the doctor. "Do you remember why you're here?"

"No."

The doctor clicked his tongue and grimaced. Obviously, not the right answer, thought Nick, his head feeling inordinately dense. Had he been drugged? The last thing he remembered was trying to free John.

"Your LSUs malfunctioned," said the doctor. "Sending you both into a coma."

"Louise?" Panic. He threw his head round to look at her. "Is she still in a coma?"

"She's come out of it. She's resting now. The pair of you have been very lucky. LSUs are not for amateurs."

"Where exactly are we?" asked Nick.

"A hospital," repeated the doctor, peering at a display panel on the wall behind Nick's bed and then tapping buttons on his handheld.

"Which hospital?"

"This one," said the doctor. "And I apologize for sounding obtuse but I shouldn't be talking to you as it is."

"Why not?"

The doctor eyed him suspiciously. "I think you know."

Nick wanted to scream, "I don't," and pursue the matter but held back. It was a slim chance but what if the hospital staff didn't know who he was? Better to play dumb, thank everyone for their help, and get discharged as soon as possible.

But what had happened? Could a sudden failure in an LSU drag them out of Upper Heywood and back to their bodies? A near-death effect. Survivors talked of something similar, didn't they? The sudden realization that it wasn't their time, that they were going to live, then the feeling of being dragged back and reconnected with their bodies. But . . .

But he hadn't felt anything like that. One second he was at Upper Heywood the next he was waking up here.

And what had gone wrong with the LSU? He'd used them before without a problem. Okay, he'd never separated before but he'd been hooked up to the units for hours at a time. Could someone have sabotaged his unit? John Bruce? Someone working for John Bruce?

In which case why was he still alive? Had Adam found them in time, recognized the problem, and called for an ambulance?

Questions. His mind was full of them. Was his identity known? The doctor was acting as though it might be. *I shouldn't be talking to you as it is.* But if he was under arrest wouldn't a police guard be in the room?

He closed his eyes. He'd separate. It was the obvious thing to do. He'd find out where they were, see if anyone was outside the door guarding the room. Maybe even fly back to the apartment and see if anyone had turned the place over.

He relaxed, settled back, willed his mind free, and . . . nothing happened. He tried again. And again. Still nothing.

"What medication have you put me on?" he asked, sitting up, trying to find a reason for his failure to separate.

"He's gone," said Louise. "And I think we should go too."

Nick agreed and began disconnecting his drip. "How long have you been awake?" he asked.

"Long enough. What the hell happened back—"

Her question was cut short by the door suddenly opening. Anders Ziegler stood in the doorway. He looked horrified. "What are you doing?" he hissed, running into the room. "Are you mad? You'll set off the alarms."

Nick and Louise froze. "What alarms?"

Ziegler ran back to the door and eased it closed. "The monitors are linked to the nurse's station. If you disconnect your heart monitors you'll have a crash team here in ten seconds flat."

Nick felt stupid. And then curious. "Why would that worry you? And what are you doing here?"

"I haven't got much time," said Ziegler. He looked nervous and his face was drawn. "I had to call in a lot of favors to get you moved here as it was."

"Where's here?" asked Louise. "Upper Heywood?"

Ziegler nodded. "It was the only place I could think of. It has secure hospital status."

"Why would we need to be in a secure hospital?" asked Nick, fearing he already knew the answer. The Oxford murders. Karen Hawkins and Vince Culley.

"You really don't know?" asked Ziegler. He looked surprised. And still very nervous. He kept glancing towards the door as though he expected someone to burst in at any moment.

"Is it because of Karen?" asked Louise. "We were miles away at the time. We couldn't—"

Ziegler cut her off. "Karen's the least of your problems. Which is why we've got to get our story straight. You say nothing about me or coming here to visit Peter. Understand?"

Nick was confused. "What's that got to do—

Ziegler glared at him. "This is not a game," he hissed. "Or a debate. You keep me and Upper Heywood out of everything and I'll do what I can to help."

He turned to Louise, his eyes pleading. "I can say you're unfit to stand trial. Make up some condition to keep them away. Anything as long as you keep my name out of it. I've destroyed all the records of your visits to Peter. But you've got to help me. You've got to."

The man was terrified.

"Keep who away from us?" asked Nick.

Ziegler stared at him, incredulous. "The Americans, of course."

"What Americans?" asked Louise.

"Bruce's Truth Commission."

"John Bruce?"

"*President* Bruce," corrected Ziegler. "He wants you extradited. His Truth Commission have named you as part of the terrorist group who had McKinley and the other political leaders assassinated."

Nick felt numbed. President Bruce. Truth Commission. Extradition.

"*President* Bruce?" asked Louise. "How long were we out?"

"Twelve months," said Ziegler. "I had you moved here the moment I could. I've done everything to keep you safe. Now you've got to repay the favor. Keep my name out of this. Don't let the Americans know I brought you together."

Twelve months, thought Nick. Twelve months and now Mr. Hyde's President.

"Has John attacked China?" asked Louise.

"Not yet," said Ziegler. "He's too busy purging his own country. Interning and deporting. But the terrorists are still getting through— fifteen Senators have been killed so far, three Supreme Court judges. Which is why Bruce set up his Truth Commission—to fast-track justice. And backed the formation of local militia—armed gangs of patriots to hunt out and interrogate subversives in their neighborhoods. It's trial by mob over there. If we're extradited we'll be dead within a week."

Ziegler turned to leave. "I've got to run," he said, checking his watch. "Remember, keep quiet. Feign memory loss if you have to. I'll be back as soon as I can."

"What are we going to do?" asked Louise as soon as the door closed.

Nick felt shell-shocked. What *could* they do? They'd had the word "terrorist" attached to their names. That changed everything: their rights, their ability to question the evidence against them, everything. Even if they could prove their innocence who'd want to listen, they were terrorists.

And it transferred their fate from the judicial arena to the political. They would become bargaining chips—political pawns dependent on the relationship between Downing Street and the White House. *You hand over those two terrorists and I'll make sure a British company's at the top of the list when the next round of defense contracts are handed out.*

If John Bruce wanted them, he'd get them.

Unless they could whip up a media campaign in their favor . . . but what chance was there of that? As terror suspects they'd have no access to the press. And how many friends or colleagues would dare speak out on their behalf? Ziegler was terrified, the scattered body parts found at Nicks' home and college had probably convinced most of Oxford of his guilt. And how many friends would Louise still have a year after being accused of killing Karen?

They were not so much in the shit as drowning in it.

Unless . . .

"Try and separate, Lou. Maybe there's still time if we can get the two Johns back together."

They both tried. Several minutes of concentrated mind-stretching to no avail. Something was holding them back. Drugs, stress, lack of practice.

"It's no good," said Louise. "I can't move an inch."

More time passed. They tossed ideas around. Whatever was preventing them from separating had to end soon. There was still hope.

And there was still despair. The silences between them grew longer. The two of them, lying shackled to beds by wires and tubes, waiting for God knows what—interrogation, torture? Imagining all kinds of futures. Most of them bad.

Time crawled. There wasn't even a clock or a watch in the room to measure it by. There wasn't even a window to look out of. It could be night outside. It could be raining, snowing, blowing a gale. And it was so quiet. No sound of life outside: no snatches of passing conversation from the corridor, no doors slamming in the distance, no squeak of wheels as a trolley rolled by. The electronic hum of the overhead light was the only sound.

Which was strange, thought Nick. He hadn't registered the fact before but now he thought about it, he couldn't remember hearing a single sound from outside the room since he'd awoken. The room wasn't soundproofed, was it?

He looked at the door. An ordinary-looking white-painted wooden door. With about an inch gap between its base and the floor. There was no way it could be soundproof.

And yet . . .

"Have you heard anything from outside since we've been here?" he asked Louise.

She sat up. "No," she said, turning her head to one side. "Why?"

"Because it's not right," said Nick. "Asylums are noisy. We should have heard someone shouting or screaming by now."

"Maybe they're all drugged. Or it's night."

He hadn't thought of that. It probably was night. But if so . . . where had Ziegler gone in such a hurry? He was hardly likely to be called to a meeting in the middle of the night.

And how long had he been gone? It seemed like hours.

Then he heard it. Footsteps. Someone was walking along the corridor, the sound getting louder. Ziegler?

Nick sat up, his eyes fixed to the door. The footsteps stopped. The door began to open, a crack at first then wider. Then . . .

A sharp intake of breath. A diminutive figure in a red uniform stood in the doorway—Pendennis—unchaperoned and smiling.

Nick tore the monitor patches from his body, pulled back the sheets. Louise was doing the same. Pendennis's smile grew wider; he ambled into the room, walked up to the foot of Louise's bed, and leered.

Louise bounced off her bed onto Nick's, two quick rubbery steps, and then she grabbed hold of Nick and bundled him away from his bed and into the far corner of the room, slamming him against the wall.

Pendennis didn't move. He just stood there, smiling.

"I only came to ask how you were," he said.

Nick pushed Louise behind him, clenched his fists, and braced himself. Would Peter be armed? He couldn't see a knife but Peter's right hand was hidden inside a pocket.

Another man appeared in the doorway—a warder from his uniform. Peter hadn't seen him. Nick waited as the warder slipped silently into the room. Any second now he'd grab Pendennis. Any second . . . why wasn't he doing anything? The warder had stopped a few feet behind Peter. He could have reached out and grabbed the little pervert, locked both his arms, and dragged him into the corridor without breaking sweat. He was twice Peter's size.

But he hadn't. He still wasn't. Was he waiting for something? The right moment, a clear corridor so he could knock Pendennis senseless without anyone seeing him?

Nick called to him. "What are you waiting for? Take him!"

The warder didn't move. Neither did Pendennis. He didn't even look round. Maybe he was unaware of the warder behind him, maybe he thought Nick was trying to trick him into turning his back.

"Get Pendennis out of here!" shouted Nick.

At last the warder moved. But not towards Pendennis. He strode past the red-clad killer, marched up to Nick, and slapped him hard across the face with the back of his hand.

Pain seared across Nick's right cheek. He'd been too shocked to move. Then the warder spoke, spitting the words into Nick's face.

"*Doctor* Pendennis to you."

CHAPTER EIGHTEEN

Louise watched in growing horror. Had the warder gone mad?

"You," he said, prodding Nick in the chest. "Move! Along the wall to the other corner. And don't try anything unless you *really* want to piss me off."

There was hate in his eyes. A blind, belligerent hate that Louise couldn't understand. Was it because he considered Nick a terrorist?

Another warder arrived. Louise's hopes soared . . . and then collapsed. He too looked to Pendennis, awaiting instructions.

"Restrain the girl," said Pendennis.

"No!" Louise was not going to be restrained. She ran at Pendennis, lunging forward, preparing to claw at his face with her hands. If she could just . . .

A warder's hand grabbed her by the left elbow, swung her around, almost off her feet, away from Pendennis and back towards the wall. She slammed into it—hard—cushioning some of the impact with her right hand, trying to push away, but the warder grabbed a fistful of hair on the back of her head and sent her forehead crashing against the wall.

Dazed, her legs buckled. She was vaguely aware of another fight to her right. Nick and the other warder. Then she was grabbed, her arms gathered up and locked behind her. She was swung round, turned to face the centre of the room where Pendennis waited, unruffled and amused.

Her head hurt, her eyes watered, and her arms felt like they were being tugged out of their sockets. She felt weak and vulnerable, a feeling exacerbated by the hospital gown. Why couldn't she have been wearing clothes! She could feel the warder press up against her. The gown open at the back. Her imagination on fire.

Nick was on the floor now. She tried not to look, tried to blot out the grunts and shouts and sickening crunches as kick after kick went into the squirming body on the ground. Why wouldn't they stop? Why wouldn't any of them stop?

"I think that's enough preop, Bobby," said Pendennis, picking at his fingernails. "Put him on the bed."

Bobby dragged Nick along the floor, hoisted him up, and flung him onto the bed, then leaned down and pulled out a series of webbing straps attached to the frame and threw them over Nick's body. Pendennis walked over to the other side and did the same, connecting the straps together and pulling them tight. Nick didn't struggle once. Louise wasn't even sure if he was conscious.

Once finished, Pendennis sauntered towards Louise.

"Make sure you watch all of this, Lulu. May I call you Lulu? Louise seems so formal."

He smiled at her, so smug, so sickening. She could have killed him. She strained forward, tried to break the lock the warder had on her arms, but was immediately tugged back. Peter reached out a hand and lightly brushed her cheek.

"Such pretty skin. Seems almost a pity . . ."

Louise tried to spit. She wanted to cover that sick bastard from ear to ear but fear had dried her mouth. Peter stepped backwards.

"I like a girl with spirit. Don't you, Tony?"

Louise leaned back against Tony and kicked out with her legs. She caught Pendennis a glancing blow on the hips. He darted backwards out of range and shook his head.

"That will not do at all, Lulu," he said and nodded to Tony.

Louise acted first. She brought her heels back against Tony's shins. If only she hadn't been barefoot! If she'd had boots she could have scraped them down his shins, done some damage. She threw her head forward then jerked it back, hoping to connect with Tony's face, hoping to hit something. But finding nothing.

Her arms came free as her captor switched holds. She struggled and twisted but an arm locked across her throat constricting her windpipe. She tried to break the hold, she pulled at the arm, dug in her nails, reached up, flailing wildly with her fingers in search of an eye, something vulnerable she could grab at or poke. She began to choke, difficult to breathe, the room spinning, feeling weak . . .

"That's enough," said Pendennis. "We don't want her to miss the show."

The pressure on her throat eased. She gulped in a lungful of air. Coughed. And once more lost the use of her arms as her captor reverted to his previous hold.

Pendennis cracked his knuckles and moved towards the bed. "Time to begin," he said.

Nick must have come to. "What are you doing?" he asked.

"Preparing you for surgery, of course," said Peter, standing in the aisle between the two beds, rolling back his sleeves. "Surely a doctor like yourself should know all about things like that?"

Louise watched in horror. Was Pendennis going to kill them? Chop them up into little pieces like he'd done to all those other people? She tried to break free. She pushed with her legs, rocked, did everything she could to throw her captor off balance.

Nothing worked. The warder whispered in her ear. "One more stunt like that and the gown comes off . . . slowly."

"Ready, Lulu?" said Pendennis, his bare forearms raised like a surgeon after scrubbing up.

She swallowed hard and looked towards the door. Surely someone had to come soon? The warders were obviously inmates. Someone must have noticed them out of their cells.

"You're making a huge mistake," said Nick, breathing hard. "We've already told Ziegler and the other doctors. We've named you. Anything happens to us and we won't be able to retract it. Understand? Kill us and the Americans will have you extradited and dead within a week. You told us to kill McKinley."

Louise held her breath. It was a desperate plan. But if it could buy them some time . . .

Pendennis laughed. "I'm not here to kill you. Look." He showed Nick his hands, spread his fingers, rotated his wrists, indicated his bare forearms. "See? No knives. I'm here to heal you. I'm your psychic surgeon."

Nick went quiet then turned his head towards Louise. "It's all right, Lou. Nothing that you're about to see is real. Psychic surgery is a con—sleight of hand. He'll pretend to dig his hand into my stomach and then palm a piece of chicken liver."

Pendennis shook his head. "No, no, no. Really, doctor, you're *so* out of date. Haven't you heard the news? Everyone swears by psychic surgery these days. Especially here. We're so good at it, aren't we, Bobby?"

Bobby grinned. "We've won awards."

Louise took a deep breath and braced herself. Pendennis was out to terrorize them. The next ten minutes or hour or however long he took would be an ordeal. A sickening, horrific, vomit-inducing ordeal. But it would pass. And someone would come. She had to believe that and she had to keep on believing it.

"This too shall pass," she shouted to Nick. "Remember that."

"How's the gown, Lulu?" asked Pendennis. "A bit draughty round the back?"

He laughed, a long, humorless, dry laugh. The kind of laugh a cat would have when moving in on a wounded, cornered mouse.

And then he turned to the body on the bed, reached down with an extravagant flourish of his right hand, traced a line along Nick's stomach and . . .

Louise blinked. She had to be seeing things. Pendennis pushed down with his hand and . . . it looked like it penetrated Nick's stomach. She couldn't see his wrist. All she could see was an arm pushing down hard on Nick's stomach; Pendennis growling and Nick struggling.

"I . . . I think I've found it," said Pendennis.

"You've found nothing," hissed Nick, his voice compressed and strained.

"I think I have," said Peter, digging deeper, twisting his arm, contorting his face. Then stopping . . . and slowly turning his head to look down at what he'd found.

"Oh," he said. "Is this yours?"

Louise screamed. She couldn't stop herself. Pendennis was pulling and pulling—something . . . something bloody and vile and over two feet long from the pit of Nick's stomach. It dangled from Peter's upraised hand like a string of sausages. He waved it in front of Nick's face, laughing, triumphant.

"*Some* chicken liver, don't you think?"

Nick retched, the two warders cheered, and Peter held his trophy aloft, the rich red blood running down his right forearm.

It's a trick, recited Louise to herself. I don't know how he did it but it was only a trick. And tricks can only hurt if you let them.

Pendennis stared in her direction and waggled his trophy. She ignored him. She was not going to break down and she was not going to be intimidated. She set her face. And waited.

"Your turn, Lulu. I expect you're looking forward to it. It always feels good when Peter takes the pain away."

Louise waited. This time she'd play submissive right up to the moment the little shit's groin came within range.

Pendennis advanced waving his trophy, his eyes burning with triumph. "Feeling peckish, are we?"

Louise looked down, watching Peter's feet, drawing imaginary lines on the floor: kicking range, kneeing range—come on you little shit, come as close as you dare.

"Don't be afraid, Lulu. Peter's not going to hurt you. There . . ." He tossed away his trophy. "Nasty mess has gone away."

Louise kept staring at the floor, waiting. He took another step forward, reached out and touched her chin with a finger and tried to lift her face to his.

It was time.

She raised her face slowly and smiled, bringing her right knee up at the same time, giving it everything she had, catching Pendennis squarely between the legs. He reeled backwards, doubling up. She leaned back and lashed out with her legs, trying to connect with his face but missing as her captor lifted her off her feet and swung her back towards the wall.

She fell against it—hard. Pain exploded across her side as a punch went into her kidneys. She started to go down, then her hair was yanked back. More pain, punches, kicks, slaps. Indiscriminate. Her forehead crashed against something solid; the next thing she knew she was on her knees, arms locked behind her back and looking towards the centre of the room through a veil of blood and tears.

Pendennis stood in front of her, looking down at her through eyes that weren't even misted over. What kind of man was he? He should have been picking his balls out of his rib cage.

But he had stopped smiling.

"You shouldn't have done that," he said. "Peter didn't like it."

"I did," she said, glaring at him defiantly.

"That's because you're in pain," he said, his smile returning. "Peter's here to take that pain away and make you whole again." He glanced down at her stomach. "Shall we see what's in there?"

"Why waste time?" she said. "Why not look in your pockets now and get it over with."

Peter's eyes brightened. He smiled at his two accomplices. "I think we have another unbeliever, gentlemen."

"Not for long," said Bobby.

Peter stepped back and patted himself down. "Look, Lulu, there's nothing here."

He unrolled his sleeves, shook them at her, rolled them up again. He twirled in front of her like a demented fashion model, patting himself down, rolling up his trouser legs.

"It's still a trick, Lou," said Nick. "Remember that."

Pendennis dismissed Nick's intervention with a wave of his hand. "What does he know," he said, looking directly into Louise's eyes. "He knows nothing of your pain, does he? But Peter does. Peter knows all about pain and loss . . . And your mother."

Louise started. Why was he bringing up her mother . . . ?

Her mind flew back to that other occasion. He'd used her mother then—to get to her—before he tried to rip her ear off. She was not falling for that twice.

He came closer, still talking. "Such a bond between a mother and child. Even death can't break it, don't you agree?"

He crouched down in front of her, looking straight into her eyes.

"Now, let's see what you've got for Peter."

She braced herself. His right hand touched her abdomen, pressing against the gown. She could feel her body starting to shake and willed it to stop. She was not going to show fear. She was not going to give the little shit the satisfaction.

His hand began to wander, higher and lower. Louise gritted her teeth, refusing to look down, refusing to look anywhere but straight ahead.

A sharp pain. His hand pressed into her, digging into her stomach and pushing under her ribs. She wanted to cry out. It felt like his hand was inside her. She knew it couldn't be but her body screamed otherwise.

"Oh," said Pendennis, pursing his lips. "What's this? What have you been doing you naughty little girl?"

This too shall pass, chanted Louise, this too.

The pressure on Louise's abdomen reduced as Peter slowly withdrew his hand. But something was coming with it. She could feel it. She could hear the dreadful sucking sound from her gut.

"It's a big one, isn't it?" said Peter. "Must be at least ten pounds."

More sucking sounds, more pain, more torment. Make it all go away. Make it all go away now!

"It's coming," said Peter. "I can see its head. One more push."

I am not pushing, thought Louise. I am not pushing and I am not looking.

There was a pop, an obscene gurgle, and a cry. A baby's cry.

Louise stared straight ahead through filmy eyes. Something wriggled on the periphery of her vision. She closed her eyes. Tight shut.

"Come on Lulu, don't you want to see your baby?"

"I have no baby," she said.

Something warm and wet touched her face. She screwed her eyes tighter. She could smell it. It was dangling in front of her face.

That's when she felt the tiny fingers pulling at her eyelids, forcing her eyes to open, forcing her to take in the full horror of the situation.

It was beyond revulsion—a mockery of life—a twisted gargoyle of a creature, more caricature than living thing. And it had hold of her eyelids! Tiny misshapen arms outstretched, grasping hold of her, forcing her to look at it.

"Ugly little thing, isn't it?" said Peter. "Wouldn't like to meet the father. Would you, Tony?"

Gratuitous laughter, pain and torment. Louise started to slip down a long dark tunnel. Someone outside retched, probably Nick.

"I'll have to keep this one at the back of my collection," said Peter. "Wouldn't want to frighten the cleaners."

She passed out soon after that.

Nick was bending over her when she came to.

"It's all right, Lou," he said. "They've gone."

All right? How could anything be all right ever again?

She lay there, smeared in memories, nausea, fear, and disbelief. A shaking hand slid down the front of her hospital gown, moving towards her abdomen. She had to know but couldn't bring herself to look. The memory burned like bile inside her.

"It's all right, Lou," he said. "There's nothing there."

She barely registered what he said as she pushed her fingers further, sliding through the coagulating mess, her stomach firm to the touch but she knew that any second it must give way, a few inches further and they'd disappear into a gaping, ragged wound.

"It's all right, Lou," Nick repeated. "There really is nothing there. Trust me. Look for yourself."

He took her hand and tried to force it lower. She snatched it back, withdrawing into herself, rolling over, hiding her face in her hands, curling into a protective fetal ball.

"Louise," he said, shaking her shoulder. "Look at me. He didn't even cut through the gown. It was nothing but a sick, disgusting trick."

She opened an eye and straightened slightly. He was showing her his gown, pulling it tight across his stomach. "See," he said. "Not even a tear. All he did was smear fake blood all over the place."

She reached down to her own abdomen, smoothing the gown out, exploring, pushing against her skin. She was whole. At least her body was.

"I saw it, Nick." she said, swallowing hard. "That . . ." She couldn't bring herself to say it. "That . . . thing! That was no sleight of hand. It was alive."

Nick stared at his feet. "I know . . . I saw it too."

"Oh, God, it's not still here, is it?" she said, jumping up and looking around in panic. She couldn't take it if that thing was hiding somewhere—maybe under the bed?

Nick grabbed her and pulled her to him. "It's gone, Lou. They've all gone. Pendennis, the so-called warders, everything."

She felt comforted for about a second.

"Are they coming back?" she asked, looking towards the door. It was closed. Maybe they could push the beds up against it and barricade themselves in?

"I don't know," said Nick. "They left soon after you passed out."

As soon as the fun dried up, thought Louise.

"And no one's been to check on us since?" she asked, pushing him away. "Ziegler? Nurses? Anyone?"

"No," he said. "I think Pendennis must have taken control of this wing." He pointed to the door. "He locked us in. I tried to pry the door open but . . ." He shrugged. "I couldn't budge it."

She walked to the door and listened. Not a sound. What kind of prison riot was this quiet? She turned to Nick.

"Have you heard anything out there?"

"Not a thing," he said. "The only thing that makes the slightest sense is that maybe some of the prisoners overpowered the night shift in this wing, took them hostage, stole their uniforms, and locked everyone else out. There have to be hostages or someone would be storming the prison right now."

It made sense. Up to a point.

"But why is it so quiet? If the prisoners are in control why aren't they rampaging up and down the corridors? Why can't I hear Pendennis torturing the occupants of the next room?"

"Maybe they've moved off into other wings? Maybe they have to keep quiet, maybe it's only a few prisoners who've got loose and they don't want to alert the guards in the other wings?"

"The entire prison is monitored, Nick. Pendennis couldn't get loose without people knowing. There are cameras everywhere."

"Not in this room."

He was right. She looked up, swung around. There wasn't a camera anywhere. Unless it was hidden?

But even if this room wasn't monitored the corridors were. She remembered seeing them, swivelling and turning—watching her—when Ziegler first brought her to Upper Heywood. They'd covered every intersection. There was no way that a prisoner could get loose and not be seen.

Unless the prisoners had total control of the site.

She couldn't believe that either. Someone would have got a message out. The police would be outside now, shouting instructions through loudspeakers, drones would be circling overhead, assault teams landing on the roof. Something would be happening. Something they could hear.

"Try and separate, Lou," said Nick. "I've tried but I'm still being blocked."

So was Louise. She lay on the bed for five minutes trying to force her mind to fly free. But all she could see was that "thing"—her "child"—staring at her, gurgling and tormenting her. Every time she closed her eyes it was there, waiting in the darkness.

"It's no good", she said, opening her eyes. "I can't . . . what are you doing?"

Nick was standing on the adjoining bed, fiddling with the ceiling light.

"Looking for a holographic projector," he said. "Something animated that gargoyle of Pendennis's."

"It touched me, Nick. I felt it grab my eyelids. It wasn't a projection."

"Maybe you thought you felt it. Suggestion is a powerful force."

"Not in my world it isn't. I smelt it, I heard, I saw it, and I felt it. And Pendennis didn't say a word about it grabbing my eyelids, it just happened."

"Because he suggested it might. He created the idea in your head that he was all-powerful. He dangled a holographic gargoyle in front of your face and 'ordered' you to look at it. Your mind created the rest."

"My mind did not peel back my eyelids. It did."

Nick stepped down from the bed. "Nothing there. Maybe he had one of those handheld devices?"

"Which he got from where?" asked Louise. "From one of the warders he just happened to overpower tonight?"

Nick shrugged. "If you've got a better explanation I'm open to suggestions. He *is* a manipulator. He could have persuaded one of the warders—"

Louise shook her head. There were too many "maybes" and "could haves." And it was far too quiet. Something was wrong. Very wrong.

And then the door opened.

CHAPTER NINETEEN

The door opened, slow and silent. Nick watched, frozen in anticipation. Was it Pendennis, a rescue team, someone else?

The door swung wider. He could see into the corridor. No one there. Unless they were hiding to the left of the door?

Louise bounced off the bed to join him. She started pulling at the wires dangling from the LSU behind him.

"What are you doing?" he hissed, keeping one eye on the door.

"Looking for something to fight with." She gave up on the wires and started pulling at the LSU itself, ripping at the structure, looking for anything she could throw or swing or stab with.

Nick watched the door. Why hadn't anyone come in? What were they waiting for? He crouched down beside the bed, using it as cover. Against what he didn't know but standing up he felt exposed.

And the hospital gown didn't help. He tugged at the back and tried to pull the two ends closer together.

Louise gave up on the LSU and squatted alongside Nick.

"Is it him?" she whispered.

Nick shrugged. It had the feel of Pendennis. Torture by threat and suggestion, drawing out the moment, letting their own minds conjure the worst.

But what if it was something else? Could the door have been opened remotely?

He peered at the door frame. He couldn't see anything that looked like a mechanism for opening the door but maybe it didn't need one. If the door was balanced to swing open it would do so the moment the lock bolt was released.

Which could be done remotely.

He whispered to Louise. "I think it's been opened remotely. The guards in the control room will have been monitoring the corridors. Maybe it's a message from them to say it's safe. Get out now and follow the open doors."

Louise wasn't so sure. "Why don't they come in and get us?"

"Maybe they're busy elsewhere. Maybe it's Ziegler giving us a chance to escape. Not just from Pendennis but from Upper Heywood as well."

He hoped what he said was true.

And the picture he had of Pendennis lurking in the corridor with his two smiling henchmen would go away.

He edged away from the bed, still crouching, trying to be as quiet as he could in that ridiculous swishing hospital gown. He crept towards the left of the door, leaning forward, trying to see as much of the corridor as he could without getting too close. It appeared empty.

He backtracked towards the beds—time to check the other side of the corridor. He inched along the foot of the first bed then the second, watching the doorway all the time, every muscle ready to fight or flee. Still nothing; an open door, an empty corridor—the small portion that he could see.

He reached the right-hand wall and crept along it—mantislike, a slight sway back and forth as his subconscious pulled him back at every step. *Prepare to flee. Prepare to flee.*

Almost there. The right-hand doorjamb a yard away. If Pendennis was out there he'd know in the next second. One more step and he'd see him.

Nothing yet. The wedge of visible corridor widened. He pressed his head flat against the wall and peered as far to the left as he could. It was empty.

Unless Pendennis had flattened himself against the near corridor wall.

Nick hovered in the doorway. He had to make that final check. He had to lean his head into the corridor. He swallowed, turned towards Louise, and forced a smile. Now or never.

He jumped through, throwing his arms out to fend off any sudden attack and . . .

Relief. It was empty. It really was empty. He swivelled on the spot. The corridor clear in both directions and—he looked harder—all the other doors appeared closed.

Was that significant? Someone had unlocked their door but no one else's? Could it have been Ziegler?

He waved Louise over.

"Do you know where we are?" she asked.

He didn't. So many of the bays looked the same and he couldn't see any signs on the walls. Even the doors weren't numbered. But the central corridor couldn't be far away. Find that and he'd have his bearings.

"This way," said Nick, selecting a direction at random. "There's got to be a sign somewhere."

They inched along the corridor, slow tentative noiseless steps. They crept past one door—closed—then another—slightly ajar. Should they look inside? Maybe there was a window? A way out?

Nick peeked through the gap. No windows that he could see. Another trademark Upper Heywood room: bare and white. And if it was occupied, Nick didn't want to know.

They moved on. There was a camera pointing towards them at the intersection up ahead—a T-junction with passages left and right. They stopped and peered around the corner. The same bare, windowless corridors in both directions. Didn't Upper Heywood believe in interior decor? A few paintings, a splash of color, a floor plan?

"Do you recognize any of this?" Louise whispered.

He still didn't. The more he looked the more the place looked like a maze. And if they didn't find a sign soon that's how he'd treat it. A maze they could escape from by always turning in the same direction.

They turned left. The camera followed them. Strip lights hummed and flickered overhead, the first real sound they'd heard for ages. They walked faster, passing closed door after closed door. They crossed an intersection, passages coming off left and right: both dead-ends, both containing a series of doors, everything unmarked.

How did people find their way around here? None of the doors were numbered or marked in any way. There were no signs or arrows, no bay numbers. All the corridors looked the same.

Voices floated down the passageway behind them.

Nick and Louise stopped dead. Pendennis? They listened. It was several voices. Yelling. And getting closer. A mob?

Nick and Louise started to run. No time for caution, they had to get away. A maze of passages lay ahead of them. They turned left, they turned right, they ran straight ahead. No plan other than to get away as far and as fast as possible.

The sound behind them grew louder: running feet, raised voices. Every corridor identical, all doorways threatening and uninviting. And not a window in sight. Not even a barred one.

They turned once more, running flat out, there had to be an exit soon! They were being pursued half-naked through a prison, hospital gowns flapping open at the back. If they were caught . . .

Nick tried to squash that thought but a hundred voices took up the cry. It sounded like the entire prison population were in pursuit, screaming and shouting.

The corridor turned to the left; he bounced off the right-hand wall in his haste to make the turn.

Then skidded to a stop.

It was a dead end. The corridor ran for another twenty yards then stopped. There were two doors—one left, one right—halfway along the passage.

A glance back the way they'd come. A few more seconds and the mob would be upon them. They had to take one of the doors. Maybe it would be an exit?

"You choose," said Nick.

"That one," said Louise. There was a lock panel to the left of the door. He hit it hard and prayed.

It opened and they dived inside.

Peter sat on the floor in the middle of the room. The blood on his hands and face matched the red of his clothes, and scattered around him lay pieces of flesh, many with fragments of clothing still attached. He looked, as he often dreamed he looked, like a small child who had crawled inside a butcher's window.

One of the larger pieces lay in his lap. He was playing with it when Lulu and her doctor friend fell into the room.

He didn't bother to look up. They'd wait. But meat had sell-by dates. If you waited too long the little voices would escape and you'd never know where they'd been hiding.

He dug his hand in and started to pull the skin away from the flesh. He liked this bit. He liked the way the skin peeled back all in one piece. You could climb inside if you were quick. Climb inside and hide for hours, dressed from head to toe in shiny red skin.

He smiled at the thought. Then remembered he wasn't alone. He could see them in the doorway, looking scared. He closed the door behind them. He could do that—open and close doors. He had the power. Always had. He loved being in control.

He felt behind him for the head on the floor. The skull extracted, only the cap of skin and hair remained. He put his hand inside and held it up like a glove puppet to show his guests.

"Have you met Doctor Ziegler?"

CHAPTER TWENTY

The room was dark; Pendennis sat in a cone of light from a central spotlight, everything else was in shadow. The room could have stretched for miles. And anyone could be lurking hidden in the shadows.

Outside, behind the door that had so recently closed, there was silence. No shouting, no running feet, no mob hammering on the door. Just silence.

Nick and Louise were rooted in the doorway, their eyes locked on the mask in Peter's hand.

"Is that really Ziegler?" asked Nick.

He had to ask, curiosity pulling the words from him. But did he really want to know the answer? Deep down, something inside him craved ignorance.

Peter didn't seem to care. He turned the grisly mask to face him, looked deep and hard into its features and said. "Looks like him to me."

He then turned, both face and mask, to Louise. "What do you think, Lulu?"

Louise didn't answer. She turned her head away, gritted her teeth, and clenched her fists. She's going to attack him, thought Nick. He placed a hand on her arm. "No," he said. "Not yet." Pendennis had to be armed. There were body parts strewn all over the floor. Something had to have been used to cut them up.

And it was too easy. Pendennis laid traps. He wouldn't allow himself to be caught alone. Someone would be in the shadows, pressed up against a far wall, waiting.

Or would they? It was a long shot but what if there were other doors in the room, maybe a way out? Wasn't that worth a look?

He whispered to Louise. "Follow the wall around. There might be a door."

"Little voices," said Peter, his voice distracted, "always whispering, thinking Peter can't hear them but Peter hears everything, doesn't he, Doctor Zee?"

Nick went right, Louise left—the pair of them sticking to the wall, their gowns swishing against the plaster, their faces turned half inward, one eye on Pendennis, the other on the shadow up ahead.

"I'm watching you," said Peter, turning Ziegler's face to stare directly at Nick. "We both are."

Nick pressed on. He'd drawn alongside Pendennis. Still no door. If the light was in the center of the room he was halfway to the far wall. If he ran, and there was a door, he could get to it before Peter. If there was a lock panel he could open it. If it wasn't guarded. If, if, if . . .

"I wouldn't go any further if I were you," said Peter.

Nick's heart thumped inside his chest. He speeded up. Not much further to go now.

"Have you seen what Peter does to bad boys?"

Yes, he had and he didn't want to think about it. He glanced across the room instead. He couldn't see or hear her but was Louise still making progress? Would she call out if she found a door?

"He bites their noses off," said Peter.

There was a growling sound from the center of the room and then a shriek. Nick turned. Peter had grabbed hold of Ziegler's nose, with his teeth and was pulling at it, shaking his head from side, trying to rip the mask to pieces, growling like a dog in a feeding frenzy.

"Peter! Stop that!" Nick's face drained. That was Ziegler's voice. The words, clear and authoritative. And they were coming from the mask.

Peter stopped, released his grip on Ziegler's nose and inclined his head. He looked spellbound, fascinated. The glove puppet spoke! Its lips, what was left of them, moved.

"That's better, Peter," said Ziegler.

Peter brought Ziegler's face closer to his. He looked mesmerized by the talking mask. His eyes filled with wonder.

"Now it's time for our little game again," said the mask. "Remember? Today, we're going back to the time when you were six years old. Do you remember when you were six years old, Peter?"

Peter nodded. "Yes, I remember."

"Good," Ziegler's voice droned on. "It's your summer holiday. You've gone to the seaside with your mother. Do you remember the day you got lost? When it was cold and showery and the wind chased you into that old funfair museum? The day you met Jack?"

Reality shuddered—as though hit by some immense force that made the room wobble like jelly. Walls and faces shimmered, began to break up, the room shattering into a myriad of dissolving fragments, leaving nothing but an all-encompassing blackness. No Peter, no Ziegler, no scattered joints of meat. Only Nick, Louise, and the dark.

"Nick, are you there?" asked Louise. She sounded close but his eyes couldn't penetrate the gloom. Not that he was looking hard. He was too busy thinking. His brain was being battered by a meteor storm of puzzle pieces. Some were actually falling into place.

"Nick?" she asked again, her voice rising half an octave.

"Over here," he said, patting himself down. One body, present and correct. At least he hadn't separated and fallen into the void.

"What just happened?" she asked, shuffling closer. "Was that a hologram breaking up?"

"No," he said, sniffing the air. A musty, stuffy smell. Definitely not Upper Heywood. Which fitted his theory.

An outstretched hand caught him under the eye. Louise apologized. "Sorry, I can't see a thing in here."

"Don't apologise. You can't hurt what's not really here."

"Are you all right?" she asked.

He was more than all right. For the first time since he'd woken up that morning—or afternoon, evening, or whatever time this pretended to be—he felt back in control. He knew where he was and he knew what to do.

"Nick, you're worrying me."

"Then prepare to be unworried," he said. If he'd been sure of his footing, he'd have added a dance. "We're not going to be extradited and John Bruce isn't President."

"What?"

"And Anders Ziegler is very much alive and regressing young Peter as we speak."

He felt the urge to pace and swing his arms. But that was tempting fate too much. Somewhere in this gloom was a funfair museum with sharp-edged metal exhibits and a six-year-old Peter Pendennis. And in this place, whatever his age, Peter would be dangerous.

Somewhere in the distance a wind howled. And was that a draft? Nick turned instinctively towards it. A horizontal line of what looked like sunlight had appeared on the floor behind him. And was that a door above it? He walked over. Louise followed, tugging at his arm.

"What are you talking about? How do you know this?"

"Peter's probably listening so I won't tell you everything but think about it . . . one minute we're on the verge of rescuing your American friend, the next we wake up in Upper Heywood and all hell breaks loose. Why? Cue simple answer: because we never left Upper Heywood in the first place. We got too close to Pendennis and instead of pulling John out, Peter pulled us in."

The ambient light must have increased; he could swear he saw Louise's mouth drop open.

"We're trapped inside Peter's head?" she said. "Like John? And you're happy about this?"

She sounded like she might be about to hit him.

"I'm ecstatic. John Bruce isn't President. The Truth Commission isn't after us. Peter Pendennis isn't running Upper Heywood and we're not being chased half-naked by rioting prisoners."

"But we're trapped inside a madman's head!"

"Temporarily. Trust me, I know the way out. In a few minutes, maybe an hour, we'll be back floating in the higher dimensions and taking John with us."

Or maybe sooner. He sat down at the base of the door, cursing hospital gown designers everywhere as a bare buttock met the cold concrete floor. The cold, gritty, concrete floor. No one could have swept the floor in ages.

"What are you doing?" asked Louise.

"Trying to separate. Peter's grip over this world could be diminished now."

"Why? Because he's being hypnotized?"

"You're catching on. He's woven a dreamworld around us. One where he's in control. As soon as that control slips he won't be able to stop us separating and out we go."

He leaned back against the door and closed his eyes. A simple stretch and he'd be free. Okay, the body leaning against the door didn't exactly exist but the principle was the same. He was connected to a physical being and needed to fly free. How he visualized that physical entity didn't matter a jot.

He relaxed, pumped hydrogen inside his brain, inflated it, cut loose every mooring, and waited for it to fly free.

It didn't. He tried again. Urging, cajoling, pushing . . .

It was no good. He was still being blocked.

He got up, dusted himself down, brushed the grit from his cheeks. And shrugged his shoulders. Pendennis would have to be made to relinquish control.

"Should we try the door?" asked Louise, searching for a handle. Anything to get out of the dark.

"No. We need to stay here. This is where Ziegler's bringing Peter and the sooner we confront Peter the sooner we get out."

"Are you sure we can do that?"

"Positive."

He sounded confident—or was that overconfidence? Surely he hadn't forgotten the encounter with the warders. Dreamworld or not, the pain had been real.

She ran a hand along the old panelled door and found a large metal ring. A door handle? She gave it a pull then a twist. The door rattled but didn't budge.

"What about Jack?" she asked. "Who do you think he is?"

"Some old wino Peter met here or an older boy who frightened him. Someone like that. Whoever it is they'll just be an illusion. It's Peter we've got to concentrate on."

Click. Louise turned at the sound. It came from deep in the gloom. Then it came again—much louder this time. A cranking sound as though a rusted metal lever had been thrown. Light. A stuttering swathe of light brought the museum into life as rows of fluorescent lights flickered across the ceiling—on, off, undecided, then on again.

Old arcade games lined the walls. Old posters above them, pictures and photographs from the Victorian era. The paintwork dingy—the walls brown and the ceiling a tobacco-stained yellow. And no sign of Pendennis or Jack. The U-shaped room was empty. For now.

"Wow," said Nick, diving towards the exhibits. "I haven't seen machines like these in years."

"You're not seeing them now," said Louise. "Remember?"

She glanced back towards the door. That had to be the way he'd arrive. Wouldn't it be better to wait here and grab him as soon as he opened the door? Just in case he brought his minders with him.

"Have a look at this," shouted Nick.

Louise reluctantly followed. Nick was standing by a bank of old fairground games: test your strength, test your passion, read your fate, try your luck. Bagatelle games with rusty ball bearings, spirals of metal runways, and strategically placed nails. Not a flashing light, electric circuit, or blaring soundtrack amongst them. Simple fun for simpler times.

And simpler people. Like Nick.

He was pointing at a tableau of a graveyard in a glass case. "This must be nearly two hundred years old," he said. "Look at that ghoul's hair. It looks like someone pulled some horse hair out of a paintbrush and glued it on his head."

It did. She couldn't imagine a modern child, used to the near-perfect holographic games imagery of today, being impressed by the standard of craftsmanship.

"Isn't it great?" said Nick. "You drop a penny in the slot here and the great god Clockwork opens all the graves and moves the monsters."

He craned his head and looked left and right, searching. "There," he said, pointing to a pile of old copper coins stacked on a display case. "I'll show you."

"No," said Louise, locking her hand around his wrist. "One thing I learned a long time ago was not to tempt fate. You put a penny in there and that thing will come alive. Trust me."

"Maybe you're right," he said, moving along to the next exhibit.

Louise walked past, peering into every gap and corner, all the little places a six-year-old boy could hide. And shouldn't there be another door? The room was U-shaped; something had to be at its center.

She tried the right-hand wing of the room. No Pendennis and no door.

"This seems to be it," she said. "The only way Pendennis can get in is through that front door."

Nick didn't answer. He was becoming infuriating. Their lives were on the line and he wasn't even concentrating! He should be planning, working out contingencies. Looking worried.

She found him by a large wood and glass cabinet.

"Do you think this could be Jack?" he said, indicating the exhibit: Jolly Jack Tar, the laughing sailor, two and a half feet of painted wood and faded cloth ready to sing and dance for a penny.

Louise took a closer look. If she were six years old and lost and came face to face with that, she'd be frightened. It was ugly; its eyes were staring and menacing. And that mouth. It looked unnatural, the way the jaw hung down as though it had been dislocated and pinned back together. She shivered. Dummies had that effect on her. She'd never seen their appeal. Give her a cuddly toy any day.

"Are you sure you can handle Pendennis?" she asked.

"Absolutely. If Ziegler can hypnotize Peter, so can I."

"But what if you can't?"

She had visions of becoming another John. Trapped inside another man's body, screaming her innocence to an incredulous Ziegler, demanding he track down all her friends from the village. If she had any left.

"Look, Lou," he said. "John managed to surface and talk to Ziegler so we know that Peter can't maintain control for ever. Sooner or later he'll sleep or whatever it is he does and we'll surface too. And when we do, we separate."

He made it sound so easy—wait, surface, and separate—no mention of the ordeal in between. Had John had to go through this? Was he still going through this? Was this Peter's initiation process for prospective new personalities—mess with their minds until they're too far gone to resist?

A wind picked up outside. It whistled through gaps in the door frame, swirled under the door. A tiny whirl of dust and fallen leaves floated across the floor. The air turned colder

Louise stared doorwards and braced herself. It wouldn't be long.

Rain beat against the outside of the door. Hail, by the sound of it. Tiny pellets of ice skittered under the door.

And then someone was calling. A child's voice, plaintive, carried on the wind, almost drowned in the noise of the storm. A small child, wet, lost and looking for shelter.

"Go to the side of the door, Lou, and stay out of sight. If Peter tries to run back outside, grab him."

The iron-ring door handle began to move. Louise took up her position to the right of the door. And behind Nick, a sailor began to laugh.

Déjà vu. Louise recognised the sound in an instant. She'd heard that laugh before. The instant before everything had gone black and Peter had pulled them into his sick, twisted world.

"Turn it off!" she shouted, her eyes dancing between the sailor and the door. Which was the bigger threat?

Nick didn't answer. He'd turned away from the door and was staring at the sailor: its head shaking with laughter, its hands outstretched, one foot raised ready to dance.

The door rattled, the wind howled, and above both rose that laugh—no hint of humor anywhere near it: a manic, mechanical, forced laugh that built and built and crackled and shrieked, threatening to burst Louise's eardrums apart.

Her hands flew to her ears. She told herself it was an illusion, to be strong, to ignore the sailor and concentrate on Pendennis.

But it was so hard. The pain! Her ears were bleeding. She was sure of it.

The door began to open. Nick hadn't noticed. He was still staring at Jack. He hadn't even covered his ears. Louise yelled at him to turn around.

And then the sailor began to dance.

Tiny feet and hands pumped out a rhythm—up and down—marching into madness. Faster now, its mouth growing wider, its rouged cheeks redder, its head thrown back with a deafening roar. Faster still, whirling and cavorting inside its glass cage, lifting its feet clear of the restraining wire until it was dancing wild and free.

The door opened. The wind came with it, flattening the heavy oak door against the wall. A small boy stood rooted in the doorway, staring at the sailor, rain beating off his head and shoulders.

Should she grab him? He was alone, stationary, an easy target. But then what? Nick was the one with the plan. What the hell was she supposed to do with the little shit? Beat him up until Nick came out of his trance?

She swayed in the wind, bent double, her hands clamped to her ears. How could she think straight with that bloody row in her head?

"Nick!" she shouted. He still didn't move, still staring at that dancing monstrosity. She staggered towards him.

"No, Jack." Another voice—Ziegler's—the words carried in on the wind, fighting against the sailor's laugh. "Stop that," he insisted. "You don't feel like laughing anymore. You want to be quiet. You're feeling sleepy."

Jack danced faster, spinning its body like a dervish whilst keeping its eyes locked on Nick's. The laughter, if anything, grew louder.

Louise felt the building shake. Tiny shards of plaster fell from the ceiling. Cracks appeared in the walls. And blood began to trickle from Nick's ears.

No! She ran towards him, grabbed him, tried to pull him away. He wouldn't budge. He'd become rooted there. She shook him by the shoulders, pulled and shoved. Still the sailor laughed, still he danced. And still the building shook.

"You're feeling tired, Jack," said Ziegler. "You have to close your eyes."

Jack didn't care. And Nick wouldn't move. Louise covered Nick's eyes with her hand. Would that break the spell? He reached up and pulled her hand away.

Large chunks of plaster fell all around them. Masonry and ceiling joists. Lights flickered, went out, clattered to the floor. The whole building was coming apart.

She glanced towards the door. Peter was still there, as transfixed as Nick, his little eyes wide, his mouth parted in a silent O.

And that bloody sailor—why wouldn't he shut up? Why wouldn't he go to sleep? He was being hypnotized, wasn't he?

Something wet trickled from Louise's ear. It's all illusion, she told herself. The blood, the sound, the pain. All illusion.

Everything except Ziegler's voice—and that was getting nowhere. "You're feeling tired, Jack," it said. "You can barely keep awake."

No effect. She had to *do* something! There was a length of wood in the rubble, she pulled it out, started swinging. Smashing the glass case then going after the sailor. Screaming at it as she did so, each sentence punctuated by a massive blow. "Go to! Fucking! Sleep!"

The sailor fell back, still laughing, got up ,and turned his gaze upon her. She looked to the side—avoiding his eyes—kept swinging, connected once . . . twice. Jack went down. The laughter stuttered. Nick moved. The spell had to be broken. She hit Jack again and again then threw down her club, launched herself at Nick and pushed him towards the door.

"Come on!" she urged, pushing and shoving, the building collapsing around them, the laughter starting up again.

Pendennis stood in the doorway, still staring at the sailor, enthralled. They barged past him, out into the rain and the wind and a seaside promenade that stretched for miles.

They ran, waves crashing against the shore to the left, the spray mingling with the wind and rain. They ran, a salty tang at the corner of Louise's mouth. They ran, on and on for ever.

Behind them a little boy grew into a man, a museum crumbled to dust, and a tiny wooden figure climbed out of the ashes.

CHAPTER TWENTY-ONE

The promenade shimmered. Cliffs rose high on the right, a wall of water on the left—the two coming together. The sky falling to meet them. White clouds, white cliffs, white foaming water. Upper Heywood; she could see the corridor forming in front of her eyes.

They were back.

Nick and Louise stuttered to a halt at the next T-junction, placed their hands flat against the far wall, and bent forward, fighting for breath. It was a while before either could speak.

"What happened to you back there?" asked Louise.

"I couldn't move," said Nick. "I looked into its eyes and that was it. I was paralyzed."

As Pendennis had been.

"It's not just Peter in here, is it?" she said in between breaths. "We've got to contend with all his personalities. Even if he falls asleep there's still . . . the other dozen to contend with. He could pass us from one to the other."

"It doesn't change anything," said Nick. "Whoever assumes control . . . can be hypnotized. Even Peter . . . we saw it. And . . ." He took another deep breath. "Once I hypnotize them, the control is broken and we can get out."

"Jack can't be hypnotized."

He turned his head towards her and grinned. "I know. Which is why we've got to flush Peter out, slip a hypnotic noose around his neck, and get the hell out."

He started to laugh, which shocked her. What was there to laugh at?

"Sorry," he said. "I was just thinking that your hypnotism technique could do with a little work."

He pushed himself off the wall, grabbed an imaginary club, and attacked a make-believe Jack. "Go to! Fucking! Sleep! Hmm, I'll have to present that to the next psychiatric symposium. Though I think the use of the surgical two-by-four might be a tad controversial."

They both laughed. Louise felt invigorated. She'd had nothing to laugh at for . . . for as long as she could remember.

"You really think you can hypnotize Pendennis?" she asked.

"I not only think it, Ms. Callander, I believe it. And belief . . ."

He stopped, his eyes taking on a faraway look.

"What's the matter?" said Louise, swinging round to check both corridors. Had Jack appeared? Had something happened?

His face snapped back into a smile and he grabbed her shoulders. "Belief, Ms. Callander. Belief and imagination. Why didn't I think of that earlier?"

He let go of her and stepped back. "This whole place is imaginary, right?" he said, emphasizing his words with a sweep of his arm.

She nodded, unsure where this outburst was leading. Didn't they already have a plan?

"Illusion," continued Nick. "A work of imagination where gargoyles can come to life and rooms fade and crumble."

"Ye-es?"

"So it's our turn to play. And, first, let's get out of these stupid gowns."

He screwed his eyes shut, concentrating. Louise watched, not sure what the hell was going to happen. He morphed in front of her. The hospital gown replaced by jeans, T-shirt, and sneakers.

"You try it," he urged. "Think clothes and force yourself to change."

She did. Anything to get rid of that ridiculous gown.

She opened her eyes. It had worked! She had her favorite sweater and her work trousers and . . . heavy boots.

"Are you cold?" he asked.

"No, I'm getting prepared." She lifted her right foot, concentrated, stared at the boot and . . .

Spikes shot out from the soles.

"You're going mountain climbing?" he asked, surprised.

"Not quite," she said, retracting the spikes. "It's a little insurance in case someone grabs me from behind again."

She flexed her feet in her boots. Perfect fit. And it was so good to be covered from head to toe again.

"What next?" she asked.

"A door, I think," said Nick. "Maybe we don't have to confront Pendennis, maybe we can tunnel our way out?"

He selected a piece of wall and started to trace the outline of a door with his fingers. A line appeared, as though drawn by a crayon. The line turned into a rectangle: five feet high and three feet broad. He stood back and admired his work.

"Some kind of mechanism to open it, I think. A button . . . about here." He pointed to a spot and a button sprang from beneath his index finger.

"Okay, Lou, now comes the moment of truth."

She held her breath. He leaned forward and pressed the button. A crack appeared in the wall, following the outline of the door. All along the line, the paint began to craze and peel off, the plaster too, tiny flakes of paint and plaster falling to the floor, forming into a long pile at the base of the skirting.

Then there was a shudder. The wall groaned . . . and opened. They'd built their first door.

Louise looked inside. There was a room: a musty, unlit, rubble-strewn room with no other door or window. They climbed inside. It looked like a building site. Cobweb-covered planks lay propped up against breeze block walls, the cement oozing out from every join. Empty pots of paint lay discarded on the floor next to misshapen buckets and stubbed-out cigarettes. It could have been a storeroom or a cellar. It could have been anything long-abandoned and never meant for show.

"Where now?" asked Louise.

"We keep on going in a straight line until we find a way out."

It sounded so easy, picking their way through the rubble to the next wall, creating another door, watching it swing open. How big could Peter's Upper Heywood be?

The door opened on another of Upper Heywood's labyrinthine corridors. They climbed through and started work on the far wall.

"How about a circular door this time? Or star-shaped?" asked Nick.

"I think door-shaped will suffice," said Louise, glancing up and down the corridor. Peter and his friends couldn't be far.

They kept going, cutting door after door, going from internal chamber to corridor to internal chamber again. The place was a warren, everything looked so similar. Louise began marking each door, giving them numbers just to prove to herself they weren't going around in circles.

As Nick started on door number eleven, she looked back the way they'd come at the long line of open doors. They had to be making progress . . . but was the maze infinite? Would Peter's imagination be working ahead of them—extending his maze as fast as Nick could cut?

That's when she heard it. An empty paint can being kicked over about six doors back.

"What was that?" asked Nick, spinning around.

Louise couldn't make anything out. She narrowed her eyes, squinted into the distance. Was that movement back there or a trick of the light?

Then she saw it; scurrying across the rubble, jumping through the next door, closing on them fast.

Jack.

"Don't look at his face," said Nick, lunging forward to grab hold of the brick and plaster door and force it closed. "You work on opening the next door. I'll seal this one shut."

Louise carved the next opening, abandoning rectangles and going for the quicker circle. She pointed her finger, concentrated, and sliced the wall with a single sweep of her arm. The door flew open—there was no time for buttons. Behind her, Nick smoothed the crack surrounding the old door into nonexistence.

Louise ran to the next wall, her right arm outstretched and carving two strides before she reached the wall. A smell hit her; something was burning. And that noise . . . what was it? She threw the door open then glanced back. A tight blue flame was shooting from Nick's fingers. He was welding the door shut.

On to the next wall, pausing to wait for Nick. They couldn't afford to get separated. All these corridors, Jack could circle round and come at them from any direction.

She had the next door open. Nick was crouching behind her working on the previous one, searing it shut, the paint curling and blackening beneath his fingers, the plaster and brick melting, specks of orange lava sparkling and spitting then cooling and hardening into an igneous bond.

A bulge appeared in the crack a foot below Nick's hand. He wasn't fast enough. The crack between door and wall was widening, a tiny hand was forcing its way through.

Nick turned up the heat and brought the flames down on Jack's hand. Flesh-colored paint cracked and crackled, tiny fingers blackened into sticks of charcoal.

The sailor screamed. Another blast of flame. Little fingers writhing, flaking off, falling to the floor. Could Nick weld Jack to the wall?

Something moved in the embers of Jack's hand. His fingers were regenerating, pushing out again, searching for something to twist and squeeze. Nick's hand spat flame but seemed to be having little effect now. Louise called to him from beyond the next door.

"Leave him. Come on!"

"You can't escape," said a new voice. Pendennis. He was in the corridor about ten yards away. Nick swung around to face him. Louise jumped back into the corridor. She'd cover Nick's back. Keep that little sailor shit behind the wall.

She filled her mind with flame, held it there, breathed deep, sucked in all the oxygen she could imagine, and then breathed it all out in one intense jet directed at the sailor's writhing hand. Jack screamed, his fingers vaporized.

But he'd be back. Thirty seconds, a minute. She'd bought Nick time and she'd keep buying him time until he put that serial-killing bastard to sleep.

"Hello, Peter," said Nick, adjusting the intensity of the flames spitting from his fingers. "How are you today? Feeling tired?"

Peter was leaning against the corridor wall, dressed in red and looking unconcerned. "Makes no difference what you do to me," he said. "The only way out's through this door and Peter's the only one who can open it."

As he spoke, a red door materialized in the wall behind him. A red door quartered with wooden panels, a gleaming brass letter box shining below a heavy door knocker. It could have been someone's front door—maybe Peter's front door. The shiny gloss paint dazzled in the reflected fluorescent light.

"Then you'd better open it, Peter," said Nick. "Before you fall asleep." He stifled a yawn. "It's so stuffy in here, don't you think?"

Nick was only a few yards away from Pendennis now. He stretched out his right hand, changing the color of the flame from blue to yellow and let it dance and flicker on his palm.

"Look into the flame, Peter. Can you see the patterns inside?"

Peter pushed away from the wall. He did appear to be looking at the flame. Louise watched. Was it working? He seemed mesmerized by it, he took a step closer, leaned forward, staring at the little flame, his eyes no more than six inches away from Nick's hand.

Then Pendennis smiled, and started to blow.

The flame on Nick's palm roared and flared, sweeping back towards his face, engulfing him. It was as though Pendennis was breathing pure accelerant. The whole of Nick's body was enveloped by flame. He staggered backwards, arms flailing. And that smell. Like no smell Louise wanted to smell again. Burnt hair, charred flesh . . .

She had to act. She had to close her mind to the smells and sounds. It was all illusion. Nick would heal. His real body was elsewhere. She had to act now.

Using the flames as cover, she leaned into the wall behind Nick, thinking herself through it, thinking herself vapor, thinking the wall permeable, a mere membrane to stretch through. She solidified on the other side, then ran along the wall of the inside chamber, towards Pendennis and a few meters beyond. Another shift, vapor again, back through the wall, into the corridor, behind Pendennis and out of his line of sight.

She solidified, thinking herself taller, thinking herself larger, thinking herself stronger. She reached down, grabbed Peter by the hair with her left hand, tugged him backwards, and struck him hard in the face with her right.

He crashed, sprawling to the ground.

"Open that door, Peter. Now!" she commanded.

He looked up at her through misted eyes, his nose bleeding. "You hit me?"

"And I'll do it again if you don't do what you're told."

He blinked. He looked surprised. He peered up at her. "Mum?"

Had she triggered a memory? He looked so small lying there by the foot of the door, and she towered above him.

"Of course it's me, Peter. Now stop playing around and open that door for your mother."

He shook his head, he looked terrified. "You don't want to go inside."

"Are you answering me back?" she said, bringing her hand back ready to strike.

"No!" he said, shuffling away from her in terror and wedging himself up against the base of the door. "It wasn't me, Mum. Honest. The cat was dead when I found it. I didn't mean to do anything wrong."

"Then open the door, Peter, and let me see. I can't help you if you don't let me."

Louise glanced at the door. Did she need Pendennis? Could she open the door herself, drift through it like she'd done to the wall? Or was the door symbolic? A switch that existed in Peter's head?

And why wouldn't the little shit open it for his mother?

"I'm counting to three, Peter," she said. "You don't want to be here when I reach three. If that door's not open by three you won't be able to sit down for a week."

The door sprang open. She looked round for Nick. The flames had gone and he'd replaced his clothes . . . But his face and hair—they were singed and blackened. Did it hurt?

He ran towards her. "Come on!" he said. "Let's go."

She ducked down and squeezed through the door after him. There were steps beyond. A stone staircase heading down and curving to the left. They ran, pushing Upper Heywood and Peter behind them, the staircase spiralling deeper and darker. The only sound, that of their fleeing feet, and the deeper they went even that sound began to fade.

CHAPTER TWENTY-TWO

"Stop!" said Nick. He'd been too busy fleeing he hadn't paid attention to where they were going.

Now he was. And he didn't like what he could see. Or, more accurately, what he couldn't see.

"Where are we?" said Louise.

He didn't want to answer. An irrational fear that in doing so he might give flesh to a situation that as yet was only a possibility. It didn't have to be the void. They'd been in dark places before. But . . .

This time he could see the faint outline of a tiny cloud of starlike lights. It could be a distant nebula, but there were no other stars in the sky. It could be another dream world of Pendennis's, but . . . he couldn't feel anything.

"We've separated," said Louise. We've escaped!"

"Could you move slightly?" he asked. "I just want to see if that's you I can see."

The cloud moved. They *had* separated. But where the hell were they? Upper Heywood couldn't be far away—twenty, thirty meters at most. But with ten planes of movement to choose from twenty meters could soon become twenty miles. He had no idea which way was up, which way was back, or anything at all. He moved by focussing on an object and thinking himself there. But in the void there was nothing to latch onto. Nothing at all.

"Are we lost?" asked Louise.

"Possibly," he said, trying to think positively. There had to be something visible out there. Something they'd see if only they concentrated more.

"Can't we just retrace our steps?" asked Louise.

"You know which direction we came from?"

"That way?" said Louise without any degree of confidence.

If Nick had had eyebrows he'd have raised them. "Are you pointing by any chance? Only I can't quite see your fingers."

The cloud moved. "This way, flame boy."

An idea came to him. "Keep going in that direction, Lou. Slowly. And keep me in sight. Use me as an anchor in case you're wrong."

"What if I fall back into one of Peter's worlds?"

"Easy answer—don't. You should see a faint light long before you get anywhere near Peter. Look for a change in the void, a patch of grey, a point of light, something like that. But make sure you keep me in sight at all times. I'll stay here."

And hope. At least doing it this way they couldn't make things worse. Wherever Louise went, they'd have a reference point that they knew was only a matter of meters away from Upper Heywood.

Unless there were currents.

He cursed his imagination. Why couldn't he have stuck on the image of himself as an anchor in an unshifting, featureless void? Why introduce the concept of currents?

"Can you still hear me?" asked Louise. He could barely make out her image—a distant smudge against an immense black blanket. But if he could hear her didn't that mean she was less than ten meters away?

"Can you see anything?" he asked.

"I can barely see you."

"Try other directions," he suggested. "Use me as your centre and spiral out. Upper Heywood can't be far."

Unless we're racing away on a higher dimensional jet stream. Which, of course, we wouldn't be able to feel as we have no sensation of movement in the higher dimensions. Or touch—we could be travelling at a thousand miles an hour and not feel the slightest wind.

Nick added sensory deficiency to his list of things to curse.

Time passed. Nick waited while Louise spiralled and orbited. She hadn't found anything but did she really know what to look for? And was she trying all ten axes of movement? Not that he knew how to discriminate between ten axes of movement but he had the feeling—the certainty—that he'd be able to do it better than Louise. He was more receptive to that kind of thing, more experienced.

He called Louise back. "You stay here while I have a go."

He threw himself into it. He imagined his mind a holoviewer and projected an image of a ten-dimensional universe inside. Then imagined moving within it. He thought up, he thought left, he thought back, he thought, a axis, b axis, c. And tried to translate that thought into movement. Whether it worked or not he wasn't sure. But he felt better for trying. He pushed himself out to the limits, pushed Louise's image to that of a vague star. And hovered, imagining himself a huge mirror, a huge mirror of infinite diameter, sucking up the faintest image from the palest, most distant light source.

But saw nothing.

They had to travel farther afield. It would be a risk, but Upper Heywood couldn't be that far away and what else could they do? They couldn't wait forever.

Louise agreed. The physical world had to be close. They couldn't have been travelling out of body for more than a few seconds.

They set out from their starting point in a slow spiral, Nick taking the lead and Louise taking a wider position, six, maybe ten meters to his side.

They scanned as they went, stopping occasionally with a surge of hope as first one and then the other thought they detected a change in the cloying blackness of the all-encompassing void.

Each time they were wrong.

They swung out wider—changed planes, changed axes—or maybe they covered the same ground as before. Who could tell?

"This isn't working," said Louise.

Nick had to agree. "There must be another way," he said. "If John Bruce managed it, so can we."

"It took John eighteen months."

"But he wouldn't have known where he was or what he was looking for—we do! There must be some way of navigating through this. Some innate skill we've forgotten about. Something that drew that part of John Bruce home."

"Like what?"

"I don't know! But there had to be something. The fact that he returned to a place he knew makes me think it wasn't coincidence. Something drew him there, a memory, maybe a memory of visiting his father at the air base, something that made him feel safe and something he latched onto at a time of need."

Or maybe not. Maybe he just orbited the Earth for eighteen months until Peter, the psychic fly trap, extended some higher dimensional snare into the void and snagged him.

He felt like screaming. The frustration of it all. He couldn't think in this void. It was like a vast blanket of thought-destroying matter. There was nothing to look at, nothing to catch your imagination and send it spinning down some unexpected path of brilliance. He liked distractions, movement, sparks to ignite his creativity.

Silence was for contemplation, thinking things through when you had a semblance of a thought that needed refining but it couldn't provide that initial spark of inspiration, and that's what he needed now. Inspiration.

Or maybe something intuitive . . .

Yes!

"What is it?" asked Louise.

"Blank your mind, Lou. It's got to be worth a try. Trust to instinct. See if something leaps in and tells you the way home."

"You call that a plan?"

"I do when I'm desperate. And I've seen what the human mind can do. I've read the case histories. Some people say we all have these latent abilities, vestigial knowledge from earlier times, that we can tap into during times of need. And all we're asking for now is a sense of direction. Just an inkling—this way or that."

"A homing instinct."

"Exactly. It's not that far-fetched, is it? Think *home* and see what happens."

They thought *home*—nothing—they cleared their thoughts, they waited, they offered up their minds as empty vessels for some arcane process to fill. Still nothing. No blinding light of revelation, no tug in an unexpected direction, no . . .

It came upon him slow and unexpected. Not the sense of direction that he'd been hoping for, but another sense entirely. And something quite unexpected.

The sense of not being alone.

Louise couldn't see anything, couldn't hear anything and couldn't smell anything. But she knew. Something was out there. Close by. Watching them.

"Nick?"

"I know. I can feel it too."

They threw their senses to the far horizons, along every plane of thought they could imagine, trying to dredge up an image of whatever was out there. They trawled their minds, their subconscious, tried to trigger some long-forgotten sense that would light up their surroundings like a sonar screen.

A silent blackness stared back.

Calm down, Louise told herself. You're letting your imagination turn shadows into monsters. There's nothing out there except Nick and the pair of you are behaving like a couple of schoolgirls swapping ghost stories at midnight.

But . . .

What if there really was something out there? Not being able to see it didn't mean it wasn't there.

Another image forced itself into her mind. Two swimmers treading water in a deep, dark ocean with sharks circling beneath them. If the sharks' fins didn't break the surface who'd know they were there? The swimmers wouldn't. Not at night. Not with everything black and fathomless.

Once started upon that line of thought, she couldn't shake it. They were being menaced by the higher dimensional equivalent of the Great White. Invisible and intangible, it circled: sometimes swimming between them, sometimes passing within inches.

The entire void might be full of them.

Flash! The void lit up for an instant. A brilliant burst of blue-tinged white. So bright it felt to Louise that it had originated from inside her. There it was again. She felt it that time. It hurt. And again. Ow! The flashes coming fast and intense. And the pain. It was like a migraine, her head exploding like a firework factory.

"Nick!" She mentally bent double. Pain, disorientation, panic. What was happening to her? Was she being eaten alive?

No word from Nick, or was that him screaming? It was like some lunatic was flipping HV channels inside her head—a confusing cacophony of voices, music, sound bites, and images.

And then it stopped. Total silence, everything black.

"What the hell was that?" she shouted. "Nick? Are you there?" She couldn't see him. "Nick!"

"I'm here." He sounded distant and in pain. And then the lights started flashing again, not as intense as before but just as disorientating. Her mind was being invaded. She . . .

"Get out of my head!" She struggled, tried to flee, tried to close her mind and squeeze whatever was in there out. Neither succeeded. She thought *move* and she stayed put. She thought *get out* and the images flashed faster.

Respite. A few seconds and then it started again. On and off. Was she being played with? Was she a mouse being tossed up in the air by a higher dimensional cat?

The bombardment continued, less painful now, and the cycle between images was lengthening. Intense flashes replaced by jerky freeze-frame views—some she recognized: people she knew, places she'd been. But others were incomprehensible—random patterns, nonsense shapes. And one—a kind of triangle within a circle but far more complex—was repeated several times.

"I think someone's . . . trying to communicate with us." Nick's words crawled inside Louise's head. He sounded exhausted and strained.

Was someone trying to communicate with them? Or were they ill? Maybe the void was poisonous to them, their brains being eaten alive, higher dimensional synapses firing and exploding and triggering all kinds of death-throe images.

Back came the triangle within a circle, the image rotating, changing shape, gaining depth, and . . . confusing the hell out of her. It looked like an optical illusion, the shape almost made sense but it hurt to look at.

Ow! Pain, sharp and sudden, then nausea, dizziness, a dull ache and—wow!—what was that? Elation, sadness, fear, trepidation, hunger—she was hurtling along an emotional roller coaster. Her mind hijacked, a thousand hands inside her head pressing buttons at random, experimenting with every facet, every feature.

Had Pendennis found them again? Was this their final rinse on the brainwash cycle to hell?

Smells hit her: some foul, some fragrant. Sounds rang out: bells, voices, laughter, gunshots. Tastes, colors, the sensation of wind in her hair, rain on her face, heat, cold . . .

And then everything stopped. She felt mentally winded, as though her brain had been in free fall and then a parachute had suddenly opened and yanked her back to reality.

And yet, she felt safe. Overwhelmingly so. For no reason at all.

Around her, the void began to lighten. Features began to appear—a landscape, fields and trees—the blackness of the void peeling back like night before day.

"Is this real?" she asked Nick. "Are we back?"

"I . . . I don't know. It looks too sharp and . . . I can't see behind me anymore."

He was right. She had to turn too. The 360-degree, all-round, up-down, left-and-right, fuzzy vision had gone. She had eyes. And a body.

And then nothing. The image broke up and the void returned. Anger. Was she being toyed with?

Her anger evaporated, back came that feeling of calm serenity. And with it a certainty that everything was going to be all right.

She tried to be suspicious of it. She could still think, she still had free will. But her emotions—they were no longer her own.

A light appeared in the distance. A blue light growing and spreading across the void towards them. She could see sea and sky and . . . was that a boat?

The light swept past them, chasing the void away like sunlight chasing cloud shadows across a windblown landscape. The boat passed beneath them. It was cutting through azure waves beneath a blue cloudless sky. Dolphins led the way. At least a dozen of them, leaping from the water at the prow of the boat.

Follow.

A voice inside her head. "Nick? Was that you?"

"I heard it too," he said. There was a pause and then he asked. "Do you feel anything?"

"I wouldn't trust anything I felt at this moment. My emotions were hijacked a while back."

The dolphins changed course, veering to the right. The boat followed. Was it a message? Dolphins lead lost boats to safety. She'd read about it. The memory of her reading about it was suddenly fresh within her mind.

The dolphins and the boat began to move away. And behind them the void was sweeping in across the sky like night.

"They want us to follow," said Nick. "I think we should."

"But what if it's a trick? Pendennis or evil aliens?"

"Can it be worse than staying here? We asked for a sign to take us home. This one's neon-lit."

The void swept past them chasing the blue bubble of light towards the horizon. They had to follow. Nick was right. It might be their only chance of finding Earth.

They chased after it, fixing their minds on the retreating bubble and dragging it towards them. As soon as the bubble filled half the sky, it accelerated, forcing them to do likewise. And again when they closed a second time, and a third, and a fourth . . . Louise had no idea at what speed they were now travelling, the void was featureless and gave no clues. But it had to be fast. Their speed increased with each iteration and how many of those had there been—ten, twelve?

And where were they going? Surely Earth couldn't be this far away?

A wave of well-being shot over here. Brilliant, she thought, someone had hit the endorphin button. She couldn't even be allowed to grumble in peace.

In the distance, on the ocean horizon, a new image appeared. A sail? Another boat? No, an island. The dolphins were heading towards it, a shimmering rock rising out of the sea. The sun glinted off craggy cliffs, shining colors of every shade of brown through red and orange.

"Is that where you're taking us?" Louise asked. "Isn't it about time you told us who you are?"

No one answered. They didn't even push a soothing image into her head. She stared at the growing island. Did it look familiar? Could it be Earth?

"I don't think so," said Nick, surprising her. She didn't think she'd transmitted the question. "I think we've travelled too far to be anywhere near Earth."

Brilliant. She waited for the endorphins to kick in and . . . there they were. She'd been abducted by aliens, experimented upon, and drugged with chocolate. Could the day get any better?

The sky began to darken. So did the sea. And the boat and dolphins disappeared. Only the island remained. And now even that began to change.

It was breathtaking. And gigantic, like a floating city of light it hung there in the void, shimmering and scintillating. They slowed as they approached. The mountain city filled half their vision. But was it a city? It looked . . . Louise struggled to work out exactly what it did look like. It looked like an artwork, sculpted out of a mountain of variegated crystals. It didn't look natural and it didn't look functional. But . . . did people live there? Well, not people obviously but . . . did someone live there? She couldn't see any signs of life: no vehicles, no spaceships, no movement—except from the city itself, which looked in a constant state of flux. Was it growing? Was it alive? Its edges wouldn't stand still. They grew; they twisted; they changed shape, color and texture. It was . . . it was as close to indescribable as anything she'd ever seen in her life.

Home, said a voice in her head.

"Your home?" she asked.

Home, came the reply.

CHAPTER TWENTY-THREE

A dolphin appeared from nowhere and started to swim towards the island city, undulating its body through a waterless black void.

"I think we're meant to follow," said Nick.

"I think I feel safer out here," said Louise.

He shared her misgivings. Up to a point. But another part of him was drawn to that incredible structure. How could anyone not want to take a closer look? It was the most amazing thing he'd ever seen. It was the most amazing thing any human had ever seen. And it was there—right in front of him.

Okay, so there was an element of danger but was that danger any less outside the island city? If the dolphin aliens meant them harm then a few miles wasn't going to provide much protection.

"If they meant to harm us, Lou, why spend so much time making us feel better?"

"To make sure we didn't try to escape."

"So why didn't they restrain us or knock us out?"

"Maybe that comes next."

"Suit yourself. But I'm going in. They're our only chance of getting back home."

He focussed on the dolphin and pulled himself towards it. Louise followed. The city loomed above them, huge towers projecting into the void like feral skyscrapers of crystal and silk—they shone, they shimmered, they rippled in both color and form. It was breathtaking. So much to look at, so much to comprehend.

The dolphin led them to a chasm—or was it a street?—between two massive iridescent towers. Nick scanned ahead, looking for doors or openings—markings, anything—some clue as to their nature. Were they buildings or crystals, alive or inert? Maybe it wasn't a city, maybe it was the higher dimensional equivalent of a coral reef.

But where was everybody? Were they waiting inside or was everyone invisible? Had Nick and Louise strayed into a part of the universe that evolution hadn't equipped them to comprehend? An infrared, ultraviolet, ultra-anything-they'd-ever-sensed-before realm cloaked from their sight?

But if so, how could they see the city? Or were they only seeing a subset of the city? Was it even more magnificent for those with full-spectrum sight?

The dolphin turned at an intersection. Another empty street cum chasm. This one appearing to narrow towards the top, the two sides of the street almost touching—hundreds, maybe thousands of meters above them.

Nick drifted to one side. He had to look closer, reach out, and touch. Were the chasm walls solid? Could he pass straight through?

"Nick? What are you doing?" hissed Louise. She sounded like a worried parent who'd just noticed her six-year-old reaching towards the most expensive vase in the shop.

"Investigating," he said. "Do you think these are buildings? I can't see any doors but maybe you just float straight through."

The wall changed as he approached. The previously flat, shiny surface suddenly incised with . . . a pattern? A triangle within a circle. Except the shape changed as he moved closer. The three sides of the triangle didn't quite meet and the circle was more like a spiral stretching impossibly back into the structure of the building. He reached out to touch it, ready to draw back at the slightest hint of danger. He . . . made contact. It *was* solid. He pushed harder. The wall didn't give.

"Come on, Nick. The dolphin's turning again."

He reluctantly left the structure. The whole city had to be made of higher dimensional matter. If only he had an imager!

He chased after Louise, reached the intersection where she'd last seen the dolphin, turned, and . . . found an empty street.

"Where did it go?"

"I don't know," said Louise.

There was a black horizontal line halfway down the far chasm wall. Could it have gone in there?

They raced towards it. It was a letterbox opening about ten meters by one and getting smaller. Nick peered inside. It was a dark and nar-rowing—a tunnel—and was that a dolphin in the distance swimming away from them? He called out.

"Are we supposed to follow?"

No answer. The mouth was closing; two feet wide, eighteen inches. He had to act.

"No," said Louise. But it was too late. He'd already swept through.

The probing started almost immediately. One second he was blur-ring through the tunnel in pursuit of the alien, the next he was immobilized and reliving old memories. But there was no pain this time. And the speed had been toned down. Images no longer flashed stroboscopically.

"What do you want?" he asked, trying to push the images aside and shout the thought at his interrogators. "You *can* speak. I've heard you."

A rush of warm fuzziness swept over him. Endorphin time. Keep the patient happy and smiling.

More images flashed by, unexpected memories tumbling out—old embarrassments, triumphs, long-forgotten friends and acquaintan-ces—all marching past in random order.

And then something even stranger happened. An art gallery appeared. One he had no memory of ever visiting. And yet there he was—Nick Stubbs—standing in front of one of the paintings. And there was Louise. She'd joined him and was pointing at a sculpture, something weird and exotic. And suddenly changing. All the exhibits were changing. And the gallery too, its walls and ceiling pushing back to double, treble its former size. A blue whale materialized, suspended from the ceiling, a dinosaur too. They were in a museum. He could see machines—cars, rockets, trains—mingled with stuffed animals and skeletons and . . .

Everything started to recede—the exhibits, the museum walls, the ceiling, everything racing into the distance. New buildings sprang up in their place; buildings he recognized, scale models of the Taj Mahal, the Parthenon, Stonehenge, various chateaux and villas, bridges and towers. Avenues of Earth's architectural heritage stretched to the horizon.

And then vanished, replaced by an image of the island city. And then that too vanished and back came the museum. The two images alternating. Was that the message? The island city was a museum?

Everything went blank and then a new building appeared—half-timbered, leaded lights. It looked like an old London coffeehouse. He was standing outside. Louise was beside him. The door opened and sucked them inside.

Inside, it was crowded and noisy. People everywhere, bustling and talking . . . or were they talking? Their mouths moved but was that speech? It was more like a sampling of speech—random words and phrases that together made no sense. And was that Einstein over there? And Newton? Da Vinci? Nick spun from face to face. Some he recognized, some had sprouted name tags. It was like a themed fancy-dress party for mankind's greatest minds. Every one of them debating with a neighbor, exchanging papers and strange objects that could have been gifts or scale models of their latest invention.

The coffeehouse faded and back came the museum, then the gallery, then the image of the triangle within the circle, then the island city. All five images cycling together. Were they one and the same? Was that the message? That the island city was this race's version of old London cafe society? A university cum museum cum art gallery, a place of learning and cultural exchange, and it had a name—one that was represented not by spoken words but by an image—the triangle within the circle?

"Is that why you've brought us here? To become exhibits?"

Louise's voice. Was that really her? Or another projection within his mind?

"Louise?" he asked. "Is that you? Are you seeing this too?"

"Nick? What's . . ."

That's all he heard. A dozen other voices started shouting in his head. Strange voices, strange words. It sounded like a Tourrette's improv night, each word shouted out like an insult. *Pig! Emblaze! Cotton! Kettle! Shingle!* Other words he couldn't catch, there were so many of them, so many people talking at the same time—men, women, children.

Images appeared—heated conversations on the street, HV debates, pages from a dictionary, pages from a book—the words peeling off and being recited in a steady stream. Pain. The volume and confusion of sound was making his head ache. The images were flashing faster, the sounds louder.

"Stop!" he commanded. "Slow down!"

He was ignored. The pain increased. No friendly shot of calming endorphins this time. But something else. A sudden adrenalinelike rush of excitement. Had they pressed the wrong button? Or was he picking up their emotions?

Images flashed furiously, sounds merging into one long shrill whine. The pain was becoming unbearable, like a dentist's drill inside his head.

Something had to have gone wrong. He had to tell them. He had to make them stop. He had to . . . communicate.

He summoned up an image—the Earth from orbit—concentrated, squeezing his mind shut to the pain, taking the image and projecting it with everything he had. If they liked pictures try this one for size. "Home!" he shouted and held on to that image, trying to force all the other pictures from his mind. "Home!" Listen, goddamn you. He took another image—Louise's cottage—thrust it at them. Home! Then Louise's lounge, a fire in the hearth, Nick and Louise sat around it, smiling. Home!

"Can't you understand that?" he shouted. "We want to go home!"

Everything went black. And silent. No sound, no pain. And then . . .

Louise's lounge materialized around them. Louise was in her favorite chair, Nick was on the sofa. A fire roared in the grate, her old clock ticking on the mantelpiece. It looked so real. . . .

She squeezed the arm of her chair. It had substance. It was warm to the touch. Were they really back? Had Nick actually persuaded the alien to return them home?

Nick leapt to his feet, he was patting his body. "Is this real?" he asked, shouting the question at the ceiling. "Have you really sent us back?"

Louise ran a finger along the leg of her jeans—brushed cotton. She hadn't worn a pair of brushed cotton jeans for years. Not since . . .

Footsteps from the hallway made her turn her head. A woman appeared in the lounge doorway.

"Hello," said the newcomer, smiling.

Louise blanched. It was her mother.

CHAPTER TWENTY-FOUR

"We thought this would make you feel more comfortable," said her mother, looking perplexed. "Were we wrong?"

"Who are you?" asked Louise, jumping to her feet. Deep down she already knew the answer. They were still in the island city.

"We are called . . ." The woman closed her eyes and immediately an image burned inside Louise's brain. A jumbled image of color and squiggles that meant nothing to her. "You have no word for it," continued the woman. "Why do you choose this strange method of communication? Don't you find it limiting?"

Louise couldn't answer. She just stared at the woman. Her voice, the way she held her head, the smile. She was attracted and repelled in equal measures. She wanted to run over and touch her face, hold her close but . . . she wanted to slap that face too. How dare they use her mother like that!

"It's the only method of communication we have," said Nick, breaking the silence.

"Untrue," said the alien. "You can converse normally. But you choose this . . . this verbal communication, which is inherently inefficient and error-prone. Why? Is it a game or, perhaps, etiquette that demands your thoughts be encoded before transmission?"

"No," said Nick. "It's a matter of necessity. Not everyone's telepathic."

"Interesting! You are telepathic but not all your people are. Does this not cause conflict? Is that why you were travelling the far reaches—in search of like minds to form a colony?"

"No, nothing at all like that," said Nick. "We were lost . . ."

Louise couldn't take any more of this. He'd be offering the alien drinks next. She cut across the conversation.

"When are you going to take us home?" she asked.

"Ah," said her mother, turning her head to face Louise. "That is the right expression is it not? To convey a mixture of regret and embarrassment?"

Louise closed her eyes. What the hell was going to happen now?

"What's the problem?" asked Nick. "I'm sure together we can find a solution."

"As indeed are we. But—" The woman shrugged, extravagantly so. "—we have other obligations as you must understand. Ours is but a small colony, to survive we must occasionally undertake work for other, larger colonies, in order to gain access to their greater pools of knowledge. We cannot afford to isolate ourselves totally from the outside world. Much as we would like to."

"Get to the point," said Louise, adding "please" as an afterthought.

"As you wish. Simply put, we were told where you would be and asked to bring you here. You were . . . expected."

Louise was back on her feet. "That's impossible!" she said. "How could anyone know where we were going to be? We arrived there by accident. We had no plans to enter the void."

"That is not for us to say. But clearly it cannot be impossible for it has happened. We were commissioned by what you would call an exploration/life science colony to monitor a particular area of space in our vicinity and bring back any life-forms we encountered. Their representatives have been informed of your coming and will be arriving soon to collect you. We thought you would be pleased—"

"How the hell could anyone be pleased about that?" shouted Louise. "We want to go home. We don't want to be collected and studied. Can't you understand that? Don't you have laws against imprisoning people against their will?"

The alien looked confused.

"There is no imprisonment involved in this transaction. You are without a colony and we have found you one. One who is prepared to take you in."

"Can't you help us find our old colony?" asked Nick.

"We are artists and theoreticians, Nicholas, not explorers. And you . . . you have no awareness of your colony's location. We searched within your memories but found no such knowledge. Your old colony is lost."

"But it's got to be close to where you found us," said Louise. "Can't you look it up on a map or something?"

"The place where we found you is a desert. There are no nearby planets. Your old colony is lost. We cannot locate it and neither can you so why not accept the inevitability of your situation? Without a colony you cannot function. Perhaps your new colony will help you in your search? We expect that is why they were looking for you. They are an explorer/life science community."

Unbelievable. Louise was ready to explode.

"Don't *we* have a say in the matter?" she snapped.

"Of course. It is your wish not to accompany your escort to the new colony, is that correct?"

"Yes," she said, glancing at Nick, ready to shout him down if he disagreed.

"Very good," said the alien, pausing for an instant. "Your views have been taken into account. We are sure that you will come to see the wisdom of our decision."

"Whoa," said Louise. "What decision?"

"The colony has voted. We are agreed. Your best interests lie with your future colony."

"When do we get a chance to put our side of the argument?"

"Your views have already been disseminated throughout the colony. We would share our viewpoint with you so that you can see the wisdom of our decision but . . . our attempts to communicate appear to give you pain. It is regrettable, yes?"

"What if we refuse to go?"

The woman looked horrified. "Individual choice must give way to the needs of the majority if anarchy is to be avoided. Surely you know this?"

Louise was lost for words. She looked at Nick. "Aren't you going to say something?"

He sat there, staring into the fire, pulling at the straggly ends of his moustache. Then he stopped and looked directly at the alien. "While we're waiting to be taken to our new colony," he said, "how about a game?"

Louise looked at him, her lower jaw probably somewhere around her ankles. What the hell was he playing at now? A game? Had he lost his mind?

"What kind of game?" asked the alien, looking intrigued. Louise shook her head in disbelief. Was she the only sane person left in the room? Or was this all part of the interrogation process? Soften the poor human up so she doesn't care what's happening to her anymore? Was that Nick over there or another alien playing the part?

"A game that would stretch even your abilities," said Nick. "And help me prove a theory of mine."

Louise snorted. Whoever was playing Nick had the part off to a tee.

"What theory is this?" said the woman, walking over to where Nick sat.

"You are a colony of theoreticians, are you not?"

"We are. Artists and theoreticians, that is our specialty."

"Well, I think you could calculate the exact coordinates of our home planet from information stored in our memories. We—"

The alien cut him off. "We have already told you. We found no awareness of universal coordinates or spatial perception within your memory."

"That's what makes it a challenge. I believe there is a way. All you have to do is analyze the image of our planet's night skies that we hold in our heads and compare those star patterns with your own charts."

Louise held her breath. Come on, say yes. Say yes and get this thing over with.

"Our charts are not extensive, and we don't discriminate between physical and nonphysical matter as you do."

"But you *can* do it," urged Nick. "Even if your charts aren't that extensive, all you need do is take us to the nearest boundary with the physical universe and take another snapshot of the star patterns from there. Take as many samples as you need, visit as many boundary points as you need. With enough data points you have to be able to calculate the exact position of our home planet."

There was a long pause. Louise watched her mother's face. It was blank, impossible to read. Was she communicating with the other Colonists? Were they voting?

Her mother spoke. "You realize that this will not change your situation. We are still contracted to deliver you to your new colony."

"Of course, but now our new colony will have the information they need to take us home."

The alien nodded. "We are agreed. This game has merit. We will extract all images concerning star configurations from your memories and begin as soon as that is concluded."

They were split up. Nick was taken to the boundary while Louise remained at the island city—the Colonists' insurance policy against flight. Not that Nick had anywhere to flee to. Unless the nearest boundary opened slap bang next to a planet he could recognize— Earth, Saturn, or Jupiter—where would he go? Aim at the nearest point of light and hope it was the sun?

The boundary layer flickered before him, hundreds and thousands of tiny shimmering stars. It was like a hazy, moonless, autumn night back on Earth. And it was wonderful.

Even if he couldn't recognize any constellations, it felt good to have left the void, to know that the physical universe was out there waiting, and somewhere—up there, down there, or over there—was Earth.

"Sufficient data has been collected," said his invisible companion. "We shall now return."

Nick returned in silence, riven between a desire to bombard the colonist with questions and the need to keep his thoughts to himself. How can you plot an escape when your mind could be read at any moment?

And how could anyone who called himself a scientist ignore the vast repository of knowledge that the Colonists had to possess?

A dilemma, replete with sharp, pointy things.

The Colonists had to be centuries, if not millennia, ahead of Earth. Wasn't it his duty, his responsibility, to find out as much as he could from them? It was a once-in-several-lifetimes opportunity, a chance to push the frontiers of human knowledge centuries into the future.

And yet . . .

He couldn't risk the prolonged contact. The longer he spent with the aliens inside his head the more likely they were to discover his intentions. Which meant he had to keep his head down *and* his distance. What good was knowledge if he couldn't get back to share it?

"Well?" asked Louise on his return. "Did you find the boundary? Did you see Earth?"

"We found the boundary but . . . we must be light years away. I couldn't even see Orion."

He projected a question towards the Colonists. "Is it okay if we fly around your colony and explore the sights?" he asked.

"By all means," said a voice in his head. "You are our guests."

Nick led Louise out of the city, not stopping until the gleaming towers covered less than a quarter of the sky.

"Well?" asked Louise as soon as he stopped.

"We've got to be careful what we think. They might even be monitoring us out here."

"Did you see Earth?" she asked, no doubt thinking he'd been lying earlier to mislead the Colonists.

"No, Lou, we really are light years away."

He looked to the horizon, wondering if he could even find the boundary again. It had been so dark he'd barely registered its existence until the colonist had told him they'd arrived. The result of being in deep space, he assumed. At least close to a star there was a wash of light.

"How are we going to get back?" asked Louise. "Even if they give us the coordinates are they going to mean anything to us?"

What did he know? He'd had an idea and run with it. He wasn't sure what he'd expected. That maybe the Colonists would relent and show them the way home? Or they'd reach the nearest boundary and it would be Earth?

"If nothing else it means that the new Colonists will know where we come from," he said. "Maybe we can persuade them to take us back."

"That's another thing I don't understand. How could they have known we were coming? It doesn't make any sense, does it?"

"Maybe they weren't expecting us, maybe they're xenobiologists conducting a survey on a particular section of space and subcontracted out the specimen collection."

"That's supposed to make me feel better? I'm a fish caught in a trawler's net waiting to see if I'll be thrown back in?"

"It could be worse," he said. "Explorer/life science colony sounds a hell of a lot better than warfare/animal experimentation colony."

A thought that triggered another. Had he put the Earth in danger? He'd been so desperate to persuade the Colonists to locate the planet he hadn't considered the ramifications. He'd given an unknown species with untold powers the means to locate Earth.

But they're friendly, he told himself. They'd gone out of the way to show that several times.

"Friendly enough to sell us on like slaves," said Louise. Again he hadn't realized he'd been projecting his thoughts. Great, how the hell was he supposed to keep secrets from the Colonists when he was leaking thoughts like a rusty sieve?

"It's different customs, Lou," he said. "You can't expect them to think like us. But they're an intelligent species and sooner or later they'll realize we are too and help us."

"As we would if the roles were reversed?"

"Yes."

He braced himself for another attack on the failings of the human race. Why was it that all animal lovers hated humans so much?

"You really believe we would? If an alien landed on Earth you think the human race would patch them up and help them on their way again?"

"I would like to think so, yes. Maybe not a few decades ago. But we're a more mature civilization now, less paranoid."

"God, you're so naïve, Nick! The military would have that alien locked away, interrogated, tortured, and its technology dissected before anyone else knew it had arrived. That's if they didn't kill it first."

He sensed her anger but couldn't share it. They were billions of miles away from Earth arguing about . . . what? The iniquities of human prejudice?

"Lou, the Colonists are an ascended species. They're beyond all that. Look around you. Have you seen a single weapon? Their city is a work of art. There are no gun turrets or space cruisers—"

"You don't need a gun to be a bully. You just have to be bigger and meaner. And as for being ascended, I judge as I find. They're not treating us as intelligent beings, they're treating us as animals to buy and sell."

Nick didn't have time to disagree. A different voice dropped inside his head. "We have completed the calculations," it said.

"You've found Earth?" asked Louise.

"We have located the source of your memories, yes. It was a stimulating exercise."

"Where is it then?" she asked. "Could you show us which direction from here?"

Subtle, thought Nick, then immediately wished he hadn't. When would he ever learn how to master his thoughts? He threw up a wall, hoping there was such a thing, a thoughtproof wall he could hide behind and plot in secret.

"It would be of no use," said the alien, hopefully to Louise's question and not Nick's. "It is better that you do not know."

"I don't understand," said Louise. "Why?"

"Your destiny lies elsewhere. Better to forget the past. Your new hosts agree it is for the best."

"You've spoken to them?"

"We have communicated. They have more experience in dealing with other species."

"They told you not to tell us, didn't they?"

"A consensus was reached."

"But no one asked us! How can you have consensus if the main party is excluded from the argument?"

"You are not the main party. There is much you do not understand. It is better to leave important decisions to those with the knowledge."

"We disagree."

"That is as may be but why distress yourself over something that cannot be changed?"

Nick saw it first, a growing speck on one of the many horizons. One of the advantages of his 360-degree, up-down, all-around, no-chance-of-being-crept-up-upon-vision.

"Lou," he said.

"What?" she snapped.

"I think our escort's arrived."

CHAPTER TWENTY-FIVE

The shape changed from speck to colossus. It was immense, hovering above them, a rippling, pulsing, jellyfish of a creature the size of a small ship—larger if you took the trailing fronds into account.

And its edges—they changed shape. Appearing, disappearing, rotating, morphing. It was like watching a multidimensional object ripple through three-dimensional space.

Louise fled, not caring where, not thinking, everything trampled in a rush to be free from that *thing* sent to fetch them.

She blurred into the void, using the creature as a point of reference and thinking *away, fast!*

Blackness surrounded her. The void, featureless and infinite. She kept going arrow-straight, not daring to think or look or doubt. *Faster*, she urged, *faster*.

A smudge of grey appeared behind her. She ignored it, thought herself into an arrowhead, sleek and smooth. *Faster*, she cried, *speed of light and beyond*.

The smudge grew, sliding towards her, slow, inexorable, swallowing the void behind her.

She veered to the right. The smudge followed. She dived, twisted, pulled left, pulled right. The smudge followed. She thought *invisible*, she thought *silent*, she thought *teleport*. *Teleport me now, anyplace, any time. Just get me out!*

The smudge followed. It covered a third of the sky and was still closing.

No!

She accelerated again, thinking *speed beyond comprehension, speed beyond imagination*.

The smudge followed, gaining all the time, beginning to flow around her, the void compressing into a shrinking jet-black tunnel.

No! There had to be a way, there had to!

Desperation. She summoned the image of a distant galaxy, the farthest object her imagination could produce, held it in her mind, and tried to drag herself towards it, tried to suck the lightyears between them into nothingness, tried to pull herself out of space-time itself.

Tried . . .

. . . and failed.

Pain exploded all around her. She felt like a sponge, picked up and squeezed dry. She couldn't move, she couldn't think, she couldn't cry out. All feelings of resistance broken and destroyed. The pain unbearable. Consciousness clouding. The dark returning.

Louise drifted in and out of consciousness. Memories played on the edge of her perception, memories of flight and capture, pain and helplessness. Sometimes she thought she heard Nick's voice, sometimes she heard herself reply. But whether it was real, a dream, or implanted, she neither knew nor cared. She was somewhere else. Disembodied and separate from all that was going on around her.

Time passed. She woke, she slept. Remembering more and hurting less with each awakening. All around her were pale, translucent walls—most times creamy but occasionally suffused with rippling color. Was she inside the creature? Had it swallowed her up?

She tried to move. Nothing more than a stretch but the pain that hit her was excruciating. She felt squeezed. She could sense a hundred tiny fronds tightening around her. The pressure unbearable, her head about to explode . . .

She slept, she dreamed, then awoke with a start. Colors! Everywhere. The creamy walls had gone but she was still moving, carried along on a current through what looked like a canal or a street between banks of intense color. Had they arrived? Was this the new colony? The structure—from the little she could see—wasn't as imposing as the island city. The banks—or buildings or whatever they were—were lower and flatter and didn't change shape. But the color . . . she'd never seen colors so intense. They had texture and depth. Yellows that oozed, reds that burned, blues so rich they made her feel sick, a green she could smell, a black so deep and cloying she knew that any hand that strayed too close would come away coated black to the elbow.

It was mesmerizing. And confusing. Painful at times, as though her senses were being overloaded with information the human consciousness could barely process let alone comprehend. She felt blinded, dazzled, and intoxicated.

She moved, inadvertently, and pain ran through her like a high-voltage cable. She froze and the pain stopped. Wherever her captor was, it wasn't far.

"Nick?" She thought she saw him, a small blurred form bobbing along behind her. But either she was mistaken or he was asleep.

Then she was falling, the current—something—sucking her down, sending her swirling towards a bright light at the base of the canal. She braced herself, tumbled through, into the light and beyond.

Wait here, commanded a voice.

Wait where? The light was so intense it blinded her. She felt like she'd been dipped—encapsulated—inside a small star. Everything around her was bleached by light.

The interrogation started almost immediately. Just as before, she felt the wrench as her mind was pulled from her grasp and her memories flipped through—forwards, backwards, fast, and slow. The same must have been happening to Nick—she caught occasional thoughts shouted across the ether. *Lou? Are you there? Did you make it?*

Yes, she was here. And she was at home, at school, riding on a bus. She was in a thousand places all at once, her life tumbling past her like pictures on a revolving drum.

What the hell did these people want? What more could they discover that they hadn't already sucked out of her brain?

And when it was over—silence. No apologies, no explanation, no soothing endorphin rush. She was trapped inside a gleaming prison—pinned by an invisible force that robbed her of all movement.

"Why don't you communicate with us?" she shouted. "We know you can."

Her words screamed across the chamber, challenging a reply that never came.

"It's no good, Lou," said Nick. "They're not listening."

"Why not!" she snapped, struggling against the invisible force that held her vicelike in position. She thought *break*, she thought *snap*, she thought *let me go*!

Frustration and anger. She felt so helpless! Her life had been one of order and self-sufficiency. She'd grown used to being in charge, never having her judgment challenged, and now this—tossed from one disaster to another, never knowing what was happening or how to make it stop.

"Why don't they communicate?" she yelled. "Why are they repeating everything that's already been done before?"

"Perhaps they don't trust the other Colonists?"

"But why? They're all the same species, aren't they?"

"*They are children!*"

The thought boomed into her consciousness, echoing and rattling into every corner of her mind. Much louder, much more insistent than anything she'd experienced at the island city.

Louise shouted back. "What do you want with us?"

"*Information.*"

"You've taken all the information we have! What more do you want?"

Louise was straining to make out some shape or substance she could yell at. Everything around her shone in such uniform brilliance. The disembodied voice held no clue. It appeared to originate from inside her head.

"*We do not have all the information we require.*"

"But we don't have anything more to give!" She spat the words out in frustration. Were they deaf as well as invisible?

"Why don't you tell us what you're looking for?" asked Nick. "Maybe we can help?"

Silence. Typical, thought Louise, run away as soon as it's your turn to answer anything.

"You still think they're an intelligent species, Nick?"

"They'll come round."

She bit her tongue. Given teeth she would have bitten a hell of a lot more. Why was he always defending the Colonists? Couldn't he recognize them for what they were?

Aaaarrrggghh! She internalized her anger, not trusting herself to project any thoughts. Her brain felt like a ransacked bedroom. So many memories pulled out of their drawers and tossed on the floor. She could see her smallholding, her animals, and wondered how they were doing. Who was looking after them? Had the spring arrived? Was the grass beginning to grow? Or had spring passed into distant memory?

And how long had they been gone? Days? Weeks? Months? Or only a few fleeting seconds. Time here was as indecipherable as their captors.

And then her mind was sucked forward again, plucked out and sent reeling into the now familiar exercise of sifting and straining. What were they looking for now? She barely had room to kindle the thought there were so many hands inside her head, pushing and prodding. Surely they'd only just finished, had time flashed by so soon?

Another voice, different this time—softer—washed over her as soon as the sifting stopped.

"Are you really as ignorant as you appear?"

Was this the merest flicker of a way out? Ignorance their savior? Too stupid to be of any use to the Colonists? Nick grabbed the opportunity.

"Thick as two short planks, us," he said. "Best to let us go, don't you think?"

"You are strange creatures. Why do you insist we let you go when you do not even know where you are? You would not survive if we released you. You must know that to be true?"

"Why don't you take us back home then?" asked Louise.

A pause.

"You want us to do that?"

There was something strange about the way the colonist spoke. Surprise, almost. Which struck Nick as bizarre. Anyone reading their minds had to know how desperately they wanted to go home.

"Of course," said Louise. "It's the only thing we do want. You must have found that out with all the scanning you've done on us."

"But you want us to accompany you?"

"We don't *want* you to come with us. If you can give us directions—fine, we'll go alone. But we thought it would be easier if you showed us the way."

"So, you would prefer our company?"

What was this? A colonist in search of friendship? A promise to swap cards at Christmas and keep in touch?

"We would be honored by your company," said Nick. "And it would be safer for us. Less chance of us getting lost again."

"Safer for you, you say. But would it be safer for us?"

This was becoming a very weird conversation.

"I don't understand?" he said. "Why shouldn't it be safe for you?"

"*It could be a trap. Why should we believe you? A creature who feigns ignorance yet regards itself as intelligent, who has the ability of image communication yet refuses to use it, who is so frightened of truth it prefers to encrypt every thought before it can be communicated and, most damning of all, whose memories belong to a totally different organism. Why should we believe you?*"

A totally different organism?

"What's he talking about, Nick?"

He wasn't sure . . . unless . . .

The separation! All their memories were physical. Human memories of their corporeal selves with arms, legs, and feet.

"But it's all there!" he said. "In our minds. How we discovered the dual nature of our existence and how we separated from our corporeal form. Surely you can't have missed that?"

"*If it's true. Isn't it just as likely you stole existing memories from one of those lesser species and grafted your transformation onto it? What better way to manufacture an identity if you knew your minds would be scanned?*"

"Why would we want to do that?" he asked.

"*That is what we are trying to find out.*"

"But wait," said Nick. "We didn't ask to be picked up. You came to us. So why would we even think of concealing our identity? It makes no sense."

"*You wish this charade to continue? Very well, the reason you were picked up is a simple one. One of our number was murdered. You were found close to the body. In a sector of space that is a desert. And now you wish us to accompany you back to that desert. In your parlance, is that not like a murderer asking the victim's brother to accompany him to a dark and lonely alley?*"

CHAPTER TWENTY-SIX

Louise couldn't believe it. "Why is it that wherever we go, someone accuses us of murder?" she said, exasperated.

"*You've been accused of murder before?*" asked the colonist.

Oh shit. Louise mentally cradled her head in her hands. When would she ever learn to keep her big thought-mouth shut?

"You already know we've been accused of murder," said Nick. "Our memories show that clearly and the reasons for the misunderstandings."

"*Convenient misunderstandings,*" said the colonist.

"Which just goes to show how ridiculous your theory is about us grafting on someone else's memory. If we wanted to hide wouldn't we choose people with spotless pasts?"

"*Not if the only beings you were in contact with were other fugitives.*"

Unbelievable, thought Louise quietly to herself. What's it going to take to convince these people?

Pain hit her as if in answer, hands inside her head delving and ripping, pulling out memories, searching and trashing. Migraine flashes, intense and prolonged. And after that, something new—a shooting, twisting pain like a team of dentists drilling her thoughts out one by one without an anaesthetic.

She hovered on the brink of consciousness. Perhaps the Colonists were delving deeper and deeper into the fabric of her mind, perhaps they were killing her, perhaps . . .

It stopped. She hung there, bracing herself, waiting for it to start up again. "Come on!" she shouted. "Is that all you've got!"

"Don't antagonize them," said Nick.

It took a while for his words to register. And when they did she started to laugh. They were being tortured and *he* was worried about antagonizing *them*.

She laughed uncontrollably—silently—her mind rocking with the absurdity, verging towards the hysterical. God, she was turning into that laughing sailor.

"*They do not believe you,*" said a voice chiming inside her head, a pre-pubescent boy's voice, each word ringing with the clarity of a cathedral-trained choirboy.

And a form appeared, bleached by the dazzling brightness of the chamber but recognizable nonetheless. A boy, human, ten, maybe twelve-years-old dressed in . . . it was difficult to see what he was dressed in—a smock, a gown—everything was so white and every edge smeared into its surroundings. He looked like a ghost. A spectral choirboy floating in a fog of dazzling white.

Louise sobered up instantly.

"Do *you* believe us?" asked Nick.

The boy avoided the question. "This language of yours," he said. "Why is it so important to you?"

The boy's lips moved out of sync. The edges of his clothes, his form, rippled and flowed behind him as though blown by a spectral wind.

"It's our method of communication," said Nick.

"Incorrect. You have other—more efficient—ways. Why is your preference for language?"

"We weren't aware of any other means."

"And yet you store memory in image format."

"Do we?"

"You do. Could it be that you store other memories in language for-mat—somewhere that we have yet to find?"

"You tell us."

"I am. You know that we have analyzed your memories and learned the mechanics of your language. But is there another layer to your language that we have overlooked?"

"How do you mean?"

"Your language has far more words than are necessary. Some words have identical meanings. Why? Could it be because there are several layers of information stored within? A technique for hiding knowledge as well as communicating it? If so, would it not make sense to engage you in conversation in order to look beneath the words?"

"Not if your conjecture is total rubbish," said Louise, unable to contain herself any longer.

"We shall see," said the boy. "You would do well to trust me. I am not like the others. Perhaps we can help each other. You say you want to leave here. That is not unreasonable to me. I want information. Perhaps we can trade. You tell me what I want to know and I will help you escape."

Louise jumped at the opportunity. "What do you want to know?"

"No, wait, Lou. We shouldn't rush into this. It could be a trap."

"But we've got nothing to hide!"

"I know that, but what if we get caught up in alien politics? We don't know anything about this . . . this new being."

"There is no trap," said the boy. "It is as dangerous for me to be here as it is for you."

"Come on, Nick, what have we got to lose?"

"I don't know—everything, nothing. There's nothing more we can tell anyone. Our new friend here might be some kind of plant to trick us. We could jeopardize the trial if we're not careful."

"What trial is this that you speak of?"

"We were told that we were suspected of murdering one of your colony. Isn't that right?"

"It is correct but there will be no trial. This is not the Earth of your . . . memories. A consensus for your guilt already exists. Did you not realize this? It is only a few individuals like myself who have prevented your disassembling. I am only here now because there are certain things that I need to know for myself. For the good of the colony, in the long run, whether they know it or not."

Disassembling . . . no trial . . . guilty. Words rained like poison arrows, but could they believe a word their new interlocutor said?

"You'll help us escape if we tell you all you want to know?" she asked.

The boy smiled, a strange otherworldly smile. "I will," he said, his lips not moving.

"Well, what do you want to know?"

"First I will put this affair in context. I note from images of previous meetings that you made a request to know what it was we were looking for in order to aid us in our search. I think that has merit.

Consensus disagreed—believing the less you knew the less tainted your answers would be—but consensus is not always right. It is a gamble, but perhaps the time for gambling is now upon us. The person you are accused of murdering was a friend of mine."

A warning light flashed inside Nick's head. They were being offered help by a friend of the victim?

"It was a close friend and colleague with, what you would call, an intuitive genius for its vocation."

"What vocation?" asked Nick.

"Xenobiology. It had an unequalled ability to understand—some would say empathize—with other species, particularly the more advanced corporeals."

Nick had a nasty feeling where this was going.

"Its work was groundbreaking," continued the boy, "but not without its critics."

"He had enemies?" asked Louise.

"It had detractors who thought its work violated the canon of separation that has protected our species since the beginning of the Isolation. They believe we should observe but not interact with other species."

"Where does torture fit in with noninteraction?" asked Louise.

"Your . . . detention is an extraordinary event. We . . . we are not used to having one of our number killed and, maybe, we have not handled this situation well. But we have little expertise in this matter. Crime is unknown to us and . . . we are learning."

"Go on," said Nick. "Your friend liked to interact with other species?"

"Indeed," said the boy, nodding his head slightly. "It would immerse itself in other cultures—maintaining that to truly comprehend another species one had to become one of them."

"It could do that?" asked Nick. "It could take on their shape and pass itself off as one of them?"

"It . . . it did not take on their shape as such. It . . . connected with them, the same way that you claim to have been connected to a corporeal entity."

"What happened to the host during all this?" asked Louise.

"The host was unharmed. My friend was acting as observer only. Albeit from inside the host's head but that was all. The host never lost free will or even knew that my friend was there."

"He didn't try and influence the host in any way?" asked Nick.

"We . . . we believe not. You must understand that my friend was a scientist. Its only motivation was to learn and it proved the efficacy of its techniques. We learned far more from its work than we'd ever learned from passive observance—even memory probing. It was—as you would say—the difference between watching a holovid of a zebra and being that zebra, tasting the grass, smelling the air."

Nick could imagine—as he could also imagine the temptation to switch from copilot to pilot. And this was an alien that specialized in advanced corporeals not zebras.

"So," said Nick. "What was he doing in our sector?"

"That," said the boy. "Is where things become confusing. My friend had been banished to a remote sensing station—it is easier to condone the flouting of rules if one does not have to witness their flouting—"

"Yes," said Nick, trying to hurry him along. "And then . . ."

"And then there is a gap. My friend suddenly left the research station and was next seen—dead—close to where you were found."

"What was the cause of death?" asked Nick.

"We do not know."

"But you must have some idea. Forensic evidence, an autopsy, something?"

"There . . . was no body—as such—we found a memory cloud, which is not unusual in such cases. Memories are difficult to destroy and often remain long after everything else has perished."

"Hang on," said Louise. "If you've got his memories, haven't you got the memory of his death as well?"

"There . . . there was no warning of death. When it came it must have been sudden and unexpected, destroying it unawares, for there are no recollections of danger."

"But it must show something," said Nick. "The reason for him leaving the station, if nothing else."

"It . . . is difficult." There was a catch in the boy's voice. And hesitance, maybe even embarrassment. He lowered his head for a second. "There . . . there are confusions."

"What kind of confusions?"

"You must understand, my friend had been . . . unwell. The prolonged physical connection to so many alien beings had . . . affected its mental well-being. We didn't realize the extent. My friend had always been . . . different. Many remarked that if there were two ways to solve a problem my friend would delight in finding a third. And the path to its solution would be bizarre, controversial, and brilliant."

The alien accompanied the final sentence with a sweep of his arms, revealing long loose sleeves that trailed and frayed in the spectral wind.

"But the memory patterns we found in the cloud, " he continued, "were . . . difficult to follow—especially towards the end. There are sequences that make no sense at all."

"Could he have become ill?" suggested Nick. "And died as a result?"

"Disease is a corporeal affliction. We do not experience it."

"Could he have committed suicide?" asked Louise.

"Impossible, my friend's final memories are dominated by intense feelings of elation."

"So what makes everyone so sure he was murdered?" asked Nick.

"Because there is no other explanation. It is the equivalent of you discovering the body of a young, healthy, well-fed man in the middle of a flat, lifeless desert."

And then finding two strangers wandering close to the crime scene. Nick joined up the dots—guilt by association and lazy logic. *Why look any further? The strangers done it.* The cry of lynch mobs throughout the ages.

"Have you discovered what it was that drew your friend away from his research station?" asked Nick.

"No . . . the station memory was erased."

"By whom?"

"There . . . there is evidence to suggest that my friend erased the entries."

"Why would he do that?" asked Nick.

There was a prolonged pause. Embarrassment? The boy's voice betrayed his reticence.

"There is some evidence of paranoia. But my friend had been banished; it was justified in its suspicion of Council interference . . ." The boy's voice trailed off.

"Would the Council have had him killed?" asked Louise.

"No!" The first hint of anger from the colonist. His image flared for an instant, blurring into the dazzling white of his surroundings. "The idea is unthinkable. My friend was held in the highest esteem even amongst the severest of its critics."

"Back to your friend's reason for leaving the research station," said Nick. "Have you determined how long ago that was?"

The boy bristled. "I begin to doubt the wisdom of this interview. All you have done is ask questions and attempt to pass the guilt onto others. This is not what I had envisioned."

He began to turn, floating rather than using his legs.

"We apologize," said Nick. "But I believe it possible that your friend visited our planet and, if so, I think it vital to find out why and when."

The boy turned back. "We found no evidence of that in your memories."

This was becoming hard going. The colonist had a very rigid way of looking at things. "That's because the possibility has only just occurred to us," said Nick. "Now, if you tell me when your friend left the research station maybe I can link that to an event on Earth that might have triggered it."

"Your nonexistent planet Earth?"

Lucky Louise was restrained, thought Nick. This would be about the time she looked around for the nearest length of two-by-four.

"Yes," said Nick. "It would help if you showed the same level of trust in me that I am placing in you."

"You have no understanding of the true measurement of time," said the boy. "Any figure I give you will be meaningless."

"Then take another look inside our heads," said Louise "and show us how clever you are by converting your measurements into ones we understand."

Nick could sense the gritted teeth surrounding Louise's words.

"Planetary rotations are arbitrary and prone to fluctuation."

"I only want to know if we're talking about days or years," said Nick. "I'm not looking for microsecond accuracy."

There was a pause and, perhaps, the merest hint of a resigned sigh. "I will scan collective memory for data on cosmic standards."

Nick waited, running through a list of potential events. Hiroshima, the first radio broadcasts, the first space flight, Voyager, SHIFT. Or would it be something small? Something accidental like the colonist just happening to scan a small patch of desert sky and receiving an unexpected burst of radio traffic . . .

"I have completed my calculations," said the boy. "My friend left the research station approximately four Earth years ago. The memory cloud was discovered nine days ago, three days before your arrival."

Four years. SHIFT launched its first unmanned space craft four years ago.

CHAPTER TWENTY-SEVEN

"You think this is tied to SHIFT?" asked Louise.

"Put yourself in the colonist's place," said Nick. "You're a scientist with an abounding interest in intelligent life and then suddenly one day a spaceship launches from the middle of a desert. Wouldn't you be interested?"

"So he drops everything and takes a look," said Louise. "That'd explain why he was there but what was he doing for four years? Was he on Earth all that time?"

"How long does it normally take for a body to degrade?" Nick asked the boy.

"It would depend upon the manner of its destruction but we would expect to find traces up to six years after the event."

"Six years? But you said he was only missing for four."

"We think that the killing took place elsewhere. You were concerned we would locate the body so you had the memory cloud moved from your colony to the desert area where it was found. Then you staged this elaborate subterfuge of falsifying your memories to make it look like you were fugitive corporeals from a nearby planet you named Earth. We are not that easily fooled. This Earth of yours will be a barren rock. Or worse, a trap."

Nick wasn't sure what to say. How can you argue with someone who regards your entire life a lie?

And there was something else. Something that had been worrying him for most of this conversation. An alien had visited Earth and shortly afterwards been killed. An unstable, paranoid alien who liked to hitch rides in people's heads—perhaps sometimes do a lot more than hitch rides. Wasn't he an accident waiting for an appointment with the U.S. military? Especially if he hung around the SHIFT project.

Which brought Nick to John Bruce and something else that was worrying him. The link between the alien and SHIFT, the damage to John Bruce's mind. Coincidence, or were they connected? Was the alien in Bruce's head during the SHIFT flight when the shielding failed? Was that how he died? Was Bruce ripped in two at the same time?

But . . . if the alien's body took six years to degrade—where was it?

"What if he's not dead?" asked Nick.

"That is not a possibility."

"Why not? All you've proven so far is how he couldn't have been killed. Why not follow up that line of thought with 'what if he's not dead'? Is there another way of creating a memory cloud?"

The boy sighed. "There is but we have dismissed the possibility."

"Why?"

The boy's image flared, impatience tinged his voice. "Because there would have been a warning attached."

"In his memories?" asked Nick.

"Yes."

"But you said yourself his memories were confused."

"In this circumstance they would not have been."

Nick felt like strangling the boy. "Why not?" he asked.

"Because jettisoning one's memories is not something undertaken lightly. It is the supreme sacrifice. A last resort which one would only contemplate if retaining those memories would jeopardize the existence of our colony. It is not something one does in a state of euphoria. It is something one does under threat of imminent capture and interrogation by a hostile, predatory species."

Like ours, wondered Nick. Then quickly stifled the thought.

"Couldn't it have happened by accident?" he asked. "If your friend was unstable couldn't he have pressed the wrong switch?"

"It is a complicated procedure. There is no switch."

"What if he 'went native'?" asked Louise. "Does that happen? If he liked to play inside the heads of corporeals and thought the Council might take that away from him, couldn't he wake up one day and say, 'Enough,' throw away his past, and start a new life."

"Impossible."

"Why?" asked Nick, his excitement building—thank you, Louise. "Wouldn't that explain his euphoria? His old life was one of banishment. He was feeling crippled, under threat, and then—suddenly—he sees a way out. Start a new life. It's classic psychology. My life sucks and it's everyone else's fault; so throw away all the bad memories and I'll be happy again."

"It is unheard of."

"But possible."

"My friend would not be so stupid." There was impatience in the boy's voice, and anger. Flecks of color—reds and pinks—suffused his image, flaring rhythmically. "It would know there would be no new life. Memory exhalation is not selective; it is all or nothing. If every memory was jettisoned then it could not function. It would be helpless with no idea who or what it was."

"It could learn. Especially if it was connected to another being at the time."

"No!" A sudden blush of dark red lined his image, spread inwards then dissipated. "I will not have this. My friend wouldn't . . ."

The boy went quiet, his image fading into the dazzling whiteout. Was he leaving or thinking? Nick prayed for the latter.

"What powers would he have?" asked Louise. "We know he can connect and disconnect and read minds. But what else could he do?"

"Nothing," snapped the boy, pulsing back into life. "Knowledge requires teaching. A being such as you describe would have no knowledge at all."

"Until he discovered them by accident," said Nick. "Trial and error is a powerful teacher."

"For lesser beings perhaps. I think conversing with you has been a mistake. I shall leave."

"Wait!" shouted Nick. "You came here looking for answers. We've given you one that you can check and if we're right your friend's alive. Can you turn your back on that?"

"You are only interested in confusing matters," said the boy.

"But what if we're right? Think about it. You can verify our story. Go to our home planet and take a look. If you're right you'll find nothing but a barren rock."

"And be killed like my friend?"

"Who by?" shouted Louise. "Look at us. If we're dangerous assassins why are we trapped here? Why haven't we killed any of you? We've had plenty of opportunity. And why haven't we escaped? Every time we've tried you've captured us easily. We're no threat."

"And we can help you find your friend. Think about it. You kill us and what have you achieved? Nothing. But what if your friend's still alive? Will consensus allow you to go and search for him or will they say, 'Keep away, it's too dangerous,' and go back to preaching isolationism and non-interference."

"Read our minds if you don't believe us," urged Louise. "Even if you think our earlier memories were grafted you have to believe what we're thinking now. We can help you. We want to help."

Nick felt a tingle inside his head. He opened his mind, attempting to project an aura of friendship and cooperation.

The silence grew. The boy's face remained impassive, unreadable, floating before them in silent judgement.

Then his image flared and doubled in size, his face looming towards them.

"I will take this gamble," said the boy. "If this Earth of yours does exit. If you can prove to me that your memories of a corporeal existence have not been fabricated . . . then . . ."

Nick waited—was the sentence ever going to end?

"*Then* you may go."

"Yes!" Louise's scream reverberated through every nook, cranny, and recess of Nick's mind. Was it really over?

"You will be restrained until then. Any attempt to escape or communicate with others of your kind will result in immediate termination of this agreement. Is that understood? I will not be taking chances."

"Understood," said Nick and Louise together.

"Then we shall leave now. I will have to flatline your life signs."

Nick was about to say, "What?" when everything went black.

Louise awoke in a panic. Where was everyone? Everything was black.

"We're cloaked," explained Nick. "To avoid detection. We can see out but no one can see us."

Stars appeared, and something else—a nebula? It filled half the sky. Thousands upon thousand of embedded stars floating in a wash of smoky pinks and reds. It was beyond magnificent.

And then it was gone. Back came the void, then a distant disc of blue and green. A planet? The Earth?

"Are we there?" she asked.

"*Not yet,*" said the colonist.

"Why are we here then?" asked Louise, growing concerned. "What planet's this?"

"*This is the quickest route to the coordinates we were given. Occasionally it passes through what you call 'physical space.' It is nothing to be concerned about.*"

The planetary disc receded to a tiny speck. Other specks grew and receded in turn. Other planets, other asteroids, other lumps of unsuspecting rocks. Then everything was gone. They were back in the void.

"Isn't this incredible?" said Nick. "We've been stepping back and forth like this for ages."

A light suddenly appeared. Dazzling. They were approaching a brilliant white star at speed. The star ballooning in size and luminosity, washing all other features from the rest of the sky.

"Shouldn't we turn?" she asked, wanting to throw a hand in front of her face and realizing for the first time that not only didn't she have any hands but she had no eyelids either. She couldn't close her eyes. She had to watch. The star getting closer and closer and . . .

A flash. White to black. The void. No, not the void. Deep space. Myriad twinkling stars surrounded them. One of them growing. Was this going to be another kamikaze run at a stellar mass?

A weak watery star turned from pinprick to small disc. Another disc, yellow and orange, spun towards them. A disc with rings. Lots of them.

Saturn? She stared at the planet, dredging back pictures from school books and holodocs. Was it Saturn? Wasn't there supposed to be a great white spot? Or was that Jupiter?

The void returned then back came the stars, one brighter than all the rest.

"*Your planet is the third, I think?*"

Before anyone could answer, the star disappeared—flash—then reappeared—flash. A cycle repeated several times, each time the star growing in size and intensity. They were stepping in and out of physical space in ten million league strides until . . .

Earth. It could be no other. A blue and white disc. Clouds and continents, oceans. They'd made it! They were home!

Emotion threatened to overwhelm her. "Thank you," she said. "Thank you."

"What do you want to see first?" Nick asked the colonist.

"One of the larger colonies—a city, I think."

"Okay, aim for that great blob of cloud and I'll direct you as we go."

"I will take a different route."

Was he really still suspicious? Surely he could see the Earth was a habitable planet? Couldn't he sense the radio traffic, the ring of man-made satellites?

They descended fast, tumbling towards the Atlantic then turning at the last second, zigzagging horizontally then flipping out of physical space altogether.

The colonist was definitely not taking any chances.

The sea appeared, its surface only a matter of feet beneath them as they skimmed over it at the speed of a small plane. It was exhilarating—even for Louise. A ribbon of grey appeared on the horizon. Land? Or a cloud? The ribbon grew and changed color—yellows, greys and greens. It *was* land. They veered towards it. A beach appeared, cliffs, a line of tall buildings, a town. Was this a large enough colony?

The colonist slowed and approached hesitantly. Below them, lines of waves threw themselves against a shelving beach of sand and pebbles. A handful of people were walking on the beach, more on the elevated promenade behind. Cars crisscrossed in the distance.

"That's our species," said Nick. "Just like our memories."

The beach disintegrated in a sudden rush of acceleration. Two faces loomed into vision: two people walking their dog. The colonist circled around them, zooming in and out in fast succession. The dog started barking. Had it seen them? It twisted around on its lead, jumping and barking, much to the annoyance of its owners.

And then it stopped, turned its head on one side, sniffed the air a few times and trotted off as if nothing had happened.

Louise felt a surge of unexpected emotion. Similar to the endorphin rush but different. Was it bleeding through from the colonist? And what was that emotion? It wasn't joy. It was like a wash of contentment or inner peace . . . was the colonist starting to relax and believe them?

Another tangential leap and they were flying up and over cliffs, past lines of hotels and offices, past roads and parks and cars and buses. A spark of recognition. Was this Bournemouth? It looked familiar. She'd holidayed on the South Coast a few times as a child.

The town ballooned in and out of focus. One second, they were flying high above the office blocks, the next, they were down at street level—nose to nose with a man, a woman, a child, a dog. Then they were inside a building, blurring through walls, pausing whenever something piqued the colonist's interest.

He had a lot of strange interests.

Electrical cables, for one. He liked them. Dogs were another—and they seemed to sense him too. Light fittings were a constant fascination. As were holoimages and goldfish. People were somewhere halfway down the list.

"*I have seen enough,*" he said.

"And?" Louise prompted.

"*I sense no danger here. This planet, these people . . . they accord with your memories. But I still need to see you connect and animate one of these corporeals.*"

Yes! The rest of the journey was lost on Louise. She was free! Or about to be any second. Roads and countryside flew by beneath her. She could hear Nick's words of navigation—intermittent *lefts*, *rights*, and *straight overs*. But they were only words. She was free. And she had a smile that stretched all the way to Saturn.

She was still smiling when they cleared the rectory's garden wall.

"Are you still with us, Lou?"

"I'm here," she said. But not for much longer. A few seconds more and she'd be reunited with her body. The Louise that she'd grown up with, the Louise that smiled back from morning mirrors and family snaps.

They passed through the apartment window. Slowing to a crawl as the colonist pushed them into the room. And let go.

"*You are now able to move.*"

Two bodies lay impassive on their beds, just as they'd left them.

"Thank God for that," said Nick. "I thought Adam might have had us moved to a hospital by now."

Louise hadn't thought of that. And she wasn't going to now. There'd be plenty of time to panic over what might have happened. In the meantime, nothing was going to spoil this moment. She was free and about to be reunited with a long lost friend.

Louise lined herself up with the top of her head. Hovered for a while, one last look at that peaceful, slow-breathing body. And then she descended. Slowly, carefully . . . successfully.

The world sprang into sharp focus. She could see, she could hear, she could move . . .

She could feel pain.

Ow! She'd tried to raise her head too quickly and her neck felt like it was attached to a lead weight. And her arms felt stiff. And her right leg had gone into spasm. Ow, ow, ow! She hopped off the bed, feeling slow and stiff. Instantaneous speed and graceful flight replaced by stuttering joints and a ponderous lurch.

She rubbed her legs and unclipped the remaining LSU leads. She felt like a giant awakening from a hundred-year sleep.

Nick didn't look any better, sitting opposite, bleary-eyed, stretching. She caught his eye and smiled. He smiled back and held out a hand.

"You'll have to help me up," he said. "I'm getting too old for this."

She pulled him up. "Can you hear us?" he asked, staring up at the ceiling.

"*I can hear you,*" came the reply, fainter than before but still unmistakably the colonist. And still originating from inside Louise's head.

"Can you sense your friend?" Nick asked.

"*No. This Earth of yours has a large population. Many signatures. I will return with help. You promised to help also.*"

"We will," said Nick.

"*Take this sign.*" An image burned inside Louise's head. The triangle within a circle. "*If you find anything, project this pictogram upwards into your atmosphere. Hold the image as long as you can and concentrate hard. If we see it, we will find you.*"

"What if you don't come?" asked Louise.

Silence.

"I think he's gone," said Nick.

Louise coughed. Her throat felt like sandpaper, she could murder a glass of water. And food too, she couldn't have had anything solid for—she checked her watch—a week! They'd been gone a whole week!

She stopped halfway towards the kitchen and ran back towards Nick, threw her arms around him and hugged him.

"We did it!" she said, a silly grin on her face. They were home and they were alive.

His arms closed around her and squeezed tight.

"Not all of it, Lou. The interesting part's just beginning."

CHAPTER TWENTY-EIGHT

Suzi Martinez had had enough. She hadn't joined the John Bruce campaign to be ignored and pushed around all day by that little pimp Arnie Fredericks. Who did he think he was? And what was a man like Bruce doing relying on a sleaze like Fredericks? There had to be a hundred better campaign managers.

She stomped along the fourteenth floor, head down and ready to snap the head off the first moron who smiled a good day at her. Vacuous Bible-bashers; the campaign was crawling with them.

To think she gave up a whole semester to work for Bruce. And for what? Did she get to talk to him, to discuss the great topics of the day, to put forward her ideas? She had so much to give and he'd seemed like the only candidate prepared to listen but she couldn't get near him. Arnie saw to that. More protective than a mother hen—shooing people away whenever Bruce looked like opening up.

What was it with that man? Was he jealous or something? Every time Bruce started to relax Arnie'd be in there pushing people out of doors, shoving them into corridors, and growling at them like some obsessive guard dog. Well, he wouldn't be doing that to her any more.

God, her father would make life hell when he found out. I warned you about that man, he'd say—all wagging fingers and father-knows-best. As though *he'd* never made a mistake. Now you get back to college, my girl, and pray they'll take you back. The hell she would. She had people to see first. People who would be very interested in what she had to say.

She knew things.

The elevator bell rang. She waited for the doors to open then stepped inside. It was empty except for the drone of Muzak and the holoback display. It must have been a shock, she mused, for the first person who stepped into one of these new elevators and found the entire back wall alive—a pseudo-holographic display that seemed to stretch back as far as the eye could see, as though the elevator was a doorway looking out on a silent woodland glade. She could see the wind moving through the trees, a deer grazing in a distant clearing. She wondered how many drunks had banged their heads trying to walk into the forest only to find a solid holoframe projector. And wasn't it a design flaw placing the display on the back wall? People always faced the doors.

She pressed the button for the lobby and watched the numbered lights descend. Behind her, something moved.

It ran along the forest floor, smoking and spitting, sending flames shooting up into the trees, running along their branches, charring the wood and curling their leaves.

Fire; swift, destructive, and silent, the wind whipping it from tree to tree, branches cracking, flaming brands falling on tinder-dry underbrush. An advancing line of fire surging across the ground like an incoming tide.

The Muzak played on, random riffs rising above the fire and smoke and the silent screams of the woodland fauna as they scurried for their holographic lives.

Suzi Martinez watched the eighth floor flash by, oblivious to the predatory tongue of virtual flame that flicked up and down her back.

By the sixth floor there was no woodland left. A black pall of death had descended. Smoldering trunks pointed skyward like charcoal fingers from a blackened palm. And the fire? Starved of fuel, the fire had spread underground, racing through the leaf mould, seeping through the layers of peat.

Searching . . .

The elevator slowed at the third floor as the deceleration program kicked in. Suzi felt the sudden pressure on the soles of her feet. Behind and below her, something moved—pushing out from beneath the forest floor into the metal structure at the base of the elevator. Fingers of cold flame tugged at the panels, explored the crevices, caressed the struts, and slid through—upwards—into the elevator floor. A tongue of flame curled around the heel of Suzi's left shoe, burnishing the soft shiny leather, caressing, waiting . . .

Two floors to go.

She didn't have time to scream. Or the oxygen to sustain it. A pillar of flame burst out from the floor with such speed that she was consumed within the flickering of a second. Her life extinguished in one hungry searing instant.

Behind what was left of her, the hologram forest awoke to a new cycle of life. Green shoots pushed through the forest floor, dancing into the daylight, their leaves unfurling. By the first floor young saplings towered above a dense underwood of shrub and fern. By the time the lift stopped, the forest floor was dappled beneath a canopy of mature oak and beech. Only the smouldering black corpse propped up against the elevator doors looked out of place.

Louise bit into the thick piece of toast and felt the hot butter run down her chin. Food. She'd forgotten how good it could taste . . . and feel . . . and smell. The tang of a mature cheddar, the gooey sensuality of a rich chocolate cake, the crunch of toast leading to that hot, yielding middle, the drool of melted butter. She could eat for the rest of the day.

"Lou," shouted Nick from the lounge. "I think you'd better come and see this."

Not yet, thought Louise, her eyes darting along the food shelves. Let me have one more minute of escapism. She threw a bag of peanuts onto the tray and a packet of biscuits—chocolate digestives. How could higher dimensional life forms exist without chocolate? Definitely an inferior species.

The two trays piled high with food, she took one in each hand and glided through into the lounge. Nick was staring at a holonews broadcast. Louise braced herself for the bad news.

"Another murder," he said. "Suzi Martinez, a campaign worker for John Bruce."

He let the newscast fill in the rest. Spontaneous combustion in an elevator, the police were calling it. The press took a more sensational line. *Republicans under fire. Assassin strikes again. Second slaying in a week. John Bruce seconds away from death.* Most of the media were convinced that Bruce had been the target; young Suzi had been in the wrong place at the wrong time. If Bruce hadn't stopped off at the cloakroom it would have been him getting into that elevator not Suzi.

Not that that stopped the tabloids from covering their pages with pictures of Suzi. She was young after all, and pretty, and dead. A heady mix. Suzi Martinez smiled and pouted from every e-news page across the globe.

"It's got to be the missing alien," said Nick. "He's latched onto Bruce and is killing anyone who gets in his way."

He could see it all. The alien exhales its memory, becomes a blank canvas, and—like a baby chick—latches onto the first thing it sees— John Bruce. What could be more natural? He was drawn to Earth by the early SHIFT flights. He had to have seen John Bruce. And it all fitted. Who else would feel so protective of John Bruce? Who else would have the ability to kill so . . . bizarrely? Who else would feel so threatened?

Imprinting—it had to be the answer. And couple that with paranoia, a penchant for the bizarre, and the gradual discovery of his alien powers and you had a recipe for a one-man killing machine ready to protect its "mother" from every threat—real or imaginary.

And he'd need to be part of John's team. Someone close. Part of his inner circle. Someone who saw John every day.

Louise stopped chewing. "Why would he kill a campaign worker?"

Nick shrugged. "Because she saw something she shouldn't? Or maybe to throw suspicion off Bruce. If our colonist friend plans to kill off every one of Bruce's rivals he's got to do something to make Bruce look innocent."

Louise cut herself a chunk of cheese. She was going to enjoy this meal. "Couldn't we talk about something else?" she said. "It would be nice to have five minutes without thinking about death."

"Shall I set my watch?"

"Only if it's slow. Aren't you hungry?"

She looked at his tray. He hadn't touched his food. His hand still clutched the HV remote. What was the matter with him? Didn't he want to relax? They'd just come back from a week in hell. If anyone deserved a break it was them.

He smiled, but not with his eyes. "Ten minutes," he said, then bit into a slice of toast and started flipping channels on the HV.

Louise tuned them out, *let the world wait for me for a change. I'm busy.*

❖   ❖   ❖

Nick checked Bruce's itinerary again. There *was* time. If they moved fast. He glanced at Louise. She looked so happy, leaning back against the box, licking crumbs off her face.

"What?" she said. "Have I got chocolate all over my face?"

"No," he smiled. "You look perfect."

He looked away and quickly changed the subject. "John's in Florida today."

"Oh, yes," she said, reaching out and taking another biscuit.

"In Orlando. I've got his itinerary here if you want to take a look. Just the one engagement. I've memorized the map."

She put the biscuit down.

"You're not thinking of going there, are you? Today? We've only just got back."

"Which is why there isn't much time. Think about it. The colonist is on his way back to his people. How long's it going to take him to collect some friends and come back? Have you thought what's going to happen next?"

Nick had. He'd thought about little else since their return.

"He'll look for his friend," said Louise, narrowing her eyes.

"And how will he do that? The truth is, Lou, we have no idea what's going to happen when he returns. He might not even be allowed to return. Consensus might say, 'No, we don't want to interfere, it's against our isolationist principles.' Or they might take several years to make up their minds. Or worse still, they turn up in force. Have you thought what might happen to the world if a couple of thousand Colonists descend upon us?"

Louise looked worried. "Wouldn't they have sensors? Wouldn't they just locate their friend and leave?"

He threw up his hands. "You tell me," he said. "The truth is, we haven't a clue. They might do just as you said. Or they might conduct a mass interrogation. You saw what it was like up there. Do you want to trust your future to them? And what if our alien friend gets wind of their arrival and escapes . . . or hides. The Colonists could be here for years."

"So, what's your plan?"

"Finish what we started. Get John Bruce back together."

"How does that help us with the Colonists?"

"It doesn't," he said, sighing, "but it does get rid of one problem. And it might stop the killing. If you're right about John being at heart apolitical then maybe he'll drop out of the election and if he does, the alien will have no need to clear John's path for him. And if we don't act now, who knows when we'll get another chance? We might be trapped inside a colonist interrogation chamber tomorrow."

Louise glanced towards the window. "It's too late to do anything today. It's afternoon. It'd be dark by the time we got to Florida. And how the hell do we get John away from Pendennis?"

"Florida's five hours behind—plenty of time to get there and back."

"And Pendennis?"

"I have a plan . . ."

"You had a plan last time. Hypnotize Peter. It didn't work."

"That's because I didn't take into account his other personalities. I realize that now. I have to hypnotize them all . . ."

She shook her head. "Won't work. Jack can't be hypnotized."

"Which is why I've come up with Plan B."

"What's Plan B?" she said, slitting her eyes.

He told her.

"No way!" she said, sitting up.

"But it'll work. I know it."

"You don't know anything of the kind. What . . ." She looked lost for words, lost for words and desperate. "What . . . what if Peter's the alien? He's powerful enough. And mad enough."

"You've changed your tune."

"And so've you. Last week you were convinced Peter was behind everything."

"That was last week. Look, Lou, what do we know about this alien? He's a scientist. A rule-bending, obsessed scientist with a streak of curiosity a mile thick and a love of the unusual. I know the type. I *am* the type. He's drawn to Earth by the early SHIFT mission and he sticks around. Hence the link to John Bruce. He's drawn to the man."

"Couldn't he *be* the man? Wouldn't that explain John's personality change? In which case we don't want to go within a million miles of John. Why don't we call the Colonists now and get *them* to check?"

"We've been through this, Lou. And anyway, the alien's not John Bruce. Think about it. The alien's a body-hopper. It's his MO. One person wouldn't be enough for him. He'd want to know what it's like to be everyone else."

"How can you *know* that? You're just projecting your own personality onto his."

"Maybe, but we know he body-hops. Think about it. Bruce couldn't have killed that burglar or Karen, he'd have been seen leaving his hotel or boarding a plane. Presidential candidates get noticed especially when the press camp outside their doors. Far easier for the alien to disconnect from his host, cross the Atlantic out of body, then search for a new host."

He could see it all. All the alien had on Nick was a name and address—the college—so he called there, asked to see Professor Stubbs and got referred to the Hall. When he arrived he surprised a burglar who, not unnaturally, made a run for it. The alien takes that as a sign of guilt, chases after him, and kills him.

Louise interrupted Nick's monologue. "Why didn't he read the burglar's mind?"

"Maybe he did," said Nick. "But as we found out, the Colonists don't always trust what they find. And this one's unstable and paranoid. So he kills the burglar convinced he's me. Then he thinks to himself, 'What if this Stubbs guy ain't working alone?'"

Louise raised her eyebrows. "The alien thinks with a New Jersey accent?"

Nick smiled back. "My alien does. Anyway, he comes up with a new plan—your plan. He cuts up the corpse and places body parts where they'll be found. Some at the college, some at my home. Covering all the bases. Anyone else in the Stubbs gang can't fail to see the warning. Mess with John Bruce and this'll be you."

"The Stubbs gang?"

"The meanest, orneriest gang west of the Pecos—wherever they are."

"So," said Louise, taking up the commentary. "Our alien disconnects and leaves one confused host wondering where the hell he is and where all the blood came from."

"Exactly. And let's hope he didn't bother to wear gloves. Not that I want the unfortunate host charged with murder but a bloody fingerprint not belonging to me or the victim would be a lifesaver."

"You think that's possible?" said Louise, brightening.

"I think it probable. I can't see our alien caring about putting on gloves. He's bound to have left traces. And then—back on story—off flies our alien only to find that the evil Professor Stubbs is not only alive but querying SHIFT again about Bruce's brain scans. So back he comes and during a search of my house he finds a name—yours—and panics."

"Why?"

"Because he's been inside John Bruce's mind. He sees the name Louise Callander on my fridge door and thinks, 'Shit, Stubbs is delving into John's past.'"

"But why did he mistake Karen for me? If he's been in John's head he'd know we don't look anything like each other."

"He'd only know what you looked like as a schoolgirl. As John remembers you. He wouldn't know what you looked like now. And, anyway, he's paranoid and unstable, you could have had plastic surgery and a memory graft."

Louise looked down at her feet.

"It's equally possible he realized she wasn't you," said Nick, softening his voice. "And killed her because she couldn't tell him where you were. I don't think he needs much of a reason to kill."

She turned towards him, her eyes misted over. "You don't know if one word of what you've just said is true," she said, quietly. "You don't even know if the alien's still on the planet."

"But we can find out, Lou. He'll be part of Bruce's inner circle. Once we've got John back together again we'll ask him if he's noticed members of his team complaining about unexpected blackouts, sleepwalking, or memory loss. Then we contact the Colonists, give them a nice small number of suspects to check out, and let them get on with it."

"What if the Colonists don't come?"

"Then we have a problem. But that's tomorrow's problem. Let's concentrate on today's."

CHAPTER TWENTY-NINE

Nick glanced at Louise as he clicked the last LSU connector home. Should he tell her or keep his concerns to himself?

Only one answer. He had to keep her focussed. Doubt was a luxury for people who had the time to do something about it.

And it wasn't as though he had any proof.

But it was a concern. When they'd been stuck in Pendennis's head, Peter had known about the LSUs, and their fears of a John Bruce presidency. How? Could he access their thoughts, their memories?

And how much could he access? Surface thoughts or everything?

If the latter then their entire plan was blown. They needed to know if they were talking to John or Peter but if Peter had access to all of John's memories . . .

Nick refused to believe it. He'd gone over their incarceration in Peter's head and there was plenty Peter hadn't known. Okay, he could have been playing a game but Peter had always referred to Nick as "doctor." Why? The only logical reason was that that's who Peter thought he was. A new member of the medical staff. The only time they'd met was during Peter's last regression—when he'd bitten Louise's ear—and they'd never been introduced.

And Peter was a manipulator—if he'd had access to all their memories he'd have used them, constructed a custom-built hell to press all their buttons. Which he hadn't, or else he'd have known that the threat

of psychic surgery was not the way to get to Nick. Spiders or wasps—
yes. In a heartbeat. But psychic surgery—never. He knew too much
about it. He'd helped expose the scam artists who still practiced it.

Which meant it had to be unguarded thoughts Peter was picking
up.

And made their mission to free John even more time critical. Every
second they delayed was an opportunity for Peter to learn more about
John.

It was time. They flowed out the window and over the garden wall.
They scudded along lane and track, over field and spinney; found the
ley and blurred everything else into a streak of watery color. Speed
and determination. This time they were going to succeed. This time
they had to.

Upper Heywood sprawled beneath them, its white walls shimmering in the afternoon sun. They swooped down, Nick taking the lead,
lining up the reception doors, and gliding through. Louise followed,
dropping down to floor level, slowing all the time. They flowed along
the corridor, passing through the legs of warders and cleaners, turning left and right, getting closer and closer until . . .

They stopped.

"Are you ready, Lou?" Nick asked.

"Ready," she said, steeling herself.

"Plan B then. It's straight down the corridor, take the second right
then first door on your left and . . . good luck."

Luck would have nothing to do with it. She set off, floating along
the corridor, imagining herself a warship sailing along a sea of white
corridors. She was impenetrable, invincible, and drawn up for battle.

"Jack," she whispered, soft and drawn out like a dying breath.

"Jack," she repeated, casting her voice ahead like a soughing wind
rustling through the topmost trees.

"Jack."

Almost there. She could see the cell door. She stretched towards it,
touched its metal surface, and slowly, ever so slowly, pushed through.

The cell appeared. Pendennis was on the bed, lying on his side, his
face turned towards the wall.

"Jack," she whispered, concentrating on Peter's head and thinking
her voice inside it.

"Jack, wake up. I'm looking for you. I'm in your museum. The one
where you met Peter when he was six years old."

She floated closer to the bed. How close did she have to get?

"Jack," she urged. "I'm here, waiting, where are you?"

Closer still. The bed only a few feet away.

"Jack . . ."

She stopped dead. Somewhere, someone was laughing. A distant, echoing, sound—as though heard through a ventilation grill in an old abandoned house when the sound and Louise were several floors apart.

Was it getting louder? Should she move closer?

"Jack," she called. "I'm waiting."

And in that instant, reality buckled. The room, Pendennis—both disappeared. And in their place, a museum stuttered into life.

Louise reacted immediately. As soon as her body materialized she clad it in armor: lightweight and flexible, its atoms fused together like diamond. A mirrored visor protected her eyes—Jack was not going to hypnotize her—and her gloved hands closed around a baseball bat studded with razor blades.

She flexed her knees, raised the club two-handed and called out:

"Bring it on, sailor boy."

The last of the overhead lights flickered into life but shadows still remained. There were no windows in the museum and the only door, the one behind Louise, was closed.

She peered into the gloom. The layout had changed. The laughing sailor exhibit was no longer by the door. She glanced left and right. Everything else looked the same.

"Come on, Jack," she called out. "What are you frightened of?"

No answer. Not even a howl of wind from outside like last time. But the smell was the same. Stale and musty. She moved away from the door, still flexed, still ready to lash out at the first sight of navy blue.

She went left, her eyes flicking from exhibit to exhibit, her ears hypersensitive. He had to be somewhere.

Then she saw it—side-on—the display case, *Jolly Jack Tar, The Laughing Sailor*. She closed on it, changing her grip on the bat to swing from the left. And stopped. The case was empty. The glass panel at the front was smashed. She swung round, expecting a trap, instinctively ducking and crouching low.

Nothing was behind her.

He had to be hiding. There were so many dark nooks and crannies in between the machines—or even behind the machines. She thought *light* and a cone of light shot from the top of her helmet. Nothing was going to stop her.

"Jack," she called. "Come on out and play. I'm waiting."

Feet scurried in the distance. It had to be Jack. Coming from the museum's right-hand bay. Louise swung round and raced back towards the door. Invulnerable, she told herself. I can't be hurt, I can't be deflected.

The sound grew louder, tiny feet skittering over the floor. Louise reached the right-hand bay and turned. Nothing visible. He was hiding, maybe to the left, maybe to the right. She stopped and scanned both walls, turning up the intensity of her beam. Nothing. No, wait . . . there *was* something. A painted mirror on the back wall. Or was it a window? Whatever it was, Jack was there, his twisted face smiling out from behind the glass. She advanced, bat held high. The sailor's image didn't move. She started to run, winding up her shoulders, ready to put everything into one devastating swing. Five yards, three, swing and . . . smash! The glass shattered, shards everywhere. A solid wall behind. And no Jack. It must have been an image etched in the glass.

Laughter. From behind. Louise started to spin around but something fastened onto the back of her left leg. Jack. She looked down. The sailor had wrapped himself around her armored leg and clamped his teeth to her thigh.

She swung down with the bat but Jack was too close. She couldn't swing hard enough. She changed grip, grabbed the bat like a kayak paddle, and stabbed down with it two-handed—once, twice, three times—hard onto the top of Jack's head.

He didn't even flinch. He stuck there, arms and tiny legs wrapped around her leg, his teeth . . . she could actually *feel* his teeth. Even through her armor!

She hit him harder. Again and again. No effect. She spun around, smashing Jack and the back of her leg against the edge of the nearest exhibit. He still wouldn't budge.

Pain shot up from her thigh. His teeth on her skin. Her armor must have given way. She threw down the bat, grabbed hold of Jack's head, and pulled . . . and twisted; thinking *strength, give it to me, as much as there is. Now!*

Jack's sailor hat ripped away in her hands but his head stayed clamped and . . . she could feel something else . . . something coming out of Jack's mouth, something sharp, something solid, pushing into her thigh. It had to be several inches long.

No! She fastened her hands around Jack's head, twisting and pulling. The pain in her leg increased. Part of Jack was now inside her—a splinter, a tongue, six inches long—and every pull on his head twisted the splinter like a knife in the wound.

Think, Louise, think! She was losing feeling in her left leg. Her thigh turning to wood, that "thing" penetrating deeper.

Flame, she thought. Emulating Nick, fire shot from the fingers of both hands. She focussed the flame, turning it from yellow to searing blue, making it hiss and roar. Then turned it on Jack, twisting her body around and sending ten jets of flame searing down on the sailor's head.

His head blackened. So did her armor. And pain . . . that thing inside her—white hot now and pushing further inside, up her leg and beyond.

No! She pushed more power into the jets from her hands. Jack crackled and peeled . . . but never let go. Charcoal Jack smouldered and clung on. Smoke everywhere, the smell of burning wood and flesh.

No! She'd lost all feeling below the waist, she was losing balance, teetering, about to fall. Think, Louise, think!

Air, she thought. I'm no longer solid; I'm a gas, inert and free. Let Jack try and grab hold of that.

She began to fade, but not her legs. *Come on*, she cried, concentrating hard, imagining herself tugging at that intricate lattice of matter—the cells and molecules and smaller still—pulling and stretching at the very fabric of her being—teasing everything apart, distending her legs from solid into gas.

Free!

She flew to the ceiling, spread out, flattening herself against the cracked plaster and paint. And looked down. Charcoal Jack blinked up at her, the whites of his eyes shining out against his blackened skin . . . and that "thing" . . . that twisted tongue that protruded some eighteen inches from his mouth.

He flexed his legs. Was he going to jump? Should she be looking into his eyes?

She shot along the ceiling, back towards the door then dived down, turning and materializing at the same time. She landed on armor-clad feet. The same armor as before but this time coated in a protecting flame. Let Jack try and sink his little wooden teeth into that.

She ran at him, her razor-tipped baseball bat reappearing in her hands. He laughed, white teeth pushing through the cracking black mask. Jack was regenerating, and growing, new paint pushing through the crumbling charcoal husk.

Not quick enough, Jack, thought Louise. And she swung, swinging from her shoulders, swinging from her biceps, bringing her wrist in at the last second and willing that bat to not only hit Jack but to go straight through him.

He tried to duck but the bat caught him on the back of his head. Louise lost her balance on the follow through, tumbled into Jack, tripped over him, kicking at him as his little hands grabbed at her legs. She fell, rolled over, and came up swinging. Jack danced away from the blows. What did it take to knock him out?

She threw away the bat, stared at her right hand—*chain saw*—then at her left—*glue hose*. Both hands morphed immediately, smoke shot from the revving chain saw exhaust, the other hand she aimed at Jack.

"What do you think this is going to be, Jack? Fire? Can your little brain feel fear?"

Jack threw back his head and roared. He didn't care. There was nothing inside him *to* care. Now, thought Louise, unleashing a jet of milky liquid—wood glue—first at Jack's mouth, then at his feet. Dance your way out of that, Jacky boy.

She lunged at him with the chain saw. He ducked from the waist but his feet had stopped moving. Her next swing connected. The chain bit, vibrating up through her arm, throwing up a stream of sawdust from Jack's neck. She had him!

He kept laughing, even when the chain saw took off his head and sent it rolling across the floor. A little hand grabbed for Louise's arm; she pulled away and brought the chain saw down hard on Jack's right shoulder. She'd lop off his arms and legs, dice him up, and feed the remains into a shredder if necessary. Nothing of him was getting away this time. Nothing!

She sliced and diced. Jack's laughter roared louder. She looked up. His head was growing another body; tiny legs had sprouted from his neck. He was running away. She aimed a glue jet at him but missed as he dashed behind one of the machines.

More laughter came from behind her. And to the sides. Jack was regenerating. All the pieces of Jack were regenerating. Even the shavings. She spun on the spot, spraying glue in an arc. There were thousands of little Jacks. All of them sprouting little mouths, all of them laughing.

She turned the floor white around her, miring as many as she could. But there were so many of them, running behind the machines, up the walls, across the ceiling. They were like ants, hundreds of insane laughing ants.

She sprayed the walls and the slot machines but couldn't keep up. They were dropping on her from above. Hundreds of them. She turned up the flames on her armor; singed them, blackened them, but still they moved—crawling and nibbling.

A tingling, tickling sensation shot from her right wrist just above the join with the chain saw. She looked down. Her wrist armour was rippling, crawling. He was inside her. Jack. Hundreds of him. The sawdust from the chain! It must have carried him inside her.

Panic. Her arm alive. *Air*, she thought. *Air now!*

She evaporated and shot to the ceiling but had Jack come with her? Was he still inside her—hundreds of tiny cuttings of Jack?

She span, thinking *tornado,* thinking *centrifugal force,* thinking *spin that thing out of me!*

She shot along the ceiling back towards the door, a spinning tornado turning right and right again into the other bay. Then stopped, she needed time to think. What kills wood? Rock, paper, scissors, what? Behind her the laughter grew . . . and the skittering. There had to be an army of Jacks racing towards her—over the floor, the walls, the ceiling.

Think, Louise, think! Acid, fire, what?

Termites, beetles, dry rot. But how could she use them? If she turned herself into a termite she'd bring Jack inside her again.

The navy blue tide swept towards her. She dropped to the floor, taking on human shape again but thinking *granite,* thinking *solid, eyeless, fissureless granite.* She'd wait him out, wait him out until she came up with a plan.

Laughter—muffled but growing. They were climbing all over her. Even through the rock she could sense their tiny feet.

An idea. Could she project her will? There was so much wood in the museum—the floorboards, joists, panelling, even the exhibits. She focussed upon them, imagined them crawling with beetles and dry rot, tendrils of fungus running through the entire structure, termites nibbling up through the floor joists, pushing into the door.

She formed two eyes of transparent quartz in her granite head, used rock hands to clear them of swarming Jacks, and started to run, her feet thundering over the vibrating floorboards. She saw the door, imagined it crawling with termites, and ran towards it. She'd wedge herself against it and trap as many Jacks as she could between her and the termite-infested door.

She pressed against the door and hoped. Time passed. Was it working? Wedged against the door, she could barely see a thing. She turned her entire body into crystal and shrank inside it. A tiny Louise standing in the stomach of a glass giant, spinning around to see what was happening around her.

The tiny Jacks *were* being eaten but others were growing—six, seven, eight feet tall and one of them was advancing on her with a sledgehammer.

She grew back into the solid quartz Louise and turned. She'd fight them to a standstill and beyond. Whatever Jack could do, she'd match. With interest.

She blocked the swing of the sledgehammer with her left arm and threw herself at the giant Jack, pushing him back against and through a test-your-strength machine.

High score.

"Come on!" she shouted. Something be in the wood. Something come out and take a bite out of Jack.

A door materialized in the wall to her left. It juddered opened, pushing one of the slot machines to the side. Nick appeared.

"This way!" he shouted. "Come on, you've done it."

Had she?

She let go of Sledgehammer Jack and fought her way towards the door, clubbing and shoving and kicking. Could it really be over? Plan B. *Jack can't be hypnotized but he can be distracted. That's your job: keep Jack busy while I take care of the others.*

And extricate John.

Her John. Was he now free?

A rotten floorboard gave way under her left foot. She sank with it, her left foot dropping eighteen inches. Several Jacks piled on top of her. So close. The door was only yards away. She couldn't fail now. She thought *water*, she thought *fountain*, she thought *through that door*.

Then she was flying, a jet of water rising from the shattered floorboard and arcing up and over Nick's head.

She'd made it.

Somewhere behind her a door slammed shut, and around her a white-walled cell materialized. She was out.

Louise moved swiftly away from Pendennis's bed. A small cloud joined her in the middle of the cell. Only the one small cloud?

Panic. "Where's John? Didn't you get him out?"

"Not here, Lou. We'll talk in the corridor. Follow me."

She followed, through the wall and out into the main corridor. There was something twenty, thirty yards away. A smudge, a mirage—was it John?

She rushed past Nick. It had to be John. A small cloud of fuzzy lights.

"John," she said. "It's Louise. Is that you?"

He didn't answer. She turned to Nick. "What's . . ."

"He can't hear anyone but me," said Nick. "I thought it safer. Which is why I brought him well away from Peter and Jack."

Relief. And surprise—when had Nick learned how to play it safe?

"Okay, John," said Nick. "Can you hear me?"

"Yes," came the sleepy reply.

"Louise is going to ask you a few questions. You can hear her voice now. Go ahead, Lou."

She questioned him thoroughly, listening to both the answers he gave and the way he gave them. It had to be John.

"Ask him about his teachers at school," said Nick interrupting.

Louise was surprised. She'd already asked seven questions. How many more did he want?

She questioned John about their school. Asked him to list as many teachers as he could and the subjects they taught. His memory was better than hers. Several she'd forgotten until John's description brought them back into memory.

"Now ask him about the house he lived in. And his family."

She complied, straining to remember enough details then resorting to asking questions about John's teenage music collection.

"Anything more?" she asked Nick, wondering if there was something he wasn't telling her.

"No," he replied. "I've heard enough."

"Okay, final question from me then John. Do you ever want to be President?"

John laughed. "Me? President? I'm a flyer, Lou. That's all I've ever wanted to be."

She turned to Nick, jubilant. "That's John."

CHAPTER THIRTY

It was Nick's turn. Out-of-Body Flight Training 101.

"Okay, John," said Nick. "Follow me just like you did before. Remember, we're in a simulator. We're not really passing through the ceiling. It's just the tech guys' idea of fun."

Nick rose slowly, watching John all the time. The small cloud started to follow.

"Up we go," said Nick, "through the roof and . . . out into the sky. Notice the 360-degree, all-round vision. It takes some getting used to but imagine the advantage it'll give our pilots in aerial combat."

So far so good. John was hovering a few meters above the Upper Heywood roofline.

"Now, let's take the new fly-by-wire system through its paces. Remember, the system's set up to react to your thoughts. You think where you want to be, and the software does the rest. You got that?"

"Roger that."

Roger indeed, Nick wondered if he should adopt a call sign. Tango Charlie something, or Wing Co. or Mad Dog . . .

"How about Rasputin?" suggested Louise.

So much for shielding his thoughts. "Okay, John, we're going to start now. See that hazy cloud moving in front of you?"

"Yes."

"That's my plane. Apologies for the crap visuals but the tech guys haven't gotten around to that yet. But imagine it's an enhanced F-84 and you're my wingman. Everywhere I go, you go. And remember you don't have to worry about G-forces, how fast you go, or how tight a turn you throw. The system's set up with inertial dampeners. All you've got to do is fix your sights on me and follow. Got that, John?"

"Copy that, wing leader."

"Okay, I'm going to start off slow, throw in a few practice turns, and see how we go."

Nick pulled away at a fast walking pace. John tucked in behind and to the left. Louise took the right. Three hazy clouds sliding along the Upper Heywood roof and then accelerating, gaining altitude, swinging left then right, up then over.

It was working.

"Okay, John, I'm going to start taking this baby through its paces. See if you can hang on."

He accelerated away, blurring Upper Heywood into the distance but flying higher than he usually did, away from the distractions of houses and trees, giving John as uncomplicated a maiden flight as he could.

Ahead, the Michael and Mary lines gilded the horizon in gold and flame. He swung towards them, maintaining his altitude, carving a long, sweeping turn until they were all pointing southwest. He slowed to check on John, wondering how long he'd stay under. Would the excitement of the flight cause the hypnotic bond to weaken? Or would it be therapeutic—John thinking he was back behind the controls of a plane after eighteen months of hell?

"Still keeping up, John?" he asked.

"Still waiting for you to show me some speed, sir."

Nick accelerated.

"This is not a race," hissed Louise. "If we lose John . . ."

"Don't worry about me, Lou," said John. "I've been doing this all my life."

Below them, the leys snaked off to the horizon like a braided molten river. Intersections came and went—Glastonbury, Avebury—and then others they hadn't seen before. New territory. Beyond their usual turn off to the rectory apartment, the Michael and Mary lines stretched all the way to Land's End, passing through the Cheesewring and St. Michael's Mount. He wondered what they'd be like. As spectacular as Avebury? Something new?

And what would the lines do at Land's End? Stop? Plunge into the sea? Shoot off across the Atlantic at wave height?

He hoped for the latter. A ley line highway all the way to America. The lines would pass just south of the Florida Keys if they maintained the same trajectory.

Time for another check on John. He slowed. "How's it going back there?"

"Like a Sunday afternoon stroll in the park."

Nick picked up the pace, skimming over moors and patchwork farms, straining to see the first line of blue on the southern horizon.

And there it was, sweeping in from the left. Mount's Bay and the Channel. And there was St. Michael's Mount, rising out of the bay like a fairy tale castle carved out of rock. A fairy tale castle only accessible at low tide.

Unless you could fly.

The leys separated. One disappeared to the right, the other headed straight for the island. They followed the latter, tumbling down the headland, over the painted cottages in their pastel blues and pinks, over the long, wide shelving beach, and across the narrow stretch of water to the mount. The ley rose on the other side. They rose with it, climbing the almost sheer cliffs and the stone slab walls of the priory that sat astride the summit.

Up and over they went. A second ley burst out of the cliff wall on the other side. The companion line—it must have travelled the last few miles underground. The two lines plunged seaward in a sinuous embrace and then turned, setting a parallel course along the bay's shallow seabed towards the next headland, looking like two shimmering torpedo trails. Magical.

Nick raced across the bay, dropping to a few feet above the waves. Below him the two leys shimmered and rippled along the seabed, their brilliance tempered by five, maybe ten fathoms of murky water.

The leys dipped and dived, split and converged. Then rose—leaping out of the sea in tandem like spawning salmon—up, up and over the headland, pushing the sea behind them, embracing the greens and browns of field and woodland.

Nick followed, tying himself to the line on the left. Its sister line veered off to the right. But not far. Nick could see it flashing through the treeline like a necklace of setting suns, paralleling their course for a mile or two before sweeping back to join its companion. The two lines entwined then suddenly . . . disappeared.

Nick stopped. They were on the edge of a cliff. But not any cliff. They were standing on the edge of the world. Or so it appeared.

"Is that cloud?" asked Louise.

He wasn't sure. It could be spray but that was impossible. If this was Land's End the sea had to be more than two hundred feet below and if it was fog why only here? Why not back in Mount's Bay or over the headland?

He stared at the sight. It was like standing at the top of Niagara Falls except this wasn't a river cascading over the cliffs but two leys. Could they have caused this? Was this higher dimensional spray sent roiling into the atmosphere as the leys plunged into the Atlantic?

He looked along the cliff line. It was difficult to pick out through the mist but they were on a promontory between two bays. Two bays lapped by cloud, no ocean anywhere in sight. He looked down. The leys followed the cliff face in a vertical plunge for ten, twenty feet and then disappeared into a shifting, billowing cloud so dense that even their light was consumed.

"We need to talk," said Louise. "Off air."

"This'll be local, Lou. I can't see it stretching right across the Atlantic."

"It's not that, Nick. It's something else."

She sounded worried.

"Okay, John, we're going to pause the simulation for five minutes to check some readings. You'll use this time to rest and won't hear anything until I say 'Westward ho.' Now what is it, Lou?"

"Have you felt anything?" she asked. "Like we're not alone?"

"We aren't alone. We've got John with us."

"No, it's more than that. Can't you feel it? It's like someone's watching us. It's the same feeling I had when we first met the Colonists."

Panic. He found himself scanning through the fog, back along the leys, above, below. Had the Colonists returned to look for their friend?

Or was their friend already here? Was he waiting in the mist?

He backed away from the cliff edge.

"How long have you had this feeling?" he asked.

"From the moment we stopped."

"Not before?"

"No. Can't you feel it?"

He couldn't. Could he? He cleared his mind . . . waited . . . and waited. Nothing. Not even the slightest sense of foreboding.

"It'll be this place, Lou. This'll be the first time you've stood at an intersection of two leys."

It had to be that. The feeling of not being alone. The feeling of presence, of spirit. The same feeling that brought ancient man to these places, that drove him to locate his temples here . . .

"But don't *you* feel anything?" asked Louise.

"It affects people differently. You feel a sense of presence; I'm bowled over by the view. Look at it, Lou. Isn't it just like standing on the edge of the world staring into the abyss? Can't you picture some ancient druid pausing here and looking over the edge just like we're doing now and wondering whether to follow the leys down into the bowels of the underworld?"

"You're not suggesting we go down there?" said Louise.

"Why not? It might cross the Atlantic. It might stop off at Lyoness or Atlantis or—"

"You are unbelievable! An hour ago you were telling me how time critical everything was. How we had to get John to Florida before the Colonists came back. Now you want to swan off to look for Atlantis!"

She had a point.

"Let's take a look over this spray," he said, focussing on a small cumulus cloud overhead and pulling himself towards it. Almost immediately a deep blue line appeared above the spray, growing with every meter he ascended and pushing along the horizon to the north and east. The Atlantic. It *was* there. The fog or spray or whatever it was was a purely local phenomenon, stretching a few hundred meters either side of the ley. Beyond that, rugged granite cliffs tumbled into the sea. A serrated coastline of promontories and small coves stretching from—if his memory served him correctly—Land's End itself, a mile or so to the north down to Carn Guthensbras a mile to the south.

And below shimmered the ancient hill fort of Carn les Boel, the westernmost edge of the great Michael and Mary Line.

He scanned out to sea. Did the line continue? If it did he couldn't see it, not even the faintest outline shone up from the seabed.

"Shall we fetch John?" asked Louise.

"Yes," he said, already diving.

Arnie Fredericks switched holovision channels for the nineteenth time in as many minutes. This time it was the WCN anchor analyzing the latest polls from the slew of Super Tuesday states. Arnie watched, looking and listening for every nuance and spin as the numbers were compared and dissected. Suarez was well in front, no surprise in that, but John still had a chance. His numbers were coming back. Not as fast as Arnie would have liked but they were coming back.

The anchor agreed.

"The polls conducted since the death of Suzi Martinez show a marked swing towards Bruce. Do you think that's a sympathy vote, Craig, or can Bruce build from here?"

The anchor faded to be replaced by the head and shoulders of the youthful and slightly windswept political correspondent, Craig Sorrensen, reporting from outside Bruce's Orlando hotel.

"It's probably too early to tell, Sasha," he said, brushing an errant hair back into place. "But I've been out and about speaking to a number of Republican voters today and I can tell you there are a lot of worried people down here who think the police and Homeland Security have been playing down the Chinese involvement in the two slayings. As one voter told me, one murder's a tragedy but two smacks of conspiracy."

"Do people really think the Chinese are behind these two deaths?" asked the anchor.

"Some do. And I think those numbers will grow until there's a definitive—some would say any—explanation from the authorities about how McKinley died. At the moment there's only one person providing answers and that's John Bruce. Last week people didn't want to believe him. Now, they're not so sure."

Arnie switched the holovision off and turned to John, sitting silently at the back of the room.

"Did you hear that, John? You can still win this."

"You think so?"

Arnie stared at the big man. He looked so . . . indecisive. And unpresidential. Head down, shoulders slumped, sitting on the edge of his bed like a teenager refusing to go to school. But that was John. Most days he was energized, overflowing with a zeal to change the world and burning to debate anyone on any topic. But other days—like today—he just wasn't there. He'd switch off, retreat into himself, and come up with all kinds of excuses why he shouldn't leave his room—he wasn't feeling well, he needed to lie down, people were after him, perhaps his candidature had been a mistake, perhaps God had other plans for him.

It was on those days that Arnie earned his money.

"I know so, John," he urged. "Every candidate has a bad week once in their campaign. You've had yours. Now it's time to come out fighting."

"But people are out to get me, Arnie. They're trying to stop me any way they can."

"No one's out to get you. Look at me, John. I'm telling you categorically—listen!—no one is out to get you. Trust me, you're the safest candidate out there."

"Really?"

"Really."

Fredericks smiled. Relief. He was getting through to the big man at last. If only John had the same belief in himself that his supporters had. He was head and shoulders the best candidate—when he wanted to be—he had vision, imagination, a gift for communication, and a head for details second to none.

And being a hero didn't hurt. He had the highest name recognition of any candidate. People liked him. There was a naïve honesty about him, a vulnerability that people found appealing. When other politicians spoke you could see the calculation behind their eyes as each word was carefully weighed, the truth secondary to dogma, presentation, and spin. But with John, what you saw was what you got. He spoke from the heart.

All he lacked was experience and self-belief. And maybe discipline—that China crack had nearly cost them the election.

But all that was trainable. Given the right team around him.

"Come on, John, get dressed. We've got to get out there and fight back. And when we've killed off Suarez, we've got to go for the Democrats. It's a kill or be killed world out there, John. Let's show them what we're made of."

Bill Suarez took his place on the sofa and smiled for the cameras. Not exactly the venue he'd have chosen but exposure was exposure and if that meant dropping in on mid-morning live talk shows then that's what he had to do. Voters had to be courted wherever they were to be found.

Missy Guzman, former child star and model, flashed her trademark smile in Suarez's direction. "Tell me, Bill," she said, leaning over and touching his knee. "How are you holding up knowing there's a crazy guy out there killing Republicans?"

Suarez smiled back. "I don't give it a second thought, Missy."

"You don't want to search Missy for a concealed weapon then, Bill?" joked cohost Sherman Zinger, turning to nod conspiratorially to the audience.

Suarez played along, holding up his hands and backing away. "I don't think *anything* could be concealed in that dress."

Laughter. Maybe a vote or two. Suarez smiled again for the cameras, imagining a room full of floating stay-at-home voters: groups C2-4, mainly women.

"So you don't think the Chinese are interfering in this election?" asked Sherman.

Suarez shook his head: time to be serious and showcase his political credentials. "I think it's laughable. I've met President Hua and I can tell you that the last thing he or his government wants is conflict with the United States."

"So who do you think killed McKinley?" asked Missy.

The answer stuck in Suarez's throat—literally. A guttural *ch* sound formed at the back of his mouth but that was as far as it got. He swallowed and tried again. Nothing. Why couldn't he speak? What was happening? Panic, a terrified internalized panic that he covered up with an apologetic smile. He was a candidate for Chrissake. He couldn't look stupid on HV.

He covered his mouth with his hand and coughed, bought himself some time, his voice had to come back soon. Had he injured his vocal cords—all those speaking engagements?

Missy looked concerned. "Are you okay, Bill?" she said, her hand once more straying towards his knee.

He tried to say "Fine" but it came out as "Ugh."

Another cough. He shrugged apologetically and pointed at this throat. Maybe he could still come out of this okay. A voice strain, nothing embarrassing, nothing that would throw doubt on his suitability for President. People lost their voice all the time, didn't they?

He swallowed again. His throat didn't feel sore. Shouldn't it feel sore if he'd hurt his voice? More panic. What if it wasn't a sore throat? Hadn't McKinley's demise started with a cough?

He looked down at his hand, a glance at his palm. No blood, thank God.

But . . . there *was* something. Something . . . strange. His thoughts were . . . echoing? There it was again. Every word he internalized reverberated as though spoken inside a vast church. Was that . . . normal? Was he fainting, losing consciousness?

What the hell was happening to him?

Water. His eyes fell on a small bottle of mineral water on the coffee table in front of him. If he poured himself a drink, maybe that would sooth his vocal cords, bring his voice back.

He reached forward, stretching towards the bottle then . . . flipped his hand at the last second, grasped the bottle by the neck, raised, and inverted it in one motion, then brought it down hard on the edge of the table. The bottle smashed, leaving a jagged glass weapon in Suarez's hand.

He turned violently, swinging and thrusting without warning, and . . . drove the bottle into Sherman Zinger's neck.

There was a moment of absolute silence. Then pandemonium. Missy started screaming. Zinger staggered to his feet, clutching his throat, falling backwards, blood spurting everywhere. Someone in the audience applauded, another laughed. Was it a stunt? It had to be a stunt, right?

"Cut!" shouted the director. "Get a doctor!"

The set exploded into activity: people rushing on, Missy screaming at the top of her voice. Suarez, confused, stared at the jagged bottle in his hand, at the blood, at the twitching, writhing body of Sherman Zinger . . .

"What's happened?" he asked. "Why . . ."

He threw the broken bottle on the floor. "It wasn't me," he shouted. "It wasn't me!"

CHAPTER THIRTY-ONE

Ziegler hurried along the corridor. A month ago an urgent summons to Peter's cell would have been a cause for excitement, now it terrified him. Bazley had been right, let Peter into your life and he'll never let go.

The blackened image of Suzi Martinez rocketed into Ziegler's mind. Peter had said he'd kill again. "Watch the news, Doc," he'd said. "There'll be another one soon. These cell walls can't contain me anymore. I only have to dream someone dead and—poof—they're gone."

Ziegler shivered. He couldn't forget that look in Peter's eye. The man was so plausible, even when he was spouting rubbish.

Which was what made this situation worse—what if it wasn't rubbish? Those two murders in Oxford—Vince Culley and Karen Hawkins—two horrific murders and the only suspects were two people with a direct link to Peter. The first murder even sounded like one of Peter's.

Coincidence? It had to be. A coincidence that Peter was now manipulating for his own purposes. Look at me, I'm a killer again. Why not call in the police, Doctor Z? I'm sure they'll want to know?

Like hell he would. The thought of Peter Pendennis insinuating himself into a major police investigation was beyond frightening. He'd turn it into a roadshow. He'd hint and twist and smile—just like he was doing with Ziegler. "See that murder in the States last night,

Doc? That McKinley bloke. The one that exploded. I did that. My Yank friend told me to do it, so I did. Do you think it was bad? Do you think you should refer me to a sleep specialist—maybe try and stop the dreams?"

If Peter had his way he'd have everyone on the planet at his beck and call. The man was an attention-seeker with an insatiable appetite.

Which begged the question—what was it going to be now? Another personality? Another murder?

A nervous and very young warder hovered outside Peter's cell door as Ziegler turned the corner.

"What's happened?" asked Ziegler.

"It's Pendennis, sir. We can't wake him. He's in some kind of coma."

Ziegler pushed past. Another warder—Mike Harris—was standing by Peter's bed. He stood back to let Ziegler through.

"We thought he was faking it or we'd have called you sooner," said Mike, biting his lip.

Nerves or a guilty conscience, thought Ziegler, wondering if he was going to find evidence of a beating. Not that there were any obvious marks on Peter's face. He looked almost peaceful. If it wasn't for his eyes staring up at the ceiling he'd have passed for asleep.

Hesitation. If this had been any other inmate, Ziegler would have rushed forward and started checking for vital signs. But this wasn't any other inmate. This was Peter Pendennis who could feign death one second and rip your ear off the next.

"Mike, could you stand at the head of the bed and hold Peter's shoulders down."

The warder obeyed without comment. Not even a raised eyebrow to his colleague. Everyone knew that Pendennis was one inmate no one took chances with.

Ziegler lifted Peter's left wrist and felt for a pulse—slow but steady. He let the wrist go and watched it flop back onto the bed, lifeless. Then he took a small flashlight from his top pocket and played the pencil-thin beam across Peter's eyes—unresponsive, fixed, but no sign of trauma. He checked his breathing—fine—he ran his hands over Peter's head. No sign of injury anywhere. But those eyes . . .

Could he be faking it?

He tried the light test again, playing the beam back and forth across Peter's eyes, watching for the slightest reaction, a blink, a dilation, a spontaneous movement. Anything!

How could anyone fake that? Even Peter couldn't control his pupils' reaction to light, could he?

Ziegler stood back, torn between his medical training and an irrational fear. Pendennis needed urgent medical attention. Something they couldn't handle at Upper Heywood. He'd have to be transferred.

And let Peter loose on the outside world?

The thought hit him like a fist to the gut. Could Peter have engineered this? Swallowed something? Another of his twisted plans—fake a medical emergency and get transferred to a less secure environment?

Hippocratic Oath. *First do no harm.* Peter had to be hospitalized.

He punched in the code on his wrist-phone and started to make the arrangements for the transfer.

"Run and get a gurney, Mike," he said. "We need to get him moved fast."

A sudden cry brought everyone's attention back to the bed.

"His eyes moved! I saw them," said the young warder, pointing at Pendennis.

Ziegler reached for his pen light and as he did so Peter's head began to turn—slowly, ever so slowly, tracking towards Ziegler—the rest of his body perfectly still.

Ziegler froze. There was something unreal—theatrical—about the whole scene. He half expected Peter's head to do a complete 360.

It didn't. It stopped the moment Peter's unblinking eyes fixed upon Ziegler's. Pendennis smiled. And spoke.

"Peter's not here at the moment, can I take a message?"

Three blurs hovered a thousand feet above the cliffs at Carn les Boel. Ahead of them lay five thousand miles of ocean. Nick extrapolated the path of the ley across the Atlantic then concentrated on a hazy area of cloud on the horizon just to the north of where the ley would have hit.

"Here we go," he said, fixing his mind on that patch of cloud and dragging himself towards it. From that cloud he hopped to the next and the next, substituting a patch of ocean when there was no cloud.

Below, the Atlantic passed in a featureless wash of blue. Clouds streaked overhead and to the sides. Faster, Nick pushed his senses further, concentrating on the horizon and clawing it towards him. Wondering, hoping that the next dark line on the horizon would be land not cloud, assembling maps within his mind: coastal charts memorized from the HV—Mexico to Maine. Any minute now they had to hit land. Any second . . .

He slowed. Was that land? False alarm. Another bank of cloud. Another bank of cloud now disappearing in the rear-view mirror of his mind. On he swept, dipping down as the clouds lowered and darkened, sweeping through the driving rain of an Atlantic depression then rising on the other side, fixing on a wisp of high cirrus and pulling himself into the stratosphere.

"Where are we going?" asked Louise.

"I need height," said Nick. "The more height, the more coastline I'll be able to see, the less chance of making a mistake."

The Earth curved below them—ocean from horizon to horizon. How long did it take to fly five thousand miles? Shouldn't they be there by now? Were they flying off course? Were they heading into the South Atlantic?

A quick check on the sun. It seemed to be in the right place. But what time zone were they in now? Should the sun be due south, east, west?

He pressed on. No time for doubt. They had to hit a coastline some time.

A line of grey appeared on the horizon, growing and stretching with every second. Other colors—twinkling whites and was that green? He slowed. It must be a coastline. It had to be! He could make out a forest and was that a city?

"Is that Florida?" asked Louise.

He wasn't sure. It looked right. But he'd expected more of a curve to it and where was Miami? Or were they further north?

"That's Jacksonville," said John. "You can just make out Cape Canaveral to the south."

Could you? Nick strained to make sense out of the hazy coastline. John could be right. Thinking about it, he probably was. He must have flown these skies countless times before.

"Let's go down and take a look," he said, aiming at a point halfway between Jacksonville and the cape. If John was right, there'd be an interstate—I95—running north-south a mile or two inland. An interstate packed with helpful road signs that even a higher dimensional traveller would have little problem making out.

The coastline grew and spread; towns appeared, lakes and forests. Down and down they dived, sucking the ground towards them. There was the interstate—a straight line parallel to the coast. Nick carved a turn towards it, sweeping in and down from the north. Slowing now, looking for a road sign, dropping to thirty, forty feet above the tarmac. And there it was. A line of green placards swung across the lanes on a gantry. He raced towards it then stopped. Large white letters shimmered in front of him—Daytona Beach 10 miles. They were almost there. Orlando couldn't be more than fifty, sixty miles away.

They followed the road, took the Orlando exit, blurred the traffic beneath them, slowed again, checking the road signs: Orlando twenty miles, fifteen, ten. Almost there, one more exit.

Nick's mind raced ahead. John was staying at the New Sheraton. He had a speaking engagement at the Metropolitan at 12:30. Then a number of interviews back at his hotel before leaving for Dallas at five. What was the time now?

Tall office blocks and apartment buildings sprung up to his right. Would one of them have a clock tower, an external digital display? He peeled off from the road, heading downtown, swinging through manmade canyons of concrete and glass, brick and stone, slowing at every intersection, reading the street names. The New Sheraton was on North Magnolia by a lake. They'd try there first.

South Magnolia. Nearly there. Nick veered right and headed north.

"Look out for a big white building," he said. "The New Sheraton. Should be at the end of this road by a lake."

A lake flashed by to the right. No hotel. How many lakes were there? The road continued, changing its name from South Magnolia to North. Nick pushed on, willing it to be morning or early afternoon, wondering if they could track John to Dallas, wondering if . . .

A large white building towered into view. He accelerated, skimming past the intervening intersections, dragging the building towards him. There was a name on the roof just like in the picture he'd seen. He . . . stopped, hovering in front of the sign. The New Sheraton, it proclaimed in ten-foot letters. Even his imperfect higher dimensional vision couldn't mistake that.

"Follow me," he said, diving down the face of the building. There had to be a clock in the foyer, or the restaurant, or on someone's wrist if he could get them to stay still long enough. He rolled through ninety degrees just before he hit street level, swinging into the recessed entrance lobby, slowing and turning and . . .

He was inside. The light level dropped instantly.

"Where are we going?" asked John.

"It's the tech guys again, John," said Nick. "They say it's an integral part of calibrating the software. Don't ask me how. I think they just like playing with our heads. You just follow me and ignore everything else you see. None of it's real."

The foyer was huge. Shops lined one wall, seats and tables and—was that a café?—lined another. And on the far wall—above the reception area—was a clock.

Nick pulled it towards him. It was a digital display. Ten-thirty-one? Or was that fifty-one? No, definitely thirty-one.

"Yes!" he shouted. Plenty of time. John might even be in the hotel now. He didn't have anything else scheduled until twelve-thirty.

"John, we're going to test the radio encryption routines for a couple of minutes," said Nick. "Follow me as before but until you hear the words 'switch frequency' you won't be able to understand a word we say."

Louise was impressed. The way Nick handled John—his speed of thought, the easy way in which he turned a mind-boggling and potentially fraught situation into something plausible and fun. Hey John, we're going to fly out-of-body across the Atlantic. Cool.

It had all gone far smoother than she'd ever imagined.

Now, they had to find the other John. Which in a hotel this size was not going to be easy. There had to be over a thousand rooms.

"It'll take ages," she told Nick. "Wouldn't it be better to wait for John at the other place? At least we know what time he's supposed to be there."

"Why wait? And think about it—you wouldn't stick a VIP like John Bruce in any old room. He'll have a suite and an entourage. Not to mention armed body guards. Even our imperfect vision couldn't miss that lot."

He was right. All candidates were assigned protection officers these days. And hotel security wouldn't want Bruce too close to their regular clientele—not after what had happened to McKinley and Martinez.

"Come on," said Nick, "We'll drift up through the floors and see what we can see."

They ascended, positioning themselves by the lift doors and rising through the ceiling into the lobby above. A long corridor ran from left to right. A woman with a cleaning trolley was knocking on one of the doors to the left. No other signs of life.

"Should we check each corridor?" asked Louise.

"Not yet. Let's start at the top and work down. Chances are that's where the VIP suites will be."

Nick was right. As soon as they hit the twentieth floor they saw him. Smart suit, heavyset, standing with his back to a door forty yards along the left-hand corridor. He had to be a bodyguard.

And was that another? There was a similarly dressed man sat in an arm chair in the lobby watching the lifts.

"How are we going to do this?" asked Louise. "Do we fly our John in and talk him through the reconnection?"

"Some reconnaissance first, I think. Remember the alien is likely to be part of Bruce's inner circle. I'd feel happier if we could get Bruce on his own. Human eyes might not be able to see us up here but who knows what alien eyes can see?"

"I'll go," she said. "You stay here and keep John out of sight."

She didn't wait for an objection. Nick was the only one who could handle John. He had to stay back. Plus, she was the careful one. If anyone was going to go blundering into a dangerous situation better it was her. Nick was more likely to do something rash.

She drifted along the corridor, wondering how large John's suite would be and how many people might be inside. Should she enter by the guarded door or slide through the walls now and approach from the side?

And could one of the security guards be the alien?

She blurred into the wall, compressing herself—or, at least, willing herself to compress. She wanted to blend with the wall, to be contained such that not one higher dimensional atom protruded into the room on the other side. She wanted to be invisible.

Everything went a speckled grey, whether it was because the plan had worked or because the wall was thick she neither knew nor cared. All her thoughts were on the next stage. And the room.

She eased forward, thinking micron small. All she needed was a glimpse of the room, nothing more. A bubble formed in the wall of grey. A droplet of light and something she couldn't make out. She pushed further. The bubble expanded. The room was empty as far as she could she. A window in the far wall bled hazy light. Tables and chairs rippled in the foreground. A large HV projector filled a corner. She pushed further. There was a table pushed against the wall below her, a bowl of fruit, flowers, a stack of what looked like files.

There were three doors. Two to the right—towards the room being guarded—and one to the left.

She slid along the wall towards the single door, reached the corner of the room, slowed, pushing and compressing herself as before. Even slower now, waiting for the bubble to appear, straining to make sense of that hazy, distorted fish-eye world.

It was a bedroom. A double bed between two windows. Something lying on that bed. A man?

She struggled to make out the man's identity. He was on his back, fully clothed, his shoes pointing into the room. She was too far way and too low to make out his face. Was it John?

She slid further into the room. Whoever it was was on his own. Or was there someone in the bathroom? There was an open door in the far wall. Anyone could be inside.

She pulled back inside the wall and rose higher. She'd find the ceiling and use that to move unseen to the point above the man's face. The speckled grey around her changed subtly. The ceiling? She flowed into and along it. It had to be the ceiling. She sampled her position, dropping microscopically into the room then pulling back. The man hadn't moved. No one else had joined him.

She stopped. This would be it. Right above his face. If it was John she'd know in the next second.

The bubble reappeared and grew and . . .

It *was* John. He . . .

She pulled away immediately. He'd been staring right at her. Could he see her?

Panic. Calm down, Louise. You're invisible. It was a coincidence. She slid two feet to the side and let the bubble form again. He was no longer looking at her. But he was still staring at the ceiling, and . . . he hadn't moved. She pushed further into the room. He didn't look right. His stare was fixed and unnatural.

She retreated back into the ceiling, slid along towards the bathroom. She had to find out if anyone was in there. There wasn't. She dropped down into the room, not caring about camouflage. Something was wrong with John. Very wrong.

She flew towards the bed, rising and hovering a few feet above John's head. He still hadn't moved. Was he resting? Was he going over his speech in his head?

Was he . . .

She didn't want to finish that sentence but why didn't he move? He hadn't even blinked. And his chest . . . it wasn't moving. He wasn't breathing!

"John," she called, projecting her voice inside his head. "Wake up, John." Then louder, drilling the words through his skull. "John! Blink your eyes, godammit. Wake up!"

Nothing.

"No!" she screamed. Not this. To have come so far, to have risked so much and then . . . to find John Bruce dead.

CHAPTER THIRTY-TWO

Nick dived into the room.

"What's happened? I could hear you from out there."

"It's John. He's dead."

Nick flew towards the body on the bed, gained height, hovering a meter or so above John's chest. Was he dead? He couldn't see any evidence of trauma—no blood, no bruises, no gaping wounds. If it wasn't for those blank staring eyes he would have said John was resting—his head was on the pillow, his arms folded across his chest. Had he been arranged?

Or wasn't he dead?

Nick dived lower, stopping inches from John's nose. Was he breathing?

Nick cursed his imperfect senses. He couldn't feel John's breath. Even if John was alive any breath would pass straight through him. And his vision—that was almost as bad—how could he tell if John's chest was moving when the whole room was rippling back and forth?

Maybe he could slip inside John's chest—see if his heart was still pumping?

He slid along John's body, paused for a second over his chest then started to push inside.

"What are you doing?" hissed Louise.

Nick didn't answer. He was too busy being amazed. And trying to make sense of what he was seeing. He was inside a human being. A

wash of red and pink and creamy white. Was it moving or was he? He
thought *stop*. The world around him continued to flex. A higher
dimensional effect? Imperfect vision? Proof that John was still alive?

He couldn't tell. Everything was too confusing.

He retraced his path, rising up through John's chest until he was
half in, half out. He'd use the room as an anchor, a reference point to
see if John's chest was moving or not. He thought *stop* and froze. Half
his world was now in the room, the other half a dark pinky red. He
watched and waited. A pink tide rose and fell like water gently lapping
against a rock.

"He's breathing," said Nick. "Just."

"But I tried to wake him," said Louise. "I shouted right into his
head. No one could have slept through that."

"Maybe that's because he's not here."

Nick rose to hover over the body. This was not what he'd expected.
Not what he'd expected at all.

"You think . . ." She paused, undoubtedly as confused as he was.
"He separated?"

That was one possibility. John could also be comatose. Or paralyzed. In a more practical universe he probably would be. But this was
a universe with a body-hopping alien in it. And two people claiming
to be John Bruce.

His mind blazed with possibility. Could the alien have seized John's
body during the *Pegasus* flight and taken it over? Could the John that
he'd left outside in a cleaner's closet be the complete John Bruce? Or
were there still two Johns—the political John having discovered the
ability to separate when . . . when what? When he'd been ripped from
his body during the space mission? Wasn't that still feasible? Likely
even. John's mind is ripped in two when the neural shielding fails, one
part's thrown free and eventually becomes ensnared by Pendennis,
the other . . . somehow it finds its way back—either because it wasn't
thrown so far or maybe the alien found it and brought it back. Either
way, it would explain his ability to separate. It would be like a drug;
once discovered how could you not want to disconnect and roam the
skies?

"He's the alien, isn't he?" said Louise, excited. "I knew he wasn't
John. I *knew* it."

"It's one possibility," said Nick.

"Come on, Nick. It's the *only* possibility. It's over, isn't it? All we've got to do is put our John back in this body, call the Colonists, and that's it."

Her voice changed. Concern. "Where is our John by the way?"

"He's safe," said Nick. "He's resting in a cleaner's closet, tucked away at the back and practically invisible."

"So, let's get him reconnected."

If only it was that easy.

"Think about it, Lou. If you're right then we have a paranoid murdering alien who's become proprietorial about John's body. He probably thinks he's John Bruce. He's probably convinced he's John Bruce. So, what's he going to do when he finds our John in his body? Rip him to shreds, cast him into the void, disassemble him?"

"So we contact the Colonists."

"What if they don't come? John wouldn't last five seconds with that alien. And have you thought what might happen if you're wrong? What if it's not the alien but John's other half. What would the Colonists make of that? Two entities each claiming to be John Bruce. They wouldn't trust a word anyone on this planet ever said again. The whole human race would be categorized as lying memory grafters."

And probably earmarked for an extensive and excruciating interrogation.

"So what do we do?" snapped Louise. "Wait here and pontificate?"

"No," said Nick. "We move John's body."

"What?"

"It's the sensible thing to do," explained Nick. "We need to know who we're dealing with—John or the alien. Whoever it is is going to be returning soon and if we leave the body here then they might blur straight in and connect—not giving us time to see who they were. But if we move the body they'll have to stop. There'll be a moment of panic while they hover over the bed. If it's John, we'll recognize him. He'll look like us."

"You don't know that! You're guessing again."

"It's what I do best. And think about it, every Colonist we've encountered so far has either been invisible or a giant pandimensional jellyfish. We'll know the difference when we see it. And, anyway, if the alien comes back and finds his body missing, he'll react."

"And then what?"

"If it's the alien we get out quick and call the Colonists, if it's John we . . . let him know where his body is and get ready to reconnect his other half."

"And how do you propose we tell him where his body is without freaking him out?" She sounded angry. "Whisper in his ear? Hey, John, try looking in the room down the hall?"

"Why not?" said Nick. "The man's a born-again Christian. Shouldn't he expect God to step in and help him when he's in trouble?"

"You are incredible."

And by Louise's tone, not in a nice way. Not that Nick cared. He knew he was right. Planting a suggestion in John's head wouldn't be difficult. Not if it was done subtly. A few whispered accentless words projected his way. *Wrong room. Try the one next door.* He'd be in such a quandary wondering where his body was he'd jump on any lead and put it down to inspiration.

"And how the hell are we going to move his body?" asked Louise.

"Connect, of course. If the alien can do it so can I."

"But . . ." Louise was speechless.

"You fly ahead and check the other rooms. I'll walk John as far as I can, hide him, then fly back here."

"No! Isn't it dangerous? What if you can't disconnect or John's body rejects you? Don't you have to be tissue-mapped or something?"

"We'll soon find out."

He focussed on a point a few inches above the center of John's forehead and flowed towards it. This'll work, he told himself. It has to.

"No!" shouted Louise. "You can't."

He tuned her protests out. He was in position, lined up. Concentrate, you've connected before. This'll be the same. Think yourself inside and . . .

He was falling, tumbling down a long dark tube, the world swimming in senseless waves, he was up, down, stretched and . . .

The room sharpened into focus. The ceiling, light fittings, wallpaper, paintings. He rolled over, pushed up with his arms, swung his legs off the bed. And almost fell over. He felt light-headed and heavy-limbed. He steadied himself, sitting upright on the edge of the bed, gripping the bedspread with both hands. Better. He massaged his thighs, stretched, flexed his shoulders. Everything felt half asleep.

He pushed away from the bed, lurching forward, stumbling.

"Can you hear me, Louise?" He projected his question towards the ceiling. No answer. And no time. John or the alien could arrive at any second. He had to leave.

He hurried towards the door, using his hands to steady his uncertain gait.

The room's empty. Louise's voice. Quiet, no louder than a whisper but at least he could hear her, even if she couldn't hear him.

He grabbed the door handle, turned, and pulled. Another large empty room. How far could he get? How far did he need to get? Into the next room, the corridor, further? And if he met someone could he make them believe he was John?

He tried speaking. Not too loud. Just the one word. "Hello." It sounded strange—deeper than his normal voice but still recognizably his. He'd have a hard time convincing anyone he was John.

There are three people in the next room and a guard in the corridor.

Louise again. He raised his thumb to let her know he'd heard. He'd have to hide John here. His eyes swung around the room. He could sit him in the corner over there or . . . there were two doors in the far wall, where did the second one lead?

He pointed to the nearest of the two doors and hurried towards it, hoping Louise was watching. "Where does this one lead?" he asked silently. "The room next door or a cupboard?"

It's a toilet.

He opened the door and slipped inside. Perfect. A small rectangular room, WC and wash basin. Easy to overlook from the higher dimensions. He closed the door, grabbed hold of the wash basin for support and eased himself down onto the blue-tiled floor. His legs felt so cramped they didn't want to bend. He stretched them out again as soon as he could—sitting on the floor, his back pressed against the wall, the cold from the tiles pressing through the thin material of his trousers.

Almost finished. He checked for stability, he didn't want John toppling over when he left and banging his head.

Perfect. He let his head slump forward. Deep breaths and relax. This'll be easy too. You got in so you can get out. Seconds passed. *Are you okay?* That was Louise. He tuned her out. He tuned everything out. The room, the situation, everything. He was floating on a gently undulating midnight sea, weightless and carefree and . . .

Out. He rose from the blurry bathroom floor; John Bruce's body shimmered below. A worried Louise sparkled near the ceiling.

"Don't you ever do that again!"

"You don't fancy having a go yourself then?" he asked, already blurring through the toilet door. "Think about it, Lou. We could ditch John and take over his body. Ever fancied being President?"

Louise snorted. "If we ever get out of this . . ."

Louise was still seething when they returned to the bedroom. When was he going to learn not to take risks? The last time he'd dived into someone else's head it had taken a week to get back. It could easily have happened again. The alien could have been faking a coma, waiting—just like Pendennis—for the first idiot to get too close.

And what was Nick going to do next? He said he was going to hide in the wall and observe but she didn't trust him anymore. Sitting back and observing was not his style. Leaping out and risking everything on a whim was.

"We're only going to observe, right?" she reiterated.

"Absolutely," he said. "If we blend into the wall no one'll be able to pick us out from the higher dimensions. You take the near wall, I'll take the bathroom wall. If it's the alien we back out quick. Forget about flying in formation, just get the hell out, send the pictogram to the Colonists, and we'll meet up as soon as we can on the roof."

"And if it's John you're going to plant a suggestion in his head."

"Exactly. Room next door. Toilet."

"And you're not going to say you're God or anything whimsical like that?"

"You think I should?"

She almost responded. He was winding her up, wasn't he? Wasn't he?

"Shhh," said Nick. "I think it best we keep quiet from now on. Think yourself invisible and silent.

She withdrew deeper into the speckled grey of the wall, leaving a small bubble of room visible. Around her she threw up walls—thick, transparent, and thoughtproof. No one would hear her.

Time passed. How long would he be? Didn't he have a speech to give at twelve-thirty? Shouldn't he be back in his body getting ready?

And how was he going to connect? If it was the alien—which she was sure it was—how could he fit inside John's head? The only Colonist she'd seen was enormous. Did it fold itself up? Did it sink a portion of itself into John's head and let the rest coil and flop around his body?

She shivered. Any second now that *thing* was going to fly into the room. It might even fill the room. Maybe she should fire off the pictogram now? After all, how long would it take to reach the Colonists? And if her hunch about the alien was right they wouldn't have to worry about confusing the Colonists with two John Bruces.

But what if she was wrong?

Indecision and foreboding. Whatever choice she made it was certain to be wrong.

CHAPTER THIRTY-THREE

The light changed. Something had rippled into the room. Something indistinct that warped the room like a heat haze. The alien? John?

Louise edged forward, expanding the bubble of light to get a better view. Was it her eyes or were those gelatinous fronds—hundreds of them, translucent to the point of near transparency?

A low rumbling roar reverberated inside her head. A scream of anguish. The room pulsed, changing color as though someone had placed a red filter over her porthole of light. Time to leave, she thought, backing away.

"Who's there?" A crazed half-human voice screamed inside her head. "Who are you? What have you done with my body?"

Louise froze. Could it see her? Was it sensing her movement, her thoughts? She threw up more walls, blended herself into the speckled grey concrete and plaster.

Something knocked against her, something solid. It was in the wall with her, searching and probing. A searing pain shot through her head. Migraine flashes. She tried to move but couldn't. She screamed.

Nick watched from his hiding place in the far wall. The alien must have found Louise. She was screaming. The air and the room were warped and writhing by the corner she was hiding. He had to do something. Now!

He thought himself solid. He thought *steel*, he thought *fast*, he thought *ram*. Aimed at the gelatinous head and launched himself at it like a bullet.

He hit it hard. Pain shuddered through him. He was momentarily disorientated and spinning. Had he bounced off? Injured it? Injured himself? A roar exploded in Nick's head. Something brushed against him. He pulled away, twisting and turning. Thinking *left, right, up, down, a axis, b*, throwing himself into every plane he could think of. Away, he had to get away!

And bring the alien with him. He had to lure it away from Louise.

He blurred through the ceiling, shouting: "I've got him. I've got John."

He shot through the roof and into the sky, casting his sight behind him watching for the roof tiles to warp and flicker. Hoping he'd be able to see the alien. Hoping he'd follow.

He was still looking when a voice rasped inside his head. "Where is it?" cried the alien. The air around Nick began to distort and bend— the cityscape below, the blue sky above. The alien was almost upon him. Dive! One thought. Down, he plunged, twisting and turning. The distortion followed.

He aimed for the nearest building, bursting through the roof tiles. He needed camouflage and cover. He veered away, tumbling through the pipes and vents, swinging through the fabric of walls and ceilings, cloaking his thoughts as best he could, trying to merge with his surroundings, to disappear, evaporate.

The alien followed. Nick could sense its pursuit; its cries, its rage— waves of raw emotion reverberating through the building. Anger, frustration, pain.

The innards of the building blurred into one streaky mass: rooms and concrete, people and furnishings. Nick carved a random path, accelerating, slowing, ducking and diving.

Light hit him. He'd burst through an external wall. He veered across the road, entered the building opposite, turned. A wall of rage followed.

Louise broke free the moment the alien released its grip. She fell backwards, throwing herself into the adjoining room, ducking down through the floor and blurring herself towards the ground. She was going to put as much concrete between herself and the alien as she could.

Then she thought of Nick and the Colonists. He'd put his own life in danger to save hers. He'd deliberately called to the alien. She'd heard him. Now it was her turn. She had to save him and she had to send the pictogram to the Colonists.

She turned at once, aiming for the roof, thinking of the sky, and pulling it towards her. Her world exploded in a wash of blue. She stopped, composed herself, summoned the image of the pictogram, and held it, fed it, filled it with as much energy as she could muster, and willed it to the stars. She turned and repeated the process, again and again, aiming at every point she could imagine, holding the image until it hurt. Wherever the Colonists were they had to see it. They had to!

She sent a prayer with the last pictogram. *Wherever you are, hurry.*

Then her thoughts turned to Nick. How long could he evade the alien? The Colonist that had pursued her had been relentless.

Nick swung through yet another office block wall and immediately turned right—flying through the skin of the wall itself, trying everything he could to throw his pursuer off. Concrete and metal reinforcing came and went, blurring into a soup of dirty grey. How could the alien follow through all this confusion? They were in a solid wall for Christ's sake! You couldn't see more than a molecule in any direction!

Unless the alien had other methods to track him? Maybe he could see through walls? Maybe he was following Nick's thoughts?

He thought *silent*, he thought *air*, he thought *blend*. He stopped running and willed himself into the cavities between matter, the interstitial gaps between atoms and reality. He spread himself, stretching, merging his essence with the fabric of the building.

Somewhere far away he could hear the alien raging, words muffled by distance and garbled by anger. The sounds came and went as the alien circled and searched. He had to know Nick was close but couldn't see where.

Nick stayed silent, covering his thoughts with layers of down. He was part of the wall, a grain of sand, a spinning electron. He was . . .

"I see you." The words burst inside Nick's head. And he could feel something else too. A wave of elation. No anger at all.

A bluff. It had to be.

"I can reach you, even in there."

The words resonated through the concrete, vibrated through Nick's elongated consciousness, brushed against his mind.

And there was something else. A fizzing, effervescing sound as though . . . acid? He felt a burning sensation. The wall was bubbling, being eaten away. Him with it. He was sure of it. He could feel the wall moving, swaying beneath him.

Out! He had to get out, escape! He drew himself back together, burst out from the wall, zigzagging wildly. Behind him, a section of wall the size of a billboard crumbled and fell like sand to the street below. No stopping to look, he buried himself in another building and another. In and out, twist and turn.

The alien followed, calling to him as the two wheeled and pitched through buildings and then up across the sky in a higher dimensional dogfight. Nick was running out of options; he'd hid, he'd run, what was left? The void? The ocean? The sun?

A pictogram image flashed across Nick's mind. Had the alien implanted it? The image disappeared. Louise? Had she sent the pictogram to the Colonists? Were they on their way?

Another thought; he had to keep the alien in Orlando, close to the pictogram's source. He had to keep the alien there until help came.

But how? The alien was gaining on him, he seemed to know every turn Nick would make before he made them.

An idea; Nick thought *left* and turned right. The pursuing distortion shot wide. Nick doubled back towards the center of Orlando, feinting turns with his thoughts, layering his mind—one for show, one for go.

Downtown Orlando gleamed in the winter sun. And something else. Something hovered above the city like a minor sun. A star in daylight?

The star was directly in his path. It hovered above the skyscrapers, a brilliant ball of light so small, so intense. The Colonists? Had they arrived so soon?

Buoyed by hope, he flew straight for it, leading his pursuer towards the light.

"John Bruce!"

The words reverberated inside Nick's head like a cathedral organ with all the stops pulled out. It wasn't the alien's voice. It was . . . higher and multilayered, more like a choir than a single person.

And was it coming from that star? The one directly in his path? The one he should be veering away from but wasn't?

He tried to turn but the light was blinding, he couldn't focus on anything else. It was sucking him in. "Turn!" he screamed. "Turn now!"

The light flashed by to his side. Somehow he'd managed to miss it. And what the hell was it? He could have sworn it had wings.

"John Bruce!" the radiance boomed again.

The alien stopped, stunned by the beauty of the shining presence that called his name, captivated by its incandescence. It had to be an angel. It had wings, it shone. It looked just like the old paintings. And that voice. The harmonics. It was like the sweetest choir he'd ever heard.

It spoke again. "I bring thee tidings of great joy."

He struggled to compose himself, to find a means of reply. If he'd had a physical form he would have thrown himself to the ground and shielded his eyes.

"Art . . . art thou an Angel?" he stuttered.

"I am the Angel of the Lord, John Bruce."

He knew it! And it had come for him just like he knew it always would. He *was* special. He'd been right all along. God *had* chosen him. The powers he'd been given had been a test, just like he'd guessed, a test to see if he was worthy to implement God's plan on Earth. To pave the way for the Second Coming.

"Thy time has come, John Bruce," sung the angel. "The Lord thy God commands thee to await him here, whereupon thy destiny shall be revealed unto thee."

John was ecstatic. He'd known since the SHIFT flight he wasn't like other men. He could project his soul. He could fly. He could hear voices. He could hear the lies that hid behind the smiles of his enemies. Satan whispering at them to say one thing while believing the other. And he could smite them when they moved against him. But he'd still had doubts. God's plan hadn't been easy to discern. Thou shalt not kill, love thy neighbor, turn the other cheek but . . . then there was the Flood, the destruction of Sodom and Gomorrah, the apocalypse. How could you tell the Just War from all the others? He'd read Revalations so many times his head hurt. The End Time had to be close. The signs were all there but . . . there were so many contradictions, so much unknown. He'd looked everywhere for the Antichrist, he'd considered the possibility that it wasn't a person but a concept, an idea, a country. A godless country like China. A godless country that had to be stopped before it took over the world.

Armageddon. That had to be why God wanted to see him. To tell him that he'd been right. To give him His blessing. Maybe a date and time. Maybe a glimpse of the paradise that was to come. The Messiah.

"Thank you. Thank you," he said, bowing as best he could in his celestial form. Whatever God decided, he was ready. He'd kill, he'd martyr himself, he'd die on a cross if necessary. Anything to serve Him.

"Thank you," he said for a third time.

The angel flickered for one last time then disappeared in a blur of wings.

Nick was waiting on the hotel roof, spread out along the roof tiles, his senses turned upwards. Where was she? This is where they'd agreed to meet. Had she been killed by the alien? He'd checked Bruce's suite, she wasn't there. Had she got lost?

Minutes ticked by. Had she been taken by the Colonists, that ball of light? And where was the alien? Had the ball of light taken him too?

"Nick?"

He heard her before he saw her, a faint whisper in his head and then there she was, dropping out of the sky, a hazy cloud of sparkling lights.

"Louise!" He burst out of the roof. "Where've you been? How'd you get away? Are you okay?" There was so much to say, so many questions, so much news to recount.

"I'm fine," she said. "But we haven't got much time. I don't know how long I can hold him there."

"Hold who, where?"

"The alien. You flew right past me. Didn't you see?"

"The ball of light?"

"Is that what I looked like? I thought *angel*, I thought *shining*, I thought *brilliant white*. Didn't I look like an angel? The alien thought I was."

He couldn't believe it. "That was you? I saw the wings but . . . you were so bright. It was like a minor sun out there. How did you . . ."

He couldn't finish the sentence, so many other thoughts pushing in. How did the process work? Illusion? Suggestion? A real physical transformation? And could he alter his form too? All those times he'd tried he was never sure if it worked or not. "You really did that just by thinking?"

"Desperation helped. I knew there was no way to outrun him so I had to come up with a plan to slow him down. Seeing he was a born-again God-fearing alien I thought I'd show him an angel. Did I really look that good?"

Louise sparkled against the deep blue sky, a thousand tiny points of lights dancing in recollection of her finest hour.

"You looked amazing but . . . what did you do to him?"

"Told him to wait there for God. I don't know how long it'll hold though. Long enough for us to get our John reconnected and into hiding, I hope. How long do you think it'll take the Colonists to get here? I sent the pictogram as soon as I could."

"Ah," said Nick. "I'm afraid it's not going to be as easy as that."

"Why not? We've got to do it now. The alien could return at any moment. He's bound to find either John or his body unless we get them away quick."

"It's not that. I forgot to tell you in all the excitement. John's gone. I can't find his body anywhere."

CHAPTER THIRTY-FOUR

"What do you mean 'his body's gone'? How could it?"

She couldn't believe it. To be so close and then . . . how could you lose a comatose body in a bathroom?

"I don't know. I was looking for you at the time . . ."

"And our John? Is he still in the closet?"

"Ah . . . let's check."

He dived into the roof. Louise followed. Could John have reconnected by himself? Some arcane sense that told him his body was close by and drew him towards it?

And wasn't that good news?

Nick dropped into the corridor, raced along the wall, and dived through a door.

"In here," he said.

Louise followed. She could barely see a thing. The closet was small and unlit.

"Where is he?" she said.

"At the back by the shelves. 'Switch frequency,' John. Can you hear me?"

"I hear you, wing leader."

Louise was confused. If John was here, where was his body? And *was* John here? She couldn't see him. She could hear his voice but that could be coming from anywhere up to eight, ten meters away. He could be in another room.

"Get John into the light. I need to see him."

"Come on, John," said Nick. "Time to follow the wing leader again."

Louise watched from the closet. Was that something moving in the shadows? She drifted back into the corridor. Two clouds of hazy lights hovered above the lush carpet. It *was* John. But . . . how? How could he be here and his body . . .

Could he have moved his body and then returned to the closet?

"Switching to radio encryption again, John," said Nick. "Same as before—follow me wherever I go but until you hear me say 'switch frequency,' you won't be able to understand a word. Now, Lou, why on Earth would John connect with his body, move it somewhere else, disconnect, and run back to the closet?"

She didn't know. But who else could have moved the body? The alien?

"He didn't have time," said Nick. "He was either chasing me or talking to you the whole time."

"Where's the bodyguard?" She'd only just noticed. The corridor was empty. The bodyguard should have been standing guard outside Bruce's room.

"He's not here, is he?" she continued, excited. "Which proves John came this way. The bodyguard wouldn't have left his post unless John left his suite."

"Uh, yes," said Nick. "I think we'd already established that. Unless you think John might have left via a window."

This was not a time for levity. She was angry and flustered. And Nick's cavalier attitude didn't help. He should be panicking too. They'd lost John and any second an enraged alien could burst through the ceiling.

"Calm down, Lou. There's a very simple way the body could have been moved without invoking anything nasty at all."

"How?"

"Think about it. John Bruce has got a major speech to make in— what do you reckon—about an hour or less by now? What's more natural than someone knocking on his bedroom door to see if he's ready?"

"So?"

"Well, what would they do? There's no answer so they open the door. The room's empty so they check the bathrooms and—voila— there he is, comatose on the floor. He's breathing but they can't wake him, so they call an ambulance. Off goes John Bruce on a stretcher and away go the security guards with him."

Relief! What had happened to her grip on reality? Someone goes missing and all she can see are little green body-snatchers dropping out of the sky in waves. Was this a taste of things to come? Normality in a sling until some future date when her brain readjusted?

"Come on, Lou. It's nearly over. All we've got to do is find that ambulance and make the reconnection."

Arnie Fredericks paced the small room. They'd had twenty minutes to rewrite John's speech. Half of that had already gone.

"No, Ricky," he said. "It's still not there. Yes, we mention Suarez but we can't be seen to be making capital. John's got to come off as shocked but statesmanlike. Everyone'll know he's the front-runner now, we don't have to rub it in."

Ricky Benitez, John's speechwriter, marked the passage and moved on.

"What about China?" he asked. "Should I cut that section? We can hardly blame China for Suarez glassing Zinger."

Arnie pushed his hair back, running his fingers through his short, wiry hair. Could they backtrack on China? After making such an issue of it?

"No," he said. "We stay on message. China's a threat and we need strong leadership."

"But what if Suarez confesses to having McKinley killed? We need to be ready to backpedal or John's going to be vulnerable to claims he's a warmonger."

"No." Fredericks was adamant. "We've got to keep America thinking about security. That's where the Democrats are at their most vulnerable and that's where John's going to win in November. Even if China didn't have McKinley killed, they could have. So, we push that." He threw up his hands. "Who knows, the Chinese might have got to Suarez and brainwashed him or tampered with his water. Where there's doubt, there's votes."

Adrenalin was pouring through Arnie's veins. John was going to win this. The nomination *and* the Presidency. A month ago it had been a crazy dream. A photogenic hero with a household name and a winning smile. Someone who might poll well enough to entice a McKinley or a Suarez to choose him for running mate, to help them woo the celebrity-obsessed voter.

But now . . . now, John was a player. Someone who had a platform to go with his looks. An unlikely platform—when John had first mentioned China, Arnie had thought he was crazy. But with three murders and an increasingly rattled electorate, John could play the China card all the way to the White House. And the beauty of it was that China would keep responding, overreacting as they always did. The American public would see that as interfering. The White House would try to smooth things over with China, John would accuse them of appeasement, and the lines would be drawn. Strong government v. appeasement. Only one winner.

As long as John kept on message.

"You okay on this, John?" he said, turning to his candidate seated by the mirror receiving the last ministrations to his hair and makeup. "No second thoughts about playing the fear card?"

John smiled at his reflection in the mirror. "No problem at all."

"You got a cold, John?" said Arnie. "Your voice sounds a bit off."

John nodded, touching his throat with his hand. "Started this morning."

Arnie froze: visions of Suarez and McKinley. "Your throat's not sore, is it? You haven't been coughing?"

John shook his head. "Nothing to worry about."

Arnie stared at his candidate. Five minutes to go to the biggest speech of John's career and . . . Was he ready? Should he postpone? If John went out there and his voice gave out or he started coughing people would panic—they'd think of Suarez and McKinley. John had to appear strong and resolute. A leader for a time of uncertainty.

There was a knock on the dressing room door.

"Five minutes, Mr. Bruce," said a voice from the corridor.

Arnie looked down at his watch. There wasn't time. Postponing the speech now would only fuel media speculation.

"I'll download the speech into the lectern," said Ricky, getting up. "You okay, Arnie?"

"Yeah, I'm fine."

Backstage, the minutes ticked down. A nervous Fredericks checked his tie, his watch, stretched his neck. Deep breaths. Had to keep calm. Every now and then his eyes shot towards the curtain. The room was buzzing, and packed. Maybe he should have booked somewhere larger? Or set up an overflow room—maybe an outside screen or a holoplatform? Everyone wanted to hear what John had to say.

Arnie shuffled some more. He couldn't settle. Nerves as taut as guitar strings. Was John okay? He seemed to be walking stiffly. Perhaps he should schedule a medical if he could slip a doctor past the media circus.

The curtains beckoned once more. Another surreptitious glance around the side. All the seats were taken and still people were arriving, lining the walls and clustering by the doors at the back.

This was going to be a day to remember.

"He's not here," said Louise. "How many more hospitals are there in this damn town?"

Three blurs hovered over a brightly lit ward; people scurried by below: doctors, nurses, orderlies, visitors. But no John Bruce, no press, and no security detail.

"Calm down, Lou, we'll find him."

"But when? We can't check every hospital bed in Orlando!"

That was becoming obvious. He'd seen enough hospital rooms to last a lifetime.

"Come on," he said. "We're not thinking straight. Let's find the Metropole. He's supposed to be giving a speech there at twelve thirty. If it's been cancelled, there'll be a sign outside, maybe a note to say where he's being treated."

"And if the speech hasn't been cancelled and he's there?"

"Then, we've got problems."

The house lights dimmed. The sudden darkness sent the crowd into a nervous hush. People and equipment were crammed into the room far beyond any fire regulation limit. They were standing ten deep around the walls, pushing against the outer seats, infiltrating the central aisle. Only the stage was empty, a thick curtain drawn a few yards from the front.

Arnie Fredericks straightened his tie, fixed his smile, and strode out from the wings. This was his moment.

"And now ladies and gentleman," he said, cranking his voice up. "I want you to give a big Orlando welcome to a real American hero, the first man to fly halfway to the stars, John Theodore Bruce!"

A crescendo of noise: applause, whistles, and shrieks. Arnie stepped back, leading the applause from the side of the stage, his hands clapping wildly, his face reddening with the effort.

John Bruce walked on from the other side. A single spotlight followed his progress from wings to lectern.

The cheering increased, cameras focussed as John's face was beamed into millions of households worldwide. A well-known face, a photogenic face. But today there was something different. Today, there was a feral quality to his eyes.

CHAPTER THIRTY-FIVE

John began to speak.

"I expect many of you today are asking the same question I am. What's happening to the world? McKinley explodes, Martinez combusts, and now Bill Suarez stabs a talk show host. What's happening?"

He milked the moment, disregarding the prepared text. He had something different to say.

"Today, I think it's time the American people were told the truth."

Another pause. He ran his eyes along the wall of network cameras and imagined his face filling their view screens. Well, not *his* face but it would do. For the moment.

"Last week, I told you of China's involvement in McKinley's murder. Today, I discovered I was only half right. Two hours ago, Bill Suarez told me the truth."

A collective gasp. Then a hush. He had them exactly where he wanted them. Intrigued and panting for more.

"I was appalled, as I know you'll be."

He looked down, shaking his head, trying to look shocked and saddened. Emotion had never been his strong point but he'd observed others. And realized its power. People preferred a story that was difficult to tell. It lent credence. A story reluctantly told and dragged from an unwilling confidant gained a provenance that no glib lie could ever match.

He shook his head again and looked directly at the camera feeds.

"Bill told me that for years senior politicians and the military have conspired to keep the truth from the American people. They know exactly what happened to McKinley and Suzi Martinez. But instead of telling the truth they lie and hide behind their veil of secrecy. Why?"

He let his head track from left to right, asking the question to each member of the room.

"Because your leaders—our leaders—think we're too stupid to handle the truth. They think we're children who'll panic. Well I know different. We're not children and we *can* handle the truth."

He took a deep breath. This was the moment. He'd laid the ground-work. Now came the fun.

"I've flown into space. I worked for NASA. I *know* that the human race is not alone. I've seen the long-range pictures of alien spacecraft. But—" He paused, giving his words time to settle. "—until today, I didn't realize they were here."

That got the reaction he'd been looking for. A real buzz. Surprise, excitement, and the cold, sweaty palm of fear.

He closed his eyes. Perhaps he should moisten them a bit, have his lower lip quiver. Look, America, I'm telling you the truth, see how it hurts.

He suppressed a smile.

"That's right," he said. "They've been here for years infiltrating our society. They slip inside our heads and take over our bodies. At first there were only a few of them—scientists and explorers—and they were careful which bodies they took over. But now, they are many and they don't care. McKinley and Martinez died because their bodies weren't suitable hosts. They couldn't take the strain so they exploded and burned. Suarez was stronger. But they had other plans for him. They knew he'd talked. So they took him over, forced him to kill, then left him to pick up the pieces."

He was flying now, driving the story towards its climax.

"China's gone. Their entire leadership's been replaced. Europe too. Now they're coming here and it's not just the leaders they're after."

Another look direct into camera. The next sentence had to hit every sitting room in America.

"They're coming for *you*," he said, stabbing a finger at the camera. "Look at the person next to you, your neighbor, your colleagues at work, your friends at school. How well do you really know them? Have they changed recently? Maybe just a little? Something you couldn't put your finger on at the time. Like forgetting something they should have known or behaving out of character. Maybe they changed their hair. That's what they do. Climb into people's heads when no one's looking. They're all around us even now. Waiting for the chance to slip inside our brains and take us over."

A girl near the front of the audience screamed, someone else jumped up. Others at the back began to move towards the exits.

Time to close.

He jerked his head up and to the left as though he'd suddenly seen something, widened his eyes in shock and parted his lips.

Then stabbed a finger at the ceiling. "There's one!" he cried, following its mythical flight with his arm, conducting its path towards the audience.

"Run!" he screamed, shouting at a woman in the audience. "It's almost on top of you."

A phalanx of the audience rose in panic, shouting and batting their arms at invisible monsters. John switched to the other side of the auditorium, picking on a man hurrying along a line of seats.

"He's one of them!" John shouted. "The man in the red tie. Don't let him get away. He's going for help."

Hands grabbed the man. A fight broke out.

"And he's another!" John pointed randomly at the audience then ducked, avoiding a swarm of mythical aliens. "There's more of them. Run for your lives!"

Pandemonium. No one remained seated. The exits were blocked by flailing masses, fights broke out, people were being trampled. Even the cameras were being abandoned.

Time for the final message.

He turned to the one remaining manned camera.

"There is hope," he said. "There's one person who can resist them. They framed him for murder. Had him locked away in a mental institution. But we can free him. We have to free him now. He's our only hope. Free Peter Pendennis!"

This was fun. Following Lulu and that idiot boyfriend of hers had opened up a new world to him. They'd shown him how to fly, how to jump inside people's heads. But they'd been so wrapped up in their own pathetic little mission they'd never once looked behind to see if anyone was following. Now he'd show them. He'd show everybody. Look at them run, look at them scream.

One person wasn't running or screaming. He was walking purposefully between the upturned chairs and abandoned possessions of the front row. Hadn't he heard? Didn't he understand English? He looked Chinese.

Peter pointed at him.

"He's one of them!" he shouted. "Look at him. He's Chinese."

No one tackled the man. Everyone was too busy trying to get out of the building.

The man drew level with the lectern, his face impassive. He raised an arm. Was that a gun? He was pointing it at Peter, from less than ten yards away.

Peter laughed, nervously. There was a flash, an explosion, pain. He was flung, spinning backwards, dumped on his backside. His right shoulder afire.

He lay there, confused. He'd been shot. He reached for his wound with his left hand. It came away stained red—a fiery, liquid red that glistened in the auditorium lights. He'd been shot in the shoulder. Out of the corner of his eye, he saw his assassin walking away. Why had the man shot only once? Didn't he want to make sure?

A pulse of pain shot through Peter/John's shoulder. And a tingling sensation, spreading down his arm, across his chest. His skin crawling as though being invaded by thousands of ants.

What was happening?

"No!" The alien's anguished cry wailed across the auditorium as he flew in from above. His body was lying on the stage, wounded and desecrated. Was this God's punishment for leaving his post?

But he'd waited as long as he could. He'd tried everything to contact the angel. He'd prayed. He'd called. But he couldn't wait forever. He had a speech to give, a body to find, and his enemies were everywhere. God would understand.

Or so he'd thought.

Anger welled within him. How dare they steal his body! Or was *this* God's plan? A test to see if he was worthy of his physical form. He swooped down. His body had staggered to its feet. Whoever was inside was laughing.

Sacrilege.

He descended upon the body of John Bruce, wrapped himself around it, readied the connection. Just like he'd done so many times before. Just like he'd done the first time.

Not that he could remember the first time. He'd jettisoned that memory along with all the others. Those unexpected disturbances picked up on the research monitors that had first drawn him to Earth. The time he'd spent monitoring humans—their loves, their fears, their hopes and desires. It had been like experiencing childhood for the first time. The freedom, the splendid anarchy, the variation of thought and action. People here lived for themselves; they didn't bend their will to serve a common good. The only consensus was that there *was* no consensus. They didn't even speak the same language.

A physical world for a physical people. Vibrant and exciting.

And when the manned mission came, he'd gone along as well, following the intrepid John Bruce into the unknown. And then it happened. A flaw in the higher dimensional shielding ripped the pilot's mind from his body.

It was so unexpected. So opportune. A chance for a fresh start, a new life—a *physical* life. All he had to do was slide forward and embrace the vacated body. It was there for the taking. It wasn't even stealing. The human pilot was almost certainly lost. It was . . . Fate. And he grabbed it with a hundred fronds.

And in that euphoric moment of rebirth, he decided to make the transformation complete, to shed the burden of his tortured past. A new start with no excess baggage to carry ever onwards towards oblivion. A new life on a new planet. All worries bundled up and tossed to the wind on the spreading cloud of exhaled memory.

And then something unexpected happened. Deprived of an identity or purpose of being, he found himself reaching out, searching for something he knew he must find but couldn't understand. He grasped the struggling pilot's mind, read it, and copied it. A complete accident. Some in-built survival mechanism that abhorred a vacuum. Whatever the reason, the memories and body of John Bruce became wedded to his own Colonist intellect and powers. Not that he had any memory of being a Colonist. He was John Bruce, the first man chosen to fly to the stars.

But a new suit of clothes was no panacea. Underneath he was still the same; instability and paranoia were not things one could exhale.

And now his physical form lay dying beneath him. One lapse of possession and his world had been invaded and abused. Anger pulsed throughout his being. He pushed inside John's head, sensed Peter's presence, grabbed hold of him, squeezed and pulled and ripped him out, spitting him into the void.

Pain hit him. And something else. His body was under attack. Hundreds of thousands of tiny machines—nanotechnocytes—were coursing through his body on a search-and-destroy mission. A wriggling army unleashed by the bullet lodged in his shoulder.

He fought them. Using whatever powers he could summon. He attacked them from the higher dimensions; burning, stripping away at the fabric of matter that held them together; ripping them out; expelling them in their hundreds.

He fell to the floor. Other bodies—humans—crawled all over him, trying to help but getting in his way. He swept them aside, sending rolling waves of paramedics crashing over the lip of the stage.

The hotel Metropole shimmered into view. Nick swung towards it, dropping to street level. People were streaming out from the hotel doors, running into the street, disrupting the traffic. What the hell was going on inside?

Nick followed the surge of people back through the hotel into the auditorium, blurring through a wall of panic-stricken people.

And stopped. John Bruce was on stage, staggering and . . . all around him the air writhed and warped and pulsed bloodred. The alien was coiled around his body.

"I'll send the pictogram," said Louise.

And pray the Colonists were already responding to the first message, thought Nick, trying to make sense of the scene. Injured people were lying everywhere. Those that could walk were trying to run and those that could run had spilled onto the street. It was chaos.

John fell down. Nick edged closer to the stage, wondering if attracting the alien's attention was a good idea or not. Could Louise pull off the angel stunt twice?

And what was the matter with John? Why was he on the floor? Was he . . .

Was that blood?

Two paramedics ran onstage. One second they were kneeling besides John's body the next they were flying through the air.

Which didn't make sense. Was the alien turning against John? Didn't he want his body to live?

A blaze of intense light flared at the back of the auditorium then flashed past Nick, heading for the stage.

It had wings.

✧   ✧   ✧

The alien was frantic, tears running down his face, insect-machines inside him, killing him while he watched and thrashed.

"Stop!" commanded the angel, its voice resonating like a hundred strong choir. "The Lord thy God commands thee!"

He glimpsed the angel through a film of tears. How could he stop? Why would God want him to stop? Wasn't human life precious?

Or was it a test? The supreme test. Accept death and prove your faith? God waiting in the wings, like he did with Isaac, waiting until the last second before stepping in and healing his disciple's poor broken body.

Or was it all a trick? Satan again, in one of his many guises—laughing at him, fooling him, making him die for nothing.

"No!" he boomed. "You're no angel. God wouldn't do this! This is Satan's work."

He lashed out, swaying unsteadily, anchored to the physical John Bruce while flailing at the false angel.

Nick watched from below. John Bruce was back on his feet. The alien pulsing bloodred and lashing out in fury. A frond must have caught Louise. She was being pulled towards the alien, her wings beating wildly.

He thought *arrow*. He thought *sharp*. He thought *cut that frond*. Bursting out of the auditorium floor he flew at the narrowing gap between Louise and the alien. Impact. He hit something, kept flying—was Louise free?

No. She was still struggling, commanding John to stop, to listen to the Word of God.

Nick turned, flew back, imagining himself the sharpest knife forged from the hardest metal. He aimed for a point as close to Louise as he dared and hit it hard. Louise came with him. The two of them barrelling away though the upturned chairs of the second row. No, the *three* of them—he hadn't noticed earlier—in his rush to free Louise he'd forgotten to tell John to stay put. The wingman must have followed Nick on his kamikaze dash.

A brilliant flash of light exploded high above them. Then another. The ornate auditorium ceiling lit up as three, four, five intense balls of light materialized.

Weapons? Colonists? Something else?

Nick melted into the carpet taking Wingman John with him. The balls of light elongated and took shape: ghostly translucent white jellyfish several meters in length, their edges warping and rippling in and out of phase. They converged over the frantic alien, their delicate fronds reaching down and caressing his writhing body.

Gradually his color dimmed, pulsing from bloodred through pink to translucent pearl. And the writhing stopped. Slowly, he began to rise. All the Colonists began to rise. Were they lifting him clear? Was he alive? Dead? Tranquillized?

John Bruce's body collapsed to the stage floor, then the auditorium shuddered and disappeared. Nick was back in his body, sitting on the sofa in Louise's lounge. Louise was by the window. A boy stood by the fireplace. A nonspectral version of the boy/Colonist who'd brought them home.

"It's over," the boy said, his face impassive, his lips still out of sync. "We are leaving."

The room vanished and back came the auditorium.

"Wait! What about all this?" shouted Louise. "Don't we get any help putting things back together again?"

The Colonists flickered once then disappeared.

"We're probably better off without their help," said Nick.

"But what about John?" shouted Louise. "The alien was killing him. You can see the blood. He's probably shredded his insides."

Nick hoped she was wrong. The alien had no reason to attack his own body but . . .

If he was insane and . . .

"Did I do this!" Louise rushed past him, streaking towards the stage, her fears spilling behind her. *Oh God, no. Not this. Please don't say I tipped him over the edge with my angel act. I told him to wait. I didn't mean . . .*

Nick followed. "It was nothing you did, Lou. We don't even know what happened. We don't even know how John got here."

Two paramedics were bent over John's body. His shirt was being ripped open, dressings applied. More people rushed in from the wings.

Nick and Louise watched, helpless. Should they reconnect John? Would that help or hinder? What if John's body died? What would they do with John then?

John was loaded onto a stretcher. Four men grabbed a handle each and rushed him offstage, passing through the wings, along a corridor towards a red-doored fire exit at the back. The doors swung open. An ambulance was waiting. More paramedics, security personnel, police.

Emergency lights flashed. John was bundled into the back of the first ambulance, the doors slammed shut, wheels began to spin.

Three blurs followed, hovering above John's body.

A heart monitor flashed numbers that Nick desperately tried to read. The numbers started to tumble. Flat-line.

"No!" shouted Louise as a paramedic worked on John's battered body, shocking him, injecting him, pummelling him back to life.

"We've got to do it now, Nick!" shouted Louise. "We've got to put him back!"

"And if he dies?"

"We've still got to do it. What life would it be for John without a body?"

"It hasn't been that bad for us, has it? Given a choice between this and nothing at all—I'd choose this every time."

"It's not your choice, Nick. It's his!"

She was right but . . . what were they going to say to John? He thought he was in a flight simulator. How did they explain that he was now in an ambulance looking down on his body fighting for its life?

What if he panicked and flew off? What if . . .

"Just do it!" screamed Louise.

"Switching frequency," he said. "No call for alarm, John. This is another drill."

He searched for the words, treading a line between the truth and something he could sell.

"This simulation tests your ability to cope with enemy counter-measures, John. They've corrupted your visuals to make you think the docking bay is your body. It's not. You need to land at a point an inch above your hairline in the center of your forehead. Approach slowly and think yourself there, John. You're cleared for landing."

"Copy that, wing leader."

Nick watched John descend, his approach made more difficult by the sudden movements of his destination as John's head jerked and spasmed.

He was in position. "Now think yourself inside, John, aim for the center of the brain below you and pull yourself in."

Did the blur disappear? John's head was jerking so much Nick couldn't tell.

John's body arched, spasming violently then collapsed. Flatline!

More paddles, more shocks, more desperate moments.

Had they killed him?

The monitor showed a pulse again. He was alive. Just. And John had to have connected. The blur had disappeared. But what kind of life would he wake up to? The John inside had no idea of the life his other half had been living. And what the hell had happened back in the auditorium? Would John have to answer for that?

"John, this is important," shouted Nick, aiming his words at John's head and willing them inside. "Listen to me. This is your wing leader."

Nick prayed John could hear. He'd been able to hear Louise when he'd taken physical form. This had to work.

"You don't remember anything after the SHIFT flight except for what I'm going to tell you now. During the SHIFT flight something went wrong. You think the neural shielding failed. You remember a violent headache then nothing. Go to SHIFT control and ask for help. Tell them to check the before and after full-spectrum brain scans from the flight. It might help get your old job back."

And provide an explanation for John's amnesia.

But it wouldn't explain everything.

"The only other thing you remember is more recent. The details are hazy but you remember a man handing you a glass of water. As you drank it you noticed the man was watching you. He looked strange—triumphant—and then he said something even stranger. He said, 'See how you like VCH, spaceman,' and then everything went blank."

"What's VCH?" asked Louise.

"Insurance," said Nick. "You're waking up now, John. Your body's injured and you need to fight."

John was now on his own.

"Insurance against what?" pressed Louise.

"Whatever happened back in the auditorium. Something tells me that John's going to need a lot more than amnesia to resurrect his credibility and VCH is a powerful hallucinogenic that clears the bloodstream in under an hour. No one'll be able to say he wasn't drugged."

Voices echoed inside John's head. Distant voices, as though he was at the bottom of a long deep well and they were at the surface shouting down to him.

"Picking up signs of internal failure! Switching to backup."

"Fight, you bastard, fight!"

Faces loomed and faded. Was he in the back of a truck? Everything was moving and swaying from side to side.

"He's coming to!"

"How much further to go?"

Someone at the front—the driver?—turned to answer.

"Nearly there. Is he gonna make it?"

John waited for the answer but everything went black. Then white. He was on a gurney being wheeled along a long white corridor. Why did that feel familiar? He felt he should know? But the feeling escaped him. Swing doors banged close to his head, a masked face peered down at him, a gentle voice, reassuring words, the smell of disinfectant, lights, even brighter lights and then darkness.

CHAPTER THIRTY-SIX

Louise was leaning against a farm gate watching her animals when Nick arrived. It was the first time he'd seen her in days. He thought she might have called but . . . it must be difficult returning to a village where a close friend and neighbor has been murdered and no one's quite sure if you're a victim or an accomplice. So many bridges to rebuild. It was bad enough at the college. People there weren't sure if he was a pariah or a celebrity. Even after being cleared by the police.

"How's it going?" he called out as he neared.

She smiled. "Better now I've got my menagerie back together again." She nodded to a couple of goats cavorting in the early spring sun. "I feel almost normal again. How about you?"

"Well, my classes are fuller. I used to be merely eccentric—with occasional flashes of brilliance, of course . . ."

"Of course," she echoed, joining in the easy banter.

"But now I have an aura of danger about me. I'm a man who discovers mutilated corpses, has human body parts lurking in his saucepan, and successfully evades a police manhunt for over a week."

"I think technically it was only four days. The DNA found on the body didn't match yours, remember. And the CCTV footage from the college showed that you couldn't have left the body parts on your desk."

He waved her argument aside. "A mere technicality. According to some of my esteemed colleagues it was all my fault anyway as I must have angered the murderer or why else would anyone want to frame me?"

"Well, you did."

"Did I?" He'd almost forgotten. He'd told so many people his whittled down version of the truth he'd begun to believe it. He was the innocent bystander who'd stumbled upon a mutilated corpse hours after witnessing a serial mutilator attack a friend. He'd been arrested, spent a night in the cells, and then came home to find human body parts in his saucepan. Of course he panicked. Of course he behaved irrationally. Who wouldn't? He was being targeted by a Pendennis-obsessed murderer.

Who, so far, had evaded capture. And always would, hoped Nick. Enough people had suffered this past month without adding another innocent. Whoever had had his body hijacked didn't deserve to be punished for a murder he had no knowledge of.

And, with the police treating Vince Culley and Karen's murders as linked, the chances of them finding evidence to link one person to both murders was remote. The alien would have used two bodies . . . maybe more.

"At least it's all over," said Louise, turning away to stare across her fields. "Look at those goats; they haven't a care in the world."

"Have you, er . . ." He paused, not sure if he wanted to know the answer, but it was a question that had nagged away at him for the past couple of days. "Have you heard from John at all?"

She looked surprised. "No, why should I?"

"I just thought . . . well, he might have contacted you."

"Why? You wiped his memory."

"Yes, but the stories in the media. He must have read them. A lot of the papers picked up on the link between the two of you. Old boyfriend/girlfriend and the fact that . . . well, Peter Pendennis figured prominently in both your statements to the press."

"I don't think John wants to be reminded of *that* speech."

Nick had to agree. John's, or more accurately, Peter's speech had eclipsed Orson Welles' *War of the Worlds* broadcast in the panic stakes. Several people had been killed, thousands injured. Riots had broken out, gun stores had been looted. It took an emergency Presidential address and the National Guard to restore order. Even now some people weren't convinced.

"Do you think he'll ever be able to resurrect his career?" asked Louise.

Nick shrugged. "I did my best."

She reached out and touched his arm.

"You were brilliant. The VCH, the headaches, the amnesia. I'd never have thought of any of that. You gave him a chance. I just . . ." She turned away. "I just wonder if anyone else'll give him a chance. He deserves better."

"Time's a great healer," he said, groaning to himself the moment the words left his mouth. Where did he find these platitudes? Time's a great healer? Why didn't he say, "Worse things happen at sea?" He was useless at giving comfort. Sarcasm and witty asides—no problem. But comfort and reassurance—send for someone else.

"NASA is looking into John's claims about the neural shields failing," he said, suddenly remembering a relevant fact. "And with the amount of publicity being generated I can't see them being allowed to keep the results secret. There's even talk about them offering John a training role in a couple of weeks when he's fully recovered."

Not that anyone would be offering him a political role anytime soon. Comics were already parodying his wild-eyed 'They're here!' speech.

"Was it . . . was it our fault?" Louise asked, looking at him pleadingly. "If we hadn't let Peter follow us he wouldn't have taken over John's body and the riots wouldn't have happened and John wouldn't be in so much trouble and—"

He cut her off. "If we hadn't intervened thousands more would have been killed. Millions if the alien had started a war with China. We had to act fast. And that meant as few stops as possible. Don't forget if we'd arrived an hour earlier we might have saved Bill Suarez and that chat show host. And if we'd stopped every five minutes to see if anyone was following we'd have risked the hold I had over John. He could have woken up or started to doubt what I was telling him."

And anything could have happened then. He hadn't told her how tenuous he believed the link was. Or how amazed he was that John had stayed under for so long.

"It was essential," he continued, "that we got John to Orlando with as few interruptions as possible. Everything depended upon it."

"Do you . . . do you think Peter's still over there?"

Not a question he liked to consider. Had the alien killed Peter or had Peter escaped? He'd watched the holorecordings so many times he knew every event off by heart. But still hadn't been able to spot the moment the alien wrested John's body back from Peter.

"I think if Peter survived we would have heard by now," he said. "Peter's not one for keeping quiet. If he'd seized another body he'd be wreaking havoc. It would be all over the news."

She seemed relieved.

"Yes, he would, wouldn't he?"

Two goat kids bounced up to the gate and stopped, staring at Nick before bleating and racing back to their mother, their back legs bouncing to the left and right like a pair of slalom skiers.

Louise smiled as she watched them go. "Have you talked to Ziegler about Peter?"

"He's not taking messages. Not from me anyway."

Which wasn't that much of a surprise. The media had camped outside Upper Heywood for two days after John's "Free Peter Pendennis" speech. One news broadcast showed a harassed Ziegler being chased across a car park, pursued by reporters shouting inane questions. *Any plans to free The Butcher, Dr. Ziegler? Is it true all his victims were aliens?*

He undoubtedly blamed Nick for every hell they were putting him through.

Louise sighed. "Do you think anyone will ever piece together what really happened?"

"No. And even if they did, who'd dare say anything? You saw what happened when Peter delivered his 'They're here!' speech. Who's going to risk a repeat by saying that there really was an alien and he lived for nearly two years undetected, body-hopping from John Bruce to Bill Suarez and God knows how many others, killing McKinley and Martinez, Karen and Culley. He nearly became President. He nearly plunged America into a global war."

"He still might," said Louise. "On the news last night they were saying the man who shot John was a Chinese national."

"Not anymore they're not. This morning he's a Chinese-American working for a U.S. Defense contractor. And China's condemned the assassination attempt and called for a 'greater understanding' between the two nations. Everyone's stepping back. No one wants war."

"I hope you're right," said Louise.

"You know I am. What politician's going to push an anti-China stance now? The moment they do, someone'll compare them to John Bruce and no politician is going to want that."

Which, ironically, made Peter Pendennis a peacemaker. His "They're here" speech had effectively negated everything the alien had said.

What price Peter Pendennis for the next Nobel Peace Prize?

Louise batted a fly away from her face. If only the world was as simple as Nick made out.

She envied him his optimism. And his ability to bounce back as though the last two weeks had never happened. Something she couldn't do. She had to pass Karen's house every time she left the village. She had to endure the stares and the awkward silences and the questions. People said they didn't blame her. People said that if The Butcher had attacked them they'd have run too. "There's no way you could have been thinking straight with all that going on,' they'd said. 'That professor ringing to tell you to lock your doors, telling you that a serial killer had escaped and killed again and was on his way over. Of course you panicked. Anyone would."

But . . .

They had to have the same doubts she had. What was she doing going to see a serial killer in the first place? Why hadn't she given Karen a stronger warning? Why?

"Talking of international intrigue," said Nick. "You never did tell me why you disabled your pickup's transponder."

"A girl has to keep some secrets," she said forcing a smile. Now was not the time to go into her animal liberationist past.

"So, what are you going to do now?" she asked, changing the subject. "Publish your findings and become famous?"

"Not a chance."

"Why not?"

"Because I'm not ready to give up my life yet. Think about it, if I published a paper on the duality of the species I'd be pitching myself into a minefield. You think Darwin had problems? Wait 'til you see what they'd do to me. I'd be lauded, attacked, and ridiculed from all sides. Science, religion, and the tabloids—every one of them interpreting my findings and twisting my words to suit their purpose."

"But you could prove it. Like you did with me. They'd have to believe you then."

"Have you ever tried arguing with a zealot? I'd have professional debunkers hounding me for the rest of my life. I'd have magicians recreating my experiments. I'd have religious nuts quoting my work as proof their child had been possessed. Hell, they might even be right."

"What?"

"Think about it, if I show people how to separate mind from body, they're going to try, aren't they? Half the teenage population would probably disappear overnight. You remember how difficult it was for us to navigate out there—what chance would they have? It would be bedlam. And those that didn't get lost forever would probably try to slip into the head of the hot girl next door or the latest Hollywood sensation or the President. The world would be taken over by body-hopping wannabees."

He had a point. For every responsible traveller there'd be tens—hundreds—of idiots.

"But if it's so easy to separate isn't it only a matter of time before someone recreates your work and goes public?"

"It's not that easy," he said. "It took me a long time to, er . . . find a way. John had his mind ripped from his body by the SHIFT flight. Peter's mind was such a mess that any membrane would have been mashed years ago—not that pain was ever a barrier to him. And you, you had me to pull you free."

"And I didn't have a membrane."

"That's true," he said, suddenly looking away.

"So, what are you going to do?" she asked. "Go back to University and research things you can never talk about?"

"Knowledge should be a goal unto itself. Besides, we've only had the smallest glimpse of what lies out there. There's so much more we skimmed past. What are ley lines? Where do they go? And why? Are those spinning rims of light natural or manufactured? Do other planets have them? Why not fly to Mars and find out. I could map Venus, travel to the center of Mercury, visit Pluto. I could leave the solar system and fly to the stars. Anything is possible and it's ours for the exploring."

"Ours?"

"Why not? We could discover Atlantis, ride comets, travel to the stars, glide with condors over the Andes. And all before breakfast. Come with me."

"And leave all this?"

"But I'm offering you the stars, Louise. And how many men can say that and really mean it?"

ACKNOWLEDGMENTS

I'd like to thank Kat Manco, Elizabeth McGlothlin, KC Heath, Francis Turner, Joe Buckley, N.R. Simpson, Shawn Thompson and Derrick Barnsdale for their helpful advice and comments.